PRETTY LITTLE LIES

ROSEHILL ACADEMY
BOOK 1

IVY THORN

PNK PUBLISHING

❀ Created with Vellum

PROLOGUE
ANYA

As I watch Nicolo Marchetti in the hallway of our high school, my daily bout of nausea brings bile to my throat. He leans toward the dimple-cheeked brunette before him, twirling a strand of her long hair around his finger. His proud lips curve into a cocky yet charming smile. The same smile he won me over with weeks ago.

The girl leans coyly back against the lockers–she's falling for his tricks just like I did, the smooth, flirtatious words, the promises of devotion. He's probably telling her how she's changed his life just by being in it.

"I've never met anyone like you. The moment I laid eyes on your beautiful face, my heart stopped, and I knew I couldn't live without you."

I close my eyes as I hear his smooth, deep voice reverberating in my mind, recalling his murmured words from our night together.

He hasn't spoken to me in weeks, but I can still hear his voice. A shiver runs down my spine, my body responding as viscerally to it now as I did then.

The intensity of his gaze, the way his dark curls fall into his hazel eyes... everything about Nicolo screams Prince Charming–at a glance.

He can only maintain the facade for so long, but when he does–it's enough for anyone to lose themselves in.

All I cared about in life was becoming a professional ballerina. But the moment his honeyed words reached my ears, I lost all focus.

I can still remember our first night together so clearly. The only thing more thrilling than sneaking out for the first time to go to his house party was the fact that the most gorgeous guy in school had asked me to. It was a party I knew I shouldn't have been at. My aunt Patritsiya never would have allowed it. And as soon as I entered the front door, I knew I was out of my element.

The cloying scent of vape pens mingled with the sweaty stench of teens who were too busy dancing and making out to notice my arrival. My shoulders curled defensively inward as the music blared too loudly in my ears. I was positive the cops would break up the party for a noise complaint. Then again, cops probably saw extravagant house parties in the rich, gated Forest Glen estates all the time.

I wandered in search of Nicolo and was almost grateful when someone shoved a red Solo cup of keg beer into my hands, though I hadn't ever drank before. Liquid courage might put me at ease. Gagging on the first sip, I looked for a place to set it down. Definitely not for me.

Then I spotted Nicolo.

In designer ripped jeans and a pale-green button-down rolled up to his elbows, he looked so cool and casual with a red cup in hand. He leaned against the doorway as he laughed with friends.

As soon as our eyes met, he pushed away from the doorframe. Heart beating loudly enough to hear clear across the room, I licked my suddenly dry lips as he approached me.

"You look beautiful," he said, toying with a lock of my blond curls.

"Thanks." I blushed profusely, suddenly shy as the most desirable guy in school complimented me.

"I'm glad you came. I wasn't sure you would, and I've been dying to get to know you better." His hazel eyes studied me appreciatively.

Thank god I chose to wear one of my few nicer dresses, though it wasn't yet spring.

"I'm glad I came too." My chin trembled nervously as I tried to smile.

Despite his reputation as a bad boy with family ties to the Italian mob, I found Nicolo Marchetti charming. His playful flirting had made him impossible to ignore. And despite my natural shyness, I liked him.

Someone stumbled into me, knocking me forward, and Nicolo gripped my forearm, steadying me. Warmth spread through my chest at his strong touch.

"Want to go somewhere a bit quieter?" he offered.

At the time, I thought he might have noticed how awkward I felt in the drunken crowd.

"Yeah," I breathed with relief.

When he took my hand, butterflies erupted in my stomach, making me thankful I didn't drink any more of that god-awful beer. I might have thrown it up. He led me upstairs with a quick smile over his shoulder, and my body melted.

Nicolo closed the bedroom door behind us, muffling the party music to a throbbing bass. He paused by the door, watching me with a playful gaze as I sat hesitantly on the baseball-themed bedspread–the only place to sit besides the floor.

I glanced nervously at the baseball paraphernalia decorating the room, unable to stand the heat of his gaze for long.

"So, you're a dancer?" he asked, returning to our conversation from the other day.

Flustered that he had even spoken to me, I'd nearly slammed my locker on his hand trying to hide the picture of five-year-old me sitting with my parents, dressed as a sugar plum fairy. Turning, I'd found myself trapped between his arms, so I'd had no choice but to speak with him. Still, I'd stumbled over my words, hardly able to respond to his witty observation. His face had been so close to mine.

"Yes, ballet," I said, pushing the embarrassing memory to the back of my mind. "It was my parents' dream for me... probably a way of carrying their culture with them, since they immigrated here from Russia before I was born."

"It *was* their dream?" Nicolo stalked toward me, settling onto the bed and making my heart flip as our knees touched. "But not anymore?"

"They died. In a car accident," I blurted nervously.

Nicolo's strong brows pressed together in concern. "I'm sorry."

I tried to shrug it off. Then dropped my gaze to hide my pain. "It was a few years ago."

"I'm sure they're proud of you." Nicolo slid closer to me, his hand resting on my thigh as his thumb stroked a comforting line across my skin.

Warm excitement pooled in my belly at his touch.

When our eyes met, I found my crackling anticipation reflected in his gaze.

Then his hand combed into my curls as he leaned in, his face mere inches from mine. The subtle, enticing scent of his cologne mingled with the hint of beer on his breath.

His lips pressed to mine, sending a jolt straight to my core. Our first kiss sucked the oxygen from the room. I lost all sense of control as excitement coursed through my veins.

"You're so beautiful, Anya. I can hardly believe you don't have guys lining up to date you," he breathed, his hand brushing my cheek.

"No one's ever tried to get to know me like you," I murmured, still in disbelief that Nicolo Marchetti was kissing *me*.

When he guided me further onto the bed and leaned me back, I didn't question it. Blinded by my attraction for him, I let him lead the way, enraptured by his passionate kiss, his gentle caress.

He took his time, kissing me passionately, putting me at ease. He touched me in ways that brought my body to life like never before. Convinced we were falling in love and sure we would end up together, I gave him my virginity.

But now, as he traps the brunette against the lockers in what must be a signature move, I can see Nicolo for what he is. A player, a snake who will say anything to get into a girl's pants. It hurts to see him toying with his next conquest while my heart bleeds over the tile floor of our high school.

Tears roll down my cheeks, and I brush them away angrily. I've been an emotional wreck since my night with him. Just thinking about it launches my body into turmoil as I shiver with unwanted desire.

The ghost of his hands exploring my body sets my skin on fire. It felt so good, so right. Sex with Nicolo had only confirmed what a perfect fit we were. And then, after he'd finished, he'd simply told me to leave.

His sudden shift was like having a bucket of ice water poured over my head. Now, it's as though I never even existed. Nicolo's gaze slides over me whenever we happen to cross paths, like I'm not even there.

I brusquely wipe at my cheeks once again, fighting to get my tears under control. At first, I thought my overwhelming emotions came from Nicolo's cold rejection combined with restless nights plagued by vivid dreams of him. always ended with Nicolo's callous gaze, his lazy command of "Get out" that sent me on my way.

But now I know better.

I'm such an idiot for thinking I could catch Nicolo Marchetti's eye. At our high school, he's a god among men, and I simply fell prey to his quest to sleep with every girl in school. *How could I have been so blind?*

Nicolo leans towards the beautiful, smiling brunette, stroking her cheek with his fingers. I can almost feel that same gentle graze across my flesh, setting my skin tingling and making my breath catch. He gave me my first kiss, and it had brought my body to life like a defibrillator.

Anger roars to life inside me as Nicolo turns from the girl, heading in my general direction. Before I can fully consider my actions, I stride forward, cutting through the crowd until I stop directly in front of Nicolo.

His gaze connects with mine, and his momentary surprise gives me a hint of satisfaction. He didn't expect to interact with me ever again.

"You used me," I accuse, my hands fisting at my sides, my lips pressed into an angry line.

"Well, hello to you, too... wait, who are you?" His tone is light, making a joke of my anger.

His friends encircle me as they chuckle at his taunting question.

"Why?" I demand, my voice quivering. "Why would you take my virginity and then just ignore me? What could you possibly–"

"Oh, riiight," Nicolo drawls, snapping his fingers as if suddenly registering how he knows me. "You're that one girl, Anna? Auna? Anya? The girl who wants to be a dancer to honor her dead parents' memory."

The sting of fresh tears threaten to spill from my eyes once more as he picks at a wound that's still fresh.

Nicolo's sneer falls into a more serious expression, his hazel eyes going flat as he looks down his proud nose at me. "Did you really believe we would be together?" He scoffs, looking at his friends as he rolls his eyes.

They respond with raucous laughter, as if this is all just a big joke. *I'm a joke to them.*

"Oh, Anya. Look, our night together was great and everything. But I'm a *somebody*. Did you really think that I, as the oldest son and heir of Lorenzo Marchetti, might end up with someone like you? My father would disown me if I brought you home to meet the family." He steps up close, his tall, muscular frame towering over me, making me feel small and weak and insignificant. "But thanks for the tight ride. I have to say, you looked pretty fucking glorious with my cum all over your face."

Despite my fury, I still respond physically to Nicolo's proximity, the masculine scent of his cologne, the heat of his body radiating from him, warming my flesh. My pulse quickens with unbidden excitement, betraying me. Tears obscure my vision along with an unwanted memory of Nicolo's strong arms wrapped around me, his naked body pressing close to mine, his full, warm lips consuming mine hungrily.

"I'm done with you," Nicolo murmurs, bringing his face dangerously close to mine. "You are nothing to me. So I suggest you remember it, and stay the *fuck* out of my way."

Standing to his full height once more, he shoves past me. His friends burst into animated speech, mocking my attempt to confront him as they make their way down the hall.

For an excruciating moment, I stand frozen, intensely aware of all the eyes staring at me. Then, I burst into horrible racking sobs. I don't care that afternoon classes are just about to start. I have to leave.

Sprinting toward the doors that lead out to the student parking lot, I flee as quickly as my feet will carry me. Crushing pain makes my lungs heave. I need to go home, to grieve the crushing loss of my innocence in peace.

I can't believe I so naively fell for Nicolo's advances. I let him have the most intimate part of me. And now I feel crushed under the full weight of the consequences.

As my anxiety intensifies, my nausea overwhelms me. Bracing one hand against the rough stucco of my high school, I bend in half and vomit up my lunch.

Stooping by the side of the building, I continue to retch until I have nothing more to throw up. Sweat coats my brow, and I shakily wipe the sweat away with the back of my hand, then spit to clear my mouth.

Sucking in a deep breath through my nose, I slump back against the building and cry. I better get used to the nausea and vomiting and this horrible feeling inside. Because *I'm pregnant*. It's time to face the cold hard truth. I've already taken multiple tests to prove it.

I'm going to have a baby.

Nicolo Marchetti's baby.

1

ANYA

Four Years Later

"Wish me luck on my first day!" I say as I sling my school bag over my shoulder and head toward the door.

Finally, after years of hard work and four semesters of a local community college, I've earned a full scholarship to the private university's elite performing arts program that I've always dreamed of attending. I still can hardly believe Rosehill College accepted me.

"Good luck," Aunt Patritsiya says in her faint Russian accent. She tilts her cheek so I can kiss it as she gives my hand an affectionate squeeze.

Average height and slightly on the plump side, my aunt is several inches shorter than me, and I have to lean down to accommodate the requested kiss she receives every day before I leave.

As I pass the kitchen table, I stop to press a kiss to my daughter's black curls, which never fail to remind me of her father's. Clara beams up at me with her innocent hazel eyes, her smile both mischievous and winning me over in a paradoxical combination. She knows she's too cute to get in trouble, and she fully uses that to her advantage.

"You be good for your auntie today, okay?" I ask, giving Clara a meaningful look.

"Yes, no more coloring on the preschool walls," Aunt Patritsiya agrees.

Though she's technically Clara's great-aunt, she always claims that title makes her feel old. I can't say I blame her, seeing as I got pregnant before my seventeenth birthday, so Aunt Patritsiya is rather young to be a great-anything at age forty-three. That's why she only ever goes by auntie.

"Draw me something on *paper* today, Clara. That way you can bring it home for me to see," I suggest as I tickle my little girl's belly.

Clara giggles, her laughter never failing to brighten my day, and she wriggles in her seat. "Yes, Mommy," she agrees. She turns her attention back to her cereal, which she spoons into her mouth sloppily.

Thanks, Auntie, I mouth, earning a kind smile from my aunt.

I don't know what I would do without her. I couldn't have done it all on my own–transferred high schools mid-semester, kept and raised Clara, pursued my dream of becoming a ballerina. The first few years of her life were particularly challenging–hard but unimaginably rewarding. Thankfully, Clara's old enough now that she goes to preschool with my aunt every day.

I give Clara one last kiss. Then, jittery with excitement, I march out the front door of our modest apartment. I race down the three flights of stairs and make it out to the bus stop just in time.

It's a beautiful August day, and the streets are bustling with activity when I exit the bus a half hour later, stepping onto Rosehill's tiny campus. It takes me no time to find the building that houses the majority of my dance classes, the studios where I'll be undergoing intense training with some of the best professors in Chicago–if not the US.

The building is made up of beautiful gray stone that forms turrets beneath steeply slanting eaves, giving it an almost castle-like appearance. The archway leading to the main entrance dwarfs me, and my chest swells with pride to know this is the school I'm attending.

My first class is choreography with a focus on ballet, and as I step into the studio, my jaw drops. The mats are already taken by numerous students stretching as they prepare for class to start. Though I'm here ten minutes early, I already feel late.

Stuffing my bag into one of the cubbies that line the wall, I remove my tennis shoes, replacing them with dance slippers. Then I pad lightly over to the mats to join my fellow students, who stretch as they converse about their summer and all they've been up to.

I choose a spot slightly away from the mix, intensely aware of how out of place I seem. Judging by the make of their clothes, I'm surrounded by students of a completely different economic echelon than me. They wear nothing but top brand dancing apparel, whereas my generic leggings are starting to look a bit threadbare from the years of use they've seen. My dance shoes are run-down as well in comparison to the other shoes in this room. But they're comfortable enough to get the job done.

"Venice was my favorite," one girl gushes as she leans into her stretch. "But they have a pasta that absolutely freaked me out. They use squid ink for sauce, so the whole dish is black. Luckily, my parents are fully on board with my trainer's meal plan, so I couldn't eat it anyway. No carbs for me."

"How long were you there?" the tall, dark-haired girl next to her asks. Her pixie cut stands out like a dark halo all around her head, making her look like a fierce fairy.

"In Venice or Europe?" the first girl asks, pausing her stretches to pull her bleach-blond hair back into a tight ponytail.

"Both?"

"Well, mostly we spent the summer in my parents' summer home in Niece. But we did a week in Venice."

My attention turns to another set of dancers stretching, as the freckle-faced guy boasts, "Oh yeah, the helicopter was just circling over the volcano. No way could we have touched down. I mean, the lava was spewing!"

"Which island was it?" his friend asks, sounding as awed as I feel at the thought of circling over a volcano.

"The big one. That's the only active volcano in Hawaii right now."

Once again, I feel out of my league. The students' blasé descriptions of extravagant vacations and summer homes in upstate New York make me highly conscious of my own financial state. I took a summer job teaching ballet to save up enough money for Clara's school. It's somewhat daunting to know I'm the only one here who needs a scholarship, generously contributed by a wealthy family's donation, to fund my education.

"I'm so excited to be in Professor Moriari's class this semester," the dark-haired pixie cut girl says, drawing my attention once more as she mentions our professor's name.

"I'm a little scared," the bleach blonde confesses with a shudder. "I hear he's really strict. I just hope I don't end up in tears."

"We'll probably all end up in tears at some point this semester, knowing his reputation," the pixie-cut girl observes dryly, finding humor in the thought.

I can't help but smile at their concerns. I know the professor's reputation is daunting, but I'm with the pixie-cut girl. The more strenuous the challenge, the better. I want Professor Moriari to be hard on us, to push us. That's what I'm here for.

Still, I feel for the blonde. I've seen many dancers' dreams crushed by mentors who pushed them too hard. I hope she can hold up under the pressure. I hope we all can.

I move through the familiar stretches, going mostly unnoticed and unbothered by the others. I don't mind. It gives me a chance to listen and learn. It's clear that they have spent the last few years getting to know each other and the program. I'm the outsider, transferring from a more affordable community college.

As the clock ticks closer to the start of class, the conversations in the room fade to a quiet focus. I can feel the shift in the air. These dancers are serious. They may be in higher social class than me, but at least we have that dedication in common.

The room goes silent as the studio doors burst open, and a man in a sharp outfit strides through the room, his hooked nose raised arrogantly. The severe line of his brow warns us to remain attentive as his shoes tap an authoritative beat across the mats. He moves with the grace of a dancer, holding a poise that commands respect, and I can only assume he's Professor Moriari.

"I expect you all to be fully stretched and prepared at the start of each class," he states, making his way to the far side of the mirrored room before turning to face his silent audience. "I waste no time with meet-and-greet practices or social interactions. You can manage all of that outside this class. Here, I expect you to be at your best, prepared to perform and learn to your utmost potential. You're upperclassmen now, and as such, you will be one of the several classes performing in the autumn showcase in a month. I expect each of your performances to properly display your talents as well as prove your potential."

My pulse quickens at the thought of dancing on stage so shortly after the school year has begun. I know I can. I've never faltered in a performance before, but learning ballet at Rosehill College is my dream, and I sense that I'm more of a little fish in a wide ocean of talent here. I only hope I can live up to the school's expectations.

"Everyone up. On your feet. I want to see how far you've progressed–or backslid–over your summer vacation."

Professor Moriari puts us through several grueling exercises, demanding more of each student as he assesses us one by one. I'm used to the pressure, to pushing myself until I'm at my body's limit, because I know I'll have to fight harder for my position than anyone with a family trust fund. I will only succeed as a dancer if I'm willing to go the extra mile, to stand out despite my economic shortcomings. It was my parents' dream to see me become a ballerina, to represent our Russian heritage and show my worth to the world. And it's my dream now. No matter the blood, sweat, and tears, I want to be the best in the world, a prima ballerina for the ages.

"Again!" Professor Moriari demands as he paces between our rows, watching our forms and figures as we execute the challenging routine he's using to assess our skills.

He pauses beside me, and I have to focus intently to stay balanced under his sharp gaze. He's had something critical to say about everyone he's stopped for so far, and I steel myself for whatever critique he has for me.

"You're the new student. Anya Orlov, is it?" he asks, his tone dry.

"Yes, sir," I respond, trying not to sound too breathless as I continue my formations.

"Very good. You show some promise." He pauses, as if to assess how I might respond to his praise.

It takes all of my strength not to wobble with the shock of his compliment.

"Keep that curve in your right arm. You're letting it get flat," he adds before moving on to his next victim.

I refocus my attention on my arm's shape, fixing its angle.

By the time he's finished assessing each student and allows us a break, I'm sweating profusely from the workout. This is exactly what I need, someone to push me, to analyze my weaknesses and tell me how I can improve.

"For the autumn showcase, you will each have a partner. I will assign them since you are limited on time to prepare. You will be in charge of choosing a performance piece that will emphasize both of your strengths. Keep in mind, this first showcase will springboard your following assignment, the winter showcase. Where you will be expected to choreograph your own piece based in the tradition of ballet. I will post a list of partners before tomorrow's class. I expect you to find your partner and choose a performance on your own time. Class time will be used to practice together. I would highly recommend you spend time practicing outside of class as well." Professor Moriari pauses to level a sharp gaze at several students in turn, and I'm thankful his eyes don't land on me following that statement.

My second class is just as challenging as my first, though this time, the focus is improv and modern dance. By my third class, my arms and legs are starting to feel the strain of continuous training, and my stomach is growling. I can't wait to get to lunch, and fortunately, I have a break between my third and fourth classes.

Heading into the school cafeteria, I pick a food line and collect a grilled chicken spinach salad–packed with nutrients–and a black coffee–no sugar or cream to disrupt my strict dietary regimen–to get me through my afternoon classes. Physical exhaustion is already creeping into my muscles, and hopefully, the boost of caffeine will keep me awake.

The woman at the register offers a kind smile as I hand her my meal-plan card.

"Part of the scholarship program?" she asks, her tone impressed.

"Yes, ma'am," I say, my cheeks warming self-consciously.

"You must be quite talented. Only a rare few get this level of aid."

I know she's just trying to be nice, but having a stranger call out one more way I don't fit in makes me squirm uncomfortably.

"I just love that the school's been able to open its doors to a few... less fortunate students with the talent for our arts program." She beams as she hands back my card, seeming oblivious to my discomfort.

"Thank you," I murmur, not sure what else to say. Then I flee.

I'm grateful that my scholarship includes a meal plan and grocery aid. It takes the financial burden off my aunt and helps provide for Clara. But I sincerely hope that my meal card won't turn into one more way to brand me as an outsider at this school.

Heading toward the tables, I carry my tray as I make my way through the throng of bodies. A familiar deep voice catches my ear as I walk, inexplicably lifting the hair on the back of my neck. Thinking my body's on overdrive from all the physical exertion, I try to calm my quickening heart.

And then he's right there in front of me.

As a student steps around me, intent on getting to the food line, Nicolo Marchetti's strong, tall, and stunningly good-looking figure appears before me.

The air leaves my lungs in a gasp as his hazel eyes meet mine, interest sparking in their depths. My body goes rigid as I come face to face with the man who hurt me so deeply. The father of my child.

Of course, he has no idea. I never told Nicolo Marchetti about the baby. He might have taken my innocence, but I wouldn't let him have her as a reward. I thought I'd escaped him when I left our high school. Now, seeing him again feels like some kind of cruel joke.

As his lips pull up into that charming, cocky smile, my body goes numb. I barely feel the tray slip from my fingers before it hits the floor.

Hot black liquid bursts upward, combining with lightly dressed salad, exploding onto me and Nicolo. The sting of scalding coffee is nothing compared to the look of utter rage that transforms Nicolo's handsome face. His strong jaw clenches, making the tendons pop dangerously beneath his lightly stubbled cheeks. His nostrils flare as his shoulders tense.

"The fuck is wrong with you?" he demands as he shakes his hands, flinging the liquid and greenery coating them back to the ground.

My heart comes to a dead standstill as I realize what I've done. But I'm so utterly shocked at seeing Nicolo that I can't seem to formulate a complete thought, let alone words.

I haven't seen him since sophomore year of high school, and I had been so thankful to be away from him then. I've spent every day since trying not to think of him. But with Clara as a living reminder, it's been hard.

And now, he's here in front of me, at the school I've always dreamed of attending, looking like he's two seconds from slapping me.

2

ANYA

Nicolo's as handsome as I remember, his hazel eyes intense, their almond shape elegant. His dark curly hair falls in a perfectly styled mess over his forehead. Since I last saw him, he's grown into his proud nose and strong jaw. The dark stubble that colors his face tells me he's more man than boy now.

His full lips twist into a sneer. "Are you deaf?" he demands as I continue to stand motionless before him. "I asked what the fuck is wrong with you."

"It seems she doesn't know how to carry a tray or speak," one of Nicolo's friends observes dryly beside him.

"I-I'm so sorry," I stutter as I stare in mortification at the mess I've made of his nice jeans.

Overwhelmed with memories, I fight the pain and rejection I felt back in high school flooding into me once again. Under his cold gaze, I feel like a self-conscious teen once again.

Nicolo looks me up and down. "You might be dressed like a dancer, but I hate to break it to you, klutz. You're too clumsy to be in *this* art

18

program." He glances at his friends. "I bet she fails out before the end of her first week."

They snort with laughter. Though they're different faces than the ones that followed him in high school, his friends are the same type of people. Tall, good-looking, muscular guys with a mean expression permanently etched on their faces.

"You must be new here. I would have noticed someone strutting around in Goodwill rags before now. Is it your first day, New Girl?" Nicolo sneers.

Suddenly, I'm struck by the realization that Nicolo doesn't recognize me. The man who made high school a living hell has completely forgotten about me. Meanwhile, my body can't seem to function properly in his proximity.

I flash back to our confrontation in the halls of our high school, Nicolo pretending he forgot my name, and I realize that while he said it then to hurt me, he really thought so little of me that he *doesn't* know who I am.

"Yes, it's my first day," I gasp, trying to regain some form of composure in front of him.

"Well, let me give you a little hint, New Girl. Stay the *fuck* out of my way," he growls, echoing his sentiment from years before and bringing back a fresh flood of memories.

"Ugh," he groans, looking down at his spinach-and-coffee-covered clothes. "I'll have to change before my next class. I guess I can just buy something from the school shops." His eyes flick back to me once more as his expression of disgust transforms into a scoff, and he leaves without another word to me.

Nicolo's friends follow, leering at me as they go.

I fight back the tears threatening to spill down my cheeks as I stare at my feet. I can't bring myself to apologize again or even clean up my mess as his words cut deep. Spinning on my heel, I race from the cafeteria, ready to crawl into the deepest, darkest hole I can find.

My eyes scan for the nearest bathroom. I rush through the door and sprint to the far stall. The moment it's closed and latched, mortified tears burst from me in gasping sobs. My back hits the wall as I sink down to the floor, trembling uncontrollably.

How is it that Nicolo Marchetti, the man who has plagued my life for years, is suddenly at school with me again? And what's somehow worse is that he doesn't even recognize me. I should be grateful, considering I have Clara to think about. I don't want him to know anything about me, but in this fresh introduction, I've clearly made Nicolo an enemy.

Huddling in the bathroom stall, I allow myself a few minutes of self-pity, releasing tears until I can regain my breath. Then I pull myself together once more. I can't afford to miss my next class over what happened with Nicolo.

When I step out of the bathroom stall and approach the mirror above the sink, I'm glad I'm alone. My face is a mess. My tears have left my cheeks splotchy, and the tip of my nose is an angry red. Turning on the cold water, I wash my face, rinsing away my salty tears and cooling my flaming skin. I dry off with paper towels and fix my hair, redoing my French braid that will keep it off my face.

I then turn to my freshly stained leggings. I do my best to blot away the worst of the coffee and salad dressing, using paper towel and water to help lift the spots, but I'll need to work on them more when I get home. I can't afford to simply replace them. At least I have a few other pairs, though these were my best ones.

My stomach growls, reminding me I haven't eaten, but I won't have time to stand in line for a salad again. Instead, I head to the expedited pre-packaged food fridge, grab a fruit bowl and bottle of water, then add it to my meal plan. Clutching my meal to my chest, I head outside to enjoy my food in peace. Finding an empty bench, I sit and eat, soaking up the summer day.

Try as I might to stop thinking about Nicolo, his face continues to swirl in my head. *What could have possibly turned him into such a mean person?* Maybe it's his life of privilege, but I bet it has more to do with his father. Don Lorenzo Marchetti all but owns this side of Chicago.

I've heard terrible things about their mafia family over the years, and from the sounds of it, they all but have the police in their back pocket. *How can anyone turn into a decent human being when their money comes from taking advantage of other people's weakness and misfortune?*

He didn't even allow me the time to feel bad for spilling hot coffee on him. I glance down at the angry red splotches on the back of my hands, massaging them delicately. I must have burned him too, but he didn't even seem to register the pain.

Finishing my meal, I head into the new gray stone building with just enough time to make it to class. I run upstairs to find the right room. This history class is one of the few remaining core classes I need for my degree. I got most of them out of the way in community college.

The room is almost full, and I rush to find an open chair in the theater-style raised seating. Slipping into my chair, I tuck my bag beneath my seat and pull out a notebook just as the professor enters the room.

"You've got to be fucking kidding me," someone says coldly behind me as I sit up straight.

Once again, the hair raises on the back of my neck, and I slowly turn to find Nicolo sitting a row behind me and a few seats to my right. My stomach drops as I realize he must be talking about me. His eyes are locked on mine, and his lip curls in utter disgust as he scoffs at me.

"What?" his blond friend with a clean-shaven face asks quietly beside him as the teacher starts to speak.

Nicolo jerks his chin in my direction, and when his friend glances my way, fresh mortification heats my cheeks. The friend snickers, and I turn to face the front of the room, willing them to ignore me now that class has begun.

I can barely focus as Professor Kennedy introduces herself, writing her name up on the board before handing a stack of syllabi to the nearest student seated in the front row. When the stack of papers reaches me, I take one and pass them down.

As the professor reviews the class expectations in depth, whispered hisses issue from where Nicolo sits. I keep my eyes focused forward, doing my best to ignore him.

Something thunks lightly against the back of my head, and I catch sight of a crumpled piece of paper tumbling to the floor in my periphery. I can't put him off any longer. Turning stiffly in my seat, I meet Nicolo's playful eyes once again, and he smiles cockily.

"Hey, New Girl, did someone forget to tell you that we don't let trailer trash into this university?" he whispers.

I glare at him, tired of the way he finds amusement in hurting me. "Then someone must have missed the memo when they sent you an admittance letter," I snap, keeping my tone low so as not to draw attention from the front of the room.

"Oh, shit, Nico! New Girl's got claws!" Nicolo's blond friend says behind his fist as he chuckles.

Nicolo backhands his friend's shoulder, shutting him up with a cold look.

"You think you're funny, klutz?" Nicolo demands, his eyes narrowing at me.

I shrug and turn to face our professor once again. His silence feels more ominous than relieving. My muscles tense as I wait for the next attack, sure that Nicolo's not done with me.

The pen that hits my head a moment later makes me jerk forward unexpectedly. *Ow.* I try not to show my pain, though I can't stop my hand from reaching up to find the tender point of contact and cover it defensively. Someone snickers, and I grind my teeth as I regain my composure, refusing to glance back and give Nicolo the satisfaction of knowing he hurt me.

"Psst, New Girl."

Another object flies past my ear, making me flinch.

"What?" I hiss, whirling to stare him down as fiercely as I can.

"Who'd you have to sleep with to get into the university? You clearly couldn't afford the tuition otherwise. Haven't you noticed you don't belong?"

"Is there a problem?" Professor Kennedy asks, her voice raising to carry more authority as it travels to the back of the room.

I turn to find her eyes on me, watching me with pursed lips that give her bespectacled face and angry librarian look.

"No, ma'am," I whisper to a round of snickers behind me. "Sorry."

"Eyes up front," she says dryly in response, no doubt thinking I must be mooning over Nicolo or something.

I struggle through the remainder of the hour, keeping my eyes locked forward despite the onslaught of paper balls thrown my way. As soon as Professor Kennedy dismisses us, I'm up and out of my chair, making my way hurriedly toward the door. But when I reach the end of my row, Nicolo's imposing figure already bars my path.

He crosses his arms over his chest, his strong biceps stretching the fabric of his blue polo. "What's your name, New Girl?"

I swallow hard, fear gripping my chest. If I tell him, he might recognize me. "Anya," I reply simply and hold my breath.

"Well, *Anya*," he sneers. "Why don't you go back to Klutzville? Chicago's my town, and I don't want you here ruining all my clothes."

A shiver runs down my spine at the threat behind his words. His family has a reputation for proving their power with violent displays.

But he wouldn't hurt me, would he? In the middle of broad daylight on a college campus? Perhaps I should just keep my head down and try not to provoke him. I don't particularly want to find out.

3

NICOLO

Tilting my chair against the back wall of my econ class, I groan. I can't get Anya off my mind. It's irritating. She burst into my life like a tornado, dumping coffee and salad all over my favorite pair of shoes and effectively ruining my day.

While I couldn't care less about the way her clumsiness burned me, it was her look that bothered me. Like I'm a viper, some poisonous snake that would surely kill her given a chance. *She spilled coffee all over me, and she had the nerve to think I'm the ass?*

As the oldest son of Lorenzo Marchetti and the heir to his business someday, I'm used to people treating me with respect and, when I demand it, fear. But Anya seemed to dislike me before she even met me. *Who is she to judge me?* No one.

She might have beautiful golden hair and captivating blue eyes. Her face is almost as delicate as a porcelain doll's. But she's a charity case, probably at Rosehill on some scholarship because no girl from a proper family would be caught dead in those rags. The runs in her leggings told me she's in desperate need of a new pair.

Anya, beautiful yet klutzy–I could almost work with that. But there's no doubt in my mind that my father would consider her beneath me.

No need to bring her home to the family. Don Lorenzo has made it perfectly clear that I'll need to set my sights higher, to a bride who can add worth to our family name.

Still, I can't get that *look* Anya gave me out of my head.

"Dude, Nico, your new car is *sick*," Jay says enthusiastically beside me, pulling me back to the present.

I smile cockily, thinking of my black Maserati parked in the garage beneath my Lincoln Park penthouse apartment. My belated birthday present from my father handles like a dream. Not that anyone in my family *needs* a car. We have drivers for that kind of stuff. But I like the extra sense of freedom when my role as Don Lorenzo's son gets too stuffy.

"It hits zero to sixty in 3.2 seconds. Makes the girls go down on my cock even faster," I brag.

I wonder if Anya might suck my cock for a ride in my new car. Immediately, I hate myself for even thinking it. Something tells me she wouldn't, and that pisses me off more. Girls don't say no to me, but from the way Anya looked at me today, I think she just might. *She thinks she's too good for me? In her threadbare clothes, a proper charity case?*

I'll teach her not to look at me that way. If she doesn't know enough to respect me, I'll make her fear me instead. The thought's reflexive, ingrained in my psyche from all the years of my father whispering in my ear. But that's the kind of power we have. If I wanted to, I could have Anya chained to my bedpost for as long as it suited me.

We fall silent for a few minutes as the professor at the front of the class drones on. Some days, I hate going to school. There's no point to it in my mind. It's all just for show.

Dad thinks a proper degree is important to maintaining the family image. We can't run the town if we don't even have a college educa-tion, in his book. Especially since a large portion of our philanthropic gestures revolve around the funding for this school. But it's not like they teach How to Run a Mafia Business 101 or Torture Techniques for the upper-division classes.

School's just all part of the facade, the lie we tell the world to cover what we really do. *Because what rich family with a proper education would commit our kind of crimes?* I've come to realize that what the world *thinks* of you is far more important than who you really are.

"Look at that prime piece of real estate," Dominic praises.

His chin juts toward the model-perfect blonde that walks through the door, her pencil skirt snuggly hugging her curves. Her heels click on the floor, making her hips sway and demanding everyone's attention. She's late for class, and I'm sure that's her intention. She's here to find a sugar daddy if I had to bet. Her outfit is too form-fitting to qualify as studious, and she's dolled up like she's looking to catch someone's eye.

Plenty of girls at Rosehill do that. Waste Daddy's money while they look for who might fund their Botox. In exchange they'll pump out a couple of kids and be the perfect trophy wife. This one's too obvious for me. But still, I can appreciate her efforts. She'll find someone to drool over her. It's just not going to be me.

"Mmm. What I wouldn't give to put that rack to good use," Dom practically pants, letting his chair fall back onto four legs as he watches her closely.

The girl's eyes flick toward the back of the room as if she can hear him, and her gaze meets mine. She gives me a sultry smile and the subtlest of finger waves. See, that's the kind of response I'm supposed to get from girls. An invitation to bend them over, spread their legs, and make them scream my name. I give her a subtle nod, returning her smile, though I can't find it in me to appreciate her. She blushes coyly and keeps peering up at me through her lashes as she finds her seat.

"Sometimes, I hate being your friend," Dom gripes.

I chuckle as he slumps in his seat and crosses his arms in a grown-man pout.

"I can't help that I'm better-looking than you," I joke, glancing his way.

I get how infuriating it must be to watch girls throwing themselves at my feet. I consider Dom and Jay close friends–close enough that they'll probably become members of my family business someday. But that won't get the same level of respect that comes with the Marchetti name. Of course, they get plenty of pussy. And I'm happy to send any girl I'm not interested in their way. But sometimes it's fun to take a girl just because I can.

"I'll tell you what," I say, clapping them both on the shoulders and drawing their eyes to me. "Dom, you can have the blonde once I've broken her in. I'll bring Jay along in my Maserati when I drop her off. Then we'll all get the ride we're looking for."

Jay chuckles, flashing his teeth to confirm his agreement.

"Fuck you, man," Dom hisses, shoving my hand away. "I don't need your sloppy seconds. I'll find a girl on my own."

I shrug. "Suit yourself."

Jay snickers. "Like how about that dumpster diver that spilled her food all over Nico today?"

My irritation spikes once again at the mention of the new girl. Her soul-piercing gaze sticks with me, tugging at the back of my brain. I don't know why, but something about her is familiar.

Dom scoffs. "I wouldn't have to stoop that low to find pussy. Even I have standards. But at least she had some fuck-worthy legs. Right? Mmm. And that ass–"

"Definitely a dancer's ass," Jay agrees.

"No one touches her," I growl.

"Easy, Nico," Dom says, raising his hands in surrender. "What, you thinking about fucking her?" he teases.

Like that would go over well with my father. Not that he gives a shit what I do with women, but he wouldn't be happy if he found out I fucked some stripper. Even my playthings should have some kind of pedigree. And it wouldn't surprise me if she's stripping to pay her way through school. I've heard some of the dancers have to do that if they don't have parents to pay their way.

"Fuck no," I scoff, making light of his suggestion. "You couldn't pay me to fuck that klutz."

Jay chuckles, combing his fingers through his short blond hair. "That's cold, man. You don't want her but we can't get any?"

I scowl at him.

"Okay, okay," he adds quickly when he sees my face. "She's probably not worth the trouble. I'm just saying, even a spaz like her might be fun for a one-time ride."

My rebellious cock twitches in my pants at the thought of Anya naked, and I shove the image from my mind. I probably just find her more interesting because I know she would be considered off limits. She's too far beneath me.

The blonde at the front of the class glances back at me over her shoulder, her lips pressing forward into a pouty smile that's become the popular seductive face. I raise an eyebrow suggestively, hinting at my interest.

The girl is beautiful enough to be a model, her hair perfectly styled in bleach-blonde curls. Her ruby lips silently suggest how good they would look wrapped around my cock. *And yet, why won't my cock respond to the thought of fucking her like it just did about the new girl?*

Again, thinking about Anya makes me start to swell, and I grind my teeth in annoyance. I need to find myself some proper pussy and fast. Plowing a couple of runway girls will do the trick, I'm sure.

I'm probably just drawn to the challenge Anya presents. From that spiteful look she gave me, I don't think she's ready to just spread her legs like the bleach-blonde currently eye fucking me. I bet Anya would take a lot more effort on my part.

She might be beautiful–and a fun challenge–but my father would never approve of her, so I shouldn't waste my time. But the thought of breaking that defiant gaze appeals to me. Maybe if I can't fuck her, I can at least have some fun. My lips curl into a smile as I think about all the ways I could make her life hell. If she wants to think I'm a monster, then I might as well show her just how horrible I can be.

And perhaps after she sees what happens when a person disrespects me, she might change her tune. By the time I'm done screwing with her head, I might just grace her with a mercy fuck. If she begs.

My cock throbs against the zipper of my jeans, and I suddenly realize that my thoughts of torturing Anya have turned sexual. I need to get my head out of the gutter and find some high end pussy fast.

4

ANYA

Pulling open the door to my next afternoon class, I scan the rows of seats and find an open spot near the back of the room. Not that I think someone like Nicolo would have anything to do with Dance Theory, but better safe than sorry.

This lecture hall is much smaller than the one for my history class, capable of holding closer to sixty students rather than a hundred, and the desks are, in fact, a long table in each tiered row.

Now that my tension from Nicolo's bullying has dissipated, exhaustion seeps into my body. Tucking my bag beneath my chair, I settle in and watch as other students start to fill the classroom.

As people trickle in, they talk happily with one other, reminding me of how alone I am. I recognize quite a few of the students from my previous dance classes, and I'm starting to feel marginally more comfortable.

The freckle-faced boy from my first class is definitely a senior, and he walks with a confident swagger. He and the guy who looks to be of Asian descent that he was talking to in my choreography class make their way to the back of the room, chatting animatedly.

"Excuse me." The freckle-faced guy pauses beside my chair to indicate he would like to pass.

"Oh, sorry." I scoot my chair forward as far as I can to allow him access.

"Thanks," his friend adds as he sidles past.

Then they promptly go back to ignoring me. Trying not to take it personally, I watch them out of the corner of my eye. *Should I even bother introducing myself since I have multiple classes with them?*

"Is this seat taken?"

I turn and tilt my head to look up at the tall dark-haired girl from my choreography class. Her wispy pixie cut frames her face, making her appear both dangerous and beautiful all at once. I glance at her hand resting on the back of the chair next to me.

"Oh. No. You're welcome to it," I say, realizing she's asking if someone will be joining me.

"Good." The girl plops into her seat with an appreciative groan.

I give her a knowing smile, literally feeling her pain. If she's a ballerina, like me, her body must be aching from the heavy load of physical classes. Of the seven I'm taking, five of them require constant motion and endurance.

"I think if I continue to repeat it enough times, I might convince myself that 'I love my major,'" the girl jokes.

I laugh. "Say it loud enough, and you just might convince me too." I do love it, truly, but the exhaustion is beyond anything I've experienced already. My previous education didn't prepare me for this level of intensity.

"I'm Whitney," she adds, holding out her hand.

"Anya." I grip her fingers eagerly.

Whitney's the first person who's bothered to introduce themselves. I was starting to wonder if I might not be invisible to everyone at this school–aside from Nicolo, who clearly hates me.

"Are you a transfer student then?" she asks.

I nod, surprised that she would jump to that conclusion so easily. "How did you...?"

"No one gets into Professor Moriari's class as a freshman, and as a dance major, I know pretty much all the upperclassmen in my degree," she explains simply.

She turns her attention to the front door and raises her hand to wave to the bleach-blond girl she was talking to in Choreography. The girl smiles broadly and waves. She and two other girls, both shorter brunettes, trek up the stairs to join my steadily growing row at the back of the class.

"Girls, this is Anya. She's a transfer student. Anya, this is Paige, Tori, and Tammy. If you couldn't guess by looking at them, Tori and Tammy are twins," Whitney explains.

"Nice to meet you," I say.

"Hey, you're the girl who Professor Moriari actually complimented today, aren't you?" Paige, the bleach-blonde, asks.

I nod shyly, embarrassed that his praise is how she would remember me.

"Yeah, how'd you manage that on our first day?" the freckle-faced boy asks as he and his friend turn their attention to me. "Did you suck his cock or something in exchange for a good grade?"

"Logan!" Whitney gasps as I feel my face burst into flames.

"It was a joke!" he says defensively. "Mostly anyway... He just doesn't go around saying nice things to students. I can't help it if I'm a little jealous."

"Well, you don't have to be a dick about it," Whitney chirps.

Logan puts a gentle hand on my shoulder. "I'm sorry. I was just teasing. I'm sure it's because you're an incredible dancer."

"Thanks," I mumble, confused by the whole exchange.

"So, you're aiming to become a ballerina?" Paige asks casually, twirling the ends of her high ponytail.

I nod. "Is that what you all are here for?"

"The boys are," Whitney explains, pointing to Logan and his friend. "As are Paige and I."

"We're here for contemporary dance," the brunette named Tammy explains.

Tori snorts. "Yeah, no way could we possibly compete with you girls when it comes to ballet. We're not 'cut out' for it," she explains, using air quotes to emphasize her words.

"They're too short," Whitney explains in a stage whisper behind her hand.

I can't help but laugh as the twins glare daggers at Whitney.

"And you all have been in this program since freshman year?" I ask.

They all nod confirmation.

"It must be nice having a tight-knit group that's all heading in the same direction," I observe with a pang of loneliness. It shouldn't bother me. I'm used to being on my own if I'm not with my daughter or my aunt. I wonder how this group would feel about me if they knew I'm a single mother, or anything at all about my past.

"Yeah, we're basically the cool kids. Stick with us, and you'll be just fine." Paige gives me a wink.

"Speaking of cool kids, we were just talking about hitting up one of the local clubs this weekend, called Danza. You want to come?" Tori offers, leaning forward in her seat to get a good look at me.

"Oh, um..." I hesitate. I don't normally go out on weekends, seeing as I have a daughter to take care of.

"Yeah, come with us," Whitney presses. "It's where all the Rosehill students go to party. You don't have to be twenty-one or anything."

"Fin and I are in," Logan says, leaning forward to join the conversation as he gestures behind him to his friend.

"We weren't inviting you boys," Paige snarks. "But I guess you can come too if you want. What do you say, Anya? Want to come out for a night of fun?"

When I hesitate once again, trying to come up with a solid reason to stay in, Tammy says, "Oh, you have to go at least once. It's one of the coolest nightclubs in Chicago. *And* it's owned by the Marchettis."

My heart stutters at the mention of Nicolo's family name. Now I'm even less inclined to go. *If his family owns the place, wouldn't I be more likely to run into him?* That's the last thing I want.

"That mafia family that basically runs Chicago's criminal underground?" Logan asks, his copper-colored eyebrows rising toward his hairline.

"Yeah, you didn't know that?" Paige asks with mild surprise. "That's part of the appeal. It gives the club a certain... mystique," she says, dropping her tone to show it's a secret.

"I don't know that I feel comfortable going to a club owned by the mob..." I hedge.

"Oh, it's not like they're ever really there anyway," Whitney insists. "And when they do come, they all sit in a separate section of the club."

"Yeah, they're far too important to mingle with the rest of us lowly college students." Paige rolls her eyes for emphasis.

"Come on, Anya. As an honorary new member of the cool kids group, you have to come," Whitney presses, widening her dark-rimmed eyes to give me a puppy dog face.

I have to admit, despite the chance of running into Nicolo unnecessarily, it feels really good to be invited to something with people I could see becoming my friends. My weak resistance crumbles as I meet their intent eyes.

"Okay, I'll come," I say, cracking a smile big enough it makes my cheeks hurt. My aunt won't mind babysitting for the night if she knows it means I'm making friends.

"Yay!" Whitney gives my shoulder a squeeze. "It'll be fun. I promise."

"We usually meet up at my place beforehand to pregame," Paige says. "It's just a few blocks from the club, so it's an easy walk from there." She scribbles her address on a slip of paper and hands it to me.

"Thanks," I say, gratefully.

We all fall silent as the professor enters the classroom and immediately begins his introduction as he hands out his syllabus. I try to focus, genuinely excited about Dance Theory. It will teach me more about the concepts behind different dance styles, something I've never known much about. Ballet is much more traditional and focuses on precision rather than the premise of the body as art.

But my mind wanders back to the invitation I just received. I have to admit, it feels kind of good to have found a group I might fit with, despite the clear separation between us economically. But my new potential friends seem grounded enough in reality to not judge me for my threadbare clothes.

And while Logan's sense of humor is a bit outside my comfort zone, his friend, Fin, actually seems quite nice. On the shy side, perhaps, just like me. But as a whole, they all seem quite nice.

My thoughts turn to the nightclub and Nicolo. Dancing does sound fun. I haven't ever been to a nightclub before, and it's been forever since I've done anything with friends.

I just have to keep my fingers crossed that I don't run into Nicolo there. It shocks me to realize how easily my old wounds could be reopened. I thought I'd buried the bad memories long ago.

What's worse is my body still seems intensely affected by Nicolo's proximity. The mere sound of his voice had sent goose bumps rippling down my arms. Fighting the shiver that races down my spine, I force my mind back onto the professor. Nicolo might be back in my life, but I refuse to let him affect me like he did back in high school.

5

ANYA

"Just one shot, Anya!" Logan presses, holding one out to me.

"No really. I'm a lightweight. You don't want to see what happens to me on shots," I insist. "I'll stick with my vodka soda. But thanks."

What with my sights set so intently on dancing and my daughter, I don't have a lot of time to spend drinking. And I don't want to make a bad impression on my first night out with friends.

"Don't worry. I'll drink it for you," Whitney offers, taking the shot as she gives me a wink.

I smile gratefully.

As we pregame in Paige's impressive apartment, I find it hard to believe one college student could merit all that prime real estate not ten minutes from campus. It's big enough to fit two of Aunt Patritsiya's apartment inside. But it was fun getting ready with the girls in her impressive master bath. And it's got a wonderful sound system for our pre-fun fun.

They take their last shot, then we make our way down to the street and walk to Danza. Feeling confident in my best summer dress and a pair of three-inch heels that accentuate my above-average height, I march toward the club with fresh courage, feeling good about tonight.

"I love those shoes," Whitney says beside me, eyes following my flashy heels.

"Thanks." I beam. "They were a birthday gift from my aunt. So was this dress."

"Aw, that's sweet." Whitney's tone is playful but somehow doesn't make me feel self-conscious. It's almost like she can see the potential for my embarrassment and is encouraging me to smile.

A line has already started to form outside the red, brick building as we arrive, telling me this place must be popular. It's not quite seven on a Friday night, and already the club must be packed. Stepping up to join the line, I listen to Logan's newest story, which he tells with animation to keep us entertained.

"I'm telling you, the fish was larger than me, and my uncle howled and thrashed as he fought to reel the thing in." Logan mimics his uncle's movements, demonstrating the struggle of trying to catch a swordfish. "Finally, the fishermen had to haul out the nets to help him, and while they were lifting this goliath out of the water, the damn thing leapt up out of the net and came flopping down onto the deck, right on top of my uncle!"

The twins howl with laughter as Paige raises a skeptical eyebrow.

"Now you're just lying," she says.

"Hey, you don't have to believe me," Logan says nonchalantly, shrugging. "But I was there. I saw it happen."

Paige rolls her eyes. "A fish as big as you? Oh, please."

"What about you, Anya?" Whitney asks. "Any great travel stories?"

I shake my head. "Not me personally. But my parents immigrated here from Russia along with my aunt before I was born."

"That's cool," Fin says. "My grandparents moved here from Japan."

"It's always nice to meet someone else from an immigrant family," I say with a warm smile.

"Yeah, totally," he agrees. "It takes a lot of courage to uproot your lives and start over again halfway across the world. Feels like a family history I can take pride in."

I couldn't have said it better myself.

Slowly, the line creeps forward as we chat and laugh, and finally we reach the silk rope separating the front of the line from our final destination. At the door, stopping people from entering without permission, are two burly men. They look like they could easily snap any one of us in half. My new friends ignore them completely, turning their backs so they're not looking toward the intimidating men. But I can't help observing the bouncers out of the corner of my eye.

The purr of a soft motor rumbles up to the curb, announcing the sleek black Maserati that makes my head turn, and my jaw drops. It's a beautiful car made of soft edges, pristine lines, and tinted windows that keep its passengers hidden from view. The driver puts the car in park, and the clubgoers behind me fall silent to see who the celebrities are.

Three heads of thick, dark curls rise from the sports car as the driver and his two passengers exit the vehicle. The boys who step from the back look to be in their late teens and similar enough in appearance that they must be twins. They have the same proud nose and confident smiles that curl the corners of their lips. The hint of a cleft lingers on their chins.

My attention turns to the driver, and my heart flutters uncomfortably. Nicolo Marchetti straightens his button-down and tosses his keys casually to a slight doorman I hadn't even noticed behind the two burly ones.

The younger guys from the back seat must be Nicolo's brothers. They look enough like carbon copies that I can't believe I didn't see it right away.

"Take care of her for me, Dino," Nicolo says to the slight man I'm assuming is a valet. "And enjoy yourself. Just don't fuck up her paint job."

The valet chuckles, striding toward the car as Nicolo and his younger brothers make their way toward the club. Mouth dry and palms sweaty, I watch him silently, hoping he won't notice me. He seems so at ease with his world, perfectly comfortable to simply pass up the line while the rest of us common people wait our turn. Of course, if his family owns the club, that comes as no surprise.

As Nicolo's long strides carry him to the entrance, one of the doormen opens the door for him, releasing a wave of club music. But Nicolo glances right, and our eyes meet. He slows as his gaze travels over my group, and a smug smile spreads across his face.

"Well, if it isn't the new girl," he sneers.

Anxiety ripples through me as Nicolo turns to face me. His brothers pause with him, their gazes landing on me with open curiosity.

"God, we just let any old riff raff in into the club these days, don't we, Brasco?" Nicolo glances over his shoulder toward the doorman still holding the door for him.

The man gives a subtle nod, though he continues to hold his pose.

"Just watch your toes," he warns my friends. "This one's got two left feet." His eyes shift back to me, dark humor dancing in their depths.

"You know this girl, Nico?" one of his brothers asks with surprise.

"This is the kind of charity case that goes to Rosehill nowadays–and apparently, our club."

His brothers exchange a glance before eyeing me with interest, as if assessing what their brother could find so distasteful about me.

Nicolo–*Nico*, apparently, to those who matter in his life–eyes me coolly before his gaze flicks to my friends once more. They stand speechless around me, all their attention turned to the Marchetti heir as if he's some kind of Roman deity.

"So, is this your best attempt to prove you're worth something, New Girl?" Nicolo asks. "Running with the rich crowd to show you can be one of them?" He steps close to me, and I can smell the woodsy scent of his cologne as he leans in to whisper, "I hate to break it to you, Anya, but nothing you do will ever make you worth anything."

My stomach knots at the combination of his proximity and the spiteful words he murmurs just for me.

Then he leans back with a smug smile. "Enjoy your evening out, Cinderella. But make sure you're home by midnight or you might just turn back into a pumpkin." He waves his brothers along, and they enter the club without a backward glance, leaving me speechless in their wake.

"Holy shit, I never realized Nicolo Marchetti was such a douche. Are you okay?" Whitney asks, her eyebrows raising.

"He and his father are nothing more than low-life criminals who buy their way out of facing jail time," Paige observes dryly.

"You can't mess with the Marchettis," Logan agrees, his voice awed. "Especially at their own club. You did the right thing by just biting your tongue until he left you alone, Anya."

I've been biting my tongue so long and hard over Nicolo, I damn near taste blood every time he's around. But I don't say as much. Instead, I shrug. "It's okay. I understand. I know who he is."

"Yeah, well, forget him. Let's go inside and dance our troubles away," Whitney says, throwing her arm around my shoulders.

In silent agreement, the doorman unhooks the silk rope barring us and gestures us into the club.

As the dim hallway opens up to the club's main area, my jaw drops. It's not so much a bar with a dance floor, like I had imagined, but rather an elaborate display of various levels holding multiple kinds of entertainment lit with golden spotlights.

The bottom level holds the dance floor, teaming with sweaty bodies rocking and swaying to the club's throbbing beat. Along the far wall is the bar, made of glass and backlit so the alcohol almost looks like it's floating. A throng of thirsty patrons shuffle against the bar, waiting on their drinks.

In the recesses of the club's alcoves, strippers perform for the men that requested them, some standing on tables or platforms, others providing personal lap dances. It's an overtly sexual display, and I'm somewhat shocked to see it so openly broadcast.

But that's not what has me in awe. Stairs punctuate the edges of the room on either side of the alcoves, leading up to separately enclosed areas decorated with fine white couches and modern coffee tables. Though the higher levels housing the VIP customers are a good distance above us, I can still see every detail of the space.

Like the liquor shelves at the bar, the VIP sections are made of glass floors and railings, revealing everything above. Sparkling flutes of champagne catch in the club's lighting, like stationary sparklers waiting for someone to consume their effervescent liquid.

And above us all, suspended by a single chain each, dangle several massive glass ornament-like cages containing scantily clad dancers. A chill runs down my spine at the thought of what paperwork they must have had to sign to be hoisted stories above the ground in a cube that could shatter and kill them if the chain should break.

"Gorgeous, aren't they?" Logan shouts in my ear.

I glance at him and realize his eyes are trained on the dancers above us.

"Terrifying," I say.

"I'm sure they're paid well, though," Whitney observes. "Nothing wrong with a little risk to make your life worth living."

When I look at Whitney, she gives me a playful wink. Linking elbows with me, she drags me toward the dance floor. "So, can a prim and proper ballerina like you get down and dirty like the rest of us?" she teases.

In all honesty, I have no clue. I've never been on a dance floor like this before. I let my new friends escort me, and we all cram into a small square of space before moving to the beat. My body's not used to the motions my friends adopt. Their hips sway and their shoulders roll rhythmically. I do my best to imitate them, but I must look entirely out of place.

As I dance, my eyes wander, trying to make sense of all the activities taking place around me. At one of the high-top tables surrounding the dance floor, a couple makes out, their hands exploring each other openly. I avert my gaze to give them privacy, though they seem unfazed by their public display.

My eyes track to the VIP section just beyond them. One of the club's dancers, dressed only in a thong made of fluorescent green fabric, lies back on a tabletop, exposing her breasts. One of the men before her taps white powder onto her flat stomach. He cuts the coke right there on her body and snorts it before letting one of his companions take a line.

It's all too much. My senses are on overload no matter which direction I turn. The heavy, sweat-soaked air, the musty smell of grinding bodies, the blaring music that throbs within my chest. The visual stimulation is overwhelming. Even on the dance floor, I'm intensely aware of the way people press together, gyrating in overtly sexual motions as men grip women's hips provocatively.

Something about it feels extremely liberating, the sight of people drinking and dancing in such a care-free way. Despite my attempt to pace myself, the atmosphere leaves me intoxicated, and I'm bordering on dizzy.

"Just relax!" Paige shouts over the music, moving her hips to show me what she means.

I smile, doing as she says and trying to follow her lead. But my eyes continue to wander, taking everything in. I feel as though I've walked into some level of the underworld, exposing myself to all the depravity of society. And while I don't know what to do with myself, I can't entirely say I hate it. It's fascinating.

Motion catches my eye on the club's highest floor–almost level with the floating dancers. I look up to find Nicolo Marchetti lounging on a white couch, his arms stretched across the back in a casual way.

Two women in short, form-fitting dresses that show off all their assets lean against him. Across the table from him, Nicolo's brothers sit, staring out at the mob of bodies on the dance floor. They watch with a youthful interest that's missing from Nicolo's gaze. When I turn my attention back to him, he looks bored. His eyes comb lazily across the club.

One of the girls slides her hand up his leg and tips her hip, exposing her thigh. Both girls are breathtakingly beautiful–models if I had to guess. Their long locks are styled to perfection, and their makeup is so artfully done, they almost look like works of art. The girl sitting on the far side of Nicolo combs her fingers into his thick curls, triggering my memory of his soft hair.

Blushing profusely, I jerk my gaze away. I shouldn't be remembering details about our night together after all these years. Then again, I haven't slept with anyone except Nicolo. I just haven't had time for romance.

And after getting pregnant from the one time, I'm not interested in casual sex. Not with my dream of dancing at stake. I'm fortunate to have found my way through one unexpected pregnancy. I barely managed to get my life back on track after having Clara. It nearly ruined my chances of becoming a professional ballet dancer. I can't afford another lengthy break like that, much less the toll I know it would take on my body. I don't dare risk another.

Forcing myself to focus on my friends, I keep my gaze locked on the dance floor. I refuse to look at Nicolo again tonight. This is my chance to have fun, even if I feel like I'm worlds away from reality.

After several minutes of uninterrupted dancing, Tori leans close and shouts so I can hear her, "Nicolo Marchetti is staring at you."

It takes all my discipline to not look up. Instead, I shrug and continue swaying to the beat. "Let him look if he wants, as long as he doesn't come down here and bother me. I'm here to have fun!"

But my stomach twists uncomfortably, and I feel his gaze burning into the back of my neck long after he must have looked away.

6

NICOLO

"You think Dad will shell out enough cash to buy each of us a new car for our birthdays?" Lucca asks.

"Yeah right. Nicolo only got his Maserati because he's twenty-one now. We probably have to wait for our twenty-first birthdays," Cassio says, rolling his eyes.

"It's probably not even that. It's probably just because he's Dad's *first born* and therefore the favorite," Lucca says.

"Maybe it's because I don't sound like a whiny baby whenever I don't get my way," I suggest dryly, leveling them with a stern gaze that makes them both shut their mouths and slouch in their seats.

Usually, I try to be more gentle with my brothers. As my father has hammered into our brains from an early age, family is the only thing I can trust intrinsically, and when I take over the family business Cassio and Lucca will likely be my best support and allies. But tonight, I don't have the patience to let them act their age.

Their whining is getting on my nerves. I've already been short tempered most of this week. It seems like Anya keeps appearing unexpectedly, which leaves her constantly on my brain. She's like a splinter, aggravating me incessantly.

And now, after I was trying to take some time away from my father's ever-growing pressure to learn the family business, all I get to hear about is how unfairly my younger brothers feel like they're being treated.

We're all relatively close in age, with Cassio and Lucca just two years behind me. Only my sister seems capable of avoiding my last nerve, but I would never bring her to the club. She's better than this place. Not to mention she's still a sophomore in high school and too young for this scene.

"You do have a gorgeous new car, Nico," the blond model under my right arm purrs, running her manicured nails up the inner seam of my slacks. "Maybe you can take me for a ride in it later?" she suggests. From her tone, I wonder if she actually means for me to drive her around or if she means I should fuck her in the back seat.

"Mmm, you could take us both for a ride," the raven-haired girl leaning into my left side offers, her fingers combing into my hair and grazing my scalp. "I'm very good at sharing."

Their heavy-handed suggestions bore me, and I grip the raven-haired model's wrist to remove her hand from my hair.

Once again, my eyes stray to Anya, who's dancing in the mob below me. Though she looks vaguely uncomfortable surrounded by all the drunken bumping and grinding, she still has a natural sway to the beat, her impressive dancer's ass moving to the rhythm in a shy but somehow tantalizing way.

She's dancing with the group of girls she stood with outside our club and seems to be trying to mirror their more aggressive hip movements. She stands out like a sore thumb in her simple floral summer dress. It looks like a hand-me-down she might have gotten from her mother or an older sister at best.

Her friends, in contrast, wear high-end nightclub fashion, glittering, sequined dresses so tight they might as well be painted on. But for some reason, I find them about as interesting as the models fawning over me. Not very.

Letting my eyes travel around the room, I search for some kind of diversion. But my gaze keeps wandering back to Anya, and it makes me impatient.

Rising abruptly from my seat, I stalk toward the back room, where my father usually attends to any business he cares to deal with at the club. My unexpected departure makes the two clingy models topple into each other before they catch themselves on the seat.

"Where are you going?" Lucca asks.

"To find some stress relief." At the door to the back room, I turn to find the two young models staring expectantly at me. "The fuck are you making me wait for?" I demand. "Get in here." I jerk my thumb over my shoulder to make it clear where they should be.

The girls jump up from their seats, straightening their dresses as they traipse flirtatiously past me.

"You two stay out here," I say to Cassio and Lucca. I jerk my chin toward our open bottle of champagne. "You can finish that one without me, but don't order another. I don't want either of you drinking too much and throwing up in my car."

"We're not babies," Lucca gripes as Cassio snickers.

I don't bother responding. Instead, I step back into the private room and close the door, turning the lock so we won't be disturbed. The girls watch me, waiting to see what I'll do next.

"Undress," I command, striding toward the couch at the center of the room.

They obey immediately, unzipping and sliding out of the skimpy sheaths of fabric until they stand before me in their lacy underwear and heels. Though their bodies are near perfection, I note that

49

neither has calves or thighs to compare with Anya's. They're just as skinny without the elegant muscle. The observation irks me.

Reaching into my pocket, I withdraw an eight ball of cocaine and pour its contents onto the coffee table before me. The models' lips curl up into mischievous smiles.

"Have at it, girls," I say, waving casually as I take a seat.

Dropping to their knees, each girl cuts a line and bends over, exposing her bare ass as she snorts the powder straight off the table. Usually, this is what I like. Getting girls coked up and making them do things to each other, then to me.

As the blond model leans back, her face taking on an expression of ecstasy, I jerk my chin toward the dark-haired girl to address her.

"Now take off her bra and panties," I command, waving toward the blonde.

The dark-haired model rises to do as I say, pulling the blonde to her feet so she can unclasp the girl's bra and slide her G-string out from between her ass cheeks.

"Turn around and bend over," I tell the blonde, my eyes intent on her fake breasts and trim waist.

She does as I say, turning so her ass is facing me, spreading her legs, and bending at the hips until her pussy is on full display. She makes a point of looking at me over her shoulder, her eyes intense with anticipation.

My cock twitches inside my slacks but doesn't come to full mast like it usually would. I grit my teeth irritably. *If that klutzy bitch has killed my hard-on, I swear to god...*

"Go on." I wave my fingers to indicate the dark-haired model should start eating the other girl out.

She stoops behind the blonde, spreading her own knees to give me a perfect view of her thong wedged between her ass cheeks as she grips the blond model's hips and buries her face in the girl's pussy.

The blonde moans with appreciation, her thighs spreading more as she rocks her ass, giving the dark-haired model better access to her clit. It's a beautiful sight, watching one perfect creature eating out another stunning girl's pussy. This would usually make me hard in about two seconds. But tonight, my cock seems determined to frustrate me.

Unbuttoning my pants, I slide my hand beneath the fabric. I grip my partially engorged dick and start to stroke it, preparing myself for some much-needed relief.

"Finger yourself while you eat her out," I order the dark-haired girl.

She runs her manicured fingers down the other girl's thighs as she makes her way to her own pussy. Pulling aside the skimpy lace of her thong, the model starts to play with herself even as she continues to lick the blonde's slit.

Both girls whimper and mewl, indicating their arousal as they pleasure themselves and each other in order to turn me on. And still, I can't find it in me to get a hard-on. Something about their performance feels so fake, almost staged. Like they're putting on a show just to please me.

My mind flashes to an image of Anya's face, her raw emotion as she stood before me, glaring in defiance after I insulted her for being unworthy of her spot at Rosehill. The blatant truth of her emotion triggers something in me.

My cock stiffens in my palm from the unexpected image, and I glare down at my cock. The fucking bastard is doing everything in its power to piss me off.

Forcing my eyes and thoughts back to the scene before me, I say, "Now stand up and finger fuck your friend's ass with the same hand you were using to play with your pussy."

The dark-haired model turns to me, wiping the blond girl's juices from her lips before she slowly rises. I can see a hint of frustration in her eyes. She doesn't like that I'm making her pleasure her friend and forcing her to wait.

My lips curl into an evil smile. Though I can tell it bothers her, she knows she's going to do as I say.

Stepping to the side, the dark-haired model caresses the blonde's ass and gives it a sharp slap, making the blonde squeal. Then she circles the blonde's asshole, teasing it for a moment as she lubes it with her own arousal.

The raven-haired girl's eyes stare pointedly at me as she shoves two fingers inside the blonde's ass without warning. Crying out, the blonde throws a sharp look over her shoulder, but she doesn't flinch from the sudden penetration.

"Harder," I command as the dark-haired girl moves her fingers in and out of the blonde's ass.

She does as she's told, thrusting her fingers into the blonde girl as her other hand braces against the girl's back. The blonde gasps dramatically, somewhere between pain and pleasure as she tries to look appealing.

But it's not her pain that consumes my thoughts. My brain shifts back to that first moment in the cafeteria when Anya's eyes found mine. Her deeply sad blue eyes had held me captive for one instant, the pain in them seeming to call to me before she spilled the contents of her lunch.

"For fuck's sake!" I shout, rising from the couch.

Both models stop abruptly, frozen in position as they watch me in alarm.

"You know what? Just get the fuck out," I say, disgust dripping from my voice.

"But–" the blonde whimpers in disbelief.

"I said get the fuck out!" I shout, snatching up their dresses and throwing them at the girls.

Startled into motion, they take up their discarded clothes and race for the doors, not bothering to dress before they slip out of the room and into the noisy club once more.

Growling in frustration, I pace. I can't seem to get the fucking new girl out of my head, and it's driving me insane. *It's not like I could ever be with such a nobody, so why the fuck does she have to haunt every second of my day?*

My balls are swollen and bruised with the need for release, but nothing I would usually use as an outlet will satisfy me. It's like Anya's wormed her way into my psyche to needle me relentlessly. Those eyes judging me–loathing me–though she doesn't even know me. Well, if she won't leave me in peace, I'll make her life a living hell.

7

ANYA

It's nearly midnight by the time I drag myself up the steps to my aunt's third-floor apartment. My ears are ringing from the club's loud music, my body buzzing from the way the beat continuously vibrated up through the soles of my feet. Despite how overwhelming the club was, I found I did enjoy the chance to be around some people my age and let loose for once.

Extricating my keys from my purse as quietly as I can, I unlock the door to our apartment and let myself in. As soon as the door clicks shut behind me, I remove my heels, relishing the sensation of the floor's cold wood beneath my throbbing feet.

While I'm used to the torturous pointe shoes required in ballet, wearing heels is a whole new world of pain. I haven't really had a chance to wear them more than once before–and definitely not for this long.

The TV flickers from the living room as images dance across the screen, but the sound's been muted so as not to disturb anyone. Aunt Patritsiya slouches in the recliner, her head tilted so her jaw rests on her shoulder, her lips parted as she snoozes in her impromptu bed. I smile fondly at her sleeping soundly. She was probably trying to stay up for me.

Padding lightly across the floor, I stop next to her chair and give her shoulder a gentle squeeze. Aunt Patritsiya's eyes flutter open, and her lips close instinctively.

"What time is it?" she asks as she takes in my face. Sitting up, she looks around in confusion. "Did I fall asleep?"

I chuckle lightly. "Yes, Auntie. But who could blame you? It's almost midnight, and I'm sure Clara's run you ragged to the best of her ability."

Patritsiya smiles. "She sure knows how to keep me on my feet. But no, she was very good tonight. Though I think she likes spending time with her mom more."

I smile sadly, thinking of what I must have missed out on. "Thank you for looking after her."

"Of course, child. You deserve a night off every now and then." My aunt rises from her chair in search of the remote to turn off the TV. "How was it?" she asks, glancing up as she shuffles through the magazines on the coffee table.

"Fun," I say unconvincingly.

She pauses to look up at me more pointedly.

"No really, it was fun for the most part. It was nice to spend some time with people my own age—dancers, who are more familiar with Rosehill's program. I had a good time." I smile to show my sincerity.

"But...?" my aunt presses knowingly.

I hesitate and drop my gaze, my fingers twining together as I try to find a way to keep my body busy. "I guess I don't quite know if I... belong. Don't get me wrong. I really did enjoy it, and they were all super nice. Whitney easily has the best sense of humor, and Paige seems perfectly accepting of me, as are the twins, Tori and Tammy. The guys were fun, too, though I... kind of kept my distance more with them. But they both seem nice enough. Fin in particular," I said, smiling affectionately. "His family is from Japan, so they're immigrants like us."

"Well, they sound nice. So why don't you feel like you belong?" my aunt asks.

"I don't know," I hedge. "I'm surrounded by rich people who don't have to think twice about bills or scholarships or how they're going to afford their dreams once they finish school. There was just so much... extravagance at the club, and no one seemed to think twice about it. Meanwhile, I didn't even consider trying to buy a drink."

Aunt Patritsiya smiles kindly. "Money's not what matters when it comes to how we live our lives."

I nod appreciatively. "I know. And honestly, I'm grateful that I even get this opportunity. I just... even at school, I feel a bit like an imposter. You know?"

Stepping close to me, my aunt gently cups my cheek. "Does it matter, when attending Rosehill will help your dream of dancing come true?"

"No," I say. "In the end, it's the program that matters. It's far more intensive than anything else I would find, and the talent around me is incredible. It will definitely drive me to get better."

"Good." My aunt pats my face lightly. "Clara drew something for you, by the way." She shuffles toward the kitchen table and picks up a crayon drawing.

My heart melts at the image of two stick figures dressed in pink tutus, one tall and blond, the other short with black hair. They smile out at me as they hold each other's hands. Tears brim in my eyes as I smile, and a sob escapes my lips.

"She's a good girl," Aunt Patritsiya says, her Russian accent growing thicker with her own emotion. "She loves her mama."

I nod, pressing my fingers to my mouth as I look down at the adorable drawing.

"She said she would only go to sleep if I promised you would tuck her in once you got home."

I pull my aunt into a hug, wrapping my arms around her short frame. "Thank you, Auntie," I breathe. Then I tiptoe toward my little girl's room and crack the door open just enough so I can slide inside.

Carefully easing the door closed, I wait until I hear its gentle click. Then I turn to feel my way across the dim room only lit by the tiny ballerina night light that spins upon its post. Clara sleeps with her tiny fist resting by her cheek. Her lips form a perfect O as she breathes from her mouth, disturbing her black curls that fall across her face.

Kneeling at the base of her bed, I comb her hair back from her face and press a soft kiss to her forehead. She's so deeply asleep, she doesn't stir. I feel as though my heart might burst with the unconditional love I have for my little girl.

Think what I might about Nicolo, I could never be angry that he blessed me with such a sweet, loving little girl. She might be a mischief maker, but she doesn't have a mean bone in her body, and I thank God for her every day.

She'll be four in a few short months, and it amazes me to think of how quickly she's growing. My little baby. She once was tiny enough to fit in the crook of my arm.

"Good night, my love," I whisper, kissing the crown of her head before I rise and carefully tiptoe back toward the door.

In the main room of the apartment, the lights are already out. My aunt left on a single hall light toward my room to guide my way. She must have gone straight to bed when I went to tuck Clara in. I can't say I blame her. Bed sounds really good right about now. But first, I feel inclined to wash off all the sweat and grime from the nightclub.

Slipping into the bathroom, I turn on the shower and strip as I wait for the water to get warm. As soon as it's hot enough, I step into the tub and slide the curtain closed. It feels good to wash away the sweat and body odor left from all those bodies pressing close around me.

While it was certainly overwhelming, I did end up enjoying myself a decent amount. The blatant sexuality intrigued me, and now that I'm alone, in the quiet of my own home, I start to process everything.

The dancers performing high above in the glass cages were truly something to behold, their bodies twisting and contorting in beautiful displays of erotic poses, and once I got past the initial horror of what might happen to them should they fall, I was able to appreciate their athletic abilities.

But more than that, I found myself intrigued by the public displays of affection, the couple making out at a table just past the edge of the dance floor, their hands exploring each other so freely. My life has been so structured and disciplined, I've never known that sense of liberation. Not beyond my one night with Nicolo.

Just his name brings back the image of him sprawled across the couch in his VIP lounge, his arms draped around two beautiful women. Though I tried to keep my eyes on anyone but him, at one point, I noticed him and the girls slip away.

In my mind's eye, I picture what I'm sure they were doing–Nicolo fucking two girls at the same time. He's clearly stepped up his game since high school, moving on from wooing virgins to having sex with multiple women simultaneously. The thought both mortifies and arouses me.

Watching the women dash down the club steps with their clothes in hand a short while later vaguely reminds me of my own experience with Nicolo, how abruptly he excused me after we were done.

The girls' expressions were a blend of scared and aroused, and I wonder just what took place in that room. When Nicolo rejoined his brothers a short while later, he was as cool as a cucumber, his face an emotionless mask.

I can only imagine how experienced he must be sexually by now. Even in high school, he managed to make me come despite the initial pain of losing my virginity. The fact that he could make me feel pleasure and mimic an intimate connection, even when he was using me, cuts me to the quick. I was so stupid.

And still, even knowing what an asshole he is, my insides start to quiver with the thought of Nicolo. My mind recalls, with perfect clarity, his gorgeously toned naked body hovering over me. The feel of his adamant lips caressing my flesh. As I stand beneath the steamy water pouring from the shower head, I run my hand across my hip bone and down between my thighs.

I'm already slick with arousal, and I don't know if that's from all the lewd dancing at the club or thoughts of my night with Nicolo. I shudder as an intense wave of guilt washes through me. I shouldn't be thinking that way about a man who only fucked me because I was a virgin, a man who could get off about taking that from me.

Pushing the image of Nicolo's playful hazel eyes from my mind, I jerk my fingers out from between my legs and grab the bar of soap from its cradle. Scrubbing my body furiously, I wash tonight's grime from my body and mind.

No matter how hard I've tried to learn and grow from my experience in high school, it seems I'm still that same naive girl. And I loathe myself for being so weak. I deserve better. Clara deserves better. And I need to keep my eye on the prize if I'm going to make my sacrifice matter.

I don't need a man in my life, especially not some selfish prick like Nicolo Marchetti.

8

NICOLO

School's becoming continuous torture in which the only relief I find is taking my frustration out on Anya. And after classes are done for the day, I've made a new habit of going for a drive before heading back to my penthouse apartment.

But today, my father's called me back to our family home in Forest Glen, so after class, I head straight there, racing across town in my Maserati, ignoring traffic safety laws to floor it down the busy streets.

I pull into our estate in record time, heading all the way up the gravel drive to the roundabout in the center of our courtyard. Parking at the foot of our pillared porch steps, I kill the motor and step out of my car.

"Welcome home, sir." The family butler snatches my keys out of the air when I toss them to him.

"Thanks, Alfie." Skipping lightly up the steps, I stride through the front doors, swinging them wide to make a grand entrance into the empty foyer.

They close with a heavy thud, and I hear the excited patter of soft feet. Moments later, my sister, Silvia, appears at the banister looking down over the foyer from the second floor.

"Nico!" she shouts excitedly. A wide smile spreads across her face, and she dashes down the stairs.

"Hey, Scout," I greet her, spinning her in a circle after she jumps into my arms. I've been calling her Scout for years now, a nickname I gave her because she's always been such a girl scout.

"I missed you," she says, squeezing my neck tightly.

I return the gesture, crushing her to my chest until I make her squeak. Then I set her gently back on her feet.

"Where's Father?" I ask, glancing around as if I think he might appear.

"In the study," she says more seriously. "He told me to send you straight there when you arrive, 'And don't disturb him for the rest of the night,'" she adds, planting her fists on her hips as she mimics his deep voice.

I chuckle and ruffle my kid sister's hair. She may be sixteen now, but she's still that same silly little girl that was always so fond of hassling me.

"But seriously, you should come home more often. It feels like I've hardly seen you since you moved out." Her tone has a hint of sadness that makes me pause.

"I will," I promise, giving her shoulder a squeeze.

"Good." Rising up onto her tippy toes, Silvia plants a kiss on my cheek before releasing me.

I give her a winning smile before turning toward the hallway that leads to the study.

I know Dad didn't call me here for a simple get-together. He's been all about business lately and ensuring I'm ready to take over the responsibilities of running it soon after I graduate.

"Nicolo, good. You're on time," he says as soon as I knock and open the door to the study. Rising from his chair behind the prominent mahogany desk, my father walks around to grip my shoulder in a formal embrace.

Two of his captains stand with their hands clasped behind their backs. I nod to each in turn before looking at my father.

"You've learned a lot over the past few years about the day-to-day responsibilities of running this family," he says. "But it's time you learn how to make the hard calls. You'll be taking command soon, and I want to make sure you can stomach the decisions you'll face."

I nod stiffly, steeling myself for whatever he has in mind.

Scuffling followed by the distressed sound of a man's voice in the adjoining chamber distracts me. Hot lead drops in my stomach as my body tenses in anticipation.

When the door bursts open a moment later, my father's lieutenant, Mazza, and two more of my father's captains enter, dragging a man between them. The man looks to be in his mid-fifties. As they haul him onto his knees, he fights fiercely despite the ropes tying his hands. A cloth gags him, muffling his words. He looks quite shaken, as though they kidnapped him from his home in the middle of dinner or something.

The sinking feeling in my chest intensifies as I recognize the man. Giuseppe Gatti, one of my father's most trusted treasurers. He and his family have shared many dinners with us in this house over the years. His younger son is roughly my age. Swallowing my anxiety, I glance toward my father and see the cold indifference clearly written on his face.

"Well, son. What do you think?" my father asks.

"From the looks of it, I would guess you're displeased with him about something." I can't bring myself to say Giuseppe's name.

"He was caught stealing from our family. Skimming off the top and spending *our* money because he thought I wouldn't notice. He thought he was untouchable, that he could get away with it," my father says flatly.

My mouth goes dry as my eyes flick between my father's unrelenting gaze and the pleading eyes of Giuseppe Gatti. He says something through his gag, but I can't understand a word.

"Well, Nicolo? What shall we do with this man who called himself our friend, who claimed he loved our family?" My father turns to look at me, his lips pressing into a thin line as his nostrils flare.

My palms start to sweat profusely, and I shove them into my pockets to hide them and dry them all at once. Then I pull them back out as I realize how inappropriate that seems. Licking my lips nervously, I glance back at Giuseppe.

"What does he have to say about it?" I ask. The last thing I want is a man's life on my hands because my father wanted to test whether I know how to come to my own conclusions.

"Ask him yourself," my father offers, waving a hand in Giuseppe Gatti's direction.

I nod to the captain holding the treasurer's left elbow, and he jerks the older man's gag down roughly.

"Please. Please, Nicolo, have mercy," he sobs, shuffling toward me on his knees. "Think of my family. Would you take their father from them?"

Though my body screams for me to step back, I clench my fists and stand my ground. I can't afford to hesitate and look weak. "I don't want to hear your pleas, Gatti. Tell me what you took from my family." Though the lead weight in my stomach makes me feel like vomiting, I grind my teeth through the nausea.

"Well, I-I-I–" he stutters, his eyes shifting from one uncaring face to the next in search of a potential ally. "I meant to pay it back," he insists. "It was only until the loan came through on my house."

Anger boils up in my chest as I listen to Gatti. He gambled his life on taking my family's money, thinking no one would notice. But stealing as much as might cover the loan on a house? He's a fool.

"And while you're *so* concerned for your family, you didn't think to come to us–your employers–and request our aid?" I keep an iron grip on my tone, forcing it to remain steady.

"P-p-please, Nicolo. Have mercy," he stutters, seeming at a loss for any other words.

No, this is not a test to see if I might ferret out the real reason Giuseppe was brought before me. This is a test of my mettle. To see if I'll kill a man when I know it needs doing. Giuseppe Gatti chose to steal from our family. Despite his years of supposed friendship, he chose to skim off the top. That's not the behavior of a man who's borrowing money temporarily.

Shaking my head, I look down at the ground. "Gag him," I command through my teeth.

Mazza does as I say without hesitation as Giuseppe Gatti tries to protest once again. The captains struggle momentarily to keep him restrained as he jerks his shoulders erratically. His eyes grow wide as he sees his fate in my face.

The gentle click of a gun cocking–my weapon of choice–draws my attention to my father's desk. A gun, a knife, a rope, a plastic bag, and brass knuckles wait for me there.

"Prove you can do it, son," my father instructs, his tone smooth and detached. "One day, you'll be rich and powerful enough that you can have someone else do the killing for you. But today is initiation day. Every man must know how to take a life if wants others to do it for him. So... which one will you choose?"

Meeting my father's gaze out of the corner of my eye, I see a flicker of anticipation there. This, too, is a test. I have to pick the *right* weapon, not just the one I might want to use. Studying my options, I run through the possibilities.

A gun would be too noisy in a house with my mother and sister and far too many people outside the family. A knife would be too bloody for the same reason. Brass knuckles might make less of a mess. Then again, they would take too long and might draw unwanted attention.

I consider the rope. Strangulation would be silent. But no, my father's testing me to see if I intend to be showy. That's not what our killings are about. Brute force is used to deliver messages, to serve as warnings. But Giuseppe Gatti is here to be executed, disposed of quietly to avoid making waves with the authorities.

Striding forward, I snatch up the sturdy plastic bag, and without giving myself time to think, I move behind Gatti. I fit the plastic neatly over the middle-aged father's head.

I cinch the bag tight.

And suffocate him.

Giuseppe Gatti thrashes violently, nearly ripping the bag, or at least yanking it from my hands. But I hold steady. Shoving my foot into the middle of his back, I apply enough force that he can no longer resist. Panicking, he tries to scream, and his remaining oxygen vanishes.

Despite his age, Giuseppe puts up a considerable fight, and by the time he's shuddered his last breath, I'm winded from maintaining my grip. When I release the bag, Gatti's head slumps forward lifelessly.

"Very good, son. You made the right choice," my father praises me emotionlessly. "We can't have a traitor running free. And disposing of this vermin will be much easier without a bloody mess."

I nod silently, my eyes lingering on the body hanging limply between my father's two captains. I don't dare speak. If I do, I might throw up, and that would only humiliate me and disappoint my father.

"Now, go clean up, and get your siblings for dinner. You'll join us tonight. To celebrate."

Giving a sharp nod, I stride toward the door and yank it open, removing myself from the room as quickly as I can manage while maintaining my cool. But as soon as the door clicks shut behind me, I race for the guest bathroom down the hall.

I barely make it to the toilet before I vomit, and I collapse against the porcelain as I heave. I don't stop throwing up until I've relieved my stomach of all its contents. When I'm finally done, I wipe my sweaty brow with a shaking hand.

I flush the toilet and rise unsteadily to stand in front of the sink. I hope no one heard me. Quickly rinsing my mouth, I also splash water on my face. Then I quickly dry off with the hand towel. When I look into the bathroom mirror, a terrifying stranger looks back at me. My face looks pale, my eyes hollow, as if what I've done has literally sickened me.

"Pull yourself together, Nico," I growl. "There's no room for weakness in the Marchetti family." Shoving away from the counter, I head back into the hall and up the stairs. My siblings are most likely hiding in their bedrooms.

I reach Silvia's room first and knock on her door frame, then lean against it as I watch the way she sprawls on her stomach across her bed, her feet swinging haphazardly in the air. At the sound of my knock, she looks up and smiles.

"Done already?" she asks brightly.

I nod, fighting the way my stomach roils dangerously. "Father said it's time for dinner," I say when I have myself under control once more.

"Are you staying?" she asks hopefully.

"Of course." I flash her a grin. "I'll meet you downstairs. I've been put in charge of wrangling Cassio and Lucca."

"Good luck," Silvia says, rolling her eyes as she sits up in bed. She closes the book she was reading. Making her way across her Paris-chic room, Silvia reaches me before I can leave. "Hey, are you okay?" She grips my wrist as she looks up into my eyes, a hint of concern in her gaze.

"Always," I promise and pat the back of her hand before pulling my arm away.

Leave it to Silvia to see right through me. I swear, for a younger sister who's supposed to be naive about the family business, she's far too perceptive sometimes.

9

ANYA

"Very good," Professor Moriari praises as he watches Fin and me practicing one of our showcase lifts. "Miss Orlov, you need to tighten your core more. You might not be a limp noodle for Mr. Tanaka to lift, but you're al dente at best. He needs more stability than that unless you want him to drop you one of these days."

A blush warms my cheeks, and I nod enthusiastically.

Fin snickers quietly beside me as Professor Moriari moves on to watch his next pair of students.

"Yes, no more cooked noodles," Fin murmurs as soon as the professor is out of earshot. "Only raw, crunchy pasta gets to dance with me on stage."

I give his shoulder a light shove and follow it up with a smile. "I promise I'll get better."

"You're already improving," Fin says more seriously. "Come on. Lighten up. This is only your second week of paired dancing, and lifts are a whole new ball game. I, on the other hand, am essentially made for this," he teases, striking a proud pose. "So I'm used to it," he adds, deflating.

I laugh, grateful that he can still make light of it, even though I'm sure he would prefer a partner who's more familiar with pairing.

Unfortunately, that's one of the few areas where my training has been less than sufficient in my other programs. Male ballet dancers flock to the prestigious schools, and since there are far fewer of them on the whole, they almost never get turned away.

"Besides, you're one of the strongest dancers here otherwise, and I'd much prefer you make us look good by bringing all the beauty. I can handle the brawn."

Chuckling, I shake my head. I don't know how I got so lucky to have Fin as a partner, but I think we might make a splash at the autumn showcase if only I can keep my core strong.

"Take three hundred and seventy-three?" Fin suggests lightly, holding out his hand.

I take it with a smile before composing myself and going en pointe.

Fin steps forward confidently, his strong hands bracing my hips as he spins me once, twice, and I extend my foot backward, arching into a swan shape as I round my arm.

We shift in tandem, Fin adjusting his center of gravity as I leap and twist, turning to face away from him. His hands find the small of my back and raise me effortlessly.

With all the strength I can muster, I tighten my core to hold myself steady as I sweep my arms up into an arc. My muscles quiver with the effort, but I refuse to be a noodle of any sort.

And then my momentary weightlessness ends as Fin lowers me gently back onto the floor. My dance slippers touch down so lightly, I almost don't hear the sound. Excitement floods me as I realize I actually did much better that time. I spin to smile broadly at my partner, who returns my grin wholeheartedly.

Slow rhythmic clapping interrupts my relief, and I look to find its source.

"Brava," Professor Moriari says from across the room. He stands next to Logan and his dance partner, but his eyes are on me and Fin.

I give a shy curtsy as the other students turn to see who's receiving our professor's acknowledgement.

"See? What'd I tell you? We'll have this routine down easy-peasy by the autumn showcase," Fin says.

I raise an eyebrow. That is definitely not what he said when we landed on this piece. "I'm pretty sure your exact words were 'Hell, it's only my senior year. When we fail at this completely, I'm sure the scouts won't laugh at me. They'll be happy to give me another chance.'"

"Me? I said that? Nooo," Fin objects. "I'm pretty sure that was you."

"Fin, I'm a junior," I remind him dryly.

"Okay, fine. I'll eat crow and admit you were right. If we can pull this off, we're going to knock their socks off."

"Come on. I want to practice transitioning from the lift into the next part of the piece."

Fin nods agreeably, shifting from his playful humor into a laser-focused performer.

I know it's still early in the year, but now that I understand how I can help Fin for our lifts, I'm more confident that we'll have enough time to put together a performance we can both be proud of. And since we're meeting every day after school for an extra hour of practice, we're certainly giving it our best shot.

"A round of applause from Professor Moriari today, huh?" Whitney bumps my shoulder encouragingly with her own as we walk to our next class.

Her Classical Technique class is a few doors down from my Contemporary Dance, and we've fallen into the habit of chatting on our way.

"Yeah, I guess so," I say, slightly self-conscious about how he singled me out once again.

"I don't know how you do it, but you sure do leave an impression on our Professor Compliment-Scrooge."

The image of Professor Moriari as a Scrooge makes me laugh. While he's certainly a drill sergeant in some ways, I don't actually think of him as miserly in his compliments, just careful to stick to constructive criticism most of the time.

"So tell me, what's your secret, *Miss Orlov*?" Whitney asks, adopting our professor's more serious tone.

I shrug. "I don't know. I mean, it's clear to me that everyone in our class is really passionate about ballet. Fin's been a great help. I was so nervous about having a partner since I'm unfamiliar with paired dancing, but I've come to appreciate Fin a lot over the past week. He's a pretty exceptional dancer, and we've been able to really push ourselves without me feeling completely out of my element."

"Yeah, you got real lucky with that one. He's got to be the best guy in our class–by miles," Whitney agrees.

I nod, smiling. "Now I'm just worried I'll let Fin down because we've chosen that impossibly difficult number from *Swan Lake*."

"Yeah, now that you mention it, you guys are crazy," Whitney jokes dryly, raising her eyebrow.

I laugh. "It'll either showcase just how good we are or send us falling back to the earth in a ball of flaming failure."

"I'm sure you won't fail," Whitney says confidently. "You're just *so good*. And it's not because you're partnered with Fin–though I'm sure that helps. But seriously, how are you such a good dancer?"

I bite my lip. "I don't know. Maybe it has to do with my background?" I suggest.

"How do you mean?" Whitney asks.

I frown, trying to find the right words. "Well, I come from a poor family whose best gift they could give me was a dream to someday become a ballerina."

"You know, I come from a poor family too," Whitney says casually, glancing at me.

That surprises me. "Really?"

She nods.

"But you're always dressed so nicely," I say, trying not to sound rude or argumentative. Still, I'm shocked that she would consider herself poor.

Whitney laughs lightly. "Let's just say I found an option to pay my way through school, and it has some added benefits. But I assure you that my dream is the only thing that's gotten me to where I am today. So as much as you want to call it the pressure of a hard background and a family you want to make proud, I don't think that's it." She grows thoughtful. "Maybe it's just in your blood. I mean, coming from Russia and all, the odds of your great-great-great-grandmother twice removed being the first prima ballerina are actually pretty good, right?" she jokes.

I snort but play along. "Maybe you're right. Wouldn't that be cool? I'd take it if that were the case."

"Pfft. I would too."

"So, how's your showcase piece coming along? You and Trent seem to be pairing up pretty nicely," I say encouragingly.

Whitney chuckles. "Let's just say I'm glad I have another year to prove I'm someone worth watching. Though I can't say the same for Trent."

"I'm sure you'll blow people away. What's the big deal about the autumn showcase anyway?" I ask, confused about how one performance could put the dancers under so much pressure.

"Well, it's kind of a make-or-break deal for aspiring dancers since scouts generally come to pick their favorite seniors and make note of up-and-coming sophomores and juniors. If you don't catch their eye this early in the year, they generally stop watching you so they can focus on the talent they want to recruit."

"That makes sense," I say.

"Aaand, our professors consider it a way to show appreciation for the family who puts on the showcase since they attend it every year. It proves that the money is being well spent."

"Oh, I didn't know that. That's pretty cool. The family must be performing arts aficionados to fund a whole showcase," I say, impressed by their generosity.

"Oh, they don't just fund the autumn showcase. The Marchettis fund almost the entire Rosehill College arts program," Whitney says, dropping a bomb on me as casually as if she'd told me today was Wednesday.

My pulse quickens as my brain tries to process what she just said. "Wait, the Marchettis are the family who fund the performing arts program?"

"Well, yeah," Whitney says as if it's the most obvious thing in the world.

If that's the case, my scholarship rides on their generosity. Anxiety pools in the pit of my stomach as something else hits me. Whitney said the Marchettis come to watch the autumn showcase every year.

With Nicolo's newfound enjoyment in torturing me daily and our shared history, I can't see how that will work in my favor. *If he sees me dance ballet, could he realize who I am? And even if my performance doesn't spark his memory, could I lose my scholarship if I perform badly in front of him?* In an instant, I'm struck by the reality that I have just as much at stake in this performance as every other dancer–if not more.

73

"You alright there, Anya?" Whitney asks as I freeze in my tracks. "You look a bit pale."

"No, I'm–I'm fine," I gasp, picking up my pace once more.

"Are you worried about the Marchettis being there because Nicolo clearly hates your guts?" Whitney asks, her tone teasing.

I bite my lip as I glance nervously her way.

"Oh my gosh, I was kidding!" She squeezes my arm reassuringly. "I'm sure he wouldn't be so big of an ass as to screw with your performance in front of his family or anything."

My eyes widen in horror at the thought. I hadn't even considered that he might sabotage me. *Hell, if he messes with my performance, could I end up losing my scholarship entirely?*

"Now I'm just giving you ideas, aren't I? Listen, Anya, I'm sure it'll be fine. After seeing you today, you have nothing to worry about. Your autumn showcase is going to go off without a hitch, and everyone will love you just as much as Professor Moriari does."

I nod silently as we reach my classroom door, my brain on too much of a downward spiral to think clearly. While my heart still pounds uncomfortably in my chest, I know that Whitney only means well, so I try to let her off the hook. But I can't help feeling twice as nervous about the autumn showcase knowing Nicolo might be there.

"I'll see you in Dance Theory?" Whitney asks, her eyes watching me with concern.

"Yes, I'll see you in Music Theory," I agree, giving her my most reassuring smile.

I like how close Whitney and I have grown since the start of school. She's probably my closest friend, and I fully appreciate her for her endless wealth of knowledge, but I can't help the way my gut twists at this most recent big reveal.

Taking a deep breath, I steel my nerves. No matter the obstacles, I can overcome them. And I'll be damned if I let Nicolo Marchetti get in my way.

10

ANYA

Hoisting my bookbag higher on my shoulder, I make my way down the crowded hall to my history class. The familiar sense of dread in the pit of my stomach comes with the anticipation of whatever new hell Nicolo will have in store for me today.

He's leaning against the wall outside our class as I approach, looking for all intents and purposes like a king among men as he lounges nonchalantly. It reminds me of the way he sprawled on the club couch weeks ago, the physical embodiment of the message that he owns everyone and everything in this town.

His friends, Dom and Jay, I believe, stand with him, the blond one talking animatedly and bringing a smile to Nicolo's face.

As if sensing my approach, Nicolo glances my way, and as soon as he registers my face, he shoves off from the wall to intercept me before I can enter the classroom.

Over the last few weeks, my body has gotten used to Rosehill's rigorous ballet program. But it's taken much more effort to adapt to Nicolo's bullying. I've learned that refusing to engage in his cruelty generally helps end it more quickly. Thank God I only have one class with him.

"Well, if it isn't the walking accident," Nicolo says, cutting off Jay's story as he walks toward me. "Nice outfit, New Girl. You hiding your stripper getup under there?" His eyes rake down my body suggestively.

Nicolo's friends follow, flanking him as they sneer down at me.

I can't help myself as I glance down at my light, tunic-length plaid shirt that I've cinched at the waist, my plain white leotard beneath it, and my simple pair of black leggings. Keeping my mouth shut, I shift to pass Nicolo between him and the wall.

But apparently, Nicolo's not willing to let me off easy today. Slapping the wall with his palm, he bars me from passing. "What are you even doing at my school, Anya? It's obvious you can't afford to go here. So who's paying for your education? The strip club you dance for?"

Anger flares in me, and my eyes snap up to Nicolo's proud, mocking gaze. I know I shouldn't talk back, but I can't help myself. "I earned my position here. I got a full-ride scholarship for ballet."

I don't rub it in his face that my scholarship means it's really *his* family paying for my education. I know if I push it that far, I'll regret it. I already regret rising to his bait.

Nicolo leans closer, trapping me against the wall with his arms as his lips curl in disgust. "Well, that explains why you're so anorexic," he sneers. "Aren't you bunheads supposed to starve yourselves or something?"

I press my lips closed. Arguing with him won't help me. Even so, the way he cages me with his strong arms, pinning me in place without quite touching me, reminds me of how he flirted with me back in high school. His face is a mere foot from mine, and the smell of his cologne makes my heart race.

"That's why the new girl has no curves," Nicolo explains, glancing back over his shoulder at his friends. "I don't think she even needs a training bra for her nonexistent breasts. Do you?" he asks me. "I mean, can you even find your breasts? I can't from just looking for them, but here, let me help."

Dropping his hands from the wall, Nicolo gropes my chest, gripping my breasts and squeezing them firmly in his palms. While my breasts might not look impressive in my athletic bra, I still do, in fact, have a modest B-cup size. His rough handling makes my nipples harden as he grips me.

"Oh, would you look at that? I found a couple mosquito bites after all," Nicolo mocks as he continues to cop a feel. His thumbs find my hardening nubs and his lips twist into a wicked grin. "And from the feel of it, I'd say you like my attention."

Hot embarrassment makes my cheeks burn, and I shove Nicolo roughly away. "You are such a fucking asshole."

Spinning, I rush back the way I came. My shoulders knock into several people trying to go the other way, but I'm so humiliated, I can't bring myself to stop and apologize. Nicolo's laughter chases me down the hall.

Hot tears of shame pool in my eyes as I race toward the bathroom. But I'm determined not to let them see me cry. Bursting into the restroom, I find an empty stall. I close myself in and slump against the wall, burying my face in my hands.

I can't believe Nicolo went so far as to grope me. He touched intimately right there in the middle of the hall. I'm mortified at how self-conscious he made me feel about my body.

But worse than that is the horrible fact that I *liked* it when he touched me. The way he cupped my breasts and teased my nipples actually turned me on. I chastise my rebellious body. But I can't deny the way my core tightened, the way my pulse pounded through my veins.

Despite the degrading treatment, I liked his hands on me.

It reminds me of our night together in high school, the way Nicolo massaged my bare breasts as he teased my nipples. My clit throbs at the memory of his lips encasing one hard peak and rolling it with his tongue. He'd been so tender with me then, murmuring about how beautiful I was.

I swallow hard as I recall the deeper connection I'd thought we had. In my naivete, I'd pictured countless nights together enjoying each other's bodies. But that connection had turned out to be a pretty little lie. He'd only ever said those things so he could fuck me.

Now, it seems I'm not even worth tricking. He can just take advantage of me in full view of everybody. And no one did anything because Nicolo is a Marchetti. He all but owns this fucking campus along with the rest of Chicago.

The heat of his body enveloping me as he trapped me against the wall flashes through my mind. The way his warm breath tickled my neck when he leaned in. Arousal floods between my thighs as a deep yearning pulses through me. It leaves me sensitive, aching, *needing* something I don't totally understand.

How can I still feel so intensely attracted to Nicolo when I know what an asshole he is? But I can't stop the sudden need for release coursing through me.

Holding my breath, I listen for anyone else in the restroom. I seem to be alone, so I slip my hand beneath the waistband of my leggings. A shiver of arousal runs up my spine as I touch myself. My panties are absolutely soaking.

Biting my lip, I struggle with my confusion and shame at knowing something so embarrassing could turn me on. But I haven't slept with anyone except that once. I've been too focused on school and Clara to waste time on romance. That must be why I'm so aroused by some-one–anyone–touching me. I have years of pent-up sexuality to account for, and my body finally found an outlet.

I stroke my fingers between my slick folds, stoking my excitement as I circle my clit. Nicolo's hazel eyes appear in my mind, and my pussy throbs. Despite how much I hate him, I can't seem to get our night together out of my mind. The memory of it turns me on even more.

I try to focus on something less masochistic, picking a random sexy celebrity to visualize. I picture him pulling me close, kissing me. Biting my lip to keep silent, I finger myself more purposefully, searching for some relief after being publicly groped.

My clit swells, pulsing with excitement as I play with myself. But my image of some stranger is weak, and my mind fills it in with the details of Nicolo's proud face, his strong stubbled jaw, his dark curly hair. My skin tingles with his phantom touch, reminding me of his hands exploring my body.

In the bedroom of his family home at his high school party, he'd fingered me as he kissed me. I mirror that same tantalizing touch that left me quivering. I can still remember the sensation of his hips spreading my legs, his soft flesh pressing against mine. That moment his silken cockhead aligned with my entrance had sent my heart racing.

The first thrust had been painful. I'd cried out as my body tensed against the sharp, overwhelming sensation of his cock filling me so completely. But as he'd ease in and out of me, new excitement had taken over. He'd made me come twice as he fucked me, his lips and teeth caressing and nipping all the most sensitive parts of my neck and face as he moved inside me.

My body creeps toward release at the memory, and I finger myself more adamantly. Heart thrumming in my chest, I breathe forcefully. Unable to stop the images of Nicolo's perfect body on top of me, pounding into my pussy, I give in to my dirty fantasy.

A flood of sensations from that night consumes me–the salty tang of his sweat, the velvety softness of his chest brushing against my nipples with every thrust. The way he moaned as he got close to his own release.

The memory of him jerking forcefully from my pussy to shoot cum all over my breasts and face launches me into ecstasy. As I reach the pinnacle of my excitement, the ghost of Nicolo's cologne fills my mind. I hear the words he whispered in my ear. My body seems completely devoid of shame as I topple over the edge, orgasming to the memory of Nicolo saying my name.

I shiver from the relief that washes through me even as tears spring to my eyes. *What is wrong with me? Orgasming to the memory of my night with Nicolo Marchetti?* I hate that I thought of him before coming. I hate that the degrading way he just treated me turned me on. It's humiliating to think my aggressor, the bully who's been treating me like shit for weeks, could excite me into touching myself at school.

Withdrawing my hand from my pussy, I straighten my outfit and go to the sink to wash my hands. In the mirror, I find a faint pink glow staining my cheeks. Burning shame roils in my belly as I make my way back to class.

I find an empty seat just as the lecture begins. Intensely aware of Nicolo and his friends snickering behind me, I lock my eyes on the front of the class. Even so, a hot blush creeps up the back of my neck. I sincerely hope my shameful arousal isn't obvious to anyone but me.

11

ANYA

This is it, the autumn showcase, my moment to shine or bring my performance down in a burning ball of flames. I shake out my arms and pace nervously backstage, in disbelief of how quickly the first month of school has flown by. I'm not ready for this moment. It's come far too fast.

And since Whitney told me that the Marchettis fund this showcase and will be in the audience today, my anxiety has only increased. My scholarship could ride on this performance. And if Nicolo happens to be watching, I imagine he'd enjoy any opportunity to trash talk me to his family. So I have no room for mistakes.

"We're going to be great," Fin says for what must be the tenth time since we arrived. He dips into another stretch, ensuring he's as limber as can be.

But I can feel the tension rolling off of him. He's just as nervous as I am, though for a different reason. It's his senior year. This is his last opportunity to catch the scouts' attention right from the starting gates. And if he can't do it now, they might not give him a second chance at the next showcase.

"We're going to do great," I echo.

I breathe deeply, inhaling the scent of cold cement and dust clinging to the velvet curtains and overwhelming the area behind the stage. Ignoring the panic in the air, I focus on the cold, imposing vastness of the theater's stage.

Sliding into the splits, I lie forward onto my leading leg, releasing the tension there. I stretch both sides equally, then rise once more to reach over my head, extending my lats. With every motion, I draw in a deep breath and release it slowly, trying to expel my anxiety.

Through the gap in the curtain, Paige's bleach-blond hair catches my eye as she twirls in place. Clasping my fingers behind my back, I stretch my chest as I peek between the velvet drapes to watch Paige and her partner on stage.

They chose a classic piece from *Coppelia* and are moving gracefully across the floor. It's nice to see them working well together. From Paige's report, she's been struggling to get her partner to cooperate about how many hours they train.

I feel lucky once more that Professor Moriari happened to pair me with Fin. When it comes to determination, he and I are quite a good fit.

I can see the slight disconnect between Paige and her partner, spots where she extends too quickly and he's not quite ready to stabilize her. But they manage well considering how little time we've had to prepare. With another few months, I bet they could make a strong team.

As Whitney steps up beside me, I admire her form-fitting emerald outfit. It sparkles as she moves, catching the light filtering back to us from the stage. She looks stunning.

Hers is a much more eye-catching display than my simple black leotard and matching tutu. At least I've done up my hair and makeup in an artistic fashion to mimic the namesake animal for my performance. Feathers frame my temples in the shape of a crown, and my eyeshadow is dark and dramatic. Meanwhile, Fin looks quite dapper in his princely white outfit and product-tamed black hair.

"How's she look?" Whitney whispers, gripping the curtains to improve her view of Paige's performance.

I open my mouth to reply just as Paige comes down from her lift with an audible thump. Not the worst thing in the world, seeing as the scouts probably can't hear over the music, but a landing like that doesn't look nearly as pretty as one would hope.

Frustration is written on Paige's face as she tries to keep her composure. If I had to guess, she's pissed at her partner. Air hisses between our teeth as Whitney and I both take in pained breaths.

"Ugh, I can't watch," Whitney breathes. "It makes me too nervous."

I agree, stepping away from the side of the stage to stand next to Fin once more. My hands tremble uncontrollably. This will be my biggest performance to date. No pressure or anything, but it could make or break my future in dance. It most likely will do so for Fin.

"We're–"

"Please don't say we're going to be great," I beg.

Fin releases a breathy laugh. "Sorry."

I give him a nervous smile. "Don't be. I'm sure you're right. I just can't hear you say it one more time."

Fin nods and silently zips his lip before throwing away the key. Thank God humor is his go-to. A small, cathartic giggle bursts from me. Then I hear the notes coming to the end of Paige's number. We're next. I feel like I might vomit the second I walk on stage.

"Break a leg," Whitney says with a smile as she stretches near her partner.

"Anya, Fin." Professor Moriari waves us toward the stage from where he stands beside our entrance.

Fin grips my fingers and gives them a reassuring squeeze. I respond with a grateful smile, and we make our way to stage left. We stand there, holding hands in solidarity, as we watch Paige's performance come to a close. The cheers that follow tell me the audience is quite large, and my gut clenches at the knowledge.

"Go, go." Professor Moriari shoos us forward as Paige and her partner bow and exit from the far side of the stage.

Taking a deep, steadying breath, I release Fin's hand and stride boldly forward, placing my feet gracefully on the stage's sparse black floor. The music may not have begun, but my performance has already started.

The bright spotlights blind me as I turn to face the audience, striking my entry pose. I can't see a single face, and that calms me. I can do this. Though I'm trembling, I remind myself to rely on muscle memory. Fin and I have practiced relentlessly for the past month. We've performed our routine so many times I've started to do it in my sleep.

The first note of our song brings me to life, and goose bumps rise on my arms. My mind goes blank, bringing with it a confident serenity. Rising to en pointe, I let my body guide my way.

The music builds, echoing around me and commanding me to move. Like a sailor drawn to a siren's song, I obey. I spin and leap and glide across the stage, drawing closer to Fin as if by magnetic force only to twirl away.

His hands close confidently on my hips for the first lift in our number. I flick my feet, launching myself upward as I tighten my now rock-solid core. The shape of my arms take on a new form as I port de bras. I move through the air weightlessly for one glorious moment before touching down again.

Each motion drives me forward into the next, and my nerves wash away as I realize I'm ready for this. Confidence pounds through my veins. The bitter scent of fear is replaced with fresh, earthy victory.

Spotting a single shadowed face in the audience, I lock my eyes on them as I pirouette, spinning again and again in a finger turn as Fin keeps me in place. A shiver runs down my spine, and I don't know why.

When Fin dips me into the final dramatic pose, I elongate my limbs, my face pointing down at the floor a mere foot below me. My feet extend toward the ceiling in a representation of my character's fall.

The silence that follows in the wake of our music's final note is deafening. Blood roars in my ears as Fin muscles me back onto my feet, righting me as gently as he can. For an instant, our eyes meet, and I can't help but smile. My grin stretches wide across my face until my cheeks ache. We did it. We made it through a flawless routine.

I can see in Fin's eyes that he feels the same.

Determined to maintain our composure, we bow formally, and the cheers that follow chase away any lingering doubt. The audience loved our performance too. My heart swells with the accomplishment, and I fight back tears of pride. We give a final bow before striding off stage, our ending touch to a knockout success.

"Brilliant!" Professor Moriari beams as we walk off stage.

His apparent approval means more to me than our audience's exuberant praise. He's the one who has seen us working every day. He's the one who can truly assess what is our best, and he's proud of the performance we gave.

Whitney's wide smile and mouthed congratulations top the cake. I squeeze her arm for encouragement as she strides out on stage for her own number.

"Fin Tanaka and Anya Orlov is it?"

We both spin, startled by the unfamiliar voice. Fin's jaw almost drops from his face.

"Uh, yes?" I say tentatively to the middle-aged woman who said our names. I cut my eyes at Fin to get him to pull it together.

He snaps his mouth closed, drawing his shoulders back as he stands up straight.

"I'm Melody Amara," the woman says, holding out her hand in a formal introduction. Her business persona matches her sharp suit and dark-rimmed glasses, her hair done up in a strict French roll. "I'm a scout for Dance New York."

It's Fin's turn to elbow me into a more appropriate response as my heart hammers in my chest.

"It's a pleasure to meet you," I say, shaking her hand emphatically.

Once I release her, Fin does the same.

"Excellent performance, both of you. *Swan Lake* is always a difficult act, but few master it at your age and with such little time to prepare. Miss Orlov, I know you still have most of your junior and senior year ahead, but I assure you, I'll be keeping an eye out for when you graduate. As for you, Mr. Tanaka, I would love the opportunity to sit down and discuss your plans for after you graduate."

"Y-Yeah, absolutely," Fin stutters.

"Great."

Melody whips out a business card so efficiently, I almost wonder if she was keeping it up her sleeve. She holds it between her first two fingers as she offers it to Fin, and he takes it enthusiastically.

"I look forward to seeing your next performance," she says before departing with a sharp nod.

As soon as she's out of sight, Fin's jaw drops once more, and he turns to me in disbelief. "Did I just get recruited to one of New York's hottest new dance companies?"

I giggle, hugging him excitedly. "I don't know about recruited, but it definitely sounds like a good window of opportunity."

Fin beams, staring down at the business card as he holds it like a golden ticket. "I can't believe that just happened."

"You deserve it," I praise.

He's a phenomenal partner and dancer, and he's taught me so much about pair dancing over the last month. In all honesty, I owe my success in this showcase to him.

He gives me a broad smile and pulls me in for a hug. "See you once I get out of these tights?"

I nod. "I think this calls for a bit of celebrating," I say happily.

"Definitely."

I head through the labyrinth of hallways toward the dressing rooms in a daze. Giddy with relief after so much stress and anxiety, I smile goofily. I feel weightless after having made it through today.

Finding the tiny dressing room with a sticky note marking it as mine, I close myself in. The resounding silence is almost deafening. Mirrors reflect my excitement from countless angles. The color in my cheeks and the light sheen on my brow mark the physical exertion I just put in. But my body vibrates with fresh energy.

Stepping up to the dressing room table, I dig through my bag of toiletries, ready to remove my performance makeup.

The door bursts open with a loud crack. I flinch, instinctively looking into the mirror to see who's behind me. My eyes lock on Nicolo Marchetti's fiery gaze. My heart leaps into my throat, and I try to swallow it back down. Suddenly, I can't breathe.

12

NICOLO

"Come on, quit fucking around," I gripe as Lucca and Cassio shove each other all the way down the carpeted hall of the Rosehill College auditorium.

The building is formidable, like most of the gray stone structures on campus, but this one reeks of stale air and about a century's worth of dust.

"Father sent us to endure this painstakingly dull performance so we could represent the family since he had to attend a meeting. Pull your shit together, and act like adults for once."

Silvia snickers beside me as she slips her dainty hand into the crook of my arm. "I believe *you* were the only one he required to come," she points out. "And I think it will be wonderful. Thanks for inviting me." She gives my arm a squeeze, hugging me on the go as we enter the main theater.

The space is open, with the seating tiered like a proper performance hall so everyone would have a view. I don't bother asking where my siblings want to sit, though the theater only seems half full. Instead, I guide Silvia further up the stairs, ready to hide at the back so no one will see me take a nap.

"Do we have to go *all* the way to the top?" she pouts. "How am I going to see anything?"

I slow my pace, hesitating, then sigh deeply. I can't deny my sister anything. "Fine, let's go in this row. It's still empty." I point her toward the row nearest us, and my brothers shuffle in first, continuing to nudge and elbow each other more subtly than before but still keeping up their antics.

"I'm not blind," I say coldly as I follow them into the seats until we reach the center.

Silvia follows me.

"Yeah, knock it off, Lucca," Cassio jokes, pretending he had nothing to do with the scuffle.

"*You* knock it off." Lucca gives Cassio a light shove.

I groan internally, kicking myself for thinking it was a good idea to bring them. I figured my suffering might be less if I had my siblings to entertain me. Silvia was a good choice, and I'm glad I asked her. She's been bubbling with excitement since I picked them up.

But Lucca and Cassio are a different story. While I have to admit their antics can be pretty fucking funny sometimes, they don't seem to care at all about responsibility or the family name. When I have one alone, I can see the potential they have. But the twins never take anything seriously, and it's driving me crazy.

Grabbing a fistful of their curly brunette locks, I clunk their heads together before they have time to stop me.

"Owwww," they groan in stereo, massaging their foreheads.

"I said get your shit together."

They slouch into their seats, crossing their arms as they turn their attention toward the stage. I catch a glimpse of Silvia smiling broadly at me before the lights dim.

A spotlight clunks on, illuminating a point on stage. I'm definitely going to fall asleep in this level of darkness. The only thing that might keep me awake is the scratchy fabric of the worn seats and the way the lumpy cushioning provides little comfort.

If I had even the remotest interest in theater or dance performances, I might consider mentioning it to my father. I'm sure we could finance their replacement.

A tall middle-aged man who carries himself with authority–his shoulders thrown back like I imagine a dancer would–strolls onto the stage. He announces that this showcase will represent his students as well as several other classes, spanning different genres. He invites us to enjoy the show before heading back off stage.

The first performers step lively into the spotlight and strike a pose that makes me snort.

Silvia elbows me. "You're supposed to behave like an adult, remember?" she whispers. Her teeth flash white even in the dim lighting as she gives me a playful smile.

"Remind me why you're not the one running this family already?" I ask, pride in my baby sister swelling in my chest.

Silvia rolls her eyes and turns her attention back to the stage. "Not that Father would let a girl run the family, but you're the oldest. It doesn't matter that I'm more emotionally mature than the lot of you."

I give a quiet chuckle and turn to watch the dancers as well. We're all silent for several minutes, and I have to admit, I didn't hate the first performance.

"The music is beautiful," Silvia breathes as the next pair of dancers come on stage and their song fills the auditorium.

I pay attention to the sounds swirling around me and have to agree. I've never thought of classical music as interesting, but when I really listen, it is pretty. We watch another set of performers take their place on stage.

"Have you been watching their faces?" I ask, leaning close to Silvia to avoid disturbing the other audience members.

Silvia shakes her head.

"Watch. You can see it when they fuck up."

Silvia glances toward me before turning her eyes back to the dancers.

"Like right there, did you see it? The guy looked like he just bit into a lemon or something. Think he fucked up? Or his partner?" I chuckle. Maybe I've found a way to stay awake for the showcase.

"You're such a jerk," Silvia scolds me. "I'm sure they've trained hard for this performance, and you're just laughing at their mistakes."

Her tone is playfully angry, but when I glance at her face a moment later, she almost looks sad. It's a marked difference from her excitement all day. My heart twists as I realize my mean humor did that. I kick myself mentally. Silvia's too kind and sweet. I need to remember that and behave while I'm with her. I don't get to see her often enough to act like an ass when I'm around her.

I can't help but notice the dancers' expressions now, but I keep the commentary to myself, leaving Silvia to enjoy the showcase in peace. On my other side, Lucca and Cassio whisper conspiratorially, and I let them be. They don't seem to be bothering anybody aside from me.

My eyes start to wander, studying the shadowed faces of the other audience members. We must be surrounded by people who actually care about this kind of thing. They all look fascinated by the performances on stage. Each pair of eyes remains focused forward like they're watching a masterpiece.

The current musical number finishes–another classical piece I don't recognize but don't dislike by any means. And as my eyes wander back toward the stage once more, my heart skips a beat.

Anya glides onto the stage in a black outfit that emphasizes the cream color of her skin and honey-blond hair. Her dramatic makeup almost makes her face unrecognizable. But I've spent weeks watching her, planning ways to torment her. So though her hair is pulled into a slick bun and crowned with black feathers that remind me of a swan's wings, I know it's her without a doubt.

I scoot forward in my chair, excitement filling me as I think about how God awful this performance will be. If her display of clumsiness on the first day of school is any mark of her agility, I give her ten seconds before she ends up on her ass.

In my periphery, I catch Silvia's gaze shifting toward me, taking note of my new posture. I don't care. I'm not about to tell her that I'm preparing for a good laugh.

Anya and her partner strike their poses, and I have to admit, I'm slightly impressed by Anya's easy flexibility.

When the first haunting notes of their song begin, the music tickles at the back of my brain. I've heard it before, but I don't know where or when. And with the first few notes, Anya comes to life.

I don't know if it's the music, but something stirs inside me. The ebb and flow of the rich symphony raises goose bumps on my arms. And my eyes remain riveted to Anya as she gracefully dances across the stage.

My breath catches in my lungs as Anya lifts lightly onto the points of her toes. In the same motion spins, she tips forward, one leg stretching behind her. Her poise captivates me, and my pulse quickens as I realize Anya is actually quite good. No, more than that. She's an extremely talented dancer.

I can't think. I can't speak as my eyes follow her across the floor. She spins and leaps so gracefully she almost looks like a bird herself, her body weightless.

The brilliant spotlight shines down on her, making her skin almost glow. Her dark tutu glares forebodingly as it matches the ominous sound of the building symphony.

I can't help but scoot forward in my seat. I'm spellbound. Cassio accidentally bumps my elbow, and anger ripples through me as I tear my eyes from the performance to shove him violently.

"Shut the fuck up and sit still," I hiss before turning my attention back to the stage.

Anya steps and spins, steps and spins, her arms held in perfect arcs as she races across stage. I think she just might be the most beautiful thing I've ever seen. I can hardly believe this is the same girl who spilled her lunch all over me.

She must have been born dancing. That's the only explanation I can find to make sense of the contradiction. She probably had to learn to walk long after she started dancing. But right now, she's art in motion. A proper masterpiece.

What I wouldn't give to know what that body feels like beneath me. I know it's impossible as soon as the thought crosses my mind. But despite the objections I'm sure my father would have, I can't help thinking about what it would be like to hold that lithe, graceful, *flexible* body.

Hell, maybe he wouldn't care all that much as long as I didn't intend to marry her...

My body throbs with sudden need. Fuck, I want to feel her, to know what it's like to have her pressed against me.

And then Anya and her partner meet. His hands close around her hips as he brings her to a halt, and a fresh level of fury washes over me. He put his hands on her. Not only that, but he's interfering with her dancing.

An inexplicable violent rage consumes me as I watch them move together. Anya gracefully leaps into the air, her body spinning until her partner's hands grip her hips from behind. He lifts her high over his head as she appears to float, practically flying.

She's intoxicating, and when she slowly descends to the floor, I wonder if her partner did anything at all. It feels like he's simply there to grope her as he taunts me. I could break every bone in his body for touching her. In truth, I've never been so tempted.

Anya leaps away from him, moving more rapidly now as the music spurs my emotion. Consumed by conflict, I'm torn between my newfound fascination with Anya and my intense jealousy every time her partner touches her.

I can't stand how violently I want Anya right now. Shoulders tight, I ball my hands into fists as I fight to contain myself. I have to have her. And when I do, no one else will dare lay a hand on her. Not even her tights-wearing partner.

It's all I can do to stay in my chair, and when the performance comes to a dramatic end, my heart stops. The final, devastating musical note concludes with Anya's body entirely suspended in her partner's arms.

Her back arches dangerously as her face hovers just above the floor. Her one foot points toward the ceiling, fully extended. The other leg bends at a sharp angle, mimicking a nocked bow. A shiver runs down my spine at the sight of the precarious and far-too-intimate hold.

After several excruciating seconds, Anya's partner rights her, setting her back on her feet as if she weighs little more than a feather. She probably does, considering her slim, athletic figure.

Silvia whistles beside me, cutting the tension as my eyes follow Anya off stage. I turn to my sister and realize she's not whistling at the performance. Her warm hazel eyes are locked on me. A knowing smile curls her lips.

"Is it just me, or did my big brother just learn to love ballet?" she teases quietly. "Or was it the ballerina that caught your eye?"

"Oh, please," I sneer, rising from my chair.

"Wait, where are you going?" Silvia asks, sitting back to stare up at me. "The showcase isn't over."

"Stay here," I say flatly. "I'll be back before the last performance." Maybe. "Just wait for me," I add in case.

Lucca and Cassio stand as well, ready to follow me, twin looks of mischief on their faces. I level a scowl at them threateningly, and they ease slowly back into their seats.

"Stay put. I won't be long, and our family has to have a presence at the performance."

My brothers slump back in their chairs, grumbling about how that's supposed to be my responsibility.

Silvia smiles knowingly. "Good luck," she breathes and winks before turning back to the brightly lit stage.

My gut twists at the genuine and entirely too-sweet support. I'm sure if she knew everything that I plan on doing to Anya when I see her, Silvia wouldn't be all for it. Regardless, her encouragement bolsters my determination, and I storm down the stairs toward the dressing rooms, ready to confront Anya and maybe break her partner's face if he happens to be in the vicinity.

Back stage is a maze of halls and doorways, some marked Props, others Dressing Room or Coat Closet. After bursting through several dressing room doors that seem to be empty, I find a hallway with brightly colored sticky notes, each with a student's name on it.

I quickly read each name as I make my way down the hall. Finally, I find the one designated as Anya's room. I don't hesitate as I grip the door handle and shove the door open so forcefully it crashes against the inner wall.

Anya stands before me, her back turned so I can see the low cut of her leotard. It scoops down until just a few inches before her tutu. Her back is slender, her skin smooth and creamy, her spine a delicate line.

Her makeup looks even more dramatic up close, the dark black and silver around her eyes making their sky-blue color stand out brilliantly. Her full red lips part in apparent shock, and the instant our eyes meet, her body tenses visibly.

Gripping the door as I step into the room, I jerk it closed behind me. Then lock it.

13

ANYA

My heart hammers erratically as dread washes through me. *Why would Nicolo come find me in my dressing room?* His reasons can't be good.

I whirl to face him. Bracing against the makeup counter, I prepare to defend myself. Like a cornered rabbit, I have nowhere to run.

Nicolo's eyes are almost crazed. They burn intensely. He strides across the small room toward me, his impressive figure striking fear in my heart.

"I can't stand other men touching you," he states, his tone filled with emotion that borders on rage. "I don't care who you are or what my family might think. I want you–and I take what I want."

The hair rises on the back of my neck as Nicolo closes the distance between. He looms over me, smooth and confident, as if he owns me– I just didn't know it.

My lips part in protest, but he's on top of me before I can say anything.

He wraps his arms around me.

His hips press me back into the makeup counter's edge.

His mouth crashes down on mine as he kisses me violently. Taking advantage of my parted lips, his tongue strokes into my mouth, exploring me intimately.

He groans as if taking his first drink of water after days in the desert. The sound makes my stomach tighten excitedly, betraying me.

The earthy, masculine scent of his cologne sends me back to our intimate night in high school. Angry tears sting my eyes even as my core tightens from the memories of our passionate sex.

Trapped against his broad, muscular chest, I push against Nicolo, futilely trying to force space between us. I might as well be shoving a wall for all the good it does. Nicolo has me trapped in such a fierce embrace, I can't move. I can't breathe.

His lips consume me, daring me to resist. I tremble beneath his ardent assault. My skin burns where we touch. It's almost painful and sinfully arousing. The way he enfolds me so entirely. He grinds against me, proving how excited he is. How turned on.

I don't want him to touch me. I desperately want to run away. His kiss brings to life all that painful rejection from years ago. But my body seems to have missed the message. My knees grow weak as my heart thrums like a hummingbird's wings.

His strong hand cradles the back of my head, locking me in place as Nicolo's tongue strokes mine. As he explores my mouth, his erection grows, pressing firmly against my hip.

Finally, he breaks our kiss long enough to catch his breath. But he still holds me close, his forehead pressed to mine. My chest heaves against him as I gulp for air.

I fight tears that threaten to fall, burning the corners of my eyes. Pushing against his chest more intently now, I try to show him I don't want him near me. He doesn't even seem to notice His strong arms just keep me locked in place.

"I bet you've never been kissed like that before, have you, *mia bella*?" he purrs, his hazel eyes molten as he leans back to meet mine.

Somehow, it cuts deeper to know that even after kissing me, Nicolo doesn't know who I am. I truly meant nothing to him in high school. My chest constricts painfully at the realization. It hurts to know that our one night together has impacted me so permanently. Meanwhile, he hasn't spared me a second thought.

He glances toward my mouth again. Licking his lower lip with anticipation, he leans in for another kiss.

I jerk my head back, fighting the light pressure of his fingers cupping the back of my head.

Nicolo's eyes flicker from lust to anger as he absorbs my rejection for the first time. The hand at the back of my neck shifts, taking my jaw firmly in his strong grip. My heart stutters, and my stomach flips as his gaze silently warns me, almost daring me to resist again.

His eyes flick down to my forcefully puckered lips. Holding my face in place with his fingers, Nicolo kisses me violently. Forcing a response from me, he strokes his tongue into my mouth once more.

The hand wrapped around my waist trails up my body, keeping me pinned against his chest. Twining his fingers into my hair, he keeps my lips locked with his. The hand gripping my jaw slides down to wrap around my throat.

Fear freezes me in place. *Will he strangle me?* I don't think I could stop him if he really chose to do it.

His fingers squeeze gently, constricting my airway for a moment. Then his hand softens to trail lower until he's groping my breast.

He leans into me so forcefully that I can't keep myself upright. But I'm determined not to let him put me flat on my back. I don't want him to think he can force himself inside me.

Throwing one hand out behind me, I brace against the counter, resisting his pressure. He seems to take it as an invitation, pushing his erection more aggressively against me as his hand explores my body.

"You'll be mine to fuck whenever I please," he breathes against my lips. "And in return, I'll dress you like a queen."

He really thinks he can break down my defenses that easily? That I would sell my body to him for some nicer clothes? I would never—especially not to a man like Nicolo. He has abused me in so many terrible ways.

A poisonous combination of anger and pain rises up inside me. I want to scream for him to get off me, to leave me the hell alone. But before I can tell him to fuck off, his lips capture mine once more.

His wandering hand wraps around my hip and moves beneath my tutu. Gripping my ass, he massages the taut muscle. A wave of arousal washes through me. Hot shame quickly follows, pooling in my cheeks. Despite the hate boiling inside me, I like the way his hands boldly explore my body.

Something about Nicolo brings me to life, compelling me into a sexual frenzy. It's unlike anything I've felt with anyone else. In that instant, I know I will always respond to him this way. But I can't let him hurt me again.

I don't think my heart would survive it.

I hate it. I hate that I'm so attracted to him, even after all the pain he's caused me.

If I agreed to be with Nicolo—if I let him have me—I would end up with another broken heart when he tossed me aside. I can't stand that. He left my life in ruins the last time he fucked me and walked away. He took my innocence and destroyed my heart without a second thought.

Nicolo continues to assault me, and resisting him clearly won't work. But I'm desperate to get him off me. My body and mind are so conflicted that I can't take it anymore.

If I don't stop him, I might just do something I'll regret. Like give in.

Nicolo's lips punish mine, consuming me as he grinds against me. Seeing my opportunity, I bite down on the soft pad of his lower lip.

He jerks away with a yelp. Eyes furious, he brings his fingers to his mouth and gingerly touches the small cut I left as a warning. "You fucking bit me," he says in surprise, looking at his hand to confirm I drew blood. He licks the blood from his lip as though the injury were an afterthought.

"I don't want you, Nicolo. You need to leave. Right now." My voice trembles despite my determination to sound strong.

"You don't want me?" Nicolo's proud lips twist into a mocking sneer. "I don't believe you. You're just a coy little prude. You like to tease men but not put out, right?"

Nicolo reaches beneath the front of my tutu. My heart stutters.

I swallow hard as his fingers find the peak between my thighs. Gripping the edge of the makeup counter, I white-knuckle it as he scoops my elastic leotard aside. He exposes my folds still thinly clad in my soft-pink performance tights.

Sliding his hand beneath the fabric of my leotard, he stretches the elastic around my hip. Then his fingers find the waist of my tights.

He yanks them down forcefully, scraping my flesh as he does.

Fresh tears sting my eyes at the sound of the delicate fabric tearing. This was my last good pair. I swallow hard as Nicolo finds my bare pussy. His fingers stroke between my slick folds. Palm pressing against my clit, he pushes one finger inside me.

I cry out as tears obscure my vision. I'm about to come from his unwanted penetration, and I fight the urge to sob. But I won't let him see how mortified I am. Biting my lip, I stop myself from making another sound. If I don't, I might just moan with pleasure.

My cheeks burn with shame. I'm so close to an orgasm despite the fact that I do *not* want Nicolo to touch me.

Nicolo releases a throaty chuckle, a smile spreading wickedly across his face. "You're fucking soaking, you little slut," he murmurs in my ear. "I bet I could make you come in two seconds flat."

The tickle of his breath on my neck makes me shiver. My clit throbs, making my pussy tighten around his finger. Nicolo inhales deeply, as if taking in the scent of my arousal. Then he releases his breath on a husky groan.

"This is how I know you want me," he purrs as he moves his hand.

His finger presses further inside my pussy. Fuck, I'm so close. I cling to the edge of the cliff, desperately trying not to clench around his invading fingers. It's so hard not to come.

"You're just playing hard to get, you little fucking tease."

I desperately blink away my tears before they fall. Then I shove Nicolo away from me as forcefully as I can, slamming the heels of my palms into his shoulders so he has to step back.

His hand slides out of my tights as his eyebrows rise in surprise. For a moment, the room falls into excruciating silence as we both absorb my actions.

"I would never want to be with you," I hiss, narrowing my eyes. "You're a soulless monster, and you must be stupid, too, to think I would ever be with you."

The tears come more quickly now, but I refuse to cry in front of Nicolo. I can hold them off, at least until he's gone.

"You've made my life a living *hell*, and I just want you to leave me the fuck alone!" I shout. My hands fist at my sides as I glare at him. I shake with the force of my anger, fueled by the arousal still blooming in my core.

"You little cunt. You're seriously going to turn me down?" Nicolo's chest expands as he pushes his shoulders back defensively. "You'll regret that, you slutty little tease. You're going to wish you were never born by the time I'm done with you."

Looking down his proud nose at me, Nicolo sneers. His hazel eyes almost look green with the intensity of his rage.

Then, without another word, he turns on his heel and storms toward the door. He yanks it open, making the hinges groan in protest. He slams the door behind him with such force that the lights above the makeup mirrors flicker.

As soon as he's gone, my knees give out. I collapse, sobbing, into the metal chair beside me. Thick tears pour down my face, marring the beautiful performance makeup I so carefully painted on my face.

With the mirrors lining the wall and the bright lights shining down on me, all my ugliness is laid bare for me to see. My silver-and-black makeup depicts the war raging inside me, blending with my tears and smudging my face to form a hideous mask.

I'm weak and pathetic. *Why do I respond so eagerly to Nicolo's touch? What is wrong with me?* Hot shame burns deep inside me because I know how easily he could have me.

Covering my face so I don't have to look at myself, I bawl. My shoulders shake as I curl in on myself, ugly-crying into my palms. I hate Nicolo and the power he still holds over me. *Why do I have to crave the touch of someone so mean?* I'm a broken person, a flawed personality.

And now that I've rejected him, I'm terrified to think of how much worse my life could get. Clearly, he thinks he can make it more miserable than he has. I shudder at the thought. *Why, of all the schools in the world, did I have to end up at the same one as Nicolo Marchetti?* No matter what I do, I can't seem to escape him.

14

NICOLO

As we sit in class, Anya maintains a stony silence. Her eyes face forward unless I absolutely force her to look at me.

The other students have stopped even trying to sit beside her, hoping to avoid a confrontation with me. That's how people are supposed to respond when a Marchetti decides they want something.

But Anya seems determined not to fold. My family could crush her, ruin her chances of becoming a dancer, even take her life if I wanted. Not that I would. I'm not that heartless.

But as I lean closer to Anya, whispering that she should just give it up since no one else will ever want her, she doesn't even blink. It fucking pisses me off, and I shove her notebook out of her hands and onto the floor. Anya's only response is to grip her pen tighter before setting it gently on her desk.

Pushing her chair back, Anya kneels on the floor. The thought of her giving me head while she's under the desk makes me instantly rock-hard.

She leans forward to grab her notebook, and I take a healthy look at her firm, round ass poking out from beneath the table. What I wouldn't give to fuck her from behind, gripping her silky blond hair as she cries out in pleasure beneath me.

As Anya shifts to climb back into her seat, I snatch the pen from her desk before she notices. Settling back into her desk, Anya sets her notebook on the table. A hint of surprise registers on her face. She glances toward my hands and catches sight of her missing pen.

I smile wickedly as her eyes slowly drag upward to my face. Her eyes hold a hint of fear. And just to get a rise out of her, I launch the pen, full force, toward the front of the class. It smacks the blackboard with a loud snap, hitting the wall less than a foot from Professor Kennedy's head.

The strict history professor's eyes snap up to glare at the class through her thick-rimmed glasses. Then she stoops to pick up the pen. "Whose is this?" she demands.

Anya sinks lower in her seat, her embarrassment radiating from her in waves. Shamelessly, I hold my hand over her head and point down at her with my finger, making it blatantly obvious that it's Anya's.

Jay and Dom snicker next to me.

"I'm confiscating this," Professor Kennedy says sharply. "I hope you value your next pen more."

"I'm so sorry, Professor," Anya apologizes breathlessly.

Ignoring the apology, Professor Kennedy shifts her eyes back down to the podium holding her lecture notes.

Satisfaction fills me at the color staining Anya's cheeks. But she doesn't turn to look at me or say anything. Instead, she reaches into the bag at her feet and withdraws another pen. Irritation flares up inside me. I want to hurt her, to make her feel as angry as she made me when she rejected me.

Reaching over while she's distracted, I take the soft flesh on the back of her arm and pinch her mercilessly. Anya gasps, jerking upright and yanking her arm out of my reach. She bites her lip as if trying to stay silent and glares at me. *Finally.* It's ridiculous how hard I have to work to get her to look at me. In response, I give her a wink.

Anya forces her gaze toward the front of the class once more. From the way her lips press together, it's taking all her self-control not to punch me. I decide to leave her be for now.

But when class is over and Professor Kennedy excuses us for the day, I can't seem to let Anya just leave. She rises so quickly to depart the room that I don't have time to stop her. But as she reaches the front of the class, our professor calls her over. That gives me time to catch up.

"Watch this," I say darkly to Jay and Dom, rising from my seat.

They follow silently, Jay smiling with anticipation as Dom watches me curiously.

I step out into the high-ceilinged hallway right on Anya's heels. Snatching her arm, I yank her back so she has to stop and face me. Anya whirls, her movement graceful even when she's thrown off balance, which surprises me. Her eyes find my hand gripping her forearm tightly. She glares, her eyes traveling up toward my face. I don't release her as I sneer.

The halls are busy with students making their way to their next class, and the flow of bodies shifts around us. The students' eyes slide over our small confrontation as they realize I'm causing the disturbance. No one wants to fuck with me. Anya's the only one who seems impervious to my family name and reputation.

"What do you want, Nicolo?" she demands coldly.

The sound of my name on her lips sends a shiver of pleasure down my spine.

I'm not sure I've ever heard her say my name before, but something about it resonates with me, rocking me to my core. I shove the feeling aside, ready to toy with her like a cat with a mouse.

"I've been thinking about how stuck up and rigid you are. You're just wound too tight. It seems to me that you could do with a good fucking to help you loosen up. Don't you think that might make her a little more bearable, boys?" I glance at each in turn.

Jay laughs and nods as Dom shrugs nonchalantly.

I turn my eyes back to Anya, taking in the hint of pink coloring her cheeks. "I'm starting to wonder, if you're so rigid because you're still a virgin," I add lightly. In truth, I am curious if that could be part of why she rejected me.

From the crimson that creeps up her neck, leaving splotches of color as it stains her cheeks, I might actually be closer to the truth than I had realized. A scoff of disbelief bursts from my lips as her reaction catches me by surprise.

"Oh my God, am I right?" I laugh as Anya squirms in my grip, her eyes dropping to avoid mine.

Jay and Dom break into peals of laughter.

"Fuck, I thought all the virgins died out sometime before the end of high school. I can't believe you're still clinging to your V card like some Catholic school girl. What are you holding out for some Prince Charming dressed in tights to ride in on a white steed and sweep you off your feet?"

Anya's eyes snap to meet mine suddenly, and the intense hatred there surprises me. It reminds me of the day I met her, when she spilled her lunch all over me. Her unbridled spite somehow seems to run deeper than a response to my bullying. She's been so unresponsive to my needling these past few weeks. I must have found a sore spot if she's reacting so visibly.

"Maybe that's why you don't want me to fuck you," I suggest, pushing her further. "No one's popped your cherry, and you've heard how big I am. You're probably scared I'll hurt you if I take your virginity." Pulling Anya closer, I speak more softly. "Don't worry, pet. I'll break you in gently."

Anya's gaze turns electric with emotion, and tears spring to her eyes. My heart twinges unexpectedly, and for an instant, I actually feel bad. I don't normally make girls cry, and seeing Anya on the verge of tears destabilizes me. I pause, my next comment dying on my lips.

Then she hisses, "You don't scare me, Nicolo Marchetti. You're just a piece of shit, and I don't want some entitled prick like you thinking you have any claim on me or my body. You probably act like such a jerk to make up for your small cock."

Her words hold such vitriol, it staggers me. Jay and Dom release shocked laughs as their eyes turn to me.

"Oooh." Jay holds his fist to his lips. "Cat's got claws, Nico. You better watch out. You might have just found your match."

"Fuck you, Jay," I snap, cutting my eyes at him.

He and Dom immediately fall silent.

If she's ready to spar, I clearly haven't pushed her too far. I'm going to break this tease, and by the time I'm done with her, she'll be *begging* me to fuck her. Squeezing her arm more tightly, I yank her forward against me.

She gasps as she collides with my chest. I grip her wrist as her hand raises to catch her fall. Her warm body presses against me, and the sweet smell of her floral perfume, the soft satin of her skin arouse me.

Forcing her wrist down to the seam of my jeans, I put her hand on top of my growing erection. "You call this small?" I ask, making her rub my cock through my jeans.

I swell further beneath her touch, my considerable girth making her eyes grow wide.

"Or maybe you can't tell since you've never seen a cock. But I promise you, pet, I could make you squeal in pain if I wanted to."

Anya pales visibly, and her lips part in horror. The look of utter mortification makes me wonder just what she's thinking. *If I fingered her again, would she be wet from feeling how turned on I am?* By her disturbed expression, I can't be sure. *Is she bothered because I'm forcing her to jack me off over my jeans right here in the school hallway?* Not that anyone would dare stop me.

Yanking free of my grasp, Anya spins on her heel. She dashes down the hallway, vanishing out the building's front doors.

Dom releases a low, astonished whistle. Jay chuckles darkly.

"Dude, I don't know why you bother. That chick seems like way more hassle than she could possibly be worth. No pussy is good enough to go to this much trouble. Not even virgin pussy," Jay says.

I shrug, turning to him as he combs his blond hair back from his face. He looks vaguely entertained. Dom, on the other hand, maintains an impassive expression. I've always found him hard to read, maybe because of his unusually light-gold eyes, which contrast with his darker complexion.

"I like a challenge," I say casually as I lead them toward the door. "Too many girls just give it up to me these days. It's fun when I find a bit of a chase. I'll probably lose interest in her once I pop her cherry, but until then, I'm not giving up."

Jay shrugs it off and shoves his hands in his pockets. "Whatever floats your boat, man."

But as we exit the building, my thoughts linger on Anya. The girl baffles me. She's like a code I'm determined to crack. I know she wants me. I can feel the attraction every time we touch.

So why is she being so difficult? Does she like the chase that much? She must get off on being a tease. I'm irritated that I've spent so many waking hours trying to understand her. I just want to break through her resistance, win this power struggle, so I can fuck her and stop feeling so goddamn obsessed.

15

ANYA

"Your transition is weak," Professor Moriari states, cutting into our demonstration as we practice after school. "Try breaking it up. Listen to the music. If you put a fouetté directly following a grand jeté, you're not acknowledging the natural build-up of the music." He gives us a nod and moves on to the next couple.

Fin and I share a look as we breathe hard, hands resting on our hips. I'm grateful Professor Moriari has set aside an extra hour after classes each day to help everyone with our choreography for the winter showcase. He's a brilliant choreographer, and we need all the help we can get.

"What if we try reversing them?" Fin suggests.

"Or maybe we're trying to fit in too much. I could fouetté as you grand jeté. That would break up the space. Then we could come back together for the lift."

Fin nods. "Let's try that."

We turn toward the mirror once more to watch the new strategy. Another dancer's motion catches my eye in the reflection, and the heavy studio door slams shut as someone enters. My gaze shifts, and my heart drops as soon as I recognize Nicolo. In my periphery, I catch Fin bristling at his sudden appearance.

"What is with him?" Fin grumbles, his eyes meeting mine in the mirror. "Doesn't he have something better to do than come gawk at you?"

I sigh. This has become Nicolo's new thing—watching me during my performance classes and now practice after school, apparently. He stares like a ravenous animal eyeing prey. This newfound torture of his unnerves me.

"I'm sorry, Fin," I apologize for the hundredth time.

Fin gives me a thin smile. "It's not your fault. But I have to say, having you as a partner was a lot nicer when your stalker boyfriend didn't watch us all the time."

"He's *not* my boyfriend," I insist.

"Whatever. Let's just dance." Fin counts off, and we start the adjusted routine.

It's challenging to focus with Nicolo's eyes burning into me. I do my best to avoid acknowledging him. At first, I thought maybe he did it to throw me off my game. But even after I stopped slipping up over his presence, he's continued to come. And afterwards, he hounds me, chasing off my friends. No one dares speak to me anymore if he's around. I hate it.

With my mind elsewhere as I spin toward Fin, I miscalculated the distance, and we crash together, abruptly halting the maneuver. Fin's hands grip my waist to stop me from falling.

"Sorry," I gasp as I cling to Fin's arms.

"It's okay. Let's try again."

I nod. We get back into the starting position, and Fin counts off again. I force myself to focus only on the dance. Kicking one leg out, I rise up onto my grounded foot's toes to porte bra and spin, using the mirror as my spot. Fin leaps behind me in his grand jeté. I feel the air move from the power of his jump.

Swiftly switching feet, I twist and spin until I'm positioned right before Fin. Together, we dance across the floor as his hands find my hips. I push off from the ground, lifting one foot as I prepare for an aerial side split.

Fin's hand firmly grips my waist, guiding me into the air. I lock my muscles in place. For an instant, I balance on his hand poised high above his head.

We wobble slightly. Fin's neck strains with the effort to hold me with one arm, but he does it. Then his elbow bends, and he eases me back to the floor. I come down a bit hard, but it's not bad for such an ambitious lift.

"I love it!" A wide grin breaks out on Fin's face.

I smile right along with him. We've already come a long way on our routine, and I'm proud of us. "With enough practice, I think we're going to knock this out of the park."

We give each other a double high five, and I glance at the time.

"I better get home," I note.

My aunt will be home with Clara anytime now.

"No worries. I don't think my arms could do much more today anyway." Fin makes his way over to the cubbies, carefully avoiding Nicolo's gaze as he collects his things.

I follow, intentionally ignoring the mobster heir. Changing from my dance shoes into my worn tennies, I wave as Fin says goodbye. Most of the students have trickled out of the classroom already. Only a few pairs remain as Professor Moriari works closely with them on their choreography.

Slinging my bag over my shoulder, I head toward the door without a backward glance. Still, I catch sight of Nicolo in the mirror. He follows me, closing the distance between us.

Ugh. I'm really not ready for another one of his bully sessions. His constant antagonism stresses me out, and my nerves are stretched to their limit. Not that I let him know it. He catches up to me just as I step out into the fall sunshine.

"You and your partner seem nice and intimate," he observes.

Golden sun rays highlight the trees' changing colors and bake the fallen leaves. The happily crackling leaves and rich autumn smell starkly contrast the icy anxiety in my heart. I keep my eyes focused on the path and turn toward the bus stop without a word.

"When he lifts you, does he ever cop a feel?" Nicolo presses. "You know, stick his finger up your pussy for extra stability?"

Fighting the urge to slap Nicolo, I press my lips together to keep my mouth shut.

"I bet you two use dance practice as foreplay. Does it make you wet to have his hands all over you?" Nicolo's tone drips vitriol. "You're both so handsy. I'm starting to wonder if you might be a thing. Is that it? You two dancing between the sheets? Maybe I was wrong about the whole virgin thing."

Fury creeps up my neck, warming my cheeks. "Fuck off, Nicolo," I snap, my hands balling into fists.

He laughs, seeming tickled that he finally got a rise out of me. "I'm not going anywhere. You might as well just give up and go out with me. I know you're having fun playing hard to get, but I find your whole prudish little act pretty fucking pathetic. It's getting old fast."

I scowl as I keep walking, wishing my legs were long enough that I could outpace him. "You're just jealous because Fin gets to touch me and I wouldn't touch you with a ten-foot pole. I'm sure you're not used to rejection, but you'll get over it. I'm nothing to you, and you'll realize it soon enough." Pain constricts my chest as I echo the words he once said to me.

"If you're looking to pop cherries, why don't you go back to high school? That seems to be your specialty." The bitter words escape before I can stop myself. My pulse quickens. *Will my words trigger his memory of me?*

"Nah. I've already been there and done that. Popping high school girls' cherries is too easy. But speaking of cherries, I still think you're a virgin. Your dance partner's not man enough to loosen up your frigidness. I bet you just go down on him. You're too much of a prude to go all the way. No, if I had to bet, I'd say your cherry's still intact, and I will take it."

Why does it cut like a knife every time he fails to remember me? I should be long past it by now. He's proven time and again that he's a jerk. He's only bothering me because he likes a challenge. But I won't fall for him again. I don't care how gorgeous he is. He's a horrible person, and getting intimate with him would only lead to more pain. Four years later, and I'm still recovering from him.

"Come on, Anya," he persuades, his voice like honey. "Just let me put it in a little bit. One time. Once you get a taste, you'll be begging for more."

Refusing to answer, I pick up my pace. I doubt I can walk faster than him, but I'm willing to give it a try. As I step ahead, Nicolo's arm snakes around my waist, stopping me abruptly as he pulls me back against his chest. His hips connect with my ass. Suddenly, I'm intensely aware of how horribly secluded our path is.

Grinding his hips into me, Nicolo traps me in place with his strong arm. His free hand curls around my hip bone, coming dangerously close to my pussy. "Come on, Anya. Just a little taste," he breathes against my ear.

I shiver as my stomach tightens, my body responding to his touch in a way that I hate. His erection digs into my tailbone, and my panties moisten with shameful anticipation. Nicolo turns me to face him, his grip like iron as he pulls me roughly against him once more. My hands land on his strong chest, and I try to push away. But he has me locked in an unbreakable hold.

"You know you want me," he purrs, his gaze electric, his smile oozing confidence.

His eyes flick down to my lips, and my heart stutters. *He's not stupid enough to go for another kiss, is he?*

He is.

He leans in, his tall frame curving against mine as he closes the remaining distance between us. Rage boils up inside me. Without thinking, I lash out, striking him soundly across the face. The slap shocks me as much as it does him. For an instant, his eyes grow wide. Then, as his cheek turns pink, he shoves me away from him.

I stumble, barely catching myself before I hit the ground, and I brace myself for further aggression.

"You little bitch," he hisses, his eyes narrowing as they flash an intense green. "I was taking it easy on you, but we can do this the hard way if you want. I tried to be patient, but I'm done. I'll show you what happens when you push me too far." His words growl from his throat as his face twists with fury.

For a fleeting instant, he reminds me of Clara during one of her rare temper tantrums–only her anger is far less terrifying. But Nicolo doesn't hurt me. He doesn't physically force me, which I half expect.

A moment of tension crackles between us.

But it's an empty threat. He doesn't do anything. "You're all talk, Nicolo. You like to pretend you're some big bad jerk who can get his way by throwing his weight around. But you're just a spoiled brat, and you don't scare me."

A white lie, but my insult seems to rock him back on his heels. When I turn to flee, he doesn't come after me. Still, Anxiety grips my chest until the bus doors close behind me and we pull away from the curb.

My hands shake with the adrenaline coursing through me, and I breathe deeply to try and steady them. God, I hope I didn't push him too far. I'm terrified he might come to my home next. *He doesn't know where I live,* I reason. He doesn't even know which bus I take to get there.

Despite my logic, I check my surroundings when I get off the bus to make sure I wasn't followed. Then I slip quickly upstairs and lock the door as soon as I'm inside.

"Mama!" Clara cries, dashing across the room and jumping into my arms.

I collect her against my chest, kissing the crown of her head and breathing in the subtle scent of her strawberry shampoo. "Hello, sweet girl. How was your day?"

"Good." She smiles widely as she plays with the simple gold chain around my neck. It has a dainty ballerina charm hanging from it, a present from my parents on my tenth birthday.

I shift Clara to my hip as I slide my bookbag off my shoulder and deposit it on the floor. Then I give Aunt Patritsiya a kiss on the cheek as she washes her hands in the kitchen sink.

"How was your day?" she asks, her soothing accent reminding me of home.

"Fine," I say simply.

I haven't told her about my conflict with Nicolo. I don't want to worry her. Aunt Patritsiya studies my face intently as she dries her hands on her apron. I stroke Clara's dark curls and hold her close.

"You look stressed," she observes gently.

I shrug it off and press one more kiss to Clara's head before setting her down. "School's just hard, but it's very rewarding." I step up to wash my hands at the sink. "What were you thinking for dinner?" I ask, changing the subject as subtly as I can.

But I know I can't keep running from my Nicolo problem forever. I'm scared to imagine what he might do next.

16

NICOLO

I slump in my chair, arms folded, scowling toward the front of my econ class without hearing a word the professor says. If I glare long enough, I just might burn a hole in the podium.

"What's got you all moody?" Dom shoves me lightly with his elbow.

"Shitty weekend," I growl. That's a vast understatement.

Since my last interaction with Anya, I haven't been able to get a wink of sleep. The girl's stubborn resistance is really starting to piss me off. And since that afternoon, she's started to ignore me completely.

I can't let that shit stand. I'm the son of Lorenzo Marchetti. And if he's taught me one thing, it's that I need to know how to control the people around me. If I expect to be don someday, I need to have a name that commands respect.

"I want you boys to do something for me," I growl, turning to face them without uncrossing my arms.

"Sure, boss, what's up?" Jay asks, always up for anything.

"Fin Tanaka, the Asian kid we see with Anya around campus, her dance partner–"

"He's Japanese," Dom says casually.

I stop to stare at him until he realizes he interrupted me.

"Sorry," he mumbles. "Just saying."

"I want you to go to the dance building after class. He and Anya practice there for about an hour. Wait for him outside the class, and when he leaves, get him alone in the bathroom just down the hall."

I'll give Anya one more chance to reconsider my offer. If not, I'll use Fin Tanaka to teach her a lesson.

"Sounds like a fun afternoon." A smile spreads across Jay's face.

Dom pauses then nods, silently agreeing.

"Good." I turn my attention back to class, my bad mood starting to dissipate.

After classes are done for the day, I open the door to the dance studio to catch the end of Anya's practice. I can't wait to get my hands on Anya–or her partner. I've got enough built-up frustration that I'm ready to send a *thorough* message.

I have to admit, Anya's dance is starting to look really good. I can tell she and her partner are making progress. Watching her moves brings me a sense of calm I haven't felt for days.

But every time her partner puts his hands on her–grasping her hips, supporting her waist, even holding her hand as she spins–I see red.

Anya's apparent determination to ignore me, not even meeting my eyes in the mirror, further escalates my ire. The little tease is going to regret that she ever went toe to toe with me. She doesn't fully grasp just how horrible I can make her life. Up until now, our games have been child's play. But no more.

When their practice comes to an end, Fin collects his things first, as usual. Our eyes meet briefly, and he trains his eyes on the floor. Then he scuttles from the room as quickly as possible. *That's* the kind of response I'm supposed to get. Something is clearly wrong with Anya that she can't figure that out. But I don't care. I have to have her. I've never wanted anyone more.

Anya approaches her cubby of personal items, and I step close to her.

"So, have you had enough time to reconsider my offer?" I keep my tone smooth and playful.

Anya flashes me a frigid look that plainly tells me to fuck off, but she doesn't say a word.

"I'll take that as consent," I prod. "I'm glad you finally came to your senses."

Anya finishes switching out her shoes and folds her arms across her chest. "That was most definitely a *no*," she hisses. "Now, will you kindly wander off a cliff so I never have to see you again?"

"You're getting vicious, aren't you?" I sneer. I lean in close until my lips almost graze her ear. She smells subtly floral beneath her salty sweat. Just the scent of her turns me on. "Well, don't worry, pet. I know how to play on that level too."

Anya jerks away from me, her eyes crackling with rage. She whisks around me, racing from the room as if she can't escape me fast enough. I watch her go, loving the sight of her long legs and perfect ass.

Well, she had her last chance. I leave the classroom right behind her, making my way down the hall to the men's bathroom.

The room's completely empty except for Jay, Dom, and Fin, so I latch the door behind me. Jay and Dom have Fin kneeling in the middle of the stained linoleum floor. They've each got one of his arms twisted behind his back so he has to lean forward slightly.

Fear flickers in his eyes as soon as he sees me, and he licks his lips nervously. "Please, whatever this is about, I'm sure we can work something out. I didn't mean to piss you off, please!" he begs, words spewing from his mouth. "I'll do anything you want if you just let me go."

A cold smile spreads across my lips. "That's good to know, Fin."

His eyes grow wide in surprise that I know his name.

"But you see, this isn't just about what *you* did." I step closer as I unbutton the cuffs of my dress shirt and roll up my sleeves. "This is about Anya. You see, I don't like other people touching my things. And whether Anya knows it yet or not, she's *mine*. Which means you have no right to touch her."

"What...?" Fin stares up at me, swallowing nervously. "I–we're just assigned dance partners. That's it. We don't have to have a problem–"

"The problem is you're touching the girl *I've* decided to fuck," I growl. "I don't care if she's sucking you off after practice or if you're just holding hands. It's time you learned your place. Anya is mine."

The blood drains from Fin's face all at once. "We didn't–I'm not–we're just dance partners! That's it! I swear to god–"

"I don't believe you," I say coolly. "And I'm going to break a bone for every lie you tell."

The stark terror on Fin's face tells me he believes me. It's intensely satisfying after so many days of Anya's rebelliousness.

"I'm sorry." Fin's voice trembles with the rest of his body. "I'm so sorry, please. I'll never do it again. I'll stop being her partner. I won't touch her again," he rants desperately.

"That's good." I nod. "I'm glad to hear it."

Fin seems to relax minutely in Jay's and Dom's grips, and I almost feel bad for the emotional roller coaster he must be on.

"I just need you to give Anya a message."

Fin nods, then his eyes widen in fear as he shrinks back from me. Jay and Dom hold him steady as I slam my fist into the dancer's jaw. His head snaps sideways as blood splatters across the floor. I follow it up with a left hook, sending his head bouncing the other direction. Then I stoop to get the proper leverage as I bury my fist in his gut.

Fin slumps forward, his forehead pressing against the floor as he wheezes for air. He barely seems to register when I take his arm from Dom. I wrench his wrist and am rewarded with a loud pop. Fin screams, and Jay kicks him in the side, knocking the wind out of him once more and effectively shutting him up.

I release Anya's partner and nod to Jay, who does the same. Dom stares down at Fin, his eyes stunned, his dark skin ashen, and for once, he's not hard to read.

"Get your shit together," I snap, irritated by his discomfort, which makes me feel guilty. "This is what your future looks like if you want to be one of my men."

"I'm up for anything, boss," Jay chimes in.

"Let's get the fuck out of here." I turn and lead the way from the bathroom, leaving Anya's partner in a crumpled heap on the floor.

"How could you?" Anya demands, stopping me dead just outside her afternoon dance class.

I managed to catch the last ten minutes of it, and by the scathing looks she gave me, I knew this was coming. Her shoulders tense, and her hands fist, her face growing bright red as she trembles with fury. Students give us a wide berth as they glance surreptitiously our way.

Raising an eyebrow nonchalantly, I look Anya up and down, admiring the way her dance clothes cling to her supple body. "How could I what?" I ask innocently.

The heat of Anya's wrath radiates from her in waves. "I went to Mercy Grace Hospital rather than my first class this morning because you put my *partner* there. He wouldn't even look at me," she hisses, tears shimmering in her eyes. "You broke his arm. His poor face... How could you hurt someone like that? He's never done anything to you?"

I glance sidelong at the students stepping around us. Several avert their eyes as soon as they meet my gaze. Gripping Anya's arm, I drag her down the hall, looking for an empty classroom. Anya resists me every step of the way.

Yanking open the door to the first vacant classroom I find, I shove Anya inside. I follow her, closing the door behind us. Dim light filters through the windows along one side, bouncing from the mirrors lining the adjacent wall. It's a small studio classroom with black rubber mats and a ballet barre running the length of the mirrors.

Anya grips the bar as if to stop herself from slapping me again.

The fire in her eyes makes my cock harden. I knew Anya was stubborn, but I kind of like this feisty side. Now that the gloves are off and I'm ready to play dirty, I wonder just how physical she might get. I bet angry sex with her would be fucking hot. And now that we're alone in a classroom, all I want to do is fuck her hard, pressed against the mirror.

"Are you seriously going to deny beating up Fin Tanaka?" she snaps. "You ruined his senior year. Scouts can't see him dance if he can't even use his arm. He might never dance professionally because of you!"

"Don't go blaming me for what happened to your partner," I scoff. "That's on you. If you had just agreed to go out with me, I wouldn't have had to send you a message."

"A message?" Anya steps away from the bar, stomping forward to get in my face. "You're a sick asshole, you know that? What kind of message does that send me? That you're not just a bully, you're a violent, sadistic prick I should stay far away from?"

I lean down until our faces are just inches away, and Anya juts her chin defiantly, refusing to back down. The scent of her floral perfume makes me harder. God, I fucking want her.

"I told you I don't like other people touching you," I breathe. "I tried to play nice. I've let you put on your coy little virgin act for long enough. You will be mine, Anya. Or I'll continue to hurt the people you care about. That's the message I was delivering. You want to try me and see if I break someone else's arm?"

Anya pales visibly, all the fight leaving her in a rush as fear fills her eyes. I've finally got her. I can see it in the way her shoulders slump, the way her full lower lip trembles. And the knowledge makes me feel powerful. I fucking love it.

"Okay," Anya agrees softly, her gaze dropping in defeat.

"Okay? What does that mean?" I demand, rubbing my victory in her face. After months of her playing coy with me, I finally got the little tease.

My mind floods with all the things I'll do to her. I can't wait to break her in. She's definitely not leaving this classroom without giving me something today.

"Okay, I'll be yours," Anya murmurs. "Just–please, don't hurt anyone else." Tears spill down her cheeks as she refuses to look at me.

A twinge of emotion tightens my chest, but I refuse to feel bad for making her cry. I might also regret that I took things so far with her partner. But that's on Anya and her fucking stubborn streak. Fin's arm will heal. And right now, I just want to enjoy my win.

"You'll do whatever I say?" I press. "You'll be my good little pet?" I hook a finger under Anya's chin and tip her face up until her eyes meet mine. They're a darker blue than usual, the color of a troubled ocean after a storm. "You'll let me *fuck* you whenever I want?" I hiss.

Anya swallows hard as her tears flow more quickly now. "Yes," she breathes.

Her chin trembles in my grip, and her breath tickles my face. *Fuck*, I want her more than I've ever wanted a girl before. My gaze drops to her full, pouting lips.

"Then let's seal it with a kiss. Convince me that you're mine," I purr.

For a fleeting moment, conflict rages in her eyes, then Anya rises onto her toes. Her hands slide up my chest, leaving a burning path in their wake as she wraps her arms around my neck.

Electric arousal crackles through my body as our lips connect. The soft warmth of her mouth makes me rock-hard in an instant. Twining my arms around her waist, I explore her slender hips. I grip her ass firmly in both hands and pull her roughly against me.

A groan rumbles up from my chest before I think to stop it. The feel of her body pressed to mine, Anya kissing me of her own volition for the first time–I'm so fucking turned on, I feel like I might just come inside my jeans.

Darting my tongue out, I trace Anya's soft lower lip. She grants my tongue access immediately. Her own tongue dances past my lips as her fingers comb into my hair. *This* is what our kiss in her dressing room should have been like. The heat of it is so intense, I'm consumed by its fire. After weeks of resistance, Anya is finally mine. And from the way she's kissing me, I'm positive she's wanted me this entire time.

17

ANYA

I kiss Nicolo with desperate passion, using my meager knowledge to convince him I'm his. I'll do anything to keep Clara and my aunt safe. Combing my fingers into his hair, I mirror his tongue's motions. His hands grope me, gripping my ass and pulling me to him. His erection grinds painfully against me.

He's an incredible kisser, not too forceful now that I'm compliant. Shame pools deep in my belly as his soft lips expertly turn me on. They contradict his hard personality, passionate and supple as he explores my mouth. It's like a dance, and his tongue lights a fire in my core, making my stomach tremble.

I hate my body for responding so eagerly, but I'm fiercely tempted to enjoy the intoxicating sensation. The electric pull to be with him is even stronger than I remember. It's what convinced me we were meant to be together in high school. That our young love could stand the test of time.

It didn't even last the night.

When Nicolo finally pulls back, breaking our kiss, we both gasp for oxygen.

"Now that"–he laughs breathily–"is how you seal a deal."

His hazel eyes dance as he continues to hold me firmly against his body. I slowly withdraw my fingers from his hair. Now that the kiss is over, I'm embarrassed for having touched him so instinctually.

Self-loathing grips my chest. I've given myself up to Nicolo Marchetti. I was so certain I would never be stupid enough to do that again. And what's worse is the way my pulse hums from being in his arms.

"Well, little bird, now that it's official, it's time for your first test."

A lead weight drops in my stomach. I'm going to regret conceding to Nicolo. I can see it in his eyes.

"Get down on your knees and suck my cock," he demands, his tone turning cold and commanding.

"Right here?" I gasp, glancing toward the studio door. "Now?" Faint music still plays in the dance studio next door, where Professor Moriari is helping students with their choreographed pieces. "Someone might walk in on us." *Please, God, don't make me do this.* I would be mortified if anyone saw.

"I don't care," Nicolo says coolly, one hand shifting to grip my chin as the other rests lightly on my waist. He slowly walks me backward toward the ballet barre and the studio's mirrored wall. "I can get away with anything. My family all but owns the city, and now I own you." His deep voice hovers just above a murmur.

I gasp as my back hits the ballet barre, bringing me to a halt.

"Do it, pet. Suck my cock," he commands more forcefully, his eyes burning with intensity.

Trembling, I slowly lower myself to my knees. Nicolo turns so he can grip the barre.

I see my profile from the corner of my eye. Shame colors my cheeks as I realize my nipples are hard. They show slightly, pressing instantly against my leotard's thin fabric.

My hands shake as I reach for the button and zipper of Nicolo's jeans, and I struggle to get them open.

Nicolo's gaze burns a hole through me as I reach into his boxer briefs to grip his cock. Slowly, I withdraw it. My core quivers as I expose his impressive rock-hard length. It's bigger than I remember. My nerves take over as I face the fact that I have no idea what I'm doing. I've never given a blowjob before.

Nicolo seems to recognize this, as he takes charge. "Wrap your lips around it, little bird," he commands, his knuckles whitening where he grips the ballet barre. "And treat it like a popsicle you don't want to let drip."

Tears of shame sting my eyes as I open wide. Wrapping my lips over my teeth, I guide his cockhead inside my mouth. The tip is silky against the roof of my mouth, and I grip the base of his cock as I realize he's too big for me to take all the way. I start to move his cock in and out of my mouth. My hand follows the motion as I try to hold him all.

Air hisses between Nicolo's teeth. His hips rock with my motion. When I look up, my eyes meet his. His cock twitches in my hand.

"Put your hands behind your back," Nicolo commands.

Anxiety constricts my chest as my pulse quickens. I do as he says, interlocking my fingers to keep them behind me. Nicolo grips my ponytail with his free hand as he cradles the back of my head.

His hips rock forward as he increases the pressure on my head. He forces his cockhead down my throat until I choke. Nicolo chuckles darkly.

"Am I too big for you, pet? You better get used to choking down my meat. I like seeing you on your knees. This is a perfect use for your smart mouth. You can't speak with my cock halfway down your throat, now can you?"

I gag as tears start to stream down my cheeks. I desperately want to move my hands, to grip his thighs at least. I need some relief, but I don't dare move.

"Use your tongue," Nicolo rasps. "Lick me." His movements grow more persistent as he fucks the back of my throat.

Fighting my gag reflex, I breathe through my nose as I flick my tongue up and down the thick vein at the base of his cock. He swells impossibly further, making my jaw ache as his breathing grows heavier.

"Ffuck," he hisses, his pace jumping up a notch.

The growing urgency in his tone makes my pussy clench. Humiliation sears my flesh as a gush of arousal dampens my leotard. As I get used to the forceful penetration, warm desire pools deep in my belly.

A subtle noise near the studio door catches my attention. My pulse hammers in my ears. Excitement trickles into my belly at the prospect of getting caught like this. And I hate myself for it. I'm not just turned on by getting throat fucked by Nicolo Marchetti. Thinking of someone walking in on us now excites me. *What is wrong with me?*

But if someone happens to be on the other side of the studio door, they decide not to come in. Nicolo's thrusts grow more erratic. I think he's about to come. Gripping my hair firmly in his hand, Nicolo removes his cock from my mouth with a sudden jerk.

The hand holding the ballet barre moves to grip his thick girth. He gives a final stroke, aiming for my face. I barely have time to close my eyes before hot cum spurts across my lips and cheek.

"Stick out your tongue," Nicolo growls as another burst coats my neck and chin.

I obey immediately, opening my mouth wide. A third spurt hits my tongue and a fourth.

"Swallow it," he commands when he seems to be done.

I close my mouth and swallow convulsively, the salty viscous substance sticking as it slides down my throat. When I open my eyes, Nicolo leers down at me. He taps my lips with the tip of his cock.

"Lick it off for me, little bird."

I dart my tongue out to clean off the pearly cum dripping from his tip, and my cheeks burn with shame. It takes me back to the night we spent together in high school. He came on my face then, too, and now I feel trapped in the same evil snare as before.

As soon as I've licked him clean, Nicolo tucks his cock back into his pants and zips them up. Without a word, he turns to leave. I remain kneeling, too stunned by what just happened to say anything. When he gets to the door, Nicolo glances over his shoulder and chuckles darkly.

"Clean yourself up. You look like a fucking mess." Then he vanishes into the hallway, leaving me alone.

Tears stream down my cheeks, mingling with his cum, but I don't want to touch my face. Looking toward the cubby area, I spot a box of Kleenex and hurry over to it. I snatch one after another until I have a thick wad. Forcefully wiping my face clean, I bite my lips to keep quiet as I sob.

I hate Nicolo. I hate him for everything he's done. But I hate myself worse because, despite how terrible he is, I'm still turned on. My clit pulses every time my leotard shifts against it. I'm so wet, I think I've soaked through every layer.

I take deep breaths as I try to calm my tears, and slowly, my sobs subside. I need to do something to release some of my stress. Glancing toward the door, I check to make sure no one's about to come in. Then I reach beneath my dance skirt and press my fingers between my thighs. My core tightens at the light contact.

Swallowing hard, I push aside my leotard and work my leggings down. Then I slide my fingers beneath the stretchy fabric. I gasp as I find my slick folds and stroke them lightly. I'm shocked at how wet I got from my confrontation with Nicolo.

I shift my fingers to graze my clit and have to bite back a moan. Slowly, I start to circle the sensitive nub, intensifying my excitement. My mind flashes back to Nicolo's soft lips crushing mine, his hands groping my ass as his cock dug into my pelvis.

I hear the air hissing between his teeth as my lips wrapped around his cock. It echoes in my mind, and my legs tremble as pleasure courses through my body. My skin lights on fire even as goose bumps lift the hair on the back of my neck.

I circle my fingers more quickly, and zings of ecstasy zip up my spine. I'm close to my release. I know it from the elastic ball of tension growing tighter in my core.

I tip my head back, gripping the barre with my free hand just as he did. Breathing deeply through my nose, I recall Nicolo's hand gripping my hair, his silky cockhead slamming against the back of my throat.

With a violent shudder, I come. My pussy clenches, and my clit throbs as I gasp from the overwhelming wave of euphoria. I continue to press against my sensitive bundle of nerves until the last of my aftershocks subside. Then I slowly withdraw my hand from beneath my leggings and adjust them back into place.

But the relief is fleeting once my reality comes crashing back down on me.

I've signed my body over to Nicolo. I'm now his toy to do with as he pleases. After today, I shudder to think of just what he might make me do.

On top of that, I no longer have a dance partner for the winter showcase. And rather than discussing my options with Professor Moriari during practice, I've been on my knees in the next room. I've been giving my first blowjob to the person I hate most in the world–who also happens to be the father of my child.

Fuck.

I desperately want to go home, take a shower, and disappear under my blankets for the rest of the night. But I need to clean myself up, get my act together, and go speak to my professor. I don't know what to do for a partner now that Fin's arm is busted. He won't be back in time for the winter showcase.

My heart aches knowing that he's in the hospital because of me. I was stupid to have put up such a futile fight. Now Fin's future is in jeopardy, and I'm in the same horrible position I would have been in anyway.

Fresh tears sting the back of my eyes, but I choke them down as I head to the bathroom. Leaning over the sink, I turn the faucet on and splash my face with water, scrubbing it vigorously to clean it. But even after it's spotless and I've dried it thoroughly, all I can see is the cum that coated it like haphazard splatter paint.

Taking deep breaths, I coach myself to suck it up as I glare into the mirror. When I'm fortified enough to speak to my professor, I turn and march out. I leave no room for hesitation. Still, in the back of my mind, I can't stop thinking about what my life has just become.

18

NICOLO

My driver pulls up to the shabby, tan-brick apartment building in Uptown to collect Anya for our first date. She sits on the front steps, waiting for me like I told her to. *Nice to see she can follow directions when the occasion arises.*

But as I take in the dilapidated structure and the poor state of the neighborhood around her, I'm intensely aware of the financial gap between us. I can't wait to see her reaction to the date I have in store for her. Now that she's agreed to be mine, I want to show her the kind of luxury she'll enjoy while she's with me.

My bodyguard Seb, who's closest to the curb, opens his door and steps out to help Anya inside my luxury SUV.

Anya slips gracefully onto the seat facing me, clad in worn jeans and a simple maroon T-shirt. The color contrasts with her cream-colored skin and emphasizes her full pink lips. I like seeing her in something other than her dance clothes. She'll look even better once I dress her.

She wears minimal makeup, as usual, though I can tell she put a bit of effort into her appearance. She wears her long hair down for once. It cascades over her shoulders in golden waves, tempting me to grab a handful and kiss her. But I remain nonchalantly reclined against my seat, eyeing her appreciatively.

Anya glances around nervously, meeting both my bodyguards' eyes before her gaze lands on me. She looks intimidated.

"Are you ready to see how the better half lives?" I ask playfully.

Anya's cheeks color slightly. "Sure," she says simply.

"I have a surprise for you," I press, wanting to get a reaction out of her.

She nods silently, and that just irks me further. She better give me more than that when she finds out what it is.

My driver pulls back out onto the street, heading toward the Magnificent Mile and the high-end luxury shopping district. Anya watches out the window, quiet the entire ride.

Her eyes grow wide when we pull up outside of 900 Shops—an impressive skyscraper by all accounts, with seven levels of brand name shops occupying the bottom floors. Her response this time is much more appropriate.

Sep opens the door once more, and I gesture for Anya to get out first.

"Be ready to pick us up when I call," I tell my driver, then I follow her from the car. I button my suit jacket once I'm standing.

Placing my hand on the small of her back, I guide Anya through the glass doors into the mall. My men will wait for me outside.

Anya slows as she takes in the grandeur of the vast space, the vaulted ceilings that loom seven floors above. A brilliant set of cohesive images give the impression of skylights, mimicking the branches of a blossoming cherry tree against a blue sky.

Anya's lips part in awe as her eyes wander up the levels of the mall. Bridges arch across the space, offering walkways from one side to the other. I smile at how round her eyes grow.

"Come on." I press her forward, guiding her toward the escalators. "We have an appointment to keep."

I lead her up to the fourth floor, and Anya keeps her head on a swivel. Clearly, she's never shopped here before. Though the mall's marble floors and plushly furnished resting areas are rather exceptional, her reaction makes my lips curl smugly. I take her to North Shore Exchange, the equivalent of Macy's but more high end.

"Afternoon," one of the sales associates says brightly, greeting us at the door.

"Hi, we have an appointment with a stylist to find a few dresses," I say.

"Wonderful." The woman ushers us to another girl dressed in a sharp black business suit and a low-cut lacy blouse that shows off her assets. "This is Amelia. She'll be helping you today."

"I look forward to working with you." The stylist eyes Anya up and down, gauging her size. "Do you have any particular styles in mind?"

"Classy," I state, "with some variety in formal and casual. Don't be afraid to pick something flattering," I hint. "Also, she needs a proper bra–something sexy that will make her breasts look nice."

Anya's cheeks redden as her eyes drop to the floor.

"No problem," Amelia says. "Feel free to look around and pull anything that catches your eye. In the meantime, I'll put together a selection of dresses in your size. They'll be ready for you in the dressing area whenever you've had enough time to look around."

Amelia gestures to the far corner of the store, where a set of comfortable-looking couches surround a coffee table and face a hall of doors. A three-way mirror occupies a large space off to the side.

"Great." Keeping my hand on the small of Anya's back, I walk her around the store, perusing.

I select several dresses just for fun, some that are probably more revealing than Anya's typical attire. I plan on fully enjoying this shopping expedition, so I pick the ones that will show me some extra skin.

Anya doesn't pick a single item, though I tell her she can. She's a closed door of emotion, and I can't make sense of whether she's intimidated or unimpressed.

When we make our way over to the dressing room, Amelia's already waiting. She shows Anya which dressing room belongs to her.

"I want to see each one, Anya." I stretch out on the blue suede couch facing the dressing rooms.

Anya blushes as she disappears into her dressing room.

"Let me know if you need anything," Amelia says. "I'll be just around the corner. Oh, I also set a pair of heels in there to finish off the look."

"Thank you, Amelia," I say.

She smiles and gives me a quick nod before walking away.

Emerging from the dressing room a few minutes later, Anya glitters in her chic club dress. Sapphire sequins glint as the lighting reflects off every inch of the knee-length form-fitting bodycon dress.

It's a simple cut meant to hug her curves with inch-wide straps that frame her collarbones. The color draws out the brilliant blue of her eyes. And in this dress, her pert breasts look really good.

Her athletic attire hasn't been doing her any favors. She actually has a decent rack when she's wearing the right bra. I imagine sliding a hand beneath the sequined fabric to palm them. My cock twitches at the thought.

Walking briskly toward me, Anya moves gracefully in her black stilettos. Her legs are to die for with the way the heels make her calves work. She gives a simple spin and pauses.

"Yes," I say simply. "Show me the next one."

Turning silently, she makes her way back to her room and closes the door.

Anya enters the hallway again after a few minutes. She's sheathed in a floor-length silk dress in a brilliant emerald color. It trails behind her as she approaches me. The waist cinches nicely, showing off her slender form, then flares again to cling to her curvy hips.

It hugs her body perfectly, hanging from her neck as a halter top and dipping just low enough to suggest cleavage. It appears she can't wear a bra with this one because, beneath the darted seams meant to mask them, her hard nipples stand out against the fabric.

"Turn around," I order, and Anya obeys.

She pulls aside her thick waves of hair to reveal the dress's open back. It shows off Anya's perfect musculature. The dress sits low enough on her hips that I can spy back dimples peeking over the green fabric.

"I like that one," I state. My cock would say it's an understatement as it bulges against my slacks. "Next."

Anya disappears into her dressing room without a word and comes out in a third dress a few minutes later. She's putting on the dresses Amelia picked out for her, I note. They appear to be more modest. And while I like this short, flowing dress with accordion pleats and a high collar, I want to see her in one of the dresses I picked out.

"Try the red dress next," I command.

When Anya strides toward me in the crimson velvet dress, my mouth goes dry. The perfectly placed asymmetrical cutouts give me a tantalizing view of her side boob, under cleavage, and flat stomach.

Her blush tells me she's uncomfortable with how much skin this dress reveals. I fucking love it. It leaves little to the imagination. The scrap of fabric is more like a mini skirt with several slivers running up her body at an angle to attach to the revealing bodice. And while the collar is high, this dress is anything but modest.

My gaze rakes down her body as my cock pulses in my slacks. Fuck, I like that dress. Anya doesn't wait for my approval this time before she spins on her toes and dashes back to the dressing room. Her arms cover as much of her exposed flesh as she can. I chuckle darkly, enjoying the way she squirms under my watchful eye.

Every dress she puts on looks stunning with her perfect body to model it. It doesn't matter the shape or style. Each one makes me harder as I imagine stripping it off her. Her final outfit is a knit long-sleeve sweater dress that clings to her curves and comes down to her midthigh.

Made of a black ribbed fabric, it looks incredibly soft. But the best part is the plunging neckline that extends down far enough to expose her belly button. Thin string crisscrosses over the opening, securely lacing it without covering her milky flesh.

It fits perfectly with her black peep-toe heels. Even Anya seems silently appreciative as she smooths the fabric over her thighs.

"Good." I rise from my seat on the couch to stride toward her. "This is your outfit for tonight. Keep it on." I circle her once, succumbing to the temptation to touch her. I brush her silky locks over her shoulder so I can see the back. A golden zipper runs up her spine.

"How did we like those?" Amelia asks when I call her over.

"Good. We'll buy them all. And the shoes. Find two more pairs that she can mix and match as well." I hand Amelia my credit card as her lips part slightly in surprise. "Oh, and several sets of your sexiest lingerie."

"R-Right away," the stylist stammers and jumps into action.

I turn to Anya, ready to remove the tag from her dress, and find her face has gone pale. The color even drains from her lips. She presses them into a thin line and swallows hard as her eyes drop to the floor. Rather than the gratitude I expected, Anya actually looks uncomfortable.

She flinches when I flip open my pocket knife. Stepping behind her, I grasp the tag and cut it off before she has time to step away. Her shoulders tense momentarily. Then her eyes land on the tag I discard in a tiny wastebasket.

I call down to the car to have one of my bodyguards collect the heavy bags of purchased items. Then we head out of North Shore Exchange. I guide Anya up a floor to the luxury jewelry store Sabbia.

If I thought Anya might be intimidated when we first entered 900 Stores, the way she peers into the jewelry display tells me she's completely overwhelmed but the decadence.

Her eyes travel over the cases of diamond rings and sapphire necklaces. Each intricate design showcases the jewels' natural beauty. Anya's face blanches as her gaze lands on the price tag behind a large single-pendant ruby necklace.

"See anything you like?" I ask.

If she picks something, I intend to buy it. I've only ever seen her wear a plain gold chain necklace with a tiny ballerina figurine. No earrings besides the simplest of studs on occasion.

"They're all breathtaking," she murmurs, her voice confirming her statement.

"You need jewelry to go with your nice dress. Pick whichever you like."

Anya's eyes snap up from the display case to meet mine, her expression panicked. "I couldn't possibly," she objects. "It's too much."

I give her a smug smile. "I promise I can afford it."

Anya bites her lip as she looks back down at the display. We wander through the store as she takes in all the fine pieces of jewelry. Finally, she lands on a pair of simple yet elegant diamond studs.

"That's it?" I ask, baffled by her complete lack of interest in the more expensive pieces. I gave her free rein to pick whichever jewelry she wants.

She nods, and her chin actually trembles, further confusing me. This girl is incomprehensible sometimes, but if that's what she wants, I suppose I won't complain. I wave over a sales associate and have them take out the earrings she picked.

"And that bracelet next to them." I point to a matching diamond-studded gold bracelet.

We head out from the store a few minutes later, Anya clad in her new wardrobe and jewelry that twinkles in the mall's overhead lights. I guide her back down the escalators and open the door for her.

In the car a moment later, we take a short ride down the Magnificent Mile to one of my favorite fine-dining spots on the strip, Cité. We take the Lake Pointe Tower elevator up to the seventieth floor. I stand next to Anya, catching glimpses of her out of the corner of my eye.

I don't know that she's said more than ten words to me today. So, tonight, I'm determined to dig further. *She's clearly a dancer, but what else makes her tick?* She has to have more to her life than ballet.

For the first time, I'm curious about what that might be. She's different from the bland supermodels I've dated. The women who like to strut their bodies and roll in the money thrown their way. Anya doesn't even seem interested in luxury. *So, what is it she wants from life?*

The elevator dings, and we make our way to the host stand.

They recognize me as I walk in. "Mr. Marchetti, your usual table is ready for you," the host says formally. "Right this way."

He takes us to the far corner of the restaurant, further from the other patrons and right near the floor-to-ceiling windows revealing the Chicago cityscape. The setting sun casts the skyscrapers in a bluish-purple glow. A beautiful contrast to the golden lights illuminating the tall buildings.

The host pulls out Anya's seat, and she thanks him as she slips gracefully into it. I order their finest Sangiovese and study Anya across the table as the host departs.

"How long have you been a ballet dancer?" I start off with something I'm sure she'll talk about.

"All my life." Anya's eyes turn toward the city skyline.

I get the sense that she's doing it as much to avoid my eyes as she is to take in the view.

I try again after taking a sip of water. "What got you into it?"

"My parents." When Anya turns to face me, her expression is guarded.

After all I've given her today, I would think conversation is the least she could offer in return. But she doesn't bite. I clench my fists in irritation.

"And what do you do besides dance?" I offer, changing direction.

"Schoolwork mostly, or sleep. I teach a children's ballet class during the summer." She circles the rim of her water glass with the tip of her middle finger.

Our server arrives at the table with our wine before I can dig further. He offers me a sample and checks to make sure I'm satisfied before he pours us each a glass.

When he asks if we're ready to order, I take over, aware that Anya hasn't even looked at her menu. "I'll have the lobster ravioli, and she'll take the filet mignon." I hand over our menus.

The waiter departs, leaving us in silence once more.

"You like children?" I press now that he's gone.

Anya's eyes flick to mine for the first time, a hint of worry in their blue depths.

"You said you teach children's ballet," I supply, reminding her of our topic before the server came over. "Try it," I insist, gesturing to her wine glass as I take a drink.

Anya picks up her wine glass and sips before setting it back on the table. I grind my teeth. She's doing everything I say and only that. She's playing with me, pushing back to see how much she can get away with. I suck in a breath of frustration as my lips press together.

"Yes, I like children." She captures her lower lip between her teeth and turns her eyes toward the now brilliant golden-pink sunset.

I let her be as I study her delicate features. *Why is this girl so infuriating? How does she know every button to push? Or am I that simple that she knows how to toy with me so easily?* No girl has ever been this difficult to understand, let alone win over.

Anger boils up inside me as I try to make sense of Anya. She doesn't seem scared of me, for the most part, and though I've gone out of my way, she doesn't seem interested in the luxury I can offer.

When the food arrives, Anya still hasn't said anything of substance. And she cuts a small piece of steak, chewing it slowly in her stony silence. The lesson I'd pictured I would teach her for being so stubborn seems to have backfired. Anya doesn't care about clothes or jewelry or fine dining despite her poor upbringing. And she's so withdrawn, I find myself growing short with her.

My lobster ravioli tastes bitter from all the frustration boiling up inside me. Anya pushes her plate further onto the table after only three bites, her eyes hooded as her expression grows uncomfortable.

"What, is the food not good enough for you?" I demand, setting my knife and fork down with enough force to make my plate jump.

"No, it's fine," she says, her eyes meeting mine.

Something snaps in my head, and I see red. "Fine?"

I wave our server over, and he approaches immediately. "You can take her plate. She doesn't like her food."

Anya visibly pales, her eyes growing wide.

"Is something wrong with it, sir? I'm happy to have the kitchen make something the lady likes," the server offers, his tone strained. He knows better than to piss me off.

Why is Anya being so fucking aggravating? The way she nervously worries her lip gives me a sense of satisfaction. Then it clicks. I've been wasting my time lavishing her with gifts today. Anya doesn't need a carrot to motivate her.

She needs the stick.

19

ANYA

My mouth goes dry. I've been so lost in my head missing Clara and worrying about what to do for a dance partner that I've pushed Nicolo too far. He was expecting lively conversation and a girl to slobber gratefully over his arm. But that's not me.

I'm grateful for the nice dresses he bought me today. But I know it's his way of turning me into his prostitute, and that turns my stomach. He's forced me into this relationship, and now he wants to make it okay by showering me with expensive things.

Well, I'm not so easily purchased.

All I want is to be at home, spending the weekend with my daughter.

But as Nicolo demands that the server take my food, I know I'll regret not trying harder to appease him.

The server scoops up my plate with a tight-lipped smile.

"You can bring us the check as well," Nicolo commands. "We're done."

My stomach twists painfully as I notice the amount of ravioli still sitting in his dish. The nearly full bottle of wine. He's proving a point.

He doesn't care how much money he spends. He has so much, he can take anything or leave it as he damn well pleases.

But if he gives me something, I better appreciate it. Because I'm the poor orphan who lives in Uptown with her aunt. I'm nothing, worth nothing, so anything I receive out of his generosity is to be accepted as a priceless gift.

As the server swiftly departs, Nicolo wipes his mouth with his cloth napkin and tosses it over his half-eaten dinner. Rising abruptly, he tosses a stack of cash on the table. It will more than cover our bill along with a generous tip–despite the vomit-inducing prices on the menu.

"If you're not in the mood for a nice dinner, then I have other plans for you," Nicolo growls.

He grabs my forearm tightly as he hauls me to my feet.

Fear grips me. He's pissed.

He drags me through the restaurant by my upper arm. I can barely stay on my feet. I try to keep up in my new stilettos that I have no idea how to walk in.

Now that I've pushed him too far, I don't know how to make it right. I've never tried appeasing him before. My stomach knots painfully as bile rises in my throat.

We make it to the elevator, and as soon as the doors open, he shoves me inside. I stumble, barely catching myself against the railing on the back wall. I feel intensely vulnerable in my fancy outfit and dressy shoes. I never wear these kinds of clothes, and I'm completely off balance.

I right myself and press my back against the elevator wall, trying to make myself small and invisible. Nicolo's jaw works furiously as he studies my face. He doesn't say a word, even as the door dings open. Instead, he grabs my arm to haul me through the hotel lobby. Somehow, his silence is more terrifying than when he chose to bully me.

His driver is waiting for us by the time we get outside. His two massively intimidating bodyguards scowl at me as if I've personally offended them. I wonder if they must suspect me of being some kind of Russian spy.

"Get in," Nicolo demands curtly. He follows me into the black tinted-windowed SUV that screams mafia.

As soon as the door shuts behind his burly bodyguards, Nicolo commands the driver to head to a place called Incognito. The ride is short, and we pull up outside another high-rise in the posh neighborhood of Lincoln Park. Incognito appears to be in the basement level of the building. Nicolo places his hand on the small of my back, guiding me down the steps into what I assume is A nightclub.

As soon as we enter the establishment, I know I'm wrong. A bell chimes quietly above us as the door opens. The woman that approaches a moment later is dressed in shiny leather that barely covers her hips, thighs, and breasts. Metal links connect the bra-like leather top to the half-sized miniskirt.

"Nico," the woman purrs. Her thickly lined eyes close partially to make her look even more seductive. "What a pleasant surprise."

"Tiffany." Nicolo nods.

Tiffany strides toward him like a runway model, her legs brushing together as she puts one thigh-high boot in front of the other. "You here for a little fun?" Her eyes flick toward me briefly.

"Yes, we're here to book a room."

Is it me, or does Tiffany look disappointed?

"Of course." She steps up to a small podium to scan a book lying open there. She scribbles a small note and flashes Nicolo a smile. "Right this way."

Tiffany leads us down the stairs into what could almost be a bar if not for the patrons. Cushy booths line the walls, and high-top tables fill the center of the floor.

Couples sit at each of the occupied tables, the women leaning toward their men, most of whom wear fancy suits and Rolex watches. But the girls are what catch my eye. If I stitched together every piece of clothing on these women, I still might not be able to make an outfit.

But the women don't seem to mind as they nibble on their partners' ears and massage the men's inner thighs. My pulse quickens as I start to wrap my mind around what kind of place this is. My palms begin to sweat.

Tiffany leads us through the lounge area to a dark hallway. Everything about this place, from the dim lighting to the dark walls and the cool air that smells faintly of salty minerals, is cave-like.

Something snaps behind a door to my left, making me jump. A cry instantly follows, making my stomach drop. Tiffany doesn't even seem to notice, and Nicolo doesn't appear to mind. He presses me forward, the palm of his hand burning into my back.

As we continue down the hall of doors, a feminine moan issues from a door to my right. I can't tell whether it's a sound of pleasure or pain. I shiver, curling in on myself as I dread where we're headed.

"This is your room." Tiffany gestures to an open door on the right near the end of the hall. "Enjoy. And don't hesitate to call if you need anything." Her voice drips honey, and her hand grazes Nicolo's shoulder as she turns to walk back down the hall.

I hesitate for a moment. But I can't refuse Nicolo as his hand presses against my back. I made a deal to protect my daughter and the people I love. I can't say no.

Wrapping my arms defensively around my stomach, I step inside the room. I find contraptions I've never laid eyes on before–some kind of bench with black leather padding along the top, a person-sized wooden X with straps attached to each corner, something that vaguely resembles a swing but with no proper seat.

One wall is dedicated to whips, handcuffs, and various forms of restraints. It also has what looks like some kind of horse bit with a rubber ball in the center. Sex toys, I realize, as goose bumps ripple across my flesh.

The door clicks shut behind me, and I whirl, feeling like a deer caught in the headlights. I meet Nicolo's burning gaze. His hazel eyes are almost green. I've come to associate that with anger. My stomach quivers at the thought of being trapped in this sex dungeon while Nicolo's angry.

"You're mine," he states coolly. "If you don't do as I say, I will punish you. And if you continue to fight me, I will punish the ones you love." He lets the silence linger to let the information sink in.

Terrified, I start to tremble uncontrollably. I don't know what's about to happen.

"Take off your dress," Nicolo demands, striding closer.

Reaching behind me, I unzip the fine fabric. Then I pull it down over my shoulders, my arms, then my hips. It pools at my feet, and I step out of it.

With the dress's plunging neckline, I wasn't able to wear a bra. Now I stand in my high heels with only a new pair of lacy black undies to cover me.

Nicolo's jaw tightens as he looks me up and down. My arms rise automatically to cover my exposed breasts.

"Don't," Nicolo commands.

He takes one last step, bringing us face to face. His eyes meet mine, the hunger in them makes my heart hammer against my ribs.

His fingers gently graze my breast, brushing across my nipple. I close my eyes, swallowing hard to choke down the shame of my excitement. His hands explore me slowly, almost tickling in their gentleness. My stomach quivers beneath his touch.

I open my eyes as Nicolo leans in to brush my ear with his lips.

"Suck my cock, little bird," he murmurs.

My breath catches, paralyzing me for an instant. I know I can't refuse. Slowly sinking to my knees, I unbuckle his belt. Nicolo sheds his fine Italian suit jacket, tossing it carelessly onto a bench. Then he goes to work unbuttoning his dress shirt.

I focus on my task, pulling his cock out of his boxer briefs. I wrap my lips around my teeth as I open my mouth. I glance up as I take Nicolo's hard length into my mouth. My heart flutters uncomfortably at the sight of his exposed chest. He was lean in high school, strong, but now, he's transformed into bulging muscle and washboard abs. A shiver of arousal trickles down my spine.

Nicolo's fingers comb into my hair as I move up and down his cock. He hasn't told me to put my hands behind my back, so I brace against his thighs as I blow him. He groans, his hips rocking at the same rhythm as my motion.

"Fuck, you're a quick learner," he groans as I run my tongue along the thick vein of his cock.

My panties dampen at the rasp in his voice. It makes me sick to my stomach. I don't want him to come on my face again. I don't want another reminder of our night together years ago. I try to harden myself to the intense rejection, but I can't stop it.

Nicolo seems oblivious to my turmoil. Or he doesn't care. That wouldn't surprise me after how angry he got at dinner. His fingers tighten in my hair. He thrusts harder, making me gag as he pushes his cockhead down my throat.

But I have better control of my body this time. Even as tears sting my eyes from the rough assault, I know I can take it.

"You like my cock in your mouth, pet?" he asks, his tone condescending. "I bet you're already *dripping*."

My clit throbs, betraying my determination not to like it. When I look up the length of his Greek god's body, my core awakens, and my pussy clenches in anticipation.

His cock swells further in my mouth, and I think that means he's close. Nicolo gives three erratic thrusts. And this time, rather than coming on my face, he shoves his cock as far down my throat as it will go. He holds the back of my head firmly to keep me in place. I gag as hot cum pours across my tongue and coats the back of my mouth.

I swallow convulsively, my throat tightening around his girth. He shoots another burst of cum into my mouth. Nicolo groans, and the sound makes my stomach tighten. Once his cock stops twitching, he slowly withdraws from my mouth.

I wipe saliva and sticky cum from my lips, then I look up at Nicolo once more. He studies me closely, and even though he just came, he looks less than pleased.

"I'm tired of that pout on your face," Nicolo growls.

My stomach drops as I realize he's just getting started torturing me tonight. Though I struggle to swallow the cum coating the back of my throat, I don't mean to pout. But Nicolo heads toward the wall of whips and restraints, and as I stay kneeling in the middle of the room, I realize it's his excuse to use one of the toys.

"Open," he commands when he returns a moment later.

He holds the odd-looking horse bit with the rubber ball to my lips.

I part them, and Nicolo presses the rubber into my mouth. He buckles the strap around my head, effectively gagging me with the horrifying contraption.

"Stand up," he says, and he actually offers me his hand to help.

My knees shake so hard, I take him up on the offer as I pull myself to my feet. Keeping ahold of my fingers, Nicolo guides me to some kind of standing picture frame that reaches a good two feet above my head. Grasping my shoulders, he positions me where he wants.

Returning to the wall, Nicolo collects a length of rope. I glance up to the frame I stand within. *Is he going to... tie me up?* My heart bursts into a full-on sprint. I glance toward the door, wondering if I might be able to outrun him. Not a chance.

Nicolo's on me in a second, his fingers deftly tying his rope around my wrist then stretching my arm above my head. He moves to my other hand, and I start to panic. I can't speak from the ball gag in my mouth, and now he's incapacitated me. I'm vulnerable, exposed, and completely at Nicolo Marchetti's mercy. The thought utterly terrifies me.

Nicolo returns to the wall, slowly examining the display of whips. He makes a show of which one he wants to use. The room's cool temperature combined with my fear makes me tremble so hard I rattle the wood frame I'm strapped to.

Nicolo decides on a simple riding crop and returns to me. "Have you ever seen one of these before, pet?"

He traces it over my nipples and breasts, making goose bumps rise in its wake. He slowly traces a curving path down my stomach, then presses the riding crop between my thighs. "Spread your legs," he demands, snapping my inner thigh lightly.

My flesh stings. I respond instinctively, stepping wider in my stilettos to avoid the crop's bite. Nicolo stoops to tie my ankles to the base of the frame as well. Then he continues to stroke and tickle my skin with the whip as he circles behind me.

The leather leaves my flesh for a moment. It reconnects with a sharp snap, and I squeal in surprise, my body tensing. I strain against the rope that holds me in place. My skin burns under the assault, and tears sting my eyes.

It's too much. I'm in over my head, but it's too late. I can't even beg him to stop. He strikes me again, this time on the other ass cheek. I sob from the intense pain that mingles with an intoxicating pleasure.

"This is what you get when you don't give me what I want, Anya," Nicolo says, his deep voice icily calm. "I will punish you until you know how to behave properly, and today, you behaved like an ungrateful brat."

He strikes me again, this time lower on my ass. I jerk as my flesh lights on fire. My pussy throbs, and I bite down on my gag, warring to gain control of my body. Nicolo strikes me a fourth time. Before I can catch myself, I moan from the overwhelming combination of pain and pleasure.

"Ha!" Nicolo scoffs, walking back around the frame to face me. His lips come within inches of my face. "Am I turning you on, little pet?" He presses his hand between my thighs, pushing aside the lace of my thong. Then he strokes my folds.

I shudder at the intense arousal that roars through my body.

"Holy fuck, you little slut. You're so wet," he breathes, his fingers pressing inside me.

A lone tear tracks down my cheek as my pussy clenches around his fingers.

"I wonder if I could make you come with just the whip," he suggests lightly.

My eyes grow wide as I silently plead for him to stop. But Nicolo doesn't seem to notice. Stroking down my chest with the tip of the whip, Nicolo circles each nipple. Then he slides the whip down to the peak of my thighs. He taps the outside of my panties playfully. My hips jerk from the jolt of electric arousal.

He hums with amusement as a wicked smile curls his lips.

Withdrawing the whip, he snaps it across my left breast, catching my sensitive, puckered nipple. I scream around the gag, my nerves lighting on fire even as my core tightens. Nicolo returns to his gentle touch, tickling my skin once more. But he's not done. He might do this until he forces me to come.

Shockingly, though all he's done is abuse me, I'm on the verge of release. I'm mortified. I would crawl into a hole and die if I could.

I anticipate the whip's snap across my other nipple, but that doesn't lessen its intensity. A scream rips from my throat as I thrash against my bindings. The worst part is how my clit pulses painfully, demanding relief.

Nicolo lightly traces the whip along my jawbone then to my sternum before traveling further down. He snaps it against my throbbing clit, and the agony is overwhelming for a split second. Then I come, my orgasm ripping through me like a tornado. Gasping and shuddering, I collapse against my wrist restraints as I ride out wave after wave of euphoria.

"Look at you, you dirty little slut. You really did come from being whipped, didn't you?"

Nicolo's hand finds my pussy once more, pushing aside my panties. I can feel the wetness slicking his fingers. He traces between my folds, collecting my arousal.

When he presses his fingers to my clit, zings of pleasure race to my core. I'm still intensely sensitive from my first orgasm. But Nicolo seems to enjoy the way I twitch and jump beneath his hand.

His thumb takes over circling my clit so his fingers can slide into my pussy. And I find I'm building to a second orgasm in no time. He touches me so expertly my body sings beneath his hands. My skin sears wherever he touches me. Nicolo fingers me forcefully, determined to get a second orgasm out of me.

I moan as the sensation overwhelms me. Insanely turned on, I feel like I might rip in half if he keeps up his grueling pace. Then he leans forward to capture my nipple in his mouth. His tongue rolls the hard nub and flicks it. The skin is raw and taut from the abuse it suffered earlier. Still, an ache throbs deep in my core.

With his free hand, Nicolo grasps my other breast and firmly kneads it in his palm. His fingers capture my nipple, and he pinches it gently, rolling it.

The overwhelming stimulation launches me into a second orgasm. I cry out as I find my release, the sound muffled by my gag. My pussy clenches around Nicolo's fingers, trying to pull him further inside of me. My chest heaves as wave after wave of ecstasy crashes down on me.

As I finally slow, I collapse weakly. My arms strain with my full weight, but I can't find the strength to stand on my own. My body has betrayed me. I shouldn't want Nicolo to touch me after all the horrible things he's done. But every time he does, my body comes alive.

Slowly, the strength comes back to my legs. As Nicolo unties my ankles, I take the weight off my wrists and stand. He unties my wrists next, and I massage the circulation back into them. Nicolo unbuckles the gag and gently pulls it from my lips.

My teeth ache from having bitten my ball gag so hard. My lips feel stretched and dry from being forced open for so long. I dare to look up into Nicolo's eyes, wondering if he might be done with me now that he's delivered his punishment.

The fire in them tells me this is not over.

"Go to the bed and take off your panties," Nicolo commands.

Anxiety grips me as I think about the last time we had sex. I got pregnant, and it changed my life permanently. I can't do that again.

Still, I do as he says, walking my death march to the black silk sheets. Hooking my thumbs into the skimpy lace, I slide the thong down over my ass. Letting it drop to the floor, then I crawl onto the bed.

I turn around to find Nicolo has stripped the rest of his clothes. From this angle, he really could be a sculpture in a museum. His body is so perfect. As he rips a condom package and rolls it down his length, a bubble of anticipation rises inside me.

He prowls toward me, climbing onto the bed and lying me back. Pressing between my knees, Nicolo shifts until his lips hover above mine. "I've been dying to find out if you're a virgin or not," he murmurs before crushing his lips to mine.

Pain lances my heart to know he still doesn't remember me. I need to get used to it if I'm going to survive this, but in the back of my mind, I still can't believe he thought so little of me. I was truly nothing to him back then, and I'm nothing more than another conquest to him now.

Grasping my wrists, Nicolo forces my hands above my head. He pins me down as his cockhead slides between my folds, pressing against my entrance. He doesn't give me a chance to accommodate him at all.

He teases me for only a second before he shoves forcefully inside me. Then he's buried in my pussy up to the hilt. He's thick and long, almost too big for me, and I stretch almost painfully around his width.

But God it feels sinfully good.

Like the first time with him, my mixture of pain and pleasure rides the perfect knife's-edge. It makes me hate myself. And it turns me on. Straining under him, I clench tighter around his length.

Nicolo groans, pausing for a moment as he closes his eyes. "Fuck you're tight," he murmurs.

Then he starts to move on top of me. Rocking in and out of my pussy, he grazes against my clit. It's so different from the first time we were together. So much more forceful. He quickens his pace, pounding angrily into me. As if he hates himself as much as I do, even as he takes the same pleasure from fucking me.

When we had sex in high school, he took his time and built up the pleasure. Even so, the way he thrusts inside me turns me on–the way he spreads my thighs and pins me down. He's completely in control, and my traitorous body *loves* it.

Each thrust sends tingles rippling out to my fingers and toes. I gasp as I try to stop myself from falling too deeply in this moment. Nicolo makes my body respond in ways I never knew it could. But he's only using me. I have to keep a clear head. And yet, my pleasure continues to intensify. The increasingly familiar impending orgasm tightens my core.

Nicolo shifts my wrists into one hand. His other trails down my arm to grope my breast and tease my nipple. His lips find the tender spot behind my ear. He sucks mercilessly, making my clit throb and my stomach quiver.

I'm so close to coming a third time.

Deep shame wars within me as I find it impossible to resist the pleasure.

The new, torturous attention sends ripples of fire licking through my veins, and I squeeze my eyes closed as I fight my building orgasm. I don't want to give him the pleasure of knowing he can make me orgasm. But I can't stop myself. I bite my lip to muffle my cry as tingling euphoria erupts from my core. My chest heaves with the intensity of it.

Nicolo releases a dark chuckle as I ride the waves of my release. "You're so fucking horny. You little tease, you clearly wanted me to fuck you all along. No one comes this many times if they don't want it."

Shame makes my cheeks flame. I have no control over my attraction toward Nicolo. He knows how to make me come even when I can't stand the thought of him claiming me. And yet here he is, fucking me for his own amusement as he rocks me to my very core.

I open my eyes to find Nicolo studying my face. Mild amusement mingles with a deep satisfaction at his accomplishment. He stills on top of me as the aftershocks of my orgasm subside.

Nicolo keeps his cock buried in me as his muscled chest expands with each deep breath. "Well, you're clearly not a virgin, little bird, but you're so tight. Is that because you're so frigid? You certainly like playing hard to get. Has anyone ever fucked you in the ass before? I bet not. I think you like toying with people and then not putting out."

His tone is light, speculative, but my heart hammers in my chest as I think of his thick cock pushing inside my untouched hole. My breathing turns frantic as my anxiety flares. Bile rises to my throat.

A wicked smile curls Nicolo's full lips. "Judging by your reaction, I must be right."

Shifting dexterously, Nicolo releases my wrists as he slides out of me. Then his hands are on my hips as he moves me. He flips me onto my stomach in one smooth motion.

His cockhead presses between my thighs as he reaches over me. He brings my hands up to the headboard. Before I know what's happening, he's looped two strands of nylon rope around my wrists. He pulls them tight, tying me in place.

Terror grips my chest, making it hard to breathe. Nicolo's hands return to my hips. He hauls me onto my knees, stretching my arms over my head. My breasts press against the black silk bed sheets as my back arches, exposing my pussy and ass.

Nicolo groans appreciatively, making my core tighten. I start to panic. His fingers trace a circle around the puckered hole of my ass. I shiver as my body responds both electrically and with an icy stab of fear.

"Maybe I should take your ass tonight since your pussy's already been filled by someone else. I want to claim your virginity. What do you say, pet? Shall I fuck this hole tonight?"

His fingers continue to tease my ass, making it perfectly clear what he means as he circles and presses against my entrance.

I can't stop the tears from pooling in my eyes. A sob bursts from my chest as my fear consumes me. Nicolo pauses for a split second–with surprise or momentary regret, I don't know. Then, whatever reaction he had vanishes as he covers it with a deep, rumbling laugh.

"Relax, my pretty little pet. I'll save that for another night." His hands shift as they part my ass cheeks further.

His cock shoves forcefully inside my pussy, filling me to my limit once more.

His hands travel over the raw flesh of my ass. Though his touch is light, I can still feel where the whip struck me. His fingers grip my hips. Bracing me, he starts to rock in and out of me. The force of his thrusts grows in intensity every time.

Pounding into my pussy, Nicolo fucks me hard. Our skin slaps each time we come together, and he rocks the bed with every thrust.

The pain is almost as unbearable as the pleasure. It builds inside me as he hammers against some hidden spot of ecstasy deep in my core. Despite how raw and abused my pussy feels, I barrel toward another orgasm. The silk sheets singe my nipples. He pulls me back onto his cock at the same time as he shoves forward with his hips.

I can't help the scream that tears from my throat, an involuntary release of the overwhelming sensations waging war inside me. Pain and pleasure, shame and earth-shattering relief.

My orgasm this time blinds me, sending black dots exploding across my vision. My pulse roars in my ears. Back arching, my muscles tense. I cling to my nylon manacles to keep me rooted in reality as I topple into an abyss of euphoria.

Nicolo groans, his thrusts growing erratic. My pussy clamps down around him, begging him to push further into my traitorous body. Nicolo shoves deep inside me, and his cock pulses as he comes. The sensation intensifies my own orgasm, prolonging the throbbing release. I grip his length again and again, shuddering with the intensity of my pleasure.

Though I know he's wearing a condom, through the haze of my lust, I think about the last time we had sex and how I got pregnant. Anxiety constricts my throat even as my body shudders with the last of my tingling aftershocks.

Nicolo stills inside me as he comes down from his own release. Then he slides out of me, rolling off the bed in one catlike move. For a split second, I think he might leave me tied to the bed to prolong my shame. But he bends over me, his masculine cologne filling my nose as he loosens the nylon straps binding me.

As soon as my hands are free, Nicolo stands to his full height and turns away. I sit up, crossing my ankles and pulling my knees against my chest to cover myself now that he's finished with me. I watch his perfectly muscled body as he strides nonchalantly across the room.

"Be ready for me again tomorrow," Nicolo commands as he removes his condom. He tosses it casually in the trash before he starts to dress. "I'm not done with you yet."

He glances over as he shrugs into his suit jacket. He observes my pathetic attempt at modesty as I remain on the bed, and a smile curls the corners of his lips. Pulling a money clip from his pocket, Nicolo counts out a considerable stack of hundred-dollar bills and approaches the bed.

Mortification burns in my cheeks as he tosses the money at my feet.

"Get an IUD or some kind of birth control so I don't have to think about it. I don't want to have to wear condoms every time I fuck you. You can use whatever money is left to buy yourself some new dance clothes or whatever."

Nicolo strolls toward the door as he shoves his money clip back into his pocket. Hand on the handle, he turns back to look at me once more. "My driver will take you home when you're ready," he adds.

Then he steps into the hall, leaving me in the room. The door clicks gently closed. Tears spill down my cheeks as soon as I'm alone. I bury my face in my knees as deep sobs rack my body.

Nicolo has done something worse to me than he even did in high school. I never thought that was possible, but it's true.

He's made me his whore.

20

ANYA

As I bend to change into my dance shoes for my first class on Monday, I bite back a groan. My muscles protest loudly, sore from my time with Nicolo this weekend. My body isn't used to the rough handling.

Anxiety kept me up most of the weekend, too, so my eyes feel tired and puffy. Stress knots my stomach every time I think about Nicolo. I haven't told a soul about our deal. I couldn't look my aunt in the eye if I did–she thinks I found a temporary part-time job–and I don't want to risk my friends' safety.

I force Nicolo from my mind despite my sore body, which serves as a constant reminder. I attempt to put on a more cheerful expression and join Paige, Whitney, and Logan already stretching on the black mats.

When I catch sight of myself in the mirrors, I realize I look as ragged as I feel. My typically tidy hair has curls already falling loose from my braid, and purple bags color the skin beneath my eyes.

"Morning," I say, sinking onto the mats to stretch with them.

Their smiles shift as soon as I join the circle. The silence that follows is awkward as their eyes follow me down to the floor. Paige's eyes narrow, and Logan's lips purse in unmistakable contempt.

"Morning," Whitney says, finally breaking the tension.

I meet her eyes, grateful that she's willing to talk to me at least. A hint of concern flickers in her gaze. The silence resumes as I stretch my legs. Spreading them into a split, I lean forward to rest my elbows on the mats like Whitney.

"How was everyone's weekend?" I ask, hoping we can move past whatever has them upset. I wonder if they spoke to Fin and hold me responsible for his broken arm.

I know Fin does. Though he told me he doesn't blame me for what Nicolo did, he hasn't returned my calls or texts since. I can't say I blame him. It is my fault, even if I didn't intend for Fin to suffer. And I can't let that happen again.

"I went to see Fin this weekend," Logan says coldly, confirming my suspicions.

"How is he?" I ask tentatively.

"He's out of the hospital at least. But he won't be back to class for a while."

The resentment in Logan's eyes cuts like a barb, and I swallow back tears as I nod.

"You look tired, Anya. Are you stressed about dating Nicolo Marchetti when he's the one who put Fin in the hospital? Is the guilt getting to you?" Paige's smirk contradicts the false concern in her tone.

I flinch, guilt twisting my stomach. I'm surprised she knows about me and Nicolo. "Where did you hear that?" I ask, defensive.

"Oh, it's been all around town," Paige says casually. "Rich future mob boss taking home a dancer with no means. Sounds like he spent a pretty penny on a new wardrobe for you."

Paige scoffs, her face turning sour. "You know, I thought you might actually be serious about ballet. But now I'm starting to wonder if you're just like the other poor girls who come to Rosehill looking for a rich benefactor. Doesn't matter if you're selling your soul to the devil as long as he'll buy you nice things."

Embarrassment flames in my cheeks as her judgment washes over me. What's worse is that I can see how she might come to that conclusion, though nothing could be further from the truth. I would give anything to steer clear of Nicolo and his money if I could. But I don't dare tell her that.

"Hey, don't sound so upset over it, Paige. Now that Anya will be spending most of her time on her back, maybe one of us can become the new class favorite." Logan reaches sideways to touch his right toes in a deep stretch.

The vitriol in their words hurts worse than I would like to admit. I fight back tears as I realize Nicolo's interest in me might have cost me my friends. "I didn't come to Rosehill looking for someone to pay my way." My objection sounds weak in the face of Paige's accusation.

Logan snorts. "Yeah, okay."

"Hey, lay off her," Whitney says as she releases from her deep stretch. "Anya's allowed to date whoever she wants. That doesn't have to change her motives for being at Rosehill. She's put in a lot of hard work to become a dancer, just like the rest of us. We can't always help who we fall for. I don't believe for a second that she knew what would happen to Fin–and we all know what the Marchettis are like. For all we know, Nicolo's not giving her much choice."

Her words come far too close to the mark. The others just roll their eyes, but I give Whitney a grateful smile. She returns a gentle one, though her eyes still hold a hint of concern.

She seems to, somehow, understand something of what I'm going through. I haven't spoken to her since last week at school, so I don't see how she could. But I get the impression that she knows more about my situation than I've told her.

"I don't know that it matters how hard Anya works. She won't find a new partner for the winter showcase. No one wants to dance with her after what happened to her last partner," Logan points out, his tone more matter-of-fact and less resentful after Whitney's interjection.

"How is your partner search going?" Whitney asks, stretching her chest and arms.

"Well, Professor Moriari suggested I look into performing with one of the underclassmen from a different class since everyone has a partner in ours. It's been a challenge finding anyone who can handle Fin's level of choreography, but I think I've found someone who can bridge that gap with enough practice."

I think of Robbie's enthusiasm when I asked him to be my partner. He's got the raw talent, just not the experience with lifts. Hopefully, I'll be able to teach him. Professor Moriari offered to hold a few closed sessions to help as well.

"We're supposed to start practice this week," I add, shifting into my next stretch.

"That's great!" Whitney says.

"Good for you," Paige agrees grudgingly. "That'll be a challenge taking on an underclassman."

Relief loosens the tension in my chest. Paige seems to be letting go of some resentment. Maybe she just needed to get her opinion off her chest. While her words hurt, I don't want to lose her as a friend.

"Yeah," I agree, "but it's a great opportunity for him. He'll get into the showcase early–extra exposure he'll appreciate. And with his enthusiasm, I think he might learn most of the choreography. I'll probably have to take out a few of the lifts though. Fin was pretty exceptional in that regard."

"Yeah, you got pretty lucky with that one," Whitney agrees. "Hey, did you guys see *Dracula* is coming to the Civic Opera House for Halloween?"

"The ballet?" Paige asks enthusiastically.

"Yeah." Whitney nods.

"I'll have to see that," Logan pipes up.

"Definitely," Paige and Whitney agree.

"I went to see it this weekend, and the performers are incredible," Whitney gushes.

I smile, grateful to have a lighter topic that everyone's enthusiastic about. It's been years since I've seen a ballet in the beautiful opera house. That was a special treat my parents could only afford a few times when I was a child. The memory of sitting in the massive theater, watching the dancers from the nosebleed section is imprinted in my mind. I loved every moment of it.

"What about you, Anya? You going to see it?" Whitney asks.

"I would love to," I say vaguely, not really answering her question.

I don't see myself splurging on a ballet performance–though seeing *Dracula* in the Civic Opera House would be incredible. But I have a daughter to think of, and while I still have a good chunk of the cash from Nicolo, I can put it to better use on ballet supplies and things my family needs. I don't need to waste it on a performance I will only get to enjoy one time.

"Hey, are you guys up for going to Danza again this weekend? We haven't been in weeks," Paige suggests, deepening her butterfly stretch.

"Heck yes," Whitney says.

"Sure," Logan agrees.

I hesitate, unsure if the invitation actually includes me after how cold Paige was when I came in today.

"Anya?" Paige turns to look at me. "Are you willing to stoop to the common folk's level for a night now that you've had a VIP experience with Nicolo?" she challenges.

"I'll be there," I promise quickly, determined to ignore her slight. Hopefully, joining them for Danza will help ease some of the tension between us.

"All right, cool."

We fall silent as Professor Moriari flings the studio door open in the same flashy style he always enters a room. He strides to the front of the class.

"Morning," he greets formally in his sharp outfit and checkered scarf. "I hope you all had a nice weekend. Let's get started. Anya, since your showcase partner will only be able to practice with you outside of class, I expect you to be working on your individual choreography."

His eyes find me, and I nod my understanding.

"Good. Then, everyone, let's get started."

Rising from our positions on the mat, everyone finds their partner. I make my way to a far corner of the room, prepared to stay out of everyone's way since I won't need as much space.

Guilt tightens my chest as I think about Fin and what he's missing because of me. I hope he'll be able to come back by next semester and recover from his injury. I miss my partner and how well we worked together.

Bitter anger turns my mouth sour when I think of Nicolo. He's done so much to hurt me. I hate him for what he did to Fin, for how he's using me. And I hate him even more for how he controls my body. He's proved that he's even the master of my pleasure.

For the hundredth time, my mind recalls his taunting words, *You little tease, you clearly wanted me to fuck you all along. No one comes this many times if they don't want it.* It makes me sick to know that I crave Nicolo's touch despite how much he's hurt me. I can't make sense of it.

Taking position, I start to practice my choreographed piece, determined to work out my pain and frustration through dance. I want nothing more than to forget about Nicolo, to have a moment of peace now that he's not here.

But my body won't let me. Every motion reminds me of him as my raw core aches and my muscles protest. Worst of all is the flicker of anticipation into my gut as I think about the next time.

21

ANYA

The sun hangs low in the sky through the studio window as Robbie and I call it quits for the evening. My new partner is proving to be a quick learner with boundless energy. I think that's the only reason I might be able to salvage my choreographed showcase piece.

"You're really getting good at spotting." I think of how far Robbie's come from our first day of practice as I towel my sweaty brow.

We've spent grueling hours trying to catch up on lost time every day after school. Finally, I think we're making some solid progress.

Robbie's considerably taller than Fin at six foot one and more gangly than muscular, which made our coordination and lifts quite challenging at first. I had to learn to jump higher to help with momentum. Robbie's worked relentlessly on the transitions so I don't get jostled or come down hard on every dismount.

"Thanks."

Robbie flashes me his toothy smile, and the dimples pop on his baby face. That smile combined with the sandy-blond hair that flops over his brow reminds me of a golden retriever. I can't help but think the two have a lot in common.

"You have plans for the weekend?" he asks as he trades out his dance shoes for black Puma sneakers.

"Some friends and I are going to Danza tomorrow night. Otherwise, I'm hoping to have an easygoing weekend."

Not likely since I'm at Nicolo's beck and call. But so far, he hasn't made any demands of me for the weekend. I can only hope that means he's starting to lose interest. My gut clenches, and I shove away the unexpected disappointment. It's pathetic that I might feel rejected over Nicolo losing interest. Not only do I anticipate its inevitability, I should welcome it.

But I look forward to clubbing with my friends. The week's been stressful, and letting loose with friends will help relieve some of it.

"What about you? Any plans?" I swing my book bag over my shoulder and walk with Robbie to the studio door.

"My mom's coming to town, so I'll be taking her around the city, doing all the touristy stuff."

"Oh, that sounds fun." I glance up at Robbie from the corner of my eye and catch his indulgent smile. "You excited to see her?"

"Very," Robbie admits. He pulls open the front door of the dance building and gestures for me to go first.

The sky has turned a dusky purple, casting long shadows on the sidewalk, and the crisp wind makes me pull my jacket closer.

"You're sure you don't want me to walk you to the bus stop?" Robbie offers.

He does every time our practice runs late.

"No, I'm fine," I promise. "I'll see you after school on Monday. Have a fun weekend with your mom!"

Robbie and I part ways, and I pull out my phone to check if I've missed any messages from Aunt Patritsiya. I open a text from Nicolo, and my heart sinks.

Be outside your house at five tomorrow evening. I'll pick you up. And wear the blue sequin dress I bought you. I'm taking you out.

I swallow hard. I'll have to cancel on my friends, which I know won't make them happy. I consider what I could possibly say to make bailing on them okay. Stepping onto the bus, I find a seat. Then, opening up a group text, I write, *So sorry, but something's come up. I won't be able to go clubbing with you tomorrow night.* I follow it with a teary emoji.

Whitney responds almost immediately, setting my anxiety at ease. *No worries, girl. Hopefully, it works out next time.*

Paige's eye roll emoji is far less forgiving. *Can't say I'm surprised,* is all she writes.

I bite my lip to fight my tears and slide my phone back into my bag. Then I rest my head against the bus seat.

At least I'll get to spend some time with Clara tonight. But I feel my relationship with Paige slipping through my fingers. By the time Nicolo's done with me, there will probably be nothing left of our friendship to salvage.

———

Standing outside my apartment complex promptly at five, I wait uncomfortably in my flashy form-fitting dress and strappy silver heels. I hug my knee-length coat tighter around me to hide the low cut of the neckline. Thankfully, it covers my dress so my aunt didn't question my attire.

The only nice thing about my outfit is that Clara thinks it makes me look like a mermaid. She said it with such awe, I could only take it as a compliment. But I can't help feeling my entire body is on display.

The dress hugs every inch of me, leaving little to the imagination. The low cut combined with the shelf bra Nicolo bought me showcase my cleavage far more than I'm comfortable with.

I left my hair down in long waves to cover my chest, much like the animated characters do in the *Little Mermaid*. I wonder if that might not have contributed to Clara's observation.

My jaw drops as a sleek black Maserati rolls up to the curb in front of me.

Nicolo rolls down his window and jerks his head toward the passenger seat. "Get in," he says by way of greeting.

Fighting to remain steady on my four-inch heels, I obey. Walking around the front of the car, I open the door. It's a challenge to slide into the soft, low-riding, leather-upholstered seat without flashing Nicolo in the short dress.

As I settle in and buckle my seat belt, I catch Nicolo watching me. I wonder if the dress-car combination might not have been so he could sneak a peek. Embarrassment warms my cheeks as I wonder if he's already gotten a good view of my lingerie.

"Ready?" Mild amusement tinges Nicolo's tone, and his lips curl in a devilish smile.

"Yes," I murmur, turning my attention to the road to avoid his gaze.

Like a rocket, the sports car leaves the curb–and my stomach along with it–pressing me back against the seat. I white-knuckle the door and squeeze my knees together, fighting the urge to squeal at the unexpected speed.

The car handles more like a plane than a car as it glides over the road. Nicolo seems more than capable with the vehicle as he shifts gears seamlessly. He weaves around traffic, rolling through yellow lights at a speed that makes the hair raise on the back of my neck.

I don't even have time to process where we're going. I'm so terrified of what we might hit at this speed. Before I know it, we pull to a stop in front of Danza.

I can't seem to get my grip to relax from the door handle as we arrive at our destination. My heart hammers as I realize Paige and Whitney–all my friends–will see me here with Nicolo after I bailed on them.

"Danza?" I breathe, anxiety constricting my chest. "Can't we go somewhere else?"

"No," Nicolo says flatly. "And take off that fucking coat. I didn't buy you nice clothes just to watch you hide them. People should know what you have to offer me."

I open my mouth to object, but he exits the car with ease. The door snaps shut before I can think of anything to say. Reluctantly, I slip the coat over my shoulders to leave it in the car. The air trapped in my lungs escapes me in a burst as Nicolo opens my door. He holds out his hand to help me from the car.

From the glint of mischief in his eyes, I suspect he enjoys my discomfort immensely. But he stands like a gentleman as he grips my fingers and supports my weight. I straighten my sapphire-colored dress as soon as I'm out of the car, hoping no one else caught a peek beneath the hem.

I glance toward the line of clubgoers waiting to be admitted. I'm struck by the realization that I used to be one of those people watching Nicolo pull up in his sleek car and toss his keys to the valet. It makes me uncomfortable. I don't belong on his arm, but when he offers me his elbow, I take it and follow him toward the club's entrance.

As my eyes move along the growing line of people, they catch on a familiar face. Paige's eyes burn with resentment. Her lips twist into a sneer that says I'm unforgivable. Guilt constricts my chest, and I drop my gaze as I follow Nicolo toward the club's dark doors.

"Nicolo?" I murmur tentatively as my stomach knots. "Could you... maybe bring my friends in as well?"

Nicolo pauses, amusement dancing around his lips. He glances back toward the line of waiting clubgoers. "Fine."

He has me point out my friends to the doorman, and I wave Paige, Whitney, Logan, and the twins toward the door. Judgment burns on their faces, condemning me even as Nicolo tells the doorman that they're to receive a private table and complimentary bottle service tonight as well.

Only Whitney's face remains soft, compassionate, like she somehow understands my discomfort. "Thank you," she says gratefully, giving my arm a gentle squeeze as she meets Nicolo's eyes.

"Not that this makes up for Fin," Logan hisses under his breath.

Still, they follow us through the doors into the club.

Throbbing music greets us inside along with Nicolo's bodyguards, who I met on our shopping day. We part ways with my friends, who are shown to a private table near the dance floor.

Nicolo's guards remain as stoic as ever. They follow us up the stairs to the Marchettis' VIP section. The golden lights make my dress shimmer, and the glass stairs and railing give us little cover. I feel as though I'm on display as Nicolo guides me to the white leather couches and coffee table that furnish our area.

I'm shocked by how soft the couch's leather is as I sink onto it. From this vantage point, as I look down on the dance floor, I feel entirely too exposed. It would take nothing for someone to look up and see me, for my friends to observe what I chose to do instead of dancing with them.

Crossing my ankles and keeping my knees pressed together, I sit up straight as I observe the club from this new angle.

Nicolo settles in beside me, his arm falling around my waist so his hand rests lightly on the side of my hip. Tingles ripple through my body at the simple yet intensely intimate touch. I fight to ignore the way my stomach flutters.

Like royalty on high, I can see everything from here, the well-lit bar, the packed dance floor, the private alcoves where couples talk and make out. I observe the female dancer trapped in her glass cube. She sits at eye level from me in this spot.

Her nipples are taped with squares of neon pink that barely cover her breasts. Her matching neon cheeky panties sit so far up her ass, they could almost be painted on. Still, as she twists and spins in time with the music, I'm mesmerized by her athletic ability.

"What do you want to drink?" Nicolo asks close to my ear, drawing my attention from the dancer.

I turn to meet his eyes, parting my lips to say I don't need a drink. Then I think better of it. "I'll have whatever you're having."

Moments later, the server pops a bottle of champagne and pours us each a flute. Nicolo presses mine into my hand, and I thank him before turning my eyes back to the caged dancer.

"Maybe I'll put you in that cage to dance one night," Nicolo suggests. "I'd love to see you like that." He murmurs so close to my ear that his warm breath tickles my skin.

Mortified, I fight the urge to wince. If he knows I would hate that, I'm sure he would be more inclined to make it happen. But I can't imagine being scantily clad and on display for everyone to see, let alone dancing on an invisible floor suspended nearly thirty feet above the ground. Despite myself, a shudder runs through my body at the horrifying thought.

Whitney's distinct pixie cut catches my attention in the mob below as she, Logan, Paige, and the twins work their way onto the dance floor. What I wouldn't give to vanish into the crowd with them, become invisible in the throng of moving bodies rather than sitting on display up here.

I sip my champagne, and the bubbles burn a trail down my throat. The dry flavor awakens my senses. From the taste of it, I'm sure this champagne is insanely expensive.

"Do you like club dancing?" Nicolo asks, demanding my attention.

I turn to face him and am immediately struck by how close we are. It would take nothing for me to lean forward and kiss him. Not that I want to. I don't think.

"Yes," I respond breathlessly. Then, recalling how angry he got over my short responses on our first date, I ask, "Do you?"

Nicolo shrugs. "I prefer to watch." His hazel eyes burn into mine suggestively.

My stomach knots.

"Nicolo!" someone shouts from the top stair of our balcony.

We both turn to see who it is.

The man is youthful, right around our age, I would guess, with black hair and dark eyes that look as Italian as Nicolo's features. One of Nicolo's bodyguards has a hand on the guy's shoulder, stopping him from entering our space. Still, the boy's expression looks friendly enough.

Nicolo's arm stiffens fractionally around my waist. Then a wide smile spreads across his face. "If it isn't Troy Gatti," he says in his most charming voice. I've only ever heard him use it on teachers when he wants his way about something. "That's all right, Sep. Let him up. He's a family friend, after all."

From the look on Sep's face, I would say there's something more to Nicolo and Troy's relationship than friendship. Suddenly, I wonder if this might not be a mafia connection. But the bodyguard drops his arm, allowing Troy to join us.

"Have a seat," Nicolo suggests, waving to the couches across from us as Troy approaches.

But Troy doesn't. Instead, he comes to stand beside me at the arm of the couch. He's close enough that I have to tip my head back to look at his face rather than his crotch.

I lean back into Nicolo slightly to gain some space. And realize that Troy's expression is less friendly than I had thought from a distance.

While a smile still curls the corners of his lips, it's a bitter one. His eyes hold a steely anger I hadn't noticed before. "Nice to see your conscience is clear and you can enjoy a night out with one of your supermodel sluts after what you did. I'm happy for you," Troy says caustically, his hands fisting.

I tense as Nicolo stiffens behind me. Suddenly, I feel trapped between a rock and a hard place.

"What do you want, Troy?" Nicolo's tone is light, but an icy coldness lingers beneath the surface.

"I want to know how you could rip my family apart like you did when we have been nothing but loyal to your family for years!" Troy growls through clenched teeth. "Our families used to spend Christmas together, and yet you killed my father in cold blood. After all he did for you, you murdered him. And you didn't even have the decency to give us his body so we might mourn him!" Troy shouts, the force of his anger misting me with spittle.

I cringe beneath his wrath, pressing back against Nicolo in my desperation to move away from Troy. For a moment, his body is warm and protective behind me.

Then Nicolo shifts to a stand. Stepping over my ankles, he puts his body between me and Troy. My heart bursts into a sprint. A muscle pops in Nicolo's jaw, telling me he's fighting to contain his anger.

"Your father chose to steal from my family even though he knew the consequences. He deserved what he got," Nicolo states flatly, making my stomach drop.

He didn't deny murdering Troy's father. He finds it perfectly justified.

"And you need to watch your mouth. You know better than to air this kind of shit in public," he hisses.

"Fuck you," Troy spits, stepping closer to Nicolo and shoving a finger into his chest.

Adrenaline floods through my veins, making me tremble as I realize Troy might get violent. Fear for Nicolo's safety grips my chest. I'm shocked by the unexpected concern that he might get hurt.

From the corner of my eye, I catch Nicolo's bodyguards stepping into action. But before they can reach Troy, Nicolo reacts. Reaching up to grab Troy's wrist, Nicolo wrenches the boy's arm around. My stomach lurches at the sickening pop. Troy howls, bending over his injury as Nicolo releases him.

My mind flashes to Fin as I realize this must be the same way he broke my former partner's arm. I scramble backward across the couch, more desperate to get away from Nicolo than I had been to get away from Troy. Fear leaves my mouth dry. My heart slams against my ribs, warning me that I'm too close to a dangerous person.

"You'll keep your mouth shut if you know what's good for you," Nicolo grits as he looks down his nose at Troy's slumped shoulders.

Troy moans in pain as Nicolo's bodyguards grab him roughly by the shoulders. They haul him down the stairs from the balcony. When Nicolo turns back to me, I flinch, unable to control my body's response to his violent behavior.

But I can't flee. Now that I've seen in person what he's capable of, I'm more terrified than ever of what he might do to my friends or family. I'm trapped with the obligation to please Nicolo in whatever way he sees fit. After witnessing his brutality, I know I can't give him any excuse to do that to someone I love.

Nicolo straightens his suit jacket nonchalantly and settles back onto the couch. He seems oblivious to my visceral response to him. Picking up his glass of champagne, he takes a drink. I stare at him, wide eyed, as I try to regain control of my heart.

22

NICOLO

Images of Giuseppe Gazzi struggling for his last breaths flash before my eyes. The altercation with Troy has soured my mood. Setting my empty champagne glass on the club's coffee table, I grip Anya's hand.

"Come with me," I command, rising from the couch.

I lead her into the back room where I entertain women often. I need a distraction, and having some fun with Anya will take my mind off the traitor and his family. Besides, from the way Anya leaned into me for protection, I wouldn't be surprised if she's already wet for me. Girls love when I put hot heads like Troy in their place. When I neutralize threats.

It turns girls on when I use my power. They like strength, and I just defended my family and protected Anya from Troy—not that he could have actually done much harm. Troy's just a stupid kid, the younger brother in a family that coddles him. He doesn't know how to hurt a fly.

I'm sure Anya is the same way. She might have played hard to get, but she's proven a good pet this week. She's done all that I ask since that first time I had to punish her. I think she's finally decided to stop fighting me.

The last time I was in the pristine private room, I watched two models play with each other while I sat frustrated over Anya. A sense of satisfaction curls my lips to know that the girl who ruined my pleasure that night is now here to satiate me.

A hub where my father might entertain business partners, the room has both a card and pool table, but I ignore both of those now. Instead, I lead Anya to the couch in the center of the room.

I pull her down onto the plush seat, and Anya obeys readily. She sits close as I snake my arm around her sequin-clad waist. The dress is eye-catching in the room's dim lighting. It reflects the light like a thousand tiny mirrors and calls attention to her perfect hips and trim waist.

I comb back her long silken locks to reveal her cleavage, and my cock starts to stiffen. Anya's blue eyes meet mine as I turn her chin to face me.

Her tongue darts out to wet her lips, calling my attention to their fullness. She trembles slightly beneath my touch, her back still rigid, probably from the confrontation. I relish the thought of wiping it from her mind.

Leaning in, I capture her lips.

Gently, I take the lower one between my teeth and nibble.

Goosebumps rise on her flesh as I slowly trail my fingers up the inside of Anya's thigh. I edge toward the hem of her tantalizingly short dress. I've been thinking about putting my hand up it since she first got into my car. She's barely managed to keep her lingerie a secret with how short and tight the club dress is.

Anya shivers as my fingers reach the peak of her thighs and the satiny fabric that covers her. Why this girl turns me on so much, I may never know, but I'm ravenous for her. Especially now that I've had a taste of her perfect lips, felt the tight warmth of her pussy.

I pull aside the thin fabric that separates us and gently stroke a finger between Anya's folds. Flicking her clit, I tease her to life. Immediately, I'm rewarded with the slickness of her arousal.

Kissing her more deeply, I urge her back against the couch, but the tension in her body resists me. Suddenly, I'm aware of her discomfort. I wonder if she's still scared after the altercation with Troy.

But after a moment's hesitation, she softens into the seat. Her resistance crumbles as her legs tremble. I circle Anya's clit with my thumb and press two fingers into her depths. I'm rewarded by her pussy clenching around me.

"Did it turn you on to see me put that prick in his place?" I purr. I draw back from Anya's lips just enough to shift my attention to her earlobe.

Anya stiffens again, leaning away just enough to meet my eyes. She studies me closely for a moment, her blue gaze penetrating. "It made me sick to see you hurt someone like that. You use your power to get what you want, and you don't seem to care about the collateral damage."

Her tone is soft, but her words snap like a whip, casting judgment on me. Her expression mirrors her words, the tension around her eyes and mouth revealing her distaste. It reminds me of the spiteful look she gave me in the Rosehill cafeteria the day we met. That same condemning look she gave before she even knew me.

Anger roils inside me. I wanted to forget my guilt over the Gatti family by fucking Anya. But Anya seems determined to make me feel bad.

With the pressure squarely on my shoulders to run the family business, I can't let emotions make me weak. I can't feel bad for killing Giuseppe when he's the one who chose to betray our family. I struggled to keep my guilt in check after, but I managed. That was supposed to be behind me.

Now Anya wants to make me feel bad for hurting Troy? She wants to pretend like I'm wrong for standing my ground?

No one gets to make me feel bad for who I am. Her honesty might have caught my eye. Her defiance was refreshing. But breaking her is part of why I wanted to make her mine. And she *will* learn her place.

"It made you sick, did it?" I demand, withdrawing my fingers from her pussy to hold them in front of her face. "You're a lying little cunt," I counter and shove her away from me.

Anya withdraws further, watching me with unmasked fear.

"If you don't think it turned you on, then you can just give me pleasure tonight. Stand up," I command.

Anya does as I say, tentatively rising from the couch.

"Now strip for me." I jerk my chin in the direction of the open space before the coffee table. "I want to see you move like the club dancers while you do."

Chin trembling, Anya takes her place where I indicated. She pauses there, looking lost for a moment. Her vulnerability makes me want to fuck her all the more. No gaudy performance in an effort to please me like so many other girls.

I know it's a contradiction—to want her more because she's different and yet be angry that she doesn't respond like other girls. But perhaps that's part of the fun.

Anya closes her eyes, and after a moment, she seems to find the music. She sways her hips to the thrumming rhythm. Keeping her eyes closed, she reaches for the hem of her dress and slowly slides it up her thighs.

She's fucking sexy, twisting and rocking gracefully as she undresses, and I unbuckle my pants. Sliding my hand beneath my boxer briefs, I grip my cock as I watch. I stroke my erection as the blue sequined sheath slides up over Anya's breasts. She guides the dress over her head before letting it fall to the floor.

Goosebumps rise across her arms and breasts. She bites her lower lip and opens her eyes to meet mine.

"All of it," I command when she hesitates. "You can keep the shoes," I amend. I fucking love the way they make her legs and ass look so lean and muscled and taut.

Anya resumes her dance, rolling her hips as she reaches back to release the clasp of her bra. Leaning forward, she reveals the perfect curve of her cleavage. The straps of her bra slide down her arms, and the lacy slip of fabric falls to the floor. The darkened pink nubs of her nipples appear.

Her toned stomach twists as she straightens. Calling attention to the top of her satin lace-lined panties, she turns to reveal the way they lace up in the back. They resemble some kind of corset.

Her back muscles flex as she sways, her fingers hooking beneath her panties. Slowly, she eases them down over her hips. My cock pulses painfully as she bends to slide them down her legs, exposing her slick pussy lips. Stifling a groan of arousal, I tell her to come to me.

Anya obeys, ending her dance as she approaches. Her heels click against the white marble floor until they find the plush rug that sits beneath the coffee table. I shove my pants down over my hips as she approaches. As soon as she's near, I take her hand, guiding her toward me.

When she stands in front of me, I grasp her hips and pull her forward until she's straddling me. Her exposed thighs spread to accommodate me as she grips the back of the couch.

I stroke my fingers between her folds, and she shudders as she lowers onto my lap. I can see it in her eyes that she's aroused. She lied to me. She might say that she dislikes my aggression, but clearly, it turns her on.

"Ride me, pet," I command. "But since you lied about getting excited, you don't get to come tonight. Only good girls get to orgasm, and it seems you need to be punished. Now fuck me good."

Anger flickers in her gaze, but Anya does as she's told. Shifting to grip the couch with one hand, she takes my cock with the other. She grips the base firmly as she guides it toward her entrance.

For someone who seems to have little more than a week of experience, she's learned the art of sex quickly. She knows how to touch me, how to move her hips, and when to adjust her pace. I like teaching her the perfect way to fuck me. Like a well-tailored suit, she fits me just right.

My balls throb as the head of my cock slides between her folds. Her slick pussy lips wet my tip as she slowly sinks onto my hard length. A gentle gasp escapes her lips as I guide her down onto me.

I grip her hips more tightly as her glorious pussy stretches to fit me like a glove. Fucking Christ she feels good. And now she has birth control, so I don't have to endure the frustrating barrier of a condom between me and her hot, wet depths.

As she takes all of me inside her tight pussy and begins to rock, her fingers move to my collared shirt. Unbuttoning it, she exposes my chest and abs. I groan as she leans in to press her lips to my neck.

She tickles the sensitive skin with light kisses, soft nips, and the teasing flick of her tongue. Her hips roll, shifting so my cock slides in and out of her. She fucks me slowly, her pussy gloriously soft and inviting.

Reaching between us, I press the pad of my thumb against her clit. I want to drive her crazy even though I've forbidden her from coming. I want to torture her, and I'm curious if she can resist me.

She said what I did made her sick. I want to prove her wrong.

She might pretend to have morals, but she wants me inside her just as much as every other girl.

Anya whimpers as she continues to ride me. Her hips grind more desperately against me as her pussy tightens. When she tries to slow down, to restrain herself from coming, I pick up the pace.

Gripping her hip with my free hand, I rock into her more forcefully.

"Play with your nipples," I rasp, and Anya shivers violently.

Sitting up straight to keep her balance, she obeys. Anya arches her back as she rolls her hips, following my motion like one might ride a horse. Her golden hair falls over her shoulders as she palms her breasts, pinching her nipples between her thumbs and forefingers. I almost lose my load right then and there as she bites her lip to keep quiet.

She's so close to coming, and I fucking love it.

"Don't you dare fucking come," I growl even as I flick her clit more adamantly and thrust deeper inside her.

Anya's breaths grow more labored as she fights it. Her hands grip her breasts as if she's clinging to her self-control. Her eyes close in concentration. Her teeth turn the pad of her lip white as she bites down hard.

Still, as I pinch and roll her clit, she can't stop herself. With an anguished cry, Anya finds her release. Her pussy clamps down around me as she milks my cock.

My balls tighten as I fight my own release. I grip Anya's hip with bruising force as I shove deep inside her again and again until her orgasm subsides.

"You little slut, you just can't help yourself, can you? Even when I told you not to come," I mock. "Well, now I have to punish you for disobeying me as well as lying. You clearly think you can do whatever you want. But that's not how this agreement works. You're my pet because that's all you're good for. You don't get to come unless I give you permission."

Embarrassment colors Anya's cheeks as she stills on top of me. Her eyes shine in the dim light, bringing her lust-filled gaze to life.

"Be honest with me this time. Did you like being fucked?"

Defiance flickers across her face, deepening her blush. Then her eyes drop to my chest. "Yes," she murmurs.

I chuckle darkly at my victory. "Good girl, maybe you did learn a little something. But you still need to be punished for coming. Lick your cum off my cock," I command.

Anya braces on the back of the couch as she dismounts me. She kneels on the plush carpet at my feet.

I scoot forward to give her better access, and she grips my thighs as she leans forward. Her breasts graze the inside of my knees as she takes my cock between her lips. Her tongue strokes down my length, making me throb in her warm mouth as she slurps up her own juices.

Fucking hell, it's hot watching her taste her own arousal. She eats it off my erection like some kind of popsicle. Gripping her golden hair in my fist, I force her head back so she has to look at me. I don't think I can take her giving me a blowjob right now. Not if I want to punish her fully.

"You know, that's how you train a dog not to pee on the carpet. Put their face in it. I *will* teach you to be a good pet that obeys me."

Fire intensifies Anya's gaze, but she presses her lips closed. I'm not sure what pisses me off more–the way she talked back to me or her newfound silence. All I know is I want to hurt her for making me doubt myself, even for an instant.

"Go bend over the edge of the pool table," I say, shoving her in the right direction.

Anya catches herself with her hands against the floor. She glares before crawling to her feet, her perfect ass on display as she walks away. Shoving off my shoes and stripping my pants the rest of the way, I rise to follow her. I discard my unbuttoned shirt as I go.

The green felt table has never looked so good as Anya's creamy skin spreads across it. Her hips bend so her pussy is at a perfect angle.

"Spread your arms and grip the sides of the table," I rasp. "Don't even think about moving," I add.

Anya hesitates for just a moment, then does as I say. I get the perfect glimpse of side cleavage as her breasts press against the pool table's surface. She looks up at me over her shoulder, her eyes suddenly worried as I massage her ass cheeks, admiring their fit roundness.

Bringing my hand down hard, I spank her with a flat palm. She squeals as her hands grip the table harder. I caress her pinkened cheek and love the way it heats from the punishment. Then I bring my hand down on her other ass cheek. This time, she seems determined to remain quiet as she turns her face from me.

Fine, if she thinks she's so tough, I know how to make her moan.

Spreading her cheeks, I shove my cock into her pussy without pause.

I thrust until I'm buried inside her up to the hilt.

Anya gasps, and her walls tighten around me, begging me to fuck her even though she's only just come.

I oblige her, thrusting hard as I take up a brutal pace.

"Remember, pet, you're not allowed to come. This is your punishment. It's not about pleasure for you tonight."

Anya cries out as I find her G-spot with my cockhead. I drive into it again and again.

She's so wet that despite how tight she is, I slide in and out of her with incredible ease, and God I want to come. But I refuse to just yet.

Her walls constrict further around me, alerting me to her impending orgasm. I have to shove forcefully every time I enter her. A victorious smile spreads across my face as Anya's hips buck back into me. She's lost all sense of resistance as her body demands release.

I oblige her. Curling my fingers around her hips, I angle her enough that my balls slap her clit with each thrust.

A desperate sob bursts from her as she orgasms violently. Pussy juice gushes out around my cock, coating her thighs.

Even as she pulses around my length, I reach forward and grip her wrists. Wrenching her arms behind her back, I pin her hands between her sexy back dimples and pull out of her pussy.

Then, using her own arousal as lube, I line my cockhead up with her tightly puckered asshole and shove forcefully inside. Even with how slick my cock is from fucking her pussy, Anya's ass is incredibly tight. I'm sure no one's ever fucked her here before.

She screams, her back arching off the table as I penetrate her.

Knowing I'm the only one who's ever been inside her ass turns me on so fucking much. And I want to teach her a lesson for guilt tripping me about who I am and what I'm born to do. I want to give her a real reason to hate me if she's going to look at me with such disgust.

And I want to punish her for thinking she's above me. She can't pretend to be all high and mighty when I'm buried inside her ass.

I'm so close to coming, I can't help but pound inside her, fucking her ass hard. I quickly find my own release and explode inside her. Releasing burst after burst of cum, I fill her up until it's oozing back out around my cock.

My hips jerk spastically with the intensity of my release, and finally, I slow to a stop, buried deeply up her ass. Chest heaving, I realize I'm holding her wrists so tightly that her fingers have started to turn purple. I release her, letting my hands rest gently on the pinkened globes of her ass. Each holds a distinct handprint.

"Fuck, Anya," I breathe as my ears ring from the force of my orgasm.

She doesn't respond as she sprawls limply across the pool table, trembling. One hand reaches forward to brush her cheek.

It takes me a moment to realize she's wiping tears from her face. It dawns on me that she's not trembling, she's crying, and a stab of guilt pierces my gut. *Maybe I took it too far.*

I shove the thought roughly aside. Anya's my pet, a new toy to play with as I please. I shouldn't feel bad about using her for my pleasure. Besides, she agreed to this, and she more than anyone should know I'm not some simpering mama's boy.

Pulling out of her unceremoniously, I stalk away from her to find my clothes. I'm ready for the night to be over now that it feels thoroughly spoiled.

"Get dressed and get the fuck out," I bark. "My driver can take you home."

Yanking on my pants without bothering to put on my boxers or shirt, I slump onto the couch. Silently, I fume over the whole shitty night.

From the corner of my eye, I watch Anya shakily push up off the table and walk unsteadily toward where she deposited her clothes.

Stepping into her undies and quickly clasping her bra, Anya doesn't waste time putting herself in order. She pulls her stunning sequin dress back on over her head. Then she heads toward the door. Her sniffles are the only sound in the deafening silence.

A burst of club music fills the room as she flees, then diminishes as the door closes behind her.

"Fuck," I groan, letting my head drop back against the couch. I close my eyes. That did not go like I'd imagined.

23

ANYA

"Hold, hold!" Professor Moriari shouts as I lock my elbow in place.

I brace against Robbie's shoulder, my opposite foot poised high in the air as he attempts to keep me aloft.

His supporting arm starts to tremble as he fails to lock his elbow before my momentum stops. Rather than pausing at the height of my leap, I sink back toward the studio mats. Robbie scrambles to catch my hips with both hands to cushion my landing.

"You have to push her!" Professor Moriari scolds, stepping closer. "She can't do the lift all by herself!" he adds as my feet touch down with surprising lightness.

Despite the frustration in my professor's tone, I'm actually quite impressed with the progress we've made. This is one of our hardest lifts, one I was certain I would have to take out of the routine. Still, Robbie's determined to practice it in the hopes that he can get it.

We still have over a month until the winter showcase, and I actually think we might get it done in that time.

"Yes, sir," Robbie breathes heavily, his head sinking with dejection.

Moriari moves on to the next pair of students who are there after school for some extra feedback on their routine, like we are.

"Don't feel bad." I pat Robbie's shoulder. "You're really improving, and even though you couldn't manage the lift, you set me down very gently. You're definitely getting stronger."

"Really?" Robbie perks up enthusiastically.

"Absolutely."

I flash him a smile, grateful for his determination and gentle nature. It so starkly contrasts Nicolo's mercurial temperament. After our night at the club this weekend, I feel exhausted, bogged down from the emotional war waging within me.

"Thanks, Anya," Robbie breathes. A wide smile breaks across his face, revealing his boyish dimples. His eyes glance over my shoulder at the clock hanging high on the wall. "I hate to say it, but I've got to head out. Eye appointment, remember?"

"Pshh. What could possibly be important about an eye appointment when we should be practicing our dance routine?" I tease as I follow him to the cubbies to collect our stuff.

"I see your point," Robbie says, catching me by surprise. "But I probably won't be able to next week when I run out of contacts."

I can't help but laugh at the cheesy joke. It feels good to have a moment of levity when I've spent so much of my time stressing over my situation lately.

My arrangement with Nicolo has challenged me morally in so many ways: I'm lying to my aunt about having a part-time job. I haven't spent proper time with my daughter in weeks, and I'm all but condoning Nicolo's violent behavior by giving in to his demands. But I can't bring myself to fight him when I know he might hurt someone else if I do.

I feel like a caged animal, and I have no means of escape except for when I dance and during these rare moments of laughter.

"I just don't get it," Paige says behind me as she changes out her shoes.

"Get what?" Robbie asks.

"How you can stand to dance with Anya when she not only sells herself to a criminal to live the good life but also seems to enjoy siccing that criminal on her dance partners for entertainment."

Paige smirks at me, her lips pursing at the look of shock on Robbie's face.

His eyes grow wide as they meet mine, and my throat constricts painfully with anxiety. Paige's attack hurts me deeply, and my mind flashes back to the expression on her face when she saw me walking into the club this weekend.

But I can't speak up to defend myself as the image of Fin in the hospital replaces Paige's face. Quickly following is the image of that boy Troy who confronted Nicolo at the club.

My gut twists as those memories shift into the pain of Nicolo shoving inside my ass. His punishment for me speaking my mind.

I'm terrified of him, and I'm utterly confused by how my body can still respond so eagerly to his attention. Even after he can be so violent and cruel. I hate that he's broken two people's arms since I came to Rosehill–and apparently killed someone in cold blood–but I can't help being aroused when he touches me.

"Nicolo was an asshole long before Anya came along," Whitney says, stepping in as she reaches the cubbies. "You can't hold her responsible for who he hurts. What he did to Fin was not her fault. And if I didn't know better, Paige, I might think you hold it against Anya that someone buys her nice things. You didn't seem too upset the other night after Anya got us into Danza without waiting in line. And she got us bottle service to boot."

"Oooh," Logan pipes in from his spot on the mats. He accidentally lets his partner stumble out of her spin. "Oops." He flinches as she topples to the floor with a squeak. Reaching down, he helps her up once more.

Paige scoffs, her mouth opening in horror. "I am *not* jealous," she snaps, flipping her bleach-blond hair over her shoulder before she storms from the room.

Robbie looks awkward as I meet his eyes reluctantly, hoping I won't find judgment there.

"I better get going, or I'll be late," he says, his expression uncomfortable. "But I'll see you after school tomorrow, right? We can put in more practice then." He heads swiftly for the door and gives me a quick wave before disappearing from the room.

My shoulders slump as I pray that Paige's comment didn't just cost me my new partner. Tears sting my eyes as I feel my cage shrinking around me. Turning my attention to my shoes, I swap them out for my boots.

"Hey, don't worry about Paige. She's just got a stick up her butt." Whitney gives my shoulder a squeeze.

A startled laugh bursts through my lips. "Thanks," I say, grateful for my one friend who hasn't completely abandoned me.

"Can I walk with you to the bus stop? Trent and I are done practicing for the day."

"We are?" her partner asks in surprise.

"Yep!" Whitney reaches for her bag and flashes me a smile.

"Isn't that the opposite way you normally go?"

Whitney shrugs. "My boyfriend's picking me up. I'll just tell him to get me on the other side of campus today."

I smile gratefully. "That would be really nice."

Crisp fall air stings my cheeks as we exit the dance building, and our breaths, still warm from practice, billow out before us as we walk.

"Are you okay?" Whitney asks after a moment of quiet. "You seem like you've been more stressed and tense since you and Nicolo got together. You seemed troubled as we went into Danza this weekend, and then you left without Nicolo. I thought maybe you two had a fight."

My stomach twists as she hits the nail on the head. I look at her with startled eyes, surprised by her observation. Everyone else seems to think I'm living the high life with all my new clothes and fancy dates.

"No, yes–I mean everything is great. Dating Nicolo is great." My words sound false, even to my ears. Still, I don't want to say anything that might put Whitney in danger.

Whitney's lips tilt skeptically as she brushes a wisp of her black pixie cut out of her eyes. Stopping in her tracks, she turns to face me as she gently grips my arm. "I know what's really going on, Anya, and that's not called dating."

My heart stutters as I see the truth in her eyes.

"You know, I was faced with a similar situation at the end of high school," she says casually, resuming our trek after a moment.

"You did?" A hint of doubt tinges my tone despite my best efforts.

Whitney glances my way with a sad smile. "I used to live in a pretty Russian neighborhood, and someone from a Bratva family took interest in me my senior year. Several years older than me, he was already out of college when he saw me walking home from school one day. He offered me a proposition of sorts. In exchange for meeting his sexual desires, which he warned me could be somewhat dark, he offered to pay my college tuition, my housing, everything I would need for as long as I gave myself to him."

Icy horror trickles down my spine as I realize the situation hits far closer to home than I would have guessed. Only, it doesn't sound like he bullied her into the agreement when she refused.

"I was poor enough, with no possibility of becoming a dancer or going to Rosehill by any other means, so I accepted." Her lips spread into a warmer smile, and she releases a gentle chuckle. "I have to admit, I ended up falling for the guy, and I quite enjoy the arrangement if I'm perfectly honest. I'm not sure I'll stop seeing him even after I graduate."

"Really?" I ask, shocked.

Whitney wraps her arm around my shoulders and gives me a squeeze. "Sometimes it can be fun to share someone's dark desires," she says. "Once I found my peace with the arrangement, I realized it could be quite pleasurable."

A deep blush warms my cheeks as my mind flashes back to the sex club Nicolo took me to on our first night together and how I came as he whipped me.

"I don't normally offer this kind of thing, but I'm worried about you, Anya, and I want you to be okay, so... would you like to come with me to a club sometime to watch us role play? That's kind of what it is, after all. It might help you feel more comfortable with the whole thing, to see what a healthy arrangement would look like."

Touched by her concern, I find I'm actually intrigued by her offer. If it will help me be more comfortable with how Nicolo is using me, perhaps I should do it. I can't keep going at this pace. I feel like I might split in two if my inner conflict continues.

"Nicolo seems like the kind of guy who finds the fight more interesting than the sex. Maybe if you find your peace with it, Nicolo will lose interest and move on. Then you could find someone kinder, someone who will treat you better."

Whitney's gentle tone is encouraging, and a spark of hope warms my chest. Maybe she's right. Nicolo did lose interest in me as soon as he got what he wanted the first time.

Even back then, it seemed more about the conquest than the sex. He liked winning me over, and now, he wants to break me. If I can find a way to accept it, he might just move on more quickly.

"If you're sure, I might really appreciate that." My blush intensifies as I realize she's offering to let me watch something incredibly intimate.

Whitney gives me another squeeze before releasing my shoulders. "Done. Let me talk to him today, and we'll find a time this week."

"Thank you, Whitney," I say. "Not just for that, but for being such a good friend. I don't know what I would do without you."

We stop in front of the bus stop, and Whitney turns to meet my eyes.

"Fortunately for you, we'll never have to find out, because you're stuck with me, friend. I'm grateful to have another real person in this school full of trust fund prima donnas." She jerks her head in the direction of Rosehill campus.

A horn honks behind Whitney, and I glance over her shoulder to watch a sleek blue Lamborghini pull up to the curb. Whitney turns and releases a giddy squeak I've never heard from her before.

"See you tomorrow!" she calls over her shoulder as she skips toward the car like a schoolgirl.

I grin, loving that she could find such happiness with this Bratva man of hers. My gut twists when I think of my own man. *How can I possibly find that same happiness when Nicolo seems so set on enjoying people's misery?*

24

ANYA

I glance up and down the street to see if anyone is watching me as I enter Incognito alone. It feels as though I'm walking into a forbidden place. As I step through the door, the quiet bell chimes above my head. Memories of my first time with Nicolo fill my mind as if triggered by a pavlovian effect.

"Can I help you?" The same girl as before strides to the door to greet me as a guest. Tiffany, I think her name is. Her gaze is far less scrutinizing than last time. I don't know that she remembers who I am without Nicolo by my side.

She wears the same fierce eye makeup that makes her look dangerous. Her shiny leather pants and matching bikini top add to that effect. I wonder if she might not be a dominatrix as well as their receptionist, but I don't dare ask.

"Uh, yes, I'm meeting a couple here. Whitney and her... boyfriend." Heat licks the back of my neck as I realize how that might sound. I don't even know Whitney's Bratva man's name.

"They're in the lounge," Tiffany says, her tone holding no judgment.

She walks me down the same path as before, and when the space opens into the lounge, I spot Whitney's dark pixie cut right away. Sitting beside her, his arm gently curling around her waist, is a man who cuts an impressive figure. He looks massive in comparison to Whitney, all brawn with a serious face and a square jaw dusted with a dark five-o'clock shadow.

The way his arm holds her against his side, his hand resting on her hip reminds me of how Nicolo put his arm around me at the club last weekend. At the time, it hadn't felt affectionate so much as sexual. But seeing Whitney's man do it makes it look more intimate.

"Have fun," Tiffany purrs. She turns back toward the reception stand, her stilettos clicking pointedly against the hard floor.

Heading into the lounge, I catch Whitney's eye, and she waves me over.

Attempting a smile, I sink into the seat across from them. "Hi," I say awkwardly. Now that I'm here, I sorely regret taking Whitney up on her offer. *Isn't this something private between these two?* I feel like I'm intruding.

But Whitney reaches across the table to give my hand a squeeze. "You look like you just walked in on your parents having sex. Relax. Just think of it as a game. We don't mind if you're here, okay? It's all part of the fun."

I nod, licking my dry lips.

"This is Ilya." Whitney gestures to the man who somehow manages to look even more intimidating up close. "Ilya, this is my friend Anya."

"Pleasure," he says, his Russian accent immediately apparent. He extends his hand to shake mine. "Whitney said you have an arrangement similar to ours and are still trying to... get comfortable," he says delicately.

His deep voice vibrates through my bones when he speaks, sending a shiver down my spine. I have no doubt this man could kill someone with his bare hands. But he flashes me a charming grin that allows me to take a breath and relax ever so slightly.

I nod, still trying to find my voice. As I wrap my head around this exchange, Whitney's warm smile sets me at ease. Ilya's Russian accent reminds me of home and my family, bringing an odd sense of comfort.

"I thought Ilya could explain a bit about how this works to help you better understand what roles you might play," Whitney suggests.

Releasing a tense breath, I smile. "That sounds good." At least we won't be jumping right into action with whips and bondage. While Whitney says she enjoys it, I'm still struggling with the idea of watching it and how that might help me feel more comfortable with Nicolo.

"BDSM is not just about punishment," Ilya starts, his dark eyes holding mine. "It is a game of power and control. My job is to create the scenarios I wish to entertain. It's Whitney's job to trust me. She must play the game, and when she does it right, I reward her." A smile spreads across his lips as he looks at Whitney with amused affection. "Sometimes, there is no right answer. Then, I punish her."

Whitney giggles. "That punishment for us usually entails forced pleasure," Whitney adds. "Making me come so many times it's almost painful."

My stomach twists at the thought of that. Nicolo makes me come multiple times when we're together. My orgasms are the only relief I get from the conflict in my brain when I'm with him. I can't imagine those moments being turned into a punishment. I also don't see how that level of euphoria could get painful. But I stay quiet as Whitney continues.

"Ilya likes to punish me so much my endurance has started to make our games last longer than the club is open. I think he's started to do our sessions at home more often to save on money."

Ilya grips Whitney's chin between his thumb and finger and turns her to face him. "That smart mouth of yours will get you in trouble if you don't watch it," he growls playfully. Then he kisses her passionately, his hand combing back into her hair as he parts her lips with his tongue.

The heat of embarrassment pools in my cheeks, and I glance down to give them a moment of privacy. Clearly, they're closer to a happy couple than I had expected after hearing about their arrangement. Seeing their connection brings me a flicker of warmth and hope.

"Would you like to come back into our room with us?" Ilya asks, drawing my eyes to him once more.

My heart stutters in my chest now that I'm faced with actually accepting the invitation to join them. *Do I just watch? They won't expect me to join in, will they?* Oh, God, I hadn't thought of that before.

"I have added you into the scenario as a passive participant. I thought it might give you a feel for role playing without having to join in the sex."

Relief floods me, and my shoulders relax. "That sounds good. Thank you."

Ilya nods. "Come."

He rises, and I follow him and Whitney down the same hall Nicolo guided me down the last time I was here.

Ilya stops at a door closer to the front of the hall and puts his hand on the handle. Then he turns to me. "In this room, we are part of a scene. Part of the fun is remaining in character, and Whitney knows her safe words to tell me if I push her too far. Otherwise, she is not allowed to disobey me in here. Not without consequences."

I swallow hard and nod my understanding. Don't interfere with his scene. Then I follow Whitney into the room. It's furnished in much the same way as the previous sex room I saw, with a wall of toys, a bed, and different benches, swings, and frames to offer variety.

Ilya closes the door behind us, and immediately, his demeanor shifts. "Take off your clothes, *rabynya*," he commands coldly. "And kneel in the center of the room." He grips the hem of his T-shirt and pulls it up over his head, revealing impressive shoulders and pecs. Tattoos mark his shoulders and chest.

He heads to a far table and sets out several toys.

Stepping to the side, I clasp my hands behind my back to stop them from shaking. Whitney strips down to a set of strappy black lingerie that resembles bondage attire more than underwear. Rather than soft or lacy material covering her breasts, a thin black band covers her nipples. The flesh of her breasts press around the top and bottom to create impressive cleavage.

Her panties are just as revealing with barely enough fabric to cover a diamond of skin at the peak of her thighs. Thin black straps stretch around her hips, resembling ropes more than elastic. A thin band cinched just above her navel serves as a garter belt. It breaks up the flat plane of her stomach and connects down to a pair of black nylons.

She's stunning in her provocative outfit, and she leaps to do as Ilya says. Stepping to the middle of the room, she kneels and bows her head subserviently.

My stomach lurches as it reminds me, once again, of how Nicolo treated me during our first night in this club. Maybe he was simply acting out a scene in his mind. But his cruelty leading up to that night and the anger he expressed before bringing me to the club doesn't fit Ilya's more mild demeanor.

Taking something from the wall of toys, Ilya latches a black leather collar around Whitney's throat. He tips her chin up so she has to look at him from her space on the ground.

"You've been a naughty pet," Ilya murmurs as he looks down on Whitney. "You've displeased me. So I've decided to send you with a trainer. She will teach you to behave properly. Unless, you can prove to me that you're a good pet, that you know how to behave. Do you want to stay with me, *rabynya*? To prove you're worthy of me today?"

"Yes, Master," Whitney breathes, her eyes growing wide.

"Good. Now get in." He points to a small metal cage before taking Whitney by the hair and leading her to it on her hands and knees.

She follows him, crawling like an actual pet and folding herself into the cage so he can close the door. It's small enough that her knees have to part and come to rest up by her shoulders if she wants to sit. It looks acutely uncomfortable, but Ilya doesn't seem to notice as Whitney peers up at him through the bars.

"Would you like a drink?" he offers me, his tone business-like as he takes a bottle of wine from a table and uncorks it.

"Um, sure, yes," I agree, unclear of what might be expected of me. But my heart's racing so fast, it might help calm me down a little.

Ilya pours us each a glass as he talks about Whitney almost as though she were an animal. "She is usually well behaved, a perfect pet, obedient, flexible, athletic, capable of enduring pain. She has been well trained for public outings, or so I thought. Lately, she seems to be testing the boundaries, pretending like she gets to run the show."

He hands me my glass of wine and gestures to the chair next to Whitney's cage. "Please, have a seat." He settles into his own chair.

I sit and take a generous gulp of wine as I wait to see what will happen next.

"She's been talking without permission, seems to think a leash is optional..." Ilya reaches between the bars of Whitney's cage to stroke her hair like one might a dog. "She's one of my favorites, but I think someone is spoiling her when I am not around. I might need your help to put her back in line. What do you think, pet? Have you been forgetting your place?" Ilya turns to look at Whitney.

"No, Master, I–"

"No? You think you know better than I do?" he demands, cutting her off.

His fingers curl into her hair to force her head back, exposing her neck and the soft curves of her breasts. He releases her with a scoff and looks at me.

"You see? I think she enjoys provoking me. She doesn't believe I'll punish her anymore. That is why I brought you here, so she knows this is her last chance to prove she can be a good pet."

Rising from his seat, Ilya looks down at Whitney, who looks adequately contrite. "Come, I'll show you what I mean about her trying to run the show." Opening the cage, Ilya latches a chain leash to a small silver loop on Whitney's collar.

Whitney starts to exit her cage, but Ilya gives her leash a gentle tug. "Down," he commands. "Your place is at my heels, *rabynya*."

He then leads her out of the cage, forcing her to crawl beside him as he guides her to the far wall of toys. Her scarcely covered ass rocks as she moves lithely across the floor in her strappy lingerie.

"That is a good pet." Ilya watches her closely, a hungry look in his eyes.

Whitney responds visibly to his praise, which intrigues me. Though I'm somewhat uncomfortable by the level of humiliation in their game, Whitney doesn't seem to mind. Instead, she seems eager to please Ilya and sad when she doesn't, just like a pet might. But his Russian term for her suggests she's more his slave than an animal.

When they reach the far wall, he unleashes her and tells her to get a toy. Whitney rises to her feet and studies the wall, almost as if his request is a test. Grabbing a set of nipple clamps, she brings them back to Ilya.

"No." Ilya's expression darkens. "You know which toy I want. Bring me the toy *I* want to play with," he insists, his tone growing more forceful.

Biting her lip, Whitney returns to the wall to find a different toy. This time, she comes back with furry handcuffs.

"No!" Ilya says again.

Whitney returns to the wall once more. She grabs a flogger more confidently and returns to Ilya. Growling, Ilya takes the flogger from her and throws it on the floor.

"You think you're funny, *rabynya*? You think this is about what you enjoy?"

"No, Master," she breathes, her eyes growing wide.

"Then what toy did I want you to get?"

Whitney scrambles over to the table where Ilya first laid out several toys and brings back a string of metal beads.

"Yes, so why didn't you bring that to me in the first place?" he demands.

Whitney swallows and shakes her head wordlessly.

Looping his finger through her collar, Ilya leads Whitney across the room to a swing. "Get in," he commands. He turns to me. "This is how I punish her for being a bad pet," he explains, withdrawing a small silicon stick from his pocket. "It is a shock collar of sorts, though I imagine you have your own more effective training tools."

Braced in the seatless swing, Whitney grips the straps that hang from the ceiling as she hooks her knees through two loops.

Clicking the silicon stick, Ilya brings it humming to life. Ilya spreads her legs and presses the tip of the stick to the peak of her thighs.

Whitney's breathing quickens.

She squeals as something crackles. Her back arches as she grips the straps above her.

Then Ilya presses aside the small diamond of black fabric covering Whitney. He eases the stick inside her. Whitney moans as her hips rock, spreading her legs further. Clearly, she's enjoying the punishment.

When Ilya asks what she has to say for herself, she cries an apology.

"Please, Master," she moans, her voice drenched in arousal. Her muscles twitch in a way that tells me she's experiencing some form of electric pulse.

Both embarrassed to watch something so intimate and fascinated by their dynamic, I can't tear my eyes from their scene. Ilya's commands and words are degrading and cruel. But he's almost entirely focused on Whitney's pleasure as he toys with her. She seems to enjoy the attention immensely.

Seeing the intensity of her pleasure makes my stomach quiver. I think about the possibility of finding that same kind of experience. An image of Nicolo comes to my mind. The memory of my forced orgasms at his club makes my panties suddenly wet.

Whitney rocks in the swing, trembling as she quickly reaches her first orgasm. I'm blown away by the way they play so naturally together. Ilya seems to love the control over Whitney, even to the point of punishing her with pleasure.

I wonder if Nicolo and I might ever be capable of reaching that level. I definitely find him attractive. My body can't seem to resist his touch, but he doesn't seem to care whether I like him or not. Even when we're in public.

Regardless of how he uses me in the bedroom, I don't see him letting go of his aggression. He's capable of being charming, but he doesn't seem to want to grace me with it.

25

NICOLO

For the fifth time in an hour, I check my phone to see if Anya's responded to my text. I don't know if she's intentionally ignoring me, but it's unacceptable. I'm about ready to track her down or march right up to her apartment and demand entrance.

Part of our agreement is that she be accessible whenever I want outside of class. And I gave her most of Saturday to do whatever the fuck she wants. *So where the fuck is she?*

Grinding my teeth, I drop my head back onto the cushion of my penthouse couch. I close my eyes to the vibrant sunset before me. The city view from the picture windows can't distract me today.

Usually, my Astor House apartment is a perfect place to find tranquility. I feel free here, high above the city bustle. But now it feels too quiet, too empty. I've hardly seen Anya this week, what with all her extra hours of practice and a new partner.

I'm trying to cooperate. I get that she needs the time since I broke her last partner's arm. But now she's ignoring me even on the weekend.

My phone dings in my palm. I snatch it up, grateful no one's around to see how quickly I respond to a text that might be Anya. But it's not. It's from Matteo, one of the guys who works with me for my father.

Grudgingly, I open the text. I'm not in the mood to think about the family business right now. My hand clenches as I study the image he sent me along with a brief note:

Saw your girl meet up with a couple at Incognito. Just thought you ought to know.

The image is of a dairk-haired girl–the one with a pixie cut I've seen in the dance studio with Anya. She leans across one of the club's lounge tables to hold Anya's hand.

The man next to her is from the Popov family. He runs the Bratva on our southern border of Chicago. He's maintained an unspoken kind of truce with our family for years. Ilya has a reputation for some pretty dark kinks, and it appears one of those is fucking two girls at once.

Fucking bitch! Anya's ghosting me to swing with one of her dance friends? Fury roars to life in my chest. I'm up off the couch before I even know what I'm doing.

The thought of that Russian's hands on Anya makes me see red. Especially when she's supposed to be with me right now. If she thinks she's ready for another taste of Incognito, I'll give her one she'll never forget.

I storm past Sep and Rocco with a cursory command for them to stay put. Then I head to the elevator and take it down to my car. I peel out a moment later, racing down the streets of Chicago to the club.

As soon as I burst through the front door, Tiffany's eyes grow wide with shock.

"What room is that piece-of-shit Russian in?" I demand.

"U-uh, f-four," she stutters, tensing from the heat of my rage.

I stalk past her without a word, heading directly for the hall of rooms. My hands fist as I consider just what I'll do. I can't start a war with Ilya's Bratva over this. But I can punish Anya so she won't dare speak to another man again.

When my eyes land on door four, I kick it open with such force that it slams against the back wall. Their scene appears to be well underway. Ilya's dark-haired girl's legs are spread wide as he penetrates her with some kind of toy.

Ilya's brows press into an irritated frown as he turns to see who's interrupting him. The look of shock on the dark-haired girl's face says I'm the last person she expected. Her eyes flick to my right as an expression of concern replaces her surprise.

I turn to find Anya sitting in a high-backed chair.

A deep blush colors her cheeks as she meets my eyes.

"Nicolo," she gasps.

She cringes as soon as she reads the fury that contorts my face.

"Is this what you want?" I demand icily, closing the distance between us in a few strides. "For a minute there, I thought you might not enjoy punishment. But you sure do search it out, don't you little slut?"

Grabbing Anya's arm, I haul her out of her chair. I'm surprisingly grateful to find she's still fully clothed. I thought she might be participating in Ilya's scene and was trying not to go completely unhinged. "If you like punishment, then I can give that to you."

I don't bother speaking to Ilya or his girl as I drag Anya from the room. I slam the door shut behind me. Stumbling in my wake, Anya tries to keep up.

Pulling her down the hall, I find an open door. I shove her inside so forcefully she falls to the floor. She barely catches herself in time to stop from faceplanting. Her hands slap against the wood boards.

"You're mine," I growl, locking the door behind me.

I strip my shirt forcefully and toss it aside as I approach her.

"You don't get to ignore my messages while you watch your little ballerina friend get fucked. No one gets to turn you on but me, you horny little flirt."

I stoop, bringing my face within inches of hers. "Did it turn you on to watch them?"

Anya shakes her head. But her blush leaves splotches of color across her chest that tell me she's lying.

"No?" I challenge, and Anya bites her lip. "Take off your panties." I hold out my hand for her to give them to me.

Anya hesitates, cringing further from me as her blush intensifies. Fear flickers in her blue eyes. She's scared of getting caught lying after last weekend.

When she doesn't do as I say, I force the issue.

Gripping Anya's knee, I shove her legs apart.

I reach beneath her simple maroon dress.

She must have bought it recently for herself. It's not one of the high-end outfits I gave her, but it's newer than the rags she used to wear. It's soft and flowing, modestly coming down to her knees and elbows.

It's a perfect dress for me to rip off her.

Anya gasps as I cup her warm pussy. I curl a finger around her panties to stroke between her folds. My cock throbs at the slick arousal I find there.

She's good and ready to be fucked, and I haven't even kissed her yet. She was turned on by watching someone else's kinks. That gets me harder even as it pisses me off.

"I thought you learned your lesson about lying to me, dirty little slut. But apparently not." Gripping her chin firmly, I pull Anya forward until I smell wine on her breath. "Stand up," I whisper, pouring every once of my fury into my command.

This time, Anya does as I say. She slowly rises, and I follow her to a stand. Her pulse races in her neck. Her pupils dilate. Her tongue darts out to wet her lips as her eyes follow me in silent question.

When she's standing, I lean down to grip the hem of her dress. Twisting it around each of my fists, I keep my eyes pointedly on hers. With a violent jerk, I rip her skirt straight up the middle. I work my way toward her collar, destroying her dress.

"You don't deserve to buy new clothes with my money when you don't know how to behave," I state coldly.

I'm rewarded by tears brimming in her eyes.

I expose her breasts, shoving the remains of her dress over her shoulders and down her arms. She's wearing a proper bra, not a sports bra. But this one is more utilitarian without an inch of lace.

"Take it off," I command, eyeing it with distaste.

Anya jumps to do as I say. Reaching behind her, she releases the clasp and tosses aside her bra before I can destroy it too. Her nipples pucker as soon as her breasts are bare.

I cup them, and my cock stiffens in my pants. The supple, soft skin and the taut nubs harden further at my touch.

"Now. Take off your panties," I repeat, glancing down at the simple cotton hip-huggers.

Anya does as I say. She places them in my hand, which I hold out to her once more. Standing straight again, she shifts her arms self-consciously to cover her naked body. I slap them away with my free hand, and she jumps at the unexpected contact.

"Put your hands behind your back," I command.

Anya does, her chin dipping submissively. The shift in behavior makes me pause, but my anger keeps me on track. I lift her panties to my nose, inhaling the tangy scent of her arousal.

Fuck, she smells delicious. I'm tempted to taste her, but I'm not about to go down on her. She needs to learn that my needs come first in our arrangement. That's what she should be focusing on, obeying me, ensuring she does as I say.

"Stick out your tongue," I order.

Anya lifts her head to obey. Her pink tongue spreads over her bottom lip. I press the wet spot of her undies against her tongue.

"Taste that?" I hiss.

Anya nods, keeping her tongue extended.

"Don't ever fucking lie to me again, Anya." Then I shove her panties into her mouth and press her jaw closed. "Get onto the bed."

I don't wait to see if she does as I tell her. Heading over to the wall of toys, I snatch a flogger from the rack along with a strand of bondage rope.

I'm pleased when I turn and find her sitting on the edge of the bed. She presses her knees together, wrapping her arms around her waist and over her breasts. Her eyes follow me, growing round as she sees the flogger. She pales visibly as I toss them onto the bed and tell her to lie in the center.

She clearly doesn't want to obey, which makes my cock ache with anticipation. Still, she crawls farther onto the bed, exposing her ass and pussy. Flipping onto her back, Anya watches me with a guarded expression.

"Grip the headboard."

Anya reaches just above her head to grasp the metal bars. I follow her onto the bed to cinch the rope around each wrist. Then I tie it to the headboard's bars. Anya shivers as I trace my fingers down the silky softness of her skin. I pause at her breasts to grope and massage them, kneading them with my palms.

They fit perfectly in my hands, the supple flesh pressing between my fingers. I squeeze them, then find her nipples with the pads of my thumbs. I roll the hard nubs.

A quiet gasp, muffled by her panties, escapes Anya's lips. She bites down hard on the fabric in her mouth.

"You like it when I play with your nipples, pet?" I murmur, a smile curling my lips.

She might not know it, but I'm testing her honesty again. I can see the defiance in her eyes. She wants to tell me no. Instead, she remains completely silent.

"You answer when I ask you a question, little bird," I growl

I pinch her nipples, intensifying the pressure until she cries out.

Her back arches up off the bed.

"Yrms!" she screams around her panties.

I release her nipples and rock back. My frustration wells inside me as she continues to fight me. Breaking her is proving a challenge I find both frustrating and deeply arousing.

But tonight, I want her to know that she's my property. She doesn't have the freedom to do as she pleases. She can't go where she wants. She's mine for as long as I want her. And the more she fights me, the more I want to claim her.

Gripping her ankles, I lift Anya's legs so her hips bend. Her knees frame her breasts, her thighs spreading wide. She folds easily until her toes touch the headboard on either side of her head. I fucking love how supple she is.

Leaning against her exposed pussy, I pin her in place. Deftly wrapping the rope around one ankle, I tie it to a bar of the headboard. Then I follow suit with the other.

Sitting up to view my handiwork, I'm impressed by Anya's flexibility. She makes the intense stretch look easy. Still, her expression says she's anything but comfortable about having her ass and pussy on full display.

"Mmm," I groan, stroking a finger down her slit and over her puckered asshole. "I love this view. Maybe I'll just rent this room indefinitely, leave you like this, a living fleshlight I can stuff with my cock whenever I want." I keep my tone light, musing.

I love the sound of her responding whimper.

Reaching over, I grasp the flogger and show it to Anya. "You see this, pet? I'm going to make you wish you never lied to me. By the time I'm done with you, you'll never want another man to look at you. You definitely won't join someone else's scene again. You're mine, Anya, to do with as I please. Not Ilya Popov's or his little toy."

Fear makes Anya's breathing rapid. Her breasts heave with anticipation, sending a thrill through my body. Shifting to the side of the bed for a better angle, I stroke the flogger's tassels up her ass crack. I graze her pussy, tickling her senses.

Anya shudders violently, and fresh arousal coats her folds. For someone who pretends she doesn't want it, she sure does fucking love the way I torture her. And tonight, I'm going to push her to her limits. I want to see just how dirty this girl really is.

I bring the flogger down across the back of her thighs. Anya releases a muffled scream as she jerks against her bindings.

"You think you can take ten lashes without coming, little slut?" I tease as I run the flogger up her ass crack and over her pussy once again.

Anya sobs in response. I bring the flogger down again, this time creeping a little higher on her thighs. Even as another cry bursts out around her panties, Anya's pussy tightens visibly. Her pearly juices start to creep down over her skin.

I don't waste time with another teasing stroke. I bring the flogger down across her ass cheeks, leaving fiery red marks in its wake.

Anya's back arches, and her legs quiver. Her toes curl from the over-stimulation of her punishment.

"Tell me you're mine, pet. I want you to say you won't come–you won't even touch yourself–unless I tell you to."

Anya nods her agreement. Rather than letting up, I bring the flogger down a fourth time.

She squeals.

"I can't hear you, little slut. What? Are you enjoying your punishment so much that you want me to keep going?" I snap the flogger across her breasts, and angry lines mar her beautiful milky flesh.

Anya shudders, her eyes fluttering closed. A deep groan escapes her as I stroke the flogger over her dripping pussy. I know this next stroke will make her come.

I fucking love watching the innocent prima ballerina joining my dungeon of dark sex and depravity. I love owning her body, making her yearn for my punishment.

"Do you want to come, pet?" I purr.

Anya's breathing is ragged as she opens her eyes to meet mine. She gives a tentative nod. Leaning over her, I press my finger between her lips, and she opens them. Hooking my finger around her undies, I slowly withdraw them from her mouth.

"Then tell me you're mine."

"I'm yours," Anya breathes. A tear escapes her eye to track down over her temple.

Those words light a fire in my soul.

I crush my mouth to hers as I consume her desperately.

Then, pulling back, I shift my stance and snap the flogger across her pussy. I'm lighter than when I struck her thighs or ass, but it's still enough force to make her scream.

Even as the pain-filled cry leaves her lips, her pussy starts to twitch. A flood of arousal trickles down her ass crack like a river.

I can't help myself. Leaning down, I stroke my tongue between her ass cheeks. Licking up her tangy juices, I make my way toward her clit. Her pussy continues to twitch even as I wrap my lips around her sensitive nub. And I suck it into my mouth.

Anya bucks, and the headboard groans as her strong dancer's legs jerk against the rope. A ragged groan tears from her chest, making my balls tighten.

I can't wait any longer.

I need to be inside of her.

Standing, I strip my jeans and boxers in one swift move then climb onto the bed just below her hips.

Fresh pussy juice trickles from her slit to coat her ass. Gripping the base of my cock, I stroke my tip through the slick viscous and up between her folds. I coat myself with as much of her arousal as I can.

"Good pets get fucked here," I murmur, hooking two fingers inside Anya's pussy and pressing against her G-spot. "But you've been misbehaving, so you don't get that tonight."

"No, Nicolo, please." Panic rises in Anya's tone as I line my cockhead up with her asshole.

Momentary guilt makes me pause. I really must have hurt her last weekend. But I can't back down now. Still, I curb my arousal. I don't want to destroy Anya. Just break her to my will.

"Don't worry, little bird. Tonight, you get to come with me inside your ass." With my free hand, I reach forward to tease Anya's clit.

She's so slick from her first orgasm that it doesn't take much to excite her once again. Anya's head tips back as I circle the sensitive bundle of nerves. I gently pinch it between my fingers. Her hips start to rock, her body instinctively craving more.

Slowly, I press inside her ass.

This time, I'll take my time, really enjoy the feel of Anya's tightness, the way her puckered anus resists my penetration. Anya's lips part. She releases a gasp that's a confused mingle of pain and pleasure.

"Fuck, you're so tight," I rasp.

I tease her clit more adamantly and press two fingers back inside her tight pussy.

Then I press my cock into her ass up to the hilt.

She feels fucking sensational as her pussy responds to the penetration. She constricts around my fingers as her ass clenches my erection. I slowly start to rock inside her, pulling out just a few inches before pressing back inside.

Anya whimpers.

Her hands grip the bars of the headrest as she presses her eyes closed.

She's so tight, I could almost lose my load even though we've only just begun. Despite my determination to take my time, I start to thrust more aggressively. I've never fucked someone so turned on and yet so tight. The thought of filling her with my cum drives me over the edge.

Crushing her clit with the pad of my thumb, I finger fuck her roughly in rhythm with my thrusts.

And I penetrate her deeply.

Anya's breasts bounce with the force of my hips as I move her body. The lean muscles of her arms tense, bracing against the headboard to stop from bumping into it with each drive.

"Ffffuck," I hiss, losing all sense of control.

Anya's pussy tightens around my fingers as she nears climax. I'm not sure I can hold on any longer.

"Come for me, Anya," I demand.

She does. A desperate sob escapes her as her back arches up off the bed. Her breasts press up between her knees. Her pussy pulses around my fingers, gripping them, milking them. Her juices gush over my hand and down onto my cock and balls.

The sight of her orgasming with me inside her ass. The smell of her warm cum. The slick feel of it coating her ass–it sends me over the edge. I slam into her as my cock swells with my release.

Burst after burst of cum erupts from me. I collapse forward, grunting as my hips convulse with the force of my orgasm.

Breathing heavily, I slow to a stop inside Anya. My shoulders press against her calves, my chest brushing her nipples when our breathing forces us closer together.

Anya's eyes slowly open. In their sky-blue depths is a deep sadness I hadn't anticipated. It completely disarms me. I have the strangest desire to alleviate that sadness.

Deeply troubled, I lean back, slowly easing out of Anya's ass. I don't know why, but I feel the need to take care of Anya now that my anger has dissipated. Where I might usually leave my sub tied until I'm finished dressing, this time, I immediately reach for the ropes tying Anya's ankles to the headboard.

It doesn't take me long to free her. I massage the circulation back into her ankles as Anya does the same to her wrists. Only after that do I retrieve my clothes and put on my pants.

Anya does the same to the best of her ability. She dons her bra and soiled underwear even though it's damp from being in her mouth. She then shrugs on her dress and grips the two shredded sides to pull them closed over her breasts.

Scratching the back of my neck, I look around the room. I have nothing to offer her for better coverage except the shirt I stripped as we entered the room. Extending my arm toward her, I offer it in place of her tattered dress.

"Thanks," she murmurs.

She averts her eyes as she takes my button-down. Quickly stripping her tattered dress, Anya replaces it with my shirt. It's just long enough to cover the tops of her thighs. Not the most coverage, but better than what the dress might offer.

She rolls the sleeves to her elbows so she has use of her hands, then she collects her ruined dress once more.

"How did you get here?" My tone is gentler than I've used with Anya before.

"The bus," she says simply.

"Come on. I'll take you home." I open the door for her, gesturing for her to lead the way.

26

ANYA

How are you today? Everything okay?

I stare down at Whitney's text for a long moment, contemplating what I might possibly say.

She called me last night, but I couldn't bring myself to answer. After what happened with Nicolo, I feel absolutely lost, my body spent.

I'm terrified of the anger he carries. I don't think Nicolo and I will ever find that balance Whitney and Ilya were talking about. For the glimmer of a second, I thought it might be possible as I watched how good Ilya and Whitney played together.

But Nicolo's abuse is something far more real, far more dangerous. I don't think he spares a second thought for how he hurts me. I can only hope that he grows tired of me and moves on like he did in high school.

Everything's fine, I finally respond. *Thanks for trying to help. I'm so sorry for causing such a disruption to your fun.*

Girl, don't worry for a second. I'm just glad you're okay. You really are, aren't you?

Yes.

I try to follow it up with something more reassuring, but I can't think of anything. The only good that came out of yesterday is that Nicolo said he would give me today off. That means I have an entire day to spend with Clara.

Speaking of which... Tiny feet patter down the hall, alerting me that my daughter is awake. My bedroom door opens a moment later, and Clara bursts in.

"Pancakes!" she cries before jumping onto the bed with me. She jostles me as she bounces on her hands and knees.

I laugh, reaching for her. Pulling her close, I tickle her belly. Clara giggles happily as she rolls on top of me.

"Will you be home today, Mommy?" Her innocent concern wrings my heart dry.

"Yes, baby. I get the day off, so we can spend the whole day together."

"Yay!" Clara wraps her arms around my neck and hugs me tightly.

"Now, go wake Auntie Patritsiya while I get dressed, and we'll make pancakes."

I give her bottom a light swat as she scoots enthusiastically off the bed. She dashes from the room without a moment's hesitation, and I swing my legs over the edge of the mattress. An involuntary groan escapes my lips at the way my body protests.

My legs are mildly sore from maintaining such a deep stretch yesterday, but what really hurts is my ass. It was far less painful this time. Nicolo took it more slowly at first, and he distracted me by playing with my clit. But he still brutalized my tender hole as he finished. Now, I'm left with a hollow ache where he filled me so utterly I felt I might tear in two.

The worst part is that I still enjoyed it. I came when he flogged me, and I came again as he fucked me in the ass. Something must be wrong with me. I still get turned on by Nicolo when all he seems to want to do is hurt me. The one kiss he gave me set my ever-loving soul on fire. That he only kissed me once was almost more punishment than the whip and forceful anal.

I feel like I'm falling apart, like my mind must be unraveling at the seams. That Nicolo could come bursting in on me and drag me from my friend's presence like he did. That he could humiliate me, ruin my clothes without batting an eye, tie me down, and flog me, and still, I could come for him? I must be broken.

I wonder if it's a weakness I've always possessed. Certainly it must have something to do with why I fell for him so naively in high school. *But why, now that I have seen him for all that he is, can I still find him attractive?*

"Mom, hurry!" Clara calls from the kitchen. She and Aunt Patritsiya start banging pots and pans in preparation for pancakes.

"I'll be right out!" Forcing my dark thoughts from my mind, I dress quickly, finding a loose pair of sweats and a T-shirt. I pick clothes that will cover the pink welts from my beating without pressing against them.

Then I step out of my room, walking the short distance down the hall toward the open living room and kitchen area. Pulling my hair up into a messy bun, I join my little girl at the fridge. She stands on her tippy toes to reach the carton of eggs.

"Mama, you get the milk," she instructs.

I grab it from the top shelf. Then we both head to the brown Formica counter, where a tiny step stool awaits Clara.

Climbing up onto it, she sets the eggs carefully on the counter. She waits patiently as I reach up into the white-painted plywood cupboards for the flour, salt, and sugar.

"Morning." Aunt Patritsiya passes me a measuring cup.

"Good morning." I flash her a tired smile.

Clara helps me measure out two cups of flour. Then comes the sugar and salt.

Clara watches closely as I crack the eggs and add them. Then we slowly stir them into the mixture together.

"Can I taste the 'nilla?" she asks as I measure out half a teaspoon of the extract.

"It won't taste like the vanilla in ice cream," I warn.

Clara's hazel eyes grow wide with fascination. Then she nods enthusiastically. I smile. Tapping a few drops of vanilla extract onto a tiny spoon, I hold it out for Clara. She slurps it up greedily, and I can't help but laugh as her face puckers in distaste.

"Eeeew!" she squeals, dancing on her stool as she waves her hands in front of her mouth.

Suppressing my humor, I grab a glass and pour her a little milk. "Here, this will make it taste better," I offer.

Clara grips the glass between her tiny hands and tilts it back to drink. When she's downed the whole thing, she releases a gasp that could rival a drunk's after slugging an entire bottle of beer.

"Better?" I ask.

"Mm-hmm," Clara agrees.

When we're finished mixing the batter, I hand it over to Aunt Patritsiya. She mans the skillet.

Clara and I set the table together as the sweet scent of cooking batter fills the kitchen. I love our Sunday routine. It's one my aunt and I set in place back when I first moved in with her in high school. When Clara was born, my daughter became a priceless addition to the quality time.

Sometimes we mix it up and cook omelets or waffles. But pancakes are our Sunday go-to simply because we all love them–each in our individual ways. I top mine with cinnamon apples, Aunt Patritsiya with fresh berries.

Clara's new favorite is smothering them in syrup, now that I've introduced her to the horribly sticky and impossible-to-clean topping. But I can't deny her the pleasure after seeing the way her face lights up after her first bite.

"What do you want to do today?" I ask Clara as we all sit around the table.

"Dance party!" Clara shouts enthusiastically.

"It's all she's been talking about this week." Aunt Patritsiya smiles gently. "She wants to see what her mommy is spending so much time on these days. Right, Clara?"

Clara nods before scooping another messy forkful into her mouth.

My heart twinges knowing that Clara's noticed how absent I've been. It kills me to think she's home missing me as much as I miss her.

"Well then, dance party it is," I agree, forcing a smile.

Aunt Patritsiya gives me a knowing smile as she meets my eyes. "I'm so proud of you for working as hard as you do to follow your dreams, Anya."

"Thank you, Auntie," I say.

"Is it too much? You've seemed so stressed lately."

Her tone holds concern, and it brings tears to my eyes.

"I'm fine. Really. Just a bit tired," I promise.

Aunt Patritsiya nods. "Well, I'm glad you get to spend the day with us today."

"Me too," I murmur. I take a bite of pancake to hide the emotion that closes my throat.

Determined to make the most of my time with my daughter and aunt, I ask all the questions I haven't been able to hear the answers to lately–what Clara's favorite thing about school is these days, how she's enjoying her new school clothes.

Clara babbles happily in her broken four-year-old's speech. She barely pauses for breath between stories and mouthfuls of pancake.

When breakfast is done, we clear the table. Then Aunt Patritsiya shoos us into the living room for our dance party while she cleans up the dishes.

Clara picks the song from among our meager collection of ancient CDs that we play on the even more ancient sound system that came with the apartment. As the tune to "I Got You, Babe" by Sonny and Cher pours from the speakers, Clara grips my fingers. She pulls me toward the open space of our living room.

Warmth fills me as the tune reminds me of my parents. They used to listen to this CD all the time when I was young. The joy of seeing my beautiful little girl spin and twirl to the music soothes my soul like a salve. I turn Clara in loops as she dances. She squeals with delight as she starts to grow dizzy.

"Mommy, you dance!" she demands as she sways unsteadily on her feet.

Laughing, I oblige. Drawing upon a few of my ballet moves she loves, I lift lightly onto my toes and flick my feet. Clara claps excitedly and begs for more.

"Okay, but you have to help me. Do as I do." I take her hands and lead her into another simple set of steps.

Clara copies me to the best of her ability. She beams when I praise her for being such a good dancer.

"I want to be a ballerina, too, when I grow up!" Clara shouts happily as she repeats the steps more confidently this time.

I feel as though my heart might burst with love. My precious little girl brings me such wonder and happiness. How I ever got so lucky to be blessed with Clara, I don't know. She lights up my life and brings me peace. Even when the weight of my circumstances feels crushing.

For Clara alone, I will be eternally grateful to Nicolo. Without my little girl, my life would have such little meaning. I live to make her life better, to see she's taken care of, well loved, and happy.

After getting to know Nicolo better, I'm more grateful than ever that I never told him about her. She's my secret, safe from his cold brutality. I will protect her from the world's evils with every drop of my strength and conviction–even if that evil is her own father.

I brim with happiness as Clara giggles freely. She throws herself onto the couch in her own special version of interpretive dance. Then she jumps into my arms to hug my neck tightly.

I cling to her, holding her close as I twirl her in a circle, extracting another of her joyful squeals. This is what I needed. One day with my daughter to fortify me for my week of torture at Nicolo's hands.

After today, I will be so full of love that nothing Nicolo does will hurt me. Clara's love and affection is as much my shield as I am hers.

27

ANYA

I feel like a streetwalker as I stand on the curb in front of my apartment building in the crimson velvet dress Nicolo told me to wear for our date tonight. Tugging on the short skirt, I try to pull it lower over my thighs.

I look up and down the street for any sign of Nicolo. A bitter gust of wind cuts across my skin like knives. I'm thankful for the dress's long sleeves. But the asymmetrical cutouts across my midriff allow the cold air to penetrate the fabric around my breasts, making my nipples as hard as glass.

I try to cover as much of my exposed flesh as I can with my arms and resist the urge to go get my jacket. I know if I do, he'll only have me take it off, like he did the other night.

Relief floods me when I spot Nicolo's black Maserati a moment later. Confused tension follows immediately. I remind myself that the warmth inside his car is what I desperately crave. Not his company.

Bending to grab the door handle, I pull it open and slide quickly into the car. I've gotten more dexterous about the maneuver. I also care less today about what he might see. All I want is to stop shivering.

"Sorry I'm late," Nicolo says flatly as his eyes follow me into the car.

A flicker of arousal disrupts the dark thunderstorm of his expression. But Nicolo seems mercurial and sullen as he pulls away from the curb.

I'm surprised to find him in such a bad mood. I actually put on the dress he found most interesting during our shopping day, the one I'd promised myself I wouldn't be caught dead in.

"Family emergency," is all he says as follow up but the tension in his tone is palpable.

As I lean closer to the heater to thaw my frozen fingers, I wonder if that means family family or mafia family. I bite my lip to stop myself from asking. Today seems like the last day I want to provoke him into punishing me.

Nicolo white-knuckles the steering wheel as he races across town.

The silence is stifling, but I can't think of anything to say.

"Are you all right?" I finally ask. I watch his reaction from the corner of my eye.

Nicolo's scowl intensifies as he glares out the windshield. "I just want you to show me a good fucking time and take my mind off of it," he growls.

My stomach knots, and I shiver as my body responds to the ice in his tone. Falling silent once more, I pick at the hem of my dress.

I don't know what he means by show him a good time. But being agreeable is probably a good idea. I choke down my internal conflict. Putting on my game face, I prepare for whatever he has in store for me.

Nicolo pulls up outside an unassuming building on the corner of Ashland Avenue and Walton Street. At first, I'm confused by it, as it almost looks like some kind of business office with odd, modern-art-decorated window.

Then I spot the small wooden sign behind the glass that names the place Temporis. My heart skips a beat as I recognize the name of the Michelin-star restaurant. Everyone at Rosehill raves about. I've never tried it, seeing as, dinner here costs almost the same as a month's rent at our apartment.

Parking the car right on the corner as though he owns the building, Nicolo kills the motor and gets out. Despite his bad mood, he walks around the car to help me get out. I'm sure I would shred my skirt if I tried to on my own.

Without a word, Nicolo guides me through the front door into the restaurant. He informs the formally dressed host of our reservation. The decor is simple and modern. Dark wood tables and simple white-cloth chairs occupy the space. The host leads us to the far end of the room, where he sits us at a quiet table.

"Ma'am," the host says, his eyes combing over my outfit apprecia-tively as he pulls out my chair.

I blush, quickly sitting before Nicolo can catch him checking me out. But Nicolo seems distracted as he settles into his own chair and orders a bottle of their finest cabernet.

The host gives a subtle bow and departs, leaving me to study Nicolo's troubled face. Gripping the stem of his wine glass, Nicolo twirls it across the table. The glass hums with the motion. He tips it so the dim lighting shines through the curved glass, reflecting onto the table.

Nicolo's hazel eyes look miles away. From the way his lips press into a tight line, I'm confident his family emergency is still on his mind.

Pushing aside my reservations, I reach across the table to cover Nico-lo's hands with mine. His head snaps up as his eyes meet mine. Mild surprise quirks his strong eyebrow.

"Nicolo, what's wrong?" I ask, trying to make my voice authoritative. It comes out as barely more than a whisper.

Sighing, Nicolo sets the wine glass aside. He removes his hands from mine in the same motion. "Someone tried to attack my sister today," he rasps. A hint of fear shines in his eye before anger takes over his face. His expression hardens as his jaw works to fight back his emotion. "Her bodyguards prevented it, but she was pretty shaken up."

"What happened?" I ask, my eyes growing round.

That he's actually opening up is almost as shocking as the way he speaks about his sister being attacked. He sounds angry but not surprised. It reminds me that his life must be so different from my own, surrounded by violence. My pulse quickens as he seems to contemplate telling me more.

Nicolo shrugs one shoulder as he glares down at his knife and fork. "Her guards say they were confronted unexpectedly outside the mall, when they were getting in the car. Silvia was able to get in safely while they dealt with the problem. But I found a note in the car saying 'Revenge is coming.'" Nicolo's expression is intense as he meets my eyes. "They went after my sister. She's barely sixteen–a child."

His fiercely protective tone disarms me. He seems to care deeply about his sister's safety. I didn't even realize he had a sister. But as he speaks about her, I'm alarmed at his level of concern.

"Do you... think this has to do with your family business?" I ask tentatively, my heart racing.

"More than likely." Nicolo picks up his butter knife and rolls it between his fingers. He's fidgeting to cope with the emotion so visibly consuming him.

He really does look like he needs a distraction. Biting my lip, I take up the menu. "So, what's good here?"

Nicolo scoffs and pulls the menu from my hands. He closes it and sets it aside. "Whatever the chef is in the mood to make."

He must not be joking. When the server arrives with a bottle of wine and offers to take our order, Nicolo tells him to have the chef decide.

Sipping my wine, I rack my brain for something to talk about that might bring Nicolo out of his mood. I quickly realize that I know little about Nicolo personally–aside from that he likes to torment me and rough sex seems to be his main MO.

"I never properly thanked you for my jewelry," I say finally. "I love it, so thank you." It's true. The simple diamond studs and matching bracelet are perhaps my favorite thing he bought me on our shopping day.

As a dancer, I can't wear big, flashy jewelry that could get caught on things or fly off as I move. But I've found myself wearing the earrings almost every day. The bracelet is a nice addition that makes me feel dressier when I want to be.

Nicolo studies me, though his brows continue to press together in a frown. "You're welcome."

We fall silent once more.

Our server delivers a beautifully decorated plate a moment later, setting the appetizer between us. "This is canapés," the server explains. "Wagyu, uni, and peach." With another subtle bow, he departs once more, leaving us to enjoy our dish.

"It looks more like art than food," I observe.

It's laid out so perfectly in the center of the white plate. It mimics some form of abstract modern art as the colors overlap and collide wonderfully.

"Hmm," Nicolo responds, gesturing that I should start.

I stare down at the plate, unsure of how I might deconstruct something so beautiful. "That's okay. You go first."

Wordlessly, Nicolo reaches into the center of the table with his knife and fork. He dissects the pretty dish into two even portions and puts one serving onto my side plate. He then dishes the other half onto his plate.

"Eat," he commands.

I do, intensely aware of how Nicolo seems to give orders without even thinking about it. I wonder if that might not have something to do with who he is and how he was raised. For the first time, I wonder what his home life must have been like growing up. *Was his father kind to him? Domineering?*

I would think Lorenzo Marchetti must be as ruthless as his son. I can't imagine how that kind of violence might have impacted Nicolo's childhood. Now that he's mentioned having a younger sister, who he's clearly protective of–and I know he has two younger brothers–I wonder if he might not be the oldest. He might feel some sense of responsibility to become the man of his family someday.

Our next dish arrives shortly after we finish our first, and it's just as artistic as the last. Despite my best attempts to distract Nicolo from his thoughts, he only seems to sink further into his dark mood.

When I ask him about his favorite things to do, Nicolo shoves his plate away forcefully.

The dishes clink together loudly.

"Fuck this," he growls. "We're leaving." Nicolo tosses his napkin onto the table and rises.

Wide eyed, I follow him up out of my chair. He tosses a stack of bills onto the table, much like he did on our first night at dinner.

My stomach tightens with nerves as I wonder if it's not a sign of what's to come. Nicolo presses his hand to the small of my back as he practically marches me from the restaurant.

"Get in," he commands when we reach the car. He yanks my door open before he stalks around to the driver's side.

I keep my lips firmly shut as Nicolo races across town. I don't know what's on his mind, but we're not heading back to my apartment complex. We're not heading to Incognito or his nightclub. He's taking me somewhere new tonight.

Nerves quiver in my belly as he pulls into the parking garage beneath a breathtaking high-rise at the edge of Lincoln Park. He helps me from the car once more. Then Nicolo leads me to an elevator. Flashing a fob to the sensor, he presses the call button.

Heart hammering in my chest, I step into the mirrored elevator. I watch Nicolo closely from the corner of my eye. He presses the button for the top floor, and the doors close, sealing us in together.

My nerves tingle as my breath catches in my lungs.

Tension rolls off of Nicolo in waves.

I don't dare break the silence after his reaction to my last attempt.

The doors open to a grand penthouse, and I gasp as the Chicago city skyline appears before me. Stained with brilliant hues of gold, pink, and deep purple, the skyscrapers glimmer in the light of sunset.

I stare, mesmerized, at the floor-to-ceiling windows that make up two full walls of the living room. Slowly, I approach the stunning sight. All thoughts of Nicolo wash from my mind as I see my beautiful home city from high above.

"You like it?" Nicolo asks, his deep voice tinged with amusement.

I turn to find him watching me. The hint of a smile tugs at his lips, though the tension still keeps his shoulders tight.

"I don't know how you ever leave," I confess, turning back to the view.

Moving closer to the window, I stop just a foot from the glass. I almost feel like I'm flying. I hover so high above the ground with only a clear barrier and a few thick metal beams to separate me from the sky itself.

Nicolo's warmth washes over me as he steps up behind me. His hands find my hips as he pulls me close. His breath tickles my neck as he dips his head to press his lips to the tender skin behind my ear. A tingle of arousal ripples down to my core from the delicate touch.

Twisting my neck to look at him, I meet Nicolo's troubled eyes. He leans in to give me a scintillating kiss. His teeth nip before his tongue presses forcefully between my lips. Nicolo intensifies the connection, tasting me passionately as his strong hands explore my body.

Their warmth sets my skin on fire as they find the bare skin of my midriff, exposed from all the asymmetrical cutouts in my dress. A wave of arousal slicks my folds as Nicolo's hand slides beneath the fabric of my top to cup my breast. This dress doesn't cover enough skin to allow for a bra. My nipples harden instantly as Nicolo pinches one lightly.

His other hand travels lower, slipping inside another cutout as he makes his way toward my panties. His fingers press beneath the lace of my thong and find my clit. I gasp into his mouth.

Nicolo groans in response. He rubs circles over the sensitive bundle of nerves, sending electric jolts of pleasure deep into my core.

The attention is surprisingly intimate, far less aggressive than I'm used to after these last several weeks with Nicolo. Though I hate myself for it, my body relaxes at his touch. I'm aroused by this new form of attention.

My body responds greedily to his gentle touch, and my panties are wet in an instant. My pussy starts to throb with anticipation.

Nicolo's hands withdraw a moment later only to grip my hips and spin me to face him. His fingers hook beneath the hem of my skirt. Dragging the dress up over my head, he forces my arms up as he strips me.

An animal growl escapes his lips as his eyes rake down my bare flesh.

Then he's on me again.

He shoves me back against the window, and his lips find mine.

His hands grope me hungrily.

"God, I fucking want to fuck you for the world to see," he rasps.

A shiver races up my spine at the feel of the cold glass, in stark contrast to his scalding touch. My stomach flips as I think about how high up we are, how only a thin sheet of glass stops me from falling.

Nicolo seems completely oblivious to that fact. He grinds against me forcefully, pressing me harder into that barrier.

I don't have time to think about it, though, as Nicolo starts to remove his pants. Shocking myself, I go to work on his shirt buttons. My fingers tremble as I undo them. Pushing the fabric over his shoulders, I help undress him.

Nicolo continues to ravish my lips as he strips down.

Next go my panties. Nicolo shoves them roughly over my hips until they fall around my ankles. My heart races as Nicolo draws back, and I take in the sight of his perfectly sculpted body, his taut muscles and tense shoulders.

As one strong hand grips my hip, his other travels up my body, feeling my curves. He massages my breasts then moves higher until his fingers wrap around my throat. Fear squeezes my chest as he pins me against the glass, constricting my airway.

In an instant, what I thought might be a healthier, more gentle night of sex transforms. Nicolo kisses me, even as his fingers tighten around my neck, making my ears ring.

His other hand slides down my thigh to grip my knee. He pulls it upward until I'm balanced on one foot. Lifting my leg, he stretches me into a spit. Then he hooks my leg over his shoulder.

"I fucking love putting you in positions like this," he groans throatily.

Lining up with my pussy, Nicolo shoves his cock forcefully inside me. My pussy clenches around him as ripples of pleasure burst through my body. Still, I can't cry out. Instead, a gasp rasps from my lips as I fight for air. Nicolo's fingers loosen as he groans. Heady relief makes me dizzy as the blood returns to my brain.

Pounding inside my pussy, Nicolo fucks me hard. My ass slaps against the cold glass with each thrust. Overwhelmed by Nicolo's firm body surrounding me, enveloping me, I feel utterly helpless. And somehow, that intensifies my arousal.

Nicolo drives into me, grinding against my clit. I throb with a ravenous need for release.

I barrel toward an orgasm as Nicolo's hands grope me.

He seems desperate to feel every inch of my body being bent and stretched for his satisfaction.

And fuck does it feel good. Wrapping his arms around my waist, Nicolo stretches me further into a split. His hips rock into me at a new angle. His cock fills me more intensely, pressing against my G-spot with relentless force.

"Fuck!" I scream as I come without permission.

My pussy explodes around his hard length. Fiery relief burns through my veins, numbing me with euphoric pleasure.

Nicolo groans. He slows as my pussy milks his cock hard, begging him to come inside me.

"You like it when I fuck you?" he rasps, his voice bordering on agony.

I'm so far gone, I don't even think to lie. "Yes!" I gasp.

Coming to a stop, Nicolo slides out of me and eases my leg to the floor. His impressive erection glistens with my juices.

Then, gripping my hips firmly, Nicolo spins me to face the window once more. He puts a foot between my high heels and shoves my legs apart. Snaking his fingers into my hair, he grabs a handful of my locks. Turning my face, he presses my cheek against the glass.

His chest crushes me to the window, pressing my breasts hard against the surface. It's begun to warm from prolonged contact with my skin. Pinning me there, Nicolo guides his cock back to my entrance.

He shoves inside my pussy once again. Every time he fucks me, my tightness stretches to accommodate him. He fills me so completely. Bracing my palms against the glass, I gasp as fresh excitement blossoms in my core. Lost in the sensation of it, I can't bring myself to hate the way he brutalizes me. I know I will have to cope with the emotional conflict later.

For now, I arch my back, allowing a better angle as Nicolo resumes his violent thrusts. My skin tingles as his lips find my shoulder. His teeth press into my flesh. He bites me just hard enough to make me cry out.

When his hand reaches around my hip to find my clit, I know I'm a goner.

"Come for me, Anya," Nicolo rasps.

His fingers circle the sensitive nub, crushing it as he does.

Sobs of ecstasy burst from me as my pussy clamps around his cock. A moment later, I come hard.

Shuddering against the window, I shut my eyes to the breathtaking view. I'm consumed by my release. Tingling pleasure crackles out to the tips of my fingers and toes, leaving my limbs weak.

Suddenly, I'm grateful for how forcefully Nicolo pins me to the window. I'm not sure I could stay on my feet otherwise.

Nicolo's cock swells and stiffens inside me as he finds his own relief. I can feel his cock pulse as hot cum shoots deep into my pussy.

The familiar anxiety over a possible pregnancy fills me once again. I have an IUD that's supposed to make it impossible now. But the fear never goes away.

We gasp as he remains buried deep inside me. Nicolo keeps me pressed against the glass for several moments.

Only then do I realize how fortunate I am that we're on the top floor of a tall building. No other skyscrapers are close enough for someone to see us here. I would have given them quite the show, my naked body pressed against the glass as Nicolo fucked me.

As my heart rate begins to calm, Nicolo eases out of me. Slowly, he transitions my weight back onto my feet. A hollow ache follows my momentary bliss as I come back to reality. I'm addicted to Nicolo's touch. I know it, and I hate it because he's done nothing to deserve my attraction.

And when he does tire of me, I'm the one who will suffer once again.

28

ANYA

As we dress in silence, I note a distinct difference in the set of Nicolo's shoulders. He still looks troubled, but the underlying tension that made him feel like a loaded spring seems to have eased.

I straighten the velvet fabric of my dress, and Nicolo rolls the sleeves of his dressy button-down. Then he studies me.

"Would you like a drink?" he offers, his tone softer than usual.

"Um, sure. Yes, please," I amend to avoid escalating his anger.

"Go ahead and take a seat." He gestures to the living room couch with his chin.

I do as he instructs, heading to the chic gray couch that sits in the shape of an L. It's angled to focus on the impressive view while still including the elaborate gas fireplace along the inner wall.

"How long have you lived here? In this apartment, I mean?" I settle onto the couch as I turn my attention back to the awe-inspiring view of the city.

Apartment doesn't even do it justice. The sun creeps further behind the horizon, and deep purples and blues take over the previous gold and pink sky.

"A few years now," he says from the kitchen.

Ice clinks followed by the sound of liquid pouring.

"I moved in the summer after high school."

"Mmm," I respond. My heart kicks up a notch at the mention of a history I don't want to revisit. "I imagine this is easy to come home to."

Nicolo chuckles. The deep rumble of it sends thrills up my spine.

I shouldn't respond to him like that, I chastise myself. It won't lead to anything good. Still, as Nicolo rounds his high-top counter holding two dirty martinis, my heart flutters. He carries them with dexterous ease. I pinch my thigh as I silently scold my body, commanding it to behave.

"Tell me something, Anya." Nicolo's his face grows serious as he hands me my drink. Then he settles onto the couch beside me.

"Yes?" I sip the chilled concoction and find the bite of alcohol impressively softened by the olive juice and something that tastes almost citric. It's enticingly delicious.

"Where were you before you came to Rosehill?"

"Um, Wilbur Wright College." I try not to squirm as he asks me something personal.

We haven't spoken like this since he took my virginity in high school. But this time, I have so much to hide–that we have a four-year-old daughter together is the biggest one.

But so many other smaller details could lead to that revelation–that we went to high school together, that he took my virginity, that I got pregnant, that I haven't had sex with anyone but him since.

His hazel eyes burn into mine with a curiosity that warms me. It might just be that his question made me think of Clara, but suddenly, I'm intensely aware of how much they look alike. She's always reminded me of him. They have the same dark hair and hazel eyes. But the intelligence behind her eyes is his as well, and the mischievous curve of her lips.

"Why did you transfer to Rosehill then?" he asks.

"Well, they have one of the best dance programs in the country." I'm surprised he wouldn't know that when his family is one of the program's main sponsors. "Plus, Wilbur Wright's only offers an associate's degree in dance. If I want to pursue a performance career–rather than teaching–I need a higher level of education. Production companies only look for the best of the best when it comes to ballerinas, and a good number of them graduate from Rosehill. When I received a scholarship into the dance program, I couldn't refuse."

The irony of it hits me in that instant. Though I've fought hard to keep Nicolo from being a part of my life and my daughter's, his family's generosity is still shaping my future. After all, they're the ones who provide the scholarship money that's putting me through Rosehill. *Does Nicolo realize that?*

"Have you always wanted to be a dancer?" he asks, seemingly oblivious to the thoughts churning inside my head.

I almost choke on my sip of martini. His question lands dangerously close to the same conversation we had in high school. I cough and force the liquid down my throat, flinching as it burns.

Nicolo watches me with mild amusement. He seems more patient to hear my answer than I think he's ever been about anything.

I clear my throat and set my martini on the coffee table before answering. "Yes, my parents inspired my love of dancing. I've always known I wanted to be a ballerina. When I was young, no more than five, they took me to a ballet. I just remember being mesmerized by the way the ballerinas glided across the stage–like they were flying rather than dancing."

A smile creeps onto my lips as I recall the way I'd stood from my theater chair, riveted by the sugarplum fairies.

"My father's always had an appreciation for the arts, my sister too," he says.

I note that he doesn't include himself in that group.

"I think that's why he puts so much money into Rosehill's performing arts program."

"What do you have an appreciation for?" I ask, curiosity getting the better of me.

Nicolo sips his martini, his eyes never leaving mine. "The way you dance," he confesses matter-of-factly.

The intensity of his gaze makes my body heat rise. I blush profusely and snatch up my martini to distract myself from the way my stomach summersaults at his compliment.

"Thank you," I murmur before taking a large gulp of my drink.

Nicolo chuckles, finding amusement in how flustered I feel. Even that makes my insides quiver. *What is he doing to me?* The thought bursts through my consciousness with a sharp edge.

I've only just started to acclimate to his irrational temper, his sadistic means of seeking pleasure. Now, I feel like he's ripped the rug out from under me once again. Only this time, he's doing it by showing interest in me, *complimenting* me. I don't understand.

"But what about you?" I ask, forcing the spotlight off of me before he can delve too far into my story. "Don't you have a sport or an interest that you're passionate about?"

Nicolo gives me a one-shoulder shrug. I'm starting to learn it's his attempt at casual disregard when something actually bothers him.

"I used to follow baseball pretty closely–when I was a kid. But my path in life has been set since the day I was born. As the oldest son of Lorenzo Marchetti, it's my responsibility to run the family business after my father."

He leans back against the couch and turns his gaze to the city skyline. But his practiced nonchalance tells me he has some underlying emotion that he's not willing to talk about.

"Did you play baseball?" I ask, rather than probing into his family's affairs.

Now that he's mentioned it, I recall the room he took me to at that high school party. It was decorated with all sorts of baseball paraphernalia.

A mischievous grin spreads across his face, and Nicolo turns to meet my eyes. "I did more than play it. I made varsity team my freshman year of high school."

"Really?" Astonishment rings in my tone. I catch myself a moment too late. But I don't recall him playing for our school.

"Yes."

Nicolo's expression darkens slightly, and at first, I think he's registered my surprise as disbelief.

But when he speaks, he doesn't sound angry with me. Instead, his tone is bitter as he explains, "But high school was when my father's expectations started to increase. I didn't have time for baseball. I needed to learn the family business, to understand the responsibilities of running the kind of enterprise we have."

Nicolo downs his martini in one gulp, as if to wash away a bad taste.

Setting his martini glass on the coffee table, he rises from the couch. "Come on. I'll take you home."

Surprised by the unexpected shift in mood, I set aside my own unfinished drink and stand as well. In silence, I follow Nicolo back to the elevator. The tension that had seemed to dwindle after our rough, passionate sex culminates once again as the lift lowers us rapidly toward the parking garage.

The doors ding open, welcoming a cold gust of autumn air into the enclosed space. And I feel as though I might have imagined the momentary window into Nicolo's mind. For an instant, it felt as though he was opening up to me. But the sullen silence that brews inside his Maserati would say otherwise. We drive back toward my Uptown apartment without a word.

Confusion wars within my mind once again. I feel like the rope in a game of tug-o-war. On one side, my mind demands I keep my distance from Nicolo. It's the only way I can protect myself from the pain and regret I'm sure to feel if I give him my heart again. It would be foolish to let down my guard around him. He's proven time again that he not only cares little about how I feel but might even enjoy my pain.

On the other side, my body is determined to revel in the sensation of his touch, to soak up every delicious moment with him. He plays me like a masterful musician. And sometimes, despite all the rational arguments on my brain's behalf, it feels as though my body might just win out.

Because no matter what I know about Nicolo, no matter how clear it is that he can and will hurt me, I can't ignore the magnetic pull I feel toward him. And now, with just the tiniest window into who Nicolo is under all his anger, I find my mind losing ground in the argument.

"Good night," Nicolo says, pulling me from my thoughts.

Startled, I look up to see we're already back at my apartment building. Reaching for the door handle, I open it quickly and climb out. I do my best to keep my skirt down around my thighs.

"Anya?" Nicolo's voice stops me just before I close the car door.

I bend at the waist to look questioningly back into the car.

"Thank you. For tonight. I know I might not be the best at showing it, but it helped."

"Oh, um." A shy smile tugs at my lips. "You're welcome... Thanks for the drink."

Straightening, I close his car door and head toward the front entrance of my building. I'm starkly aware of the way he waits for me, his car idling at the curb until I step inside my apartment building.

Not only has he taken the time to drive me home, but for the first time, he seems to consider my safety. An odd tingling at the base of my neck accompanies this realization. I push the thought from my mind as I make my way up the stairs to my door.

I just don't know what to make of it all. No matter how roughly Nicolo handles me, he still manages to make me orgasm multiple times when we're together. That makes me feel even more conflicted about our arrangement since I've been so adamantly against it from the start.

And now that he's started to ask about my personal life, things are even more baffling. I can only imagine he's pretending to care. *But why?* He's already getting what he wants.

It had to be that he needed a distraction tonight. Still, after our first real conversation in years, I find myself incapable of getting Nicolo off my mind.

I'm sorry, Anya. Something came up. I won't be able to come to practice today...

It's the fifth time Robbie's canceled our dance practice in a week. I can't do this anymore. His excuses are growing increasingly more flimsy, and they started shortly after Paige's comment. I'm sure she scared him away.

As I stare down at my phone, fighting back the tears. Strengthening my resolve, I yank my bag from the cubby where I'd stored it. I ignore Whitney's question that follows me as I march out the studio door.

I don't waste time changing out my shoes as I race toward the stairs. Instead, I make my way down to Robbie's improv dance class on the floor below. It's his final class of the day, one that should have ended minutes ago, when he sent the text. On the off chance that he hasn't left campus for the day, I plan on confronting him to see what's really going on.

I'm in luck. As I round the corner of the stairwell, I spot his lanky form at the far end of the long hallway.

"Robbie!" I call.

It looks as though he was on his way out the side door. He cringes as my voice carries, turning several people's heads. Stopping in his tracks, he slowly turns and faces me. He doesn't try to meet me halfway as I stride down the hall with purpose. But he doesn't make a run for it either.

Breathless and flustered when I finally reach him, I plant my fists on my hips. I look up into his bashful baby face. "What is going on with you?" I demand. "You've bailed on me five times now. Is this your way of telling me you're not up for being my partner anymore? Because if it is, it's a pretty lousy way of doing it. I don't have time to waste being yanked around, Robbie."

Robbie flinches from the harsh accusation in my tone, and his eyes drop to the floor.

"What's 'come up' this time that's so important you can't spare a second to tell me face to face? I'm one floor above you, for God's sake. I've waited almost an hour to start practice. I could have gone home to do something else with my family if you'd given me any kind of notice." I take a deep breath, trying to control my temper.

Robbie's lips press together in discomfort, making the dimples pop on his cheeks. "You're right. I'm sorry." His eyes meet mine tentatively, brimming with apology. "I just..."

He releases a deep sigh, his shoulders dropping in resignation. "I kind of panicked after what your friend said the other day–you know, about your mafia boyfriend going after your partners. I keep trying to get past it. I know it's not your fault–that you would never hurt someone intentionally. But I just... kind of... freaked out and didn't know what to do."

My chest tightens as a knot sticks in my throat. *How can I possibly be mad at him now?* I would be scared, too, if I were in his shoes. Hell, I'm terrified, and I'm not even the one Nicolo has threatened to physically harm. Though I do know what he is capable of better than most.

Dropping my hands from my hips, I release my anger on a breath. "I understand why you would be scared. And I get it if you don't want to be my partner anymore." My voice trembles, and I fight the urge to cry. "I wish you would have told me sooner."

"I'm sorry, Anya. I really do want to be your partner. I just... don't want to end up in the hospital, you know?" Robbie's lips twist into a conflicted expression.

"I know." I give him a sad smile. "Not that I'm trying to change your mind–or even think I can–but just so you know, I don't think Nicolo would hurt you. What happened to Fin... well, it was because I was being stubborn. I know that now, and I would never risk your safety like that."

Robbie's eyebrows press together in confusion, clearly baffled by my vague explanation as I try not to give away too much. Then his expression softens. "I really do love being your partner. I feel like I've grown so much these past few weeks working with you."

A glimmer of hope flickers to life inside me. "I've really enjoyed being your partner as well. We make a good team."

"You don't think your mafia boyfriend is going to chop me up into little pieces or anything if I keep dancing with you?" he asks hopefully.

I laugh. "No, I don't think so. I promise I won't let that happen," I add more passionately. I never want to see someone I care about get hurt again, not if I can help it. And with Nicolo, I find that the less I resist him, the more amenable he's become.

"Well, then. If you'll forgive me for being such a dick lately, what do you say we put in a few hours of practice?"

A broad smile splits my face. "That sounds great."

29

NICOLO

"I miss you," Silvia says, her tone melancholy as it crackles through the phone. "Will I get to see you again soon?"

"This weekend," I promise. "Sunday probably. And I miss you too. You're sure you're feeling better?"

"Yes, Nico. I'm fine. I just got home from school. Call you later?"

"Sounds good." I end the call, releasing a heavy sigh as I walk across campus to my car.

I've been checking on my little sister regularly since she was attacked. While she wasn't physically harmed, I've never seen her that rattled.

I can still hear the anxiety lingering in her voice, the slight wobble when she says anything about emotion. It's taken a big toll on her. In truth, it's taken a toll on me too. We haven't been able to find the bastards who attacked her.

I've been on edge all week, hardly able to bring myself to attend classes when someone targeted my sister. They're still out there. They could try again. Our family has so many enemies, so many potential suspects. I don't know where to direct my gaze, who to punish, crush, destroy beyond repair. I'm trapped in a perpetual state of helplessness, and that infuriates me.

The only thing that seems to ease my restless discontent is Anya. I've spent every night with her since this weekend. I've called her every evening after spending as many hours as I can resisting the urge.

It doesn't suit a man of my position to need someone like her. Pets are meant to be beautiful playthings to show off and take to events. They prove my wealth and power. They're a pussy to fuck when it amuses me. I'm not supposed to feel more for her.

But this week, her presence has become something almost therapeutic. Our sex is the only outlet I can find for my tension. It seems to give me a sort of reprieve.

Rather than taking her to the club or out to fancy dinners, I've had my driver bring her to my penthouse late each evening. We fuck, and when I can't bring myself to send her home right away, we talk.

I've never cared to listen to anyone but Silvia before, but somehow, the hours I've spent with Anya this week have only heightened my interest in her.

Normally, I would have fucked my pet and moved on within a few dates, bored by the vanilla drivel about the supermodel lifestyle they dream of living. But I never know what to expect from Anya.

She doesn't tell me what she thinks I want to hear. She says what's on her mind. And fuck if I don't find that as sexy as it is infuriating sometimes.

My cock twitches in my jeans just thinking about Anya as I make my way across the tree-studded campus of Rosehill College. As if drawn by her presence, my gaze drifts toward the dance building up ahead to my left.

It's been a while since I've seen Anya dance. In truth, I haven't watched her since the day she agreed to be mine. Perhaps I let the knowledge that she would do whatever I said whenever I said it get to my head. I've enjoyed having her at my beck and call.

But today, I want to see her dance. Changing course, I head toward the turreted gray stone building and climb the steps. She'll be out of class now, practicing in her after-hours session if I had to guess.

From the sound of it, she's been working relentlessly on her dance for the winter showcase. Anticipation bubbles inside my chest as I think about seeing her progress.

Heading up to the second floor and the now-familiar studio where her professor teaches, I pull open the door and pause. It looks as though most students are wrapping up for the day. A few still occupy the dance mats. Most are collecting their bags and saying goodbye to their friends.

Anya's dance professor is nowhere in sight, his strict, no-nonsense tone notably absent.

More unexpected is that I don't see Anya anywhere in the room. Did she go home already? that doesn't seem like her. Just yesterday she mentioned she would need to practice late for the next few weeks since she had fallen behind.

My eyes land on Anya's dancer friend, the tall, dark-haired girl with a pixie cut. She's the one I stormed in on at Incognito when I found Anya at the club with her and Ilya Popov. Whitney, I think Anya called her.

Whitney's sharp gaze meets mine as she pulls on her street shoes, and her eyes narrow accusingly. Whether she's pissed at me for barging in during the middle of their scene or for dragging Anya out of the room to punish her, I don't know. Nor do I particularly care.

"You looking for Anya?" she asks, her tone bordering on accusatory.

She's feisty. I can see why Ilya likes her–and why she and Anya get along.

"Yes. Where is she?"

"Professor Moriari couldn't stay late today, so we broke off into smaller groups to have more space. I think she's in a studio down the hall." Whitney jabs her thumb over her shoulder as she stands and collects her bag.

"Thanks," I say, turning to leave.

"Hey," she says, her tone cold and commanding.

Surprised by her gall, I turn toward her once again and find anger in her expression.

"Anya is a good person," she says. "Don't hurt her."

She doesn't wait for my response. In truth, I'm not sure what I would say. An unbidden twinge of guilt twists my gut. Shoving the emotions down, I turn to follow Whitney from the room.

I head down the hall toward the smaller dance studios.

I know it's Anya as soon as I spot her lithe form through the small window in the door. I open it without knocking. An intriguing musical score greets me, an intricate combination of classical music and a more modern beat. The tune is both haunting and powerful, catching my interest immediately.

Anya twirls across the floor as the music crescendos. Her legs twine, seeming to meld into one limb as she spins faster and faster. Her arms shift in a mesmerizing flow that holds my attention.

Suddenly, one of her legs shoots back, halting her progress across the floor. She dips her body low. Her legs split, one foot arcing up toward the ceiling. At the same moment, the beat drops.

My heart stops, affected by the perfectly timed choreography.

Only then do I notice the tall blond dancer who steps forward. He captures her ankle in his grasp, freezing her motion. He looks younger than her last partner, more gangly than muscled and almost as tall as I am.

He seems like the kind of guy who might spend nights playing Call of Duty with his friends and go home every Sunday for lunch with his mom.

But that doesn't stop the burning jealousy from ripping through me as his hand forces Anya back into motion. Her leg swings back down until she tips backward, falling into his arms. Her legs strike a gracefully angular pose.

"The fuck?" I demand as they pause there.

The guy's face is turned to look longingly down at Anya. Her own gaze turns toward the floor.

"Nicolo!" Anya gasps, her face paling as her eyes find mine.

The music continues to blare from the speakers as her partner rights her in an instant. He steps back, like a kid caught with his hand in the cookie jar.

"What are you doing here?" she asks breathlessly as she rushes to turn off the music.

"I could ask you the same thing." I eye her partner with dislike.

"We're practicing." Anya's tone is defensive as she turns to face me, her frustration evident. "This is Robbie. He's my new partner. He's helping me with the winter showcase since Fin won't be back before the end of the semester."

A hint of accusation lingers there. I know she's thinking about how I'm the reason she has a new partner.

"Nice to meet you, Robbie. Now get the fuck out," I say flatly.

Robbie jumps into motion, doing as I say without a moment's hesitation. He's out the door in several long strides. Anya's gaze doesn't waver from mine as he disappears into the hall. She's pissed. Her lips press into a thin white line. Her arms tense as her hands ball into fists.

"What is wrong with you?" she explodes as soon as we're alone. "You can't keep chasing away my partners! I have to dance with someone, Nicolo."

"I don't see why." I stride closer until we're face to face.

"If you won't let me dance with anyone else, then, do you plan on being my dance partner?" She closes the distance further to glare up at me with intense fury.

I scoff. The thought of me donning a pair of tights to dance with her is so utterly ridiculous. I can't help but find it humorous. "Why don't you dance alone?"

"Because that's not the requirement. We're supposed to have a choreographed *duet*," she snaps. "And just because you decided to go all Al Capone on my last partner doesn't mean I can up and change my piece to a solo act!"

Anya trembles with rage. I've never wanted to fuck her more.

"I think you can," I murmur. Brushing a stray golden curl back from her temple, I tuck it behind her ear. "In fact, I want you to prove it." Tracing her jawline with the pad of my thumb, I make my way toward her chin. Gently, I stroke across her full pink lips.

Anya swallows visibly. Her sky-colored eyes dilate in response. My cock stiffens, knowing I can turn her on with just one touch.

"Come on, little bird. Dance for me." I step back toward the speaker her phone is plugged into so I can start the music from the beginning. Then I turn to Anya, crossing my arms over my chest as I scrutinize her closely.

Anya hesitates, still standing in the same spot where I left her. As the first tones of the violin filter into the room, Anya bites her lip, but she doesn't move.

"Dance, Anya," I command more assertively.

Anya flinches, my order seeming to bring her out of her frozen stance.

Obeying, she takes her position. She holds her pose for the brief symphonic introduction. When the first pulsing tones of the contemporary beat fill the air, they bring her body to life.

Bending and twisting, Anya brings shape to the deeply melancholic tune overlaid with bursts of violin. The song has a steady rhythm, an unmistakable pulsing beat. But Anya's fluid movements, her graceful arcs and twirls, refine it. She transforms it into a masterpiece.

I see the moment she becomes swept up in her art. She gets lost in the music. Her face relaxes as her body responds to the song as though she were born to dance it.

Something inside me shifts as Anya dances for me alone. I'm bewitched by her captivating movements. I find myself unable to look away, unable to speak, unable to breathe. I'm intoxicated as she transforms into an otherworldly being right before my eyes. The music reveals the goddess she keeps locked inside.

Anya rises up onto her toes, and her eyes meet mine as the music begins to crescendo. She spins again and again, faster and faster with every turn. Slowly, she makes her way across the room to me. And with every turn, her eyes find mine.

A shiver runs down my spine as an inferno roars to life in my chest. Pulled forward by an indisputable force, I step toward her. Like a powerful magnet, we're drawn together. Anya twirls weightlessly across the floor as I reach for her.

And when the beat drops, it's me who stops her. Our chests collide, and my hands find her slender waist to steady her. She remains poised on her toes, her arms curved gracefully above her head.

Like a moment suspended in time, we stand frozen. Our eyes lock as Anya's warm breaths burst from her lips to tickle my face and neck.

The fire in her eyes is something I've never seen before. It's not the anger or resentment I've come to consider my constant companion. This is a yearning, a hunger I never thought I would find in her. Instantly, I'm rock-hard in my jeans. I've never wanted to taste Anya more than I do in this moment.

I don't hesitate. Snaking my arms firmly around her waist, I pull Anya to me as I kiss her. And the kiss she returns sets my soul on fire. Her arms fall around my shoulders as her tongue strokes hungrily between my lips.

She explores me like never before. I groan with the intensity of my arousal and pull her closer still, lifting her off her toes.

Her legs wrap around my waist as Anya grinds into me with vigor.

"I fucking have to have you. Right here. Right now," I rasp.

Anya nods, making my cock throb.

Sinking onto the studio's mats, I lower Anya to the floor without breaking our kiss. The taste of her honey lips is driving me crazy. She seems to have lost all sense of restraint as she nips and kisses me in return.

I yank her ballet skirt down over her hips and growl with frustration when I find her leotard blocking my path to her heavenly pussy. But that doesn't deter me.

Rocking back onto my knees, I run my hands up over Anya's heaving breasts. I reach the top of her sleeves. She doesn't object when I pull her leotard down forcefully, exposing her perfect nipples. I strip her of her top and bottoms all at once. The leggings go next. Then she's lying fully exposed in the middle of the dance studio.

Anya's hands reach for my shirt as he rises up off the mats. She lifts just enough to grab the hem and haul it over my head. Several buttons break free, pinging across the floor from the assertive maneuver.

Fucking Christ she's sexy when she wants me.

I don't wait for her to take off my jeans.

Instead, as she flings my shirt aside, I dip my shoulders between her thighs.

I spread them as my lips find her pussy. Tangy juices coat my tongue as I stroke between her folds.

"Oh, God!" Anya gasps, making my balls tighten almost painfully.

She slumps back onto the studio mats with a thump. When I raise my gaze to look across the flat planes of her body, her pert breasts swell, arching upward as she breathes heavily.

The sight of her enthusiasm, the taste of her arousal drives me mad with need. I love this new side of Anya. More than breaking her with my punishments, I find her wild abandon intoxicating. Exhilarating.

Stroking my tongue up over her clit, I circle it. I relish the way her legs shudder around me. Her hips rise up off the mats in response, and I grip them firmly. I massage her soft flesh as I repeat the pattern. Licking her pussy lips, I then circle her clit with my tongue.

"Oh, fuck," Anya moans breathlessly.

Though I doubt anyone can hear us over the music, I can tell she's fighting to stay quiet.

I hum with amusement as I suck her clit into my mouth. Then I flick my tongue across the tiny bundle of nerves. Anya's hips jerk. Her fingers comb into my hair as she grabs it. Her clit throbs against my lips every time I increase my suction.

Wanting to taste Anya's cum before I fuck her, I slide two fingers into her wet pussy. I finger her even as I keep my lips locked around her clit. Anya mewls, her fingers spasming in my hair. My cock pulses against the zipper of my jeans.

Curling my fingers to press against her G-spot, I egg her on. I can tell she's close as her walls tighten around me, restricting my movement.

I finger fuck her harder in response. Thrusting forcefully forward into that hidden spot, I send her over the edge.

Anya's back arches up off the mats. Her lips part in a silent cry of ecstasy. Her pussy clamps down around my fingers and starts to pulse. Her clit twitches against my tongue as she orgasms hard. Fresh cum slicks my fingers.

Withdrawing them, I replace my fingers with my tongue. I stroke inside her tight pussy as I lap up her juices. Anya shudders as she collapses back onto the mats. When I rise to look at her, her eyes are glazed with lust. Her chest heaves, beckoning to me. Her legs go limp, spreading her knees further.

Unbuttoning my pants, I shove them down quickly, letting my erection spring free.

Then I fall between her thighs.

Anya's so wet that I slide inside her easily. She gasps from the sudden penetration. Then her head rises from the mat until her lips meet mine.

The thought of her tasting her own arousal on my tongue excites me. I thrust more forcefully as my balls throb.

Anya's groan of pleasure zings down my spine, making me tingle with anticipation.

I won't last long at this rate.

"You feel so fucking good," I grit between my teeth.

"Nico!" she moans as her walls tighten around my cock.

Fucking Christ. The sound of my name on her lips is like a bolt of lightning through my chest.

Her fingers press into the flesh of my back as I crush her beneath me. I feel every inch of her soft skin sliding against mine as I move on top of her.

And I rock deep within her wet depths.

"Come for me, *mia bella*," I rasp.

I feel my own orgasm building at the base of my spine.

Anya cries out, burying her face in my shoulder to muffle the sound. And as her walls clamp down around my hard length, I shove deep inside her, filling her with my seed.

Shuddering together, we gasp as we collapse onto the black mats.

30

ANYA

I don't know what we're doing for our date tonight, but as I slip into my green silk dress–the halter-top one with a small train that Nicolo bought for me–I find I'm actually excited.

Something's shifted. Over the last week, Nicolo has shown genuine interest in me. He's opening up, too, telling me details about his life that give me glimpses deep into his soul. Still, they never touch on his family's business or his responsibilities within it.

I think the fear of losing his sister shook Nicolo more than he's willing to admit. And at the same time, it's like his whole motivation for being with me has changed. He still fucks me every time we're together, but even that has changed into something more passionate, less forceful.

I pin my hair up into a loose bun that allows a few golden curls to fall casually around my face. Then I turn in the mirror to admire the cut of the dress. It scoops low enough in the back to reveal my dimples there, and while I might usually be shy about the amount of exposed skin, this dress is so elegant, I hardly mind.

Not to mention, I find the thought of Nicolo's eyes on me far more enticing now.

The memory of Nicolo commanding me to dance for him sends a shiver down my spine. The way his eyes followed me, the lust burning within them. I couldn't hold onto my anger over him treating Robbie like shit.

In that studio, as I danced for Nicolo, I felt the connection crackling between us. I *wanted* to dance for him. And when our eyes met, it rocked me to my core.

As though all my passion for ballet had somehow fused with my undeniable attraction toward Nicolo, I couldn't stop myself.

I wanted him. And fuck did it feel good. No one had ever gone down on me like that before, and the sex was something else entirely. As though he was turned on by my need for him. He fucked me with a passionate kind of tenderness he's never shown before.

I had wanted him to come inside me for the first time. And the feel of our simultaneous orgasms had made me lightheaded, it was so over-whelming.

I'm still conflicted about the whole arrangement–selling my body to ensure my loved ones' safety. And yet, with this new, more vulnerable side of Nicolo, I find myself drawn to him more and more. Without reason and against my better judgment, I have found myself succumbing to my attraction.

I take the time to apply a hint of eyeliner and mascara as I contemplate what we could possibly be doing for our date tonight. Nicolo has been unusually secretive about it. He's dropped hints, giving me a sly smile as he promises I'm going to like it.

He told me I should wear my best dress. But no matter how many times I've asked, he's chosen to leave me in the dark.

My stomach quivers with anticipation as I slip into my peacoat and head toward the front door. He can't possibly refuse me a jacket today, when frost still lingers on the windows and trees well past noon. My dress has no sleeves or back to it, and I would be frozen in no time.

The house is exceedingly quiet as I walk through the living room toward the front door. Aunt Patritsiya has taken Clara to the Children's Museum for the day, and already, I miss my little girl.

A smile tugs at my lips as I lock our apartment and carefully make my way down the stairs in my black high heels. I'm still not quite used to walking in glamorous shoes. It seems somewhat ironic that I can balance on the tips of my toes without a second thought, but I wobble slightly with every step on the pencil-thin stilettos.

Nicolo's driver is supposed to pick me up today–part of the surprise–so I stand on the curb a few minutes before four and look down the road in the direction he should come from. My breath plumes before me, and I pull my coat tighter around me to ward off the chill.

As I wait, my mind wanders to Nicolo once more and this mysterious date he has planned. I don't know why, but I feel as though something has changed for him. He never would have planned a date like this for me when we first got together. *Would he?*

I wonder if that might not have been his intention with the shopping date, only he hadn't cared to understand me back then. He thought he might impress me simply by buying me nice things. The notion intrigues me.

While we haven't changed anything about our arrangement, I do find I'm starting to enjoy our time together. I even feel like we're starting to form a connection, in some strange way. He's sharing more with me emotionally and actually seems to care about what I think.

Still, I can't let myself fall for him. Not again.

He could too easily drop me as soon as my feelings get real.

A cold gust of wind cuts through the thin fabric of my dress. I shiver, glancing down the road to see if Nicolo's driver is almost here.

A black SUV turns the corner onto my street, and I release a sigh of relief. I feel like my lips might be turning purple with the cold. The

SUV pulls up to the curb. Classic tinted windows make it impossible to see if Nicolo waits inside. It's all part of the surprise.

The door pops open a moment later, and a burly bodyguard steps out to usher me inside. I don't hesitate to slide across the fine leather seat, anticipating the warmth within. As the guard follows me back into the car and closes the door, I glance up for the first time.

And meet the familiar hate-filled gaze of Troy Gatti.

My heart stops.

I recognize him from that night at Danza, but if I had any question in my mind, the cast encasing his right arm confirms it. My pulse jump starts back to life. A cold sweat breaks out across my brow.

From the look in his eyes, he has something in store for me, and I won't like it one bit.

"Well, look what the cat dragged in," Troy drawls, leaning back against the seat and turning to look at the guy next to him.

"I'd say we caught ourselves some proper bait," the man says.

My heart skips a beat as I absorb the meaning behind his words. I study his face, searching for any hint of empathy there, but all I find is cold rage. He has the same strong, Italian features as Troy, the same almond eyes and sneering lips.

Though he looks several years older than Troy, I can only assume they're related–brothers would be my guess. Which means that Nicolo killed their father, and I've just willingly entered their vehicle.

Panic floods my brain. Without a second thought, I scramble for the door, desperate to escape. The brothers release a bone-chilling chorus of laughs as the guard sitting next to me snatches up my wrists. He effectively restrains me before I even have a chance to fight back.

The second guard reaches across my shoulders and shoves me back against the seat. The driver pulls away from the curb, taking me away from my home, from safety.

"Where are you off to in such a hurry?" the older Gatti sneers. "We just want to have a bit of fun."

Troy chuckles darkly. "Alexia, don't toy with the poor girl. She'll be begging us for death by the night's end. It's just cruel and unusual to give her a sense of false hope."

Alexia flashes a look toward Troy that says Troy ought to keep his mouth shut. "You'll have to excuse my younger brother," he says, turning his cold eyes back to me. "He can be a bit... crass sometimes."

"What do you want from me?" I demand, putting as much strength into my voice as I can. I don't know what I can possibly do to get out of this situation. But I can't bring myself to cower, to give them the pleasure of watching me beg.

"What do we want?" Alexia's tone drips with false confusion. "Well, we want our father back. But seeing as neither you, your boyfriend, nor God Almighty has the power to deliver him to us, we'll take what we can get."

"Now who's toying with her?" Troy gripes, casting a sideways glance at his brother.

Alexia completely ignores the rib as he keeps his eyes leveled on mine. A shiver runs down my spine as I see the intense hatred within their depths.

I swallow hard as I cast my mind for any means of escape. But I'm surrounded by men almost twice my size. They seem completely at ease with the thought of hurting me–killing me, even.

"What are you going to do to me?" I ask, and this time, my voice quivers.

Alexia slides forward on his seat, his gaze more intent now, as if he's glad I asked. "We're going to torture you," he says gleefully.

"We're going to cut you up bit by bit and send pieces of you back to your self-righteous fuck of a boyfriend. And when we're done with you, Nicolo will know not to fuck with the Gattis ever again. He took my father from me. Now I'm going to take what he cares about."

The snort that escapes my lips surprises even me. "You think I'm what Nicolo cares about?" I ask in disbelief.

These guys clearly don't understand the arrangement.

A flash of uncertainty dances across the brothers' faces.

Alexia quickly recovers, masking his moment of hesitation with a dark chuckle. "You're trying to play games with us, to convince us that we've got the wrong person. But I assure you, short of Silvia Marchetti–who's impossible to get to after our botched attempt to kidnap her–"

He flashes Troy a withering look that makes his younger brother scowl.

"You are what Nicolo cares most about in this world. He spends more time focused on you than he does the *family business*."

Alexia's words unsettle me. That can't be true. Sure, Nicolo was obsessed with tormenting me at the start of the year, and yes, we've spent a considerable amount of time together lately–especially after what happened to his sister.

But that was about Nicolo finding a way to release the stress of his situation. It has nothing to do with me personally. He's already made it perfectly clear that I'm completely disposable to him. Forgettable, even.

Still, my pulse quickens. At one point in my life, I would have given anything to be what Nicolo cared for most. But right now, I'm faced with the cold, hard reality that not only do I not mean something to him–even the possibility of it has put my life on the line. I'm going to die, and I don't even get the added benefit of knowing that Nicolo loves me.

Instead, my body turns to ice as I realize that I will be leaving Clara an orphan when she's little more than a baby. I don't relish the thought of dying, but the thought of leaving my beautiful baby girl behind is unbearable. And she will be an orphan, because when I die, the knowledge of who her father is dies with me.

"You know, I think I'm going to like the sound of your screams," Alexia taunts, a smile spreading across his lips.

Irrational anger consumes me as I look across the car at the Gatti brothers' sneering faces.

I do the only thing I can think of to show them just how much I hate them.

I spit.

My saliva lands on Alexia's cheek, and his head jerks back in shock. His fingers go to his face as he wipes away the fluid. Troy laughs at the unforgivable sign of disrespect.

Alexia's dark eyes burn with a new form of fury, and his hand comes out of nowhere. He backhands me so hard, it flings me sideways across the lap of a bodyguard. A loud ringing fills my ears as I see stars.

31

NICOLO

My foot taps impatiently as I sit in the intimate dining establishment of Oriole, one of the chicest fine-dining restaurants Chicago has to offer.

I have to admit, I'm nervous about this date. Tonight, I want to do something I know Anya will like. She's helped me work through my anger and stress over the thwarted attack on my sister. The thought that one of our enemies got so close to harming Silvia has been more than a small hurdle for me to overcome.

And through it all, Anya has been there. She's even talked with me in a way I don't talk with anyone. It's been really nice.

And after the way she danced for me at school, I'm more drawn toward her than ever, more connected. I crave her approval, something I've never sought in the girls I've dated. So tonight, I'm taking her to see *Dracula* at the Civic Opera House. It's a ballet, and at some point in our conversations, she mentioned how much she enjoyed seeing them as a child.

Reaching for my glass of wine, I take another sip and realize it's empty. *Where the hell is she?* She should be here by now. It's nearing five o'clock, and my driver was supposed to pick her up at four. Glancing at my watch yet again, I confirm the time.

It irks me that she's making me wait. A niggling thought that she might have stood me up worms into the back of my mind. She wouldn't dare. Not when she knows I'm willing to punish her. *Would she? I've even conceded to her keeping her new dance partner, so why would she choose to piss me off now?*

Lifting my phone off the table, I dial Anya for the third time in the last twenty minutes. It rings. And rings. And rings. I grind my teeth when I get her voicemail once again. Pounding the red button, I end the call with unnecessary force.

No one makes me wait over a half hour–definitely not my pet who's finally earned a reward. If this is how she's going to behave, perhaps I was too hasty to think she deserved something nice.

I call my driver, who was supposed to pick her up.

"Where are you?" I growl when he answers on the third ring. "Why are you making me wait? If she's taking this long, go up to Anya's apartment and drag her out by her hair."

"This is Sep."

My bodyguard's deep voice rumbles gravely across the line, giving me pause. *Why would he be answering my driver's phone?*

"I'm sorry, sir. Just as we were pulling around the corner to pick up Miss Orlov, she got into a strange vehicle. It looked like one belonging to the Gattis."

My stomach drops as the air leaves my lungs in a whoosh.

"We're in pursuit now. We won't lose sight of her, sir."

"What direction are they heading?" I demand.

"South, toward the shipping yard if I had to guess."

Ilya Popov's territory. He won't like us crossing boundary lines, but I won't let that stop me if the Gattis have Anya.

"Keep me informed. I'll meet you there," I growl and hang up before he can respond.

The next number I dial is my father's, and I give him a rapid-fire explanation of the situation. "I'm going after them," I finish gruffly, brooking no argument.

"Good. No one takes what belongs to the Marchettis and gets away with it," my father says. "I'm sending men for reinforcements."

If I can say one good thing about my father, it's that he never fails to back me up when a demonstration of strength is necessary. He has always backed me if I think violence is the best answer. And in our line of work, it's often the only answer.

I don't even count the bills as I toss them onto the table. I make a beeline for the door. Snatching my Maserati's keys off the valet board, I stride out into the cold evening air and head straight for the parking garage.

Thankfully my car is built for speed. I floor it as soon as I'm free of the parking structure. Racing down the city streets of Chicago, I weave in and out of traffic. I don't bat an eye when I run a red light.

I thought I'd been furious with Anya for making me wait. All kinds of elaborate punishments had flashed through my mind as I sat there, feeling her rejection with every passing moment.

But now that I know she's in danger, that I could lose her, all that pent-up rage is laser-focused on the men responsible. I will kill every last one of the Gattis for what they've done.

If I had a doubt that they were responsible for Silvia's attack, I'm confident now. And I plan on ripping them limb from limb when I find them. A location pings on my phone a moment later. Sep dropping a pin at the warehouse just blocks from the shipping yard.

"Fuck!" I shout, slamming my hand against the steering wheel as I urge my car faster down Highway 41.

The warehouses there are perfect spots to kill victims and dispose of them without getting caught. They're practically abandoned and far enough from traffic to avoid notice.

Anxiety chokes my throat in an iron grip as I think about Anya in the hands of the Gattis. I killed their father. I have no doubts they took Anya to exact revenge. I did this. I put Anya in danger, and if something happens to her, I will never forgive myself.

Putting my phone on speaker as I race against the clock, I call Sep directly.

"Talk to me," I demand as soon as he picks up.

"They're parked outside the warehouses. Haven't gone in yet. We're just down the street, watching to see which building they enter. I don't think they know we're here, so that will give us a slight advantage. You give the word, boss, and we'll make a move."

I glance down at my car's GPS. Ten minutes out as I blow through ninety. The speedometer creeps closer to a hundred miles an hour. "Wait for me. I'm almost there. Observe and report for now. Let me know if they take her inside. I want to hear about her condition as well–as soon as you find out. Will she need medical attention? Is she conscious?"

"Yes, sir."

Hanging up, I drum the steering wheel nervously. I feel like I might snap from the tension building inside me. Those fuckers are dead. No one lays a hand on Anya. She's mine. I don't care what I've done. She doesn't deserve what they plan on doing to her.

They took her to hurt me. It puts my stomach in knots to realize they must have been watching me, waiting, analyzing how they could inflict the most pain. And they've done it. All I see is red as I barrel across town, smashing every speed limit. I've never wanted to kill someone so badly in my life.

When the warehouse lot finally comes into view, I bring my car down to a more acceptable speed. It won't do me any good to get spotted before I've had a chance to meet up with my men. We need to form a strategy.

My phone pings as I round the corner and spot the Escalade that was supposed to pick Anya up tonight. Glancing down, I see the image of Anya, bound and gagged as several men lead her into the warehouse nearest us.

From the grainy sunset-lit picture, I can faintly make out her expression. She looks utterly terrified, but at least she's conscious. This must have happened just minutes ago.

Pulling up behind the Escalade, I throw my Maserati in park and dash the short distance to join Sep and Rocco in the back seat of the SUV.

"Your father's men are still about ten minutes out," Rocco says as soon as I close the door behind me.

"We're not waiting for them," I state. "That looked like four men—two of which are the Gatti brothers. And Troy's got a broken wing. We can take them easily with the element of surprise."

My guards nod agreement, no question, no hesitation in their gazes. They trust me, and they are trained professionals. They would follow me into the pits of hell if I asked them to.

"My father's men can join the festivities when they arrive," I add, attempting levity to ease my own tension.

Sep smiles darkly. "We'll be halfway back to town by the time they show up," he jokes.

I bark a laugh, accepting the two Sig Sauers Rocco passes me. "We move fast, stay low. Stick to the building until I can assess the situation. Then move on my signal," I say.

Short and sweet. Once we get inside, I'm sure all hell will break loose, so I don't plan what to do from there.

"And don't *fucking* shoot my girl," I add, putting force behind my words.

Slipping silently from the back seat into the growing dusk, I lead my men across the bare expanse of parking lot. We move noiselessly, making it to the warehouse. I hug the metal siding as Sep and Rocco fall in behind me.

Muffled voices come from within the basic structure, one distinctly female, as we pass by the closed garage door. I can't help the sense of pride that swells within my chest at the sound of Anya's defiance. Her words are obscured by a gag, I assume. But her cadence is rebellious. If I had to guess, she just told someone to go fuck themselves.

The resounding snap that follows makes my blood boil.

I creep quickly closer to the warehouse's side door where we'll enter.

"Tie her up," comes the muffled command as I reach the door.

I recognize Alexia's voice. The fucking bastard. He's going to regret messing with my family–if he survives long enough to face my wrath.

I hear scuffling through the door. Then Anya's cry spurs me into action. Gripping the door handle, I force myself to turn it slowly.

First, I have to find the men's positions. Then we can attack.

If we go in guns a-blazing, we're as likely to kill Anya as we are the Gattis and their men.

32

ANYA

"No one's coming for you, little ballerina," Troy taunts as my eyes flit desperately toward the warehouse door.

My cheek stings from the fresh blow, Alexia used to silence me. I swallow around the cloth that gags my mouth. I know no one is coming for me. *How could anyone know where I am? That I'm in trouble?*

I got into their car without a second glance. My aunt and daughter weren't even there to see me leave. I'm sure Nicolo is furious with me by now for not being where I'm supposed to be. But that could mean any of a thousand things to him.

Why would he automatically assume these psychos have driven me to a warehouse on the outskirts of town with the intention of chopping me into little pieces?

That doesn't stop me from searching for a means of escape.

When my eyes land on the table where Alexia and Troy stand, my heart breaks into a sprint. Knife after cruel-looking knife is laid out methodically across its surface. An overwhelming panic fills me as I scream.

I twist forcefully against the bindings holding me in my chair, fighting to break free. The skin around my wrists stings as the coarse rope chafes my flesh. Alexia releases a cruel laugh at my fruitless efforts.

I'm trapped, completely helpless as I face my own death. All I can think about is my daughter and Nicolo. They will never know their connection because the truth of it will die with me.

Tears of rage sting the back of my eyes. It's probably best that Nicolo never knows about Clara. Not when this could happen to the people he might care about. I'm just his fuck toy, and look where it's gotten me.

Picking up a wickedly curved knife, Alexia turns to face me. He holds the blade up so it shines in the light. "Are you ready, Anya?" he taunts.

From the corner of my eye, Troy looks rather pouty. He wanted the opportunity to cut me up himself. I imagine Alexia might let him have a turn once he's gotten his pound of flesh. Those words take on new meaning for me. Now that I'm faced with true and actual pain at the hands of a madman.

Alexia slowly stalks toward me, a vicious grin spreading across his face. Blood roars in my ears as my heart pounds a mile a minute. My ribs ache with the force of its hammering.

"Where shall we start?" he asks conversationally. He traces the blade down my cheek to my jaw. "Your face? It's so pretty. I'm sure Nicolo will hate to see it cut up beyond recognition."

The tip of the blade skims lower, down past my collar bone to follow the valley between my breasts. I close my eyes and swallow hard. Fighting back my nausea, I prepare for the blade's bite. With a flick of the wrist, Alexia draws it away from my skin, leaving me unblemished.

I dare to open my eyes, and the fury that twists his face makes me wish I hadn't.

Gripping my hand forcefully, Alexia crushes my palm to the chair arm I'm bound to. "Let's start with a finger," he growls, bringing the knife down with conviction.

My lungs burn with the force of the scream that rips from me. I turn away, unable to endure the sight of my impending dismemberment.

Then pain explodes in my ear as deafening sounds echo through the warehouse.

Frozen in fear, I can't bring myself to look. I hunch down in my chair, leaning as far away from my ensnared hand as possible. Another deafening report fills the space, then another. And suddenly, chaos surrounds me. Men shout and dive for cover.

The pressure on my hand releases at the same moment as something hot and wet spatters my cheek and chest. It brings me back to my senses.

Turning, I try to make sense of the scene around me. My eyes grow wide. Alexia's open, unseeing eyes stare up at me. Blood oozes from a wound in his neck. I flinch as bullets ping and ricochet around me. Each shot drills into my ears with deafening force.

Troy's panicked shouts call from behind the table that had once been covered with torture devices. It's now upturned to serve as a meager shield. I curl in on myself to make my body as small as possible. Bullets fly by me in either direction.

Something heavy falls behind me—one of their bodyguards I would guess. Screams quickly follow. They sound like what I can only imagine is the younger Gatti brother dying painfully.

The gunfire slows. Then I hear a deep grunt followed by an immediate ceasefire.

Cautiously, I unfold my body enough to look around the back of my chair. The two burly bodyguards who had restrained me lie dead in a pool of their own blood.

Uncontrollable shivers rack my body. I can't seem to process what just happened. For an instant, I wonder if I'm not going into shock after losing a finger. But when I muster enough courage to look down at my hand, all my digits are still attached.

Fresh commotion draws my gaze to the side entrance the Gatti brothers brought me through. A wave of utter panic consumes me.

Then I see Nicolo.

Overwhelming relief leaves me dizzy. How he knew to come for me–let alone how to find me–I have no clue.

"Are you alright?" Nicolo demands as he kneels in front of me.

He pulls my makeshift gag from my mouth.

Behind him, his two bodyguards fan out. They keep their guns raised as they check the men for pulses and search the warehouse for others.

My ears ring from the ghost of gunshots. I can barely make out Nicolo's words as my eyes follow his lips. Buzzing numbness tingles across my skin. Still, I try to make sense of his question.

Am I alright? I don't know.

Nicolo's hands and eyes examine me gently. His fingers graze lightly across my throbbing cheek. He wipes at the liquid that's started to cake on my face and chest.

"Did they hurt you?" he persists.

Fighting to break through the fog of numbness, I shake my head. I'm not seriously injured anyway. Relief washes across his face, and the hint of a smile pulls at his proud lips.

"Well, little bird. What do you think about my violence now?" he asks, gesturing to Alexia's deathly still body. "Does it still sicken you?"

I know he's teasing me, calling back to the night he broke Troy's arm. But the full weight of what just happened comes crashing down on me then.

I burst into tears.

Overwhelmed with emotion, I sob. My breaths rasp in and out of my burning lungs. I screamed so loudly in my fear that I left them raw.

Nicolo's face falls. Humor fleeing, he gently cups my face in his hands. His thumbs smooth away my tears as quickly as they fall.

"Shh, you're alright, Anya. It's over. You're safe. Shh," he soothes. "I won't ever let anyone hurt you," he promises adamantly.

He reaches for the cruel knife that lies beside Alexia's hand. I shudder violently as it gleams in the fluorescent lighting. Cautiously, Nicolo slides the blade between the chair and my wrists. He cuts through my bindings with ease, freeing me.

Blood pumps back out to the tips of my fingers, making my hands tingle. I massage my wrists as Nicolo stoops to cut the ropes tying my ankles to the chair.

Then Nicolo scoops me effortlessly into his arms. I wrap my arms around his neck, clinging to him, desperate for his protective warmth.

I don't know when they arrived, but around ten other men, all dressed in fine Italian suits, stand near the warehouse entrance. Some look out, as if to keep watch. Others sweep the area for lingering danger.

"I'll leave this for you boys to clean up," Nicolo says authoritatively.

He carries me toward the door, cradling me close to his chest.

I let him, sure that if he tried to set me on my feet, my legs would be too weak to stand.

Armed men escort us to his sleek black Maserati. I don't know why that particular detail shocks me, but I'm surprised to find Nicolo drove here himself.

With all the men at his disposal, he could have just handed my rescue over to them. *Why didn't he?*

Carefully easing me into the passenger seat, Nicolo ensures I'm fully inside the car. Then he closes the door and rounds the front of the vehicle to get into the driver's side. The Maserati purrs to life, and we're on our way.

The warehouse where I almost died fades into the distance moments later.

"How... how did you find me?" My words come out on a whisper when I finally find my voice.

"The car I sent for you. They were just around the corner and saw you get into the Gattis' car. They followed you to the warehouse and alerted me."

Well, that explains a lot. Deep gratitude warms me. I'm alive because of his men's astute observation and quick action. Then my brow presses into a frown. "But then, how did *you* get here so quickly?"

Even if his men had called Nicolo right away, he would have been somewhere else entirely. Probably at whatever location he was supposed to meet me. His reaction time must have been quite fast.

Nicolo shrugs casually. "This car was built for speed," he says lightly.

My eyes grow round as I consider that. It took me and my captors a considerable amount of time to get to the warehouse. And we weren't going particularly slow. Nicolo must have been flying to make up for lost time.

"Thank you," I breathe as my emotions overwhelm me once more.

In response, Nicolo simply reaches across the console and takes my hand, enveloping my icy fingers in warmth.

In what feels like no time at all, we're back in the city. I register my surroundings for the first time in the dim evening light as Nicolo pulls into the underground garage of his penthouse.

"You're not taking me home?" Surprised, I turn to face him.

Nicolo parks his car before meeting my eyes with a hint of concern. "I thought you might like to get cleaned up before you went back to your family." He hesitates. "And if I'm perfectly honest, the thought of letting you out of my sight tonight is more than I can bear."

My heart quickens, thrumming an irregular pattern at the meaning behind his words. "Okay," I murmur, unsure of what else to say. Then my mind shifts to Clara and my aunt. "I should just let my family know."

Nicolo's eyes soften. "Of course. Let's get you upstairs, and you can call whoever you need."

I nod gratefully as fresh tears sting the back of my eyes. He's being so gentle, so kind, and I don't know what to make of it. After everything that's happened tonight, it leaves me feeling like I'm in some kind of dream.

33

ANYA

"Would you like a drink?" Nicolo offers as we step into the open layout of his penthouse.

"Yes, please." My voice is slowly coming back to me.

He leaves me in the living room to make my calls, heading into the kitchen to fix us cocktails.

I don't trust myself not to cry if I hear Aunt Patritsiya's voice, so instead, I text her. *Out for a drink with a friend. Might not make it home tonight, so don't wait up. I'll see you in the morning.* I send the text with a heart emoji.

Glancing up, I watch Nicolo bring me a generous tumbler of amber liquid.

He presses the glass into my hand and clinks it with his own. I sniff the drink, unfamiliar with it, and wish I hadn't. The scent burns the inside of my nose.

Nicolo smiles. "It's whiskey. It'll burn on the way down, but it'll warm you up. You haven't stopped shivering."

I look down at my hands and realize he's right.

"Thanks," I say gratefully and watch him down the shot like a glass of water.

I imitate him, taking the drink in one large gulp. Immediately, I regret it. I force the flaming liquid down my throat, then cough and sputter as my face contorts. Holding the back of my hand over my lips, I will myself to not spray the whiskey all over Nicolo's carpet.

Nicolo's chuckle warms me as much as the drink does, burning its way down to my belly. I'm surprised at how effectively it chases away the bone-chilling cold.

"Did you talk to whoever you needed to reach?" he asks.

I glance down at my phone and see my aunt's reply. *See you tomorrow. Be safe.*

The cautionary words bring tears to my eyes, and I sniff them back before I start crying.

"Yes. All set." I tuck my phone back into my jacket pocket and look up to meet Nicolo's hazel gaze.

It's so gentle, my breath catches in my lungs. I stand momentarily stunned.

"Let's clean you up," he offers.

He takes my glass from me, setting it aside. Then he gathers my frigid fingers in his.

I follow him wordlessly as he leads me into the back of his condo, through the impressive master bedroom, and into the master bath that never fails to astound me. It's spacious and decorated with the finest marble and stone. A clawfoot tub occupies one corner. A glass shower with two ceiling-mounted showerheads occupies another.

Nicolo leads me to the tub and turns on the water. He tests its temperature before he turns his attention to me.

Carefully, he eases my jacket over my shoulders. He lets it drop to the floor, uncovering my beautiful silk dress for the first time this evening.

A flicker of desire fills Nicolo's gaze as he admires how the dress hugs my body. Reaching around my neck, he takes the ends of the halter-top ties and pulls, releasing them.

The top falls from my shoulders, revealing my bare breasts. Encouraging the soft fabric down over my hips, Nicolo lets it pool around my feet.

Then he holds my hand to stabilize me so I can step out of it.

A shuddering breath escapes my lips as he kneels before me. But rather than removing my panties, he takes one high-heeled foot and slides my shoe off. Then the next.

His touch is gentle, careful almost, and not meant to explore or arouse.

Still, it sends tingles of pleasure racing across my flesh.

As he comes to a stand, he shrugs out of his dress coat and rolls up the sleeves of his shirt. Then he checks the water once more. As a last step, he slides my panties down around my ankles. Taking my hand, he supports me as he leads me into the tub.

Goosebumps burst across my flesh as the deep cold of my shock meets the hot water. I shiver more violently as I slowly lower into the tub. Then I'm encompassed by warmth. My heart pounds more confidently in my chest as my blood slowly thaws. For the first time in hours, my muscles start to relax.

Nicolo busies himself in the cabinet, pulling out a washcloth and bath soap. It smells like eucalyptus and lavender as soon as he opens the bottle.

Then he starts to clean my body. He begins with my face, dipping the rag into the hot water before brushing the washcloth over my forehead, my nose, my lips, my cheeks. The dried blood tugs on my skin before he washes it away. Alexia's blood, I realize for the first time.

He moves on to my neck and chest, gently washing away the events of the night, and his touch is so careful and patient.

A flicker of fury turns his hazel eyes green when he reaches my wrists. The skin is raw from where I struggled so hard against my bonds. He gently massages each angry-pink bracelet of flesh before setting them back into the water.

The soothing scent of the soap fills my nose, calming me with every breath. As Nicolo moves to wash my back, I pull my knees to my chest and rest my cheek on them. Suddenly, I'm bone tired. The whiskey combined with the hot bath and the lavender soap as Nicolo sponges me clean... I start nodding off.

"Let's get you to bed," he murmurs, bringing me back to the present.

He rises to bring me a towel.

I don't ever want to get out of this tub, but I know I can't sleep here. It's so wonderfully deep and full; I could easily drown if I did. Rising, I step from the tub and into the waiting terry cloth as Nicolo towels me dry.

"You can borrow one of my shirts for the night," he offers.

He walks me into the bedroom and opens his dresser.

Pulling out an oversized blue-and-red Cubs T-shirt, Nicolo helps me into it. It's large enough to hang down around my thighs.

"Why are you being so nice?" I ask, my sleep-addled brain short-circuiting my filter.

Nicolo pauses, as though I've asked him an exceptionally deep question. "Well, I guess... I just want you to be okay," he says finally, his tone laced with concern.

I smile drowsily as he puts me in his bed and pulls the covers up around me.

"Why are you smiling?" he asks, amusement and confusion in his voice.

"It's nice," I say simply, already halfway asleep.

"What?"

"That you care."

I think he chuckles, but I'm already asleep, so I can't be sure.

It's a warm summer's day, the heat hovering around me like a heavy blanket. I stand in the sunshine, my face turned up to feel it kiss my skin. As I wait on the street corner, I don't have a care in the world. I'm waiting for someone, but that doesn't matter.

Nicolo's black Maserati pulls up. It must be him who's picking me up. My heart flutters with excitement, and I make my way around the car to slide into the passenger seat.

He must have the AC turned up full blast because, as I sit, I feel as though I've stepped into a freezer. Sweat from the heat of the day turns to frost on my skin. I turn to Nicolo to ask him to turn the air down.

But it's not Nicolo. It's Alexia Gatti.

"You did this to yourself," he mocks, his eyes murderous.

Suddenly, I'm in a nightmare of my own making.

Alexia throws the car in drive, and we speed away. Terror freezes me to my chair, and my lungs feel as though I've swallowed cement. I can't breathe, can't speak. I'm trapped in my immobility.

Then the frigid car transforms. Tied to a hard wooden chair, I try to make sense of my surroundings. But all I see are lights and shadows. Alexia approaches, knife in hand.

"Where shall we start?" he asks conversationally. "Your face?"

The cold blade slides across my skin like a sliver of ice.

"No," he rasps. "I think we'll start with your throat."

Fire rips across my vocal chords as he slices my neck wide open.

I try to scream, but I can't. He's silenced me forever.

Wet blood spatters across my cheeks as my head falls back. Overwhelming fear consumes me as I bleed out.

The bloodcurdling shriek jolts through my body like a defibrillator. It sounds like some otherworldly being coming to drag me to hell. I thrash as strong arms wrap around me, pulling me down.

I wake with a start, the sound of my own scream bringing me back to consciousness. My pulse pounds through me at a thousand miles a minute.

"Easy, easy! It's just a dream, Anya. Just a dream."

Nicolo's deep, urgent voice calms me. His muscular arms hold me close against his chest, warming me as he brings me back to reality.

My scream peters into a sob as I realize I'm not dead. I'm no longer at Alexia's mercy. I shudder violently at the image of the older Gatti brother's sneering face burned into my mind.

"You're okay," Nicolo promises, his soft hand brushing hair away from my face. He leans up onto one elbow so he can look at me. His fingers stroke the tears from my cheeks.

My throat burns from how hard I screamed.

The deep concern in his eyes fills me with a smoldering fire. All I want to do is wipe the memory of the Gatti brothers from my mind. I want to forget everything. Without taking a moment to think, I lean up off my pillow and capture Nicolo's lips with mine.

He tenses, seeming momentarily shocked by my adamant kiss. Then he shifts on top of me as I roll beneath him, turning so his body aligns with mine. My fingers tangle in his dark curls as I close my eyes. And I kiss him with all the emotion building inside me.

His lips are passionate yet tender. They bend to my hunger as he strokes his tongue to twine with mine. He tastes of spearmint toothpaste.

The deeply masculine scent of his cologne fills my nose. It surrounds me, rooting me in the moment.

His arms encompass me as his body presses me into the mattress. I can feel him growing hard against my hips. Releasing his hair, I run my hands down over his well-muscled back.

He's not wearing a shirt.

My heart hammers against my ribs, bruising them with its force.

I don't care. All I want is for Nicolo to wipe away my nightmare.

"Fuck me," I murmur in his ear. My brush with death makes me feel more bold than I've ever been before.

Nicolo shivers violently in response.

Shifting my attention to my makeshift nighty, I grip the hem of the oversized T-shirt and pull it up over my hips, my waist, my ribs.

Nicolo lifts up off of me to help me along. I shove the fabric over my head, then sit up to help Nicolo out of his basketball shorts.

"You're sure?" he murmurs as I pull him down on top of me once more.

"I want you, Nico," I gasp. "Please."

Nicolo responds with enthusiasm. His lips find my neck as he trails feather kisses from my ear down to my shoulder. Bracing on one forearm, he massages me gently with his other hand. He kneads my breasts, tickles over the planes of my stomach, then presses between my thighs.

I gasp as he runs a finger along my wet slit. His shuddering breaths wash across my skin, warm and comforting.

Turning my head, I find his mouth in the dark. I demand kisses, tracing my tongue along his lower lip. The fire in his response sets my skin alight.

His fingers tease my clit, building my arousal into a roaring inferno.

"Please, Nico," I breathe against his lips, begging him this time.

I want all of him, filling me, stretching me, consuming me so entirely that I can't think of the horrible dream lingering in the back of my mind.

His cockhead presses between my slick folds, and my breathing quickens with anticipation. He eases into me, so I feel every inch of his impressive girth. I groan as he pushes inside of me up to the hilt. I relish the warmth of him everywhere all at once.

He rocks slowly in and out of me, and the soft way he fucks me makes my heart ache. My stomach quivers. He's never shown this level of tenderness during sex before. It brings tears prickling to my eyes. Fuck, I love it.

"Yes!" I gasp as I barrel toward an orgasm. "Oh, God. Nico!"

Nicolo's cock swells inside me, and I find my release. As the first wave of ecstasy grips me, I feel hot cum spurt deep inside my core.

A groan reverberates through Nicolo's chest and into my body as we come at the same time. His lips crush mine in a fierce kiss. His arms cradle me. His hips press me into the soft mattress.

Wave after wave of tingling euphoria consumes me, washing away all the anxiety and tension. Deep contentment from my powerful orgasm leaves my limbs limp, my skin electric to the lightest touch.

Nicolo's gasping breaths mingle with mine. He rests on his forearms, looking down on me, and his eyes shine with intense emotion.

"I love it when you call me Nico," he confesses, his lips turning up into a grin.

I hum contentedly, rising from my pillow to kiss him.

After several glorious moments, Nicolo eases out of me. Collapsing onto the bed beside me, he stares up at the ceiling.

I study his strong, devastatingly handsome face. Something has definitely shifted between us. For me, I know what it is. I'm falling for him.

The protective care he's shown me tonight has shattered all my hard-won defenses. He came for me, saved me from certain death when he could have handed the job off to his men. Hell, he could have left me to die. But he didn't. *He* rescued me. And that affects me on a deep, resounding level.

Despite our conflicts, despite all his cruelty along the way, I can't stop it.

Even if it means I end up hurt again.

I'm falling for Nicolo fast and hard.

Snaking his arm around my waist, Nicolo pulls me against his side, holding me close. I rest my cheek on his chest, using him as my pillow. There, wrapped in his arms, I listen to his heart beat a steady rhythm. Slowly, I drift into a deep, dreamless sleep.

34

ANYA

Inhaling deeply, I wake to the warmth of Nicolo's powerful arms still holding me close. His chest presses against my back. His hips curl around mine as he spoons me tenderly.

A bubble of emotion bursts in my chest to know he held me all night. In his arms, I wasn't plagued by nightmares. I slept more soundly than I have in months, actually.

A yawn parts my lips, and I fight to do so quietly. Nicolo stirs behind me, releasing a deep, satisfied breath. His muscles tense, pulling me tight against his chest for a moment. Then he releases me, allowing me to sit up in bed.

I do so, pulling the bed covers up around my breasts as I turn to face Nicolo.

"Good morning," he groans as he stretches his arms languorously above his head.

A smile pulls at my lips. "Good morning." The warmth of a blush tinges my cheeks. This is the first time I've spent the night with a man–actually slept in the same bed. Somehow, that makes what we have feel all the more intimate.

His perfect mess of curls cascades over his forehead after a night of sleep, and the ruffled look fills me with butterflies. Suddenly, I wonder if my hair is a complete rat's nest. I don't remember removing the pins from it before falling asleep.

Reaching up with my free hand, I feel the loose knot at the base of my neck. My heart sinks. I'll need to give it some serious attention to retrieve all my pins from the mess I find.

Humor lights Nicolo's eyes as he catches me checking my hair. "You look beautiful," he says. "Especially after the night you had."

His gaze shifts to my cheek, and he brushes soft fingers across the bruised skin. His expression turns inscrutable.

It releases a flood of images that come crashing into my brain, wiping the smile from my face. I'm lucky to be alive. When faced with that fact, a tiny thing like the state of my hair–even my bruised cheek– seems completely inconsequential.

Then my mind fast-forwards to the terrible dream that woke me in the middle of the night. My core tightens just thinking about the gentle way Nicolo calmed me. The passionate yet tender sex that followed.

Sliding from beneath the covers, Nicolo stands and collects his basketball shorts. He pulls them up over his naked body, hiding his sheer perfection.

Glancing around, I search for the T-shirt he lent me and snatch it up off the floor. Fighting the unreasonable shyness that turns my skin warm, I drop the covers to don the Cubs logo.

"Are you hungry?" Nicolo asks. "Or would you rather I take you home?"

My heart skips a beat as I realize it's Sunday. "Oh, um. Actually, if you don't mind, home would be great... Sunday breakfast is kind of a big deal with my family."

My pulse quickens as I tread dangerously close to the secret I've been keeping from him for months now.

Miraculously, Nicolo seems unbothered by my response. "No problem. If you don't mind, I'm going to take a quick shower. Then I'll drive you home."

"Thanks." I smile shyly and watch him disappear into the bathroom.

Glancing down at my apparel, I realize I can't go home wearing this. While I don't necessarily want to put my green dress back on, it would be better than walking into our apartment wearing a man's clothes.

I find my dress folded on the gray leather reading chair that occupies one corner of his room. My panties are placed neatly on top. Something about the simple, thoughtful gesture tugs at my heartstrings.

Reaching for the lace thong, I pull it on then strip the T-shirt once more to replace it with my dress. Despite all the horrendous events of yesterday, the dress is in almost perfect condition. Aside from a small tear at the top of the thigh-high slit, there isn't even dirt or blood staining the beautiful fabric.

That means my coat must have taken the brunt of Alexia's gore. I shudder to think of what it must look like. It's not included in the stack of clothes Nicolo left me. Probably for a good reason.

The running water shuts off as I sit to put on my shoes. Nicolo exits the bathroom with a towel wrapped around his waist. His skin glistens from the beads of water on his shoulders and chest, and my mouth goes dry.

Now that all my defenses have been battered down, I can't seem to stop noticing just how gorgeous Nicolo is. Like a god among men, his body is pure perfection. His muscles are lean and toned, his abs the dictionary definition of washboard.

He flashes me a playful smile as he catches me ogling him, my hands frozen at my ankle. I had forgotten all about putting on my shoes. I blush profusely and focus on the task at hand as he finishes dressing.

Before we leave, Nicolo wraps a warm coat around my shoulders. Then he hands me my house keys and phone. "I'll buy you a new coat. In the meantime, you can borrow mine."

Why does that make me feel like crying?

In no time, we're pulling up to the curb outside my building. Nicolo puts his Maserati in park.

"Thank you, Nico," I say, turning to meet his gaze. I use his nickname intentionally. Now that I know he likes it, the name sends a thrill through me. "Thank you for everything. I..." I falter as the reality of my intended words brings a lump to my throat. "I owe you my life."

Nicolo's fingers brush softly across my bruised cheekbone and curl behind my ear as he combs a stray lock from my face.

Then he leans across the console to graze a kiss over my lips.

As I turn to open my door, Nicolo kills the motor of his car and follows suit. Taken aback, I watch in stunned silence as he makes his way around the hood of his car.

"What are you doing?" I ask as he helps me from the low front seat. Confusion presses my brows into a frown.

"I thought I would walk you up." Humor makes the corner of his lips twitch up into a smile.

My heart stutters, and I swallow hard. The thoughtful gesture both disarms and terrifies me. It's such a simple, nice act, but if he walks me to my door, he might just see Clara. And as the spitting image of her father, nothing good would come of that.

My brain short circuits.

I can't think of a single reason for why he shouldn't walk me up if he wants to.

Struck dumb, I follow Nicolo helplessly as he tucks my hand into the crook of his arm.

"The elevator's broken," I explain nervously as he walks me toward the front door of my building.

"It's been that way since before I moved in."

"We can take the stairs," Nicolo says lightly. He doesn't seem to mind.

I worry my lip nervously on our way up. But every time I glance at Nicolo from the corner of my eye, he seems perfectly at ease.

"Now I get why you have such killer legs," he jokes lightly as we finish the final flight of steps.

A breathy laugh escapes me, but I'm too distracted by the nausea over what might happen that I don't fully register his words.

My ears roar with my hammering pulse.

Then we're standing in front of my apartment door.

Nicolo turns to face me, his eyes a brilliant shade of green as he looks deep into my soul. He leans in to press a scintillating kiss to my lips. Warmth floods me, and I melt into his embrace.

"I'll see you soon?" Nicolo says when we finally break apart.

"Yes."

A smile tugs at my lips as he reaches up to pinch my chin between his thumb and forefinger. He brushes my lips gently with his. Then he turns to head back down the stairs alone.

Heady relief makes me dizzy, and I lean against our apartment door for support. My secret's safe. Only after Nicolo is safely out of sight do I turn and slip the key into the lock.

"There she is!" Aunt Patritsiya says as I walk through the door, her familiar Russian accent wrapping around me like a warm hug.

"Mama!" Clara exclaims, jumping down from her stool at the countertop to greet me.

"Careful, Clara. Your hands are all covered in flour! You don't want to ruin your mother's beautiful dress."

But I don't care. Letting Nicolo's coat fall from my shoulders, I scoop up my baby girl in my arms and hold her close. Breathing in the fruity scent of her shampoo, I soak up the feeling of her tiny body.

"I missed you," I say fiercely, fighting to contain my tears.

"Where were you?" she asks, leaning back so she can take in my fancy dress.

"Nowhere nearly as fun as when I'm here with you. Sorry I'm late. Let me go change, and I'll be right back out to help with breakfast."

I set Clara on her feet, and she scampers back into the kitchen to help her auntie. Stooping, I collect Nicolo's coat in my arms and head toward my bedroom. It takes me no time at all to shed my beautiful dress. I toss it aside before pulling on a comfortable pair of joggers and a sweatshirt.

Before I head back out, I double-check my cheek. It's slightly swollen and rosy but hasn't started to bruise visibly. Hopefully, it will stay that way. If it does, I doubt my aunt will notice.

I head back into the communal area to make pancakes with my family. My heart overflows with happiness to be spending time with my little girl. I can't keep my eyes off of her today. It's astounding just how much she looks like her father.

I can see it now more than ever. And for the first time, that knowledge fills me with joy rather than pain or sadness. I have loved every moment of raising my little girl. But her dark curls and hazel eyes, her mischievous smile and a thousand little details in her personality remind me of Nicolo.

For the past four years, she has been a constant reminder, bringing him to the forefront of my mind. And once again, my heart twinges as she answers my question with a cheeky response. It reminds me of her dad.

For the first time, I'm less confident in my decision to keep Clara a secret from Nicolo. Until now, I've been sure that it was the right thing to do. I did it to protect my daughter from a man who could hurt her.

But after nearly losing my life last night, I don't know what to think. If something were to happen to me, Nicolo would never know he has a daughter. And that knowledge weighs on me. Clara would never know who her father is. That fact causes me far more pain than I realized it could.

I'm falling for Nicolo, and now I wonder if this might not turn into a more long-term arrangement than I had anticipated. While I don't know how long he might want to be with me, I suddenly find myself drawn to our new connection.

I need to decide what I'm doing with my life. If I want to make things work with Nicolo, I can't keep hiding Clara from him. Our daughter will need his protection. After last night, that much is glaringly obvious. And I can't continue to lie to him if our connection has any hope of becoming something more.

But the thought of telling Nicolo I've been hiding something so monumental utterly terrifies me.

35

NICOLO

The simplicity of Anya's shimmering rose gold dress for our date tonight somehow makes her look even more stunning than usual. The color draws out the natural blush of her creamy cheeks. The long sleeves and V-neck transition down to a form-fitting waistline.

I appreciate the slit that runs from the bottom of the knee-length skirt all the way to the top of her thigh. It's subtly sexy, and I love watching her descend the final flight of steps from her third-floor apartment. It gives me a full understanding of just how much leg that slit has to offer.

Her golden curls are swept to the side in a half updo. They cascade over one shoulder. She almost seems to glow, she's so beautiful.

"Nice," I say as she reaches the bottom step.

I give her an obvious once over.

"You like it?" Anya gives me a spin.

My gut tightens as I realize the simple front hides a tantalizing back. It fully exposes her skin from the top of her neck down to her adorable back dimples. Only a thin strap laces back and forth across the expanse to ensure a snug fit.

"Definitely." I pull her into my arms. Crushing her against me, I arch her back and kiss her to prove how much I appreciate her new dress.

She releases a breathless laugh when I finally release her.

"You ready for our date do-over?" I never told her what her surprise was supposed to be on our date when she got kidnapped.

I'm excited to see her reaction tonight when she finally finds out. And to ensure nothing goes wrong, I chose to pick her up myself.

"More than," she says with a playful smile.

I have to admit, I like this new side of her, one where she's smiling and witty. I could get used to the sound of her laugh.

Putting my hand on the small of her back, I guide her through the front doors of her building and out to my waiting Maserati.

"Before you get in, I have something for you." I pause by the back door of my car.

"Nico, you didn't have to," she says, surprised.

"This time, I really think I did," I counter.

I lean into the back seat and retrieve the new coat I bought to replace her worn peacoat that got ruined. Standing, I reveal the top-of-the-line REDValentino coat. I hold it so she can put it on.

"It's beautiful," she gasps, sliding into the warm layers of fabric. She stops to admire the quality of the wool. "Thank you."

"You're welcome."

I take her to Cité for a culinary treat before the show.

I'm surprised when a wave of memories crash over me as we step out of the elevators. This is the same place I took Anya after our shopping date. I haven't been here since. We hadn't stayed long enough to eat that meal. And I'd been so furious with her that I'd manhandled her on our way to Incognito.

I glance at Anya to gauge her reaction to the familiar location. Her eyes linger on our table from our first date. A jumble of emotions flicker across her face, ending with a question that she keeps locked inside.

I'm dying to know what it is.

The host seats us at a table on the far side of the room, closer to the pianist, who plays a gentle melody for the dinner guests. I order us a bottle of sauvignon blanc. My eyes linger on Anya's face as she looks out over the city. Her attention shifts to the musician seated at the white baby grand piano.

"What are you thinking?" I ask as soon as we're alone.

Anya's blue eyes meet mine. The question still lingers there. "You said this was a date do-over, and I had assumed it was the date we were originally going to do last weekend, before..." She trails off, not wanting to breathe life into that hellish night again.

I cock my head, not sure where she's going with this.

"Did I misunderstand? Are we redoing our first date?"

I detect an underlying worry in her tone, and an unexpected twinge of guilt tightens my belly. I fight to keep the emotion from my face, giving her a smile instead.

"No, your first thought was right. We're doing the date I had intended for last weekend. Only... I picked this restaurant over Oriole," I admit.

When it came down to it, I didn't want to sully the night with reminders of last weekend. But I hadn't considered that bringing her here might drum up bad memories.

Anya's shoulders relax, dropping ever so slightly as a smile returns to her face. She clearly has some lingering pain over our first night together.

I focus back on it now to consider what I might have done to hurt her so badly. Sure, I'd been rough with her, but our attraction had a contentious beginning. And I'm confident it wasn't her first time with a man, so it's not like I took her virginity that forcefully.

I wonder if I pushed it too far, if I hurt her. She'd pissed me off enough that I hadn't been too concerned about it at the time. But even as I punished her, she'd clearly liked it. She came from being spanked for fuck's sake. Not every girl can do that, but damn was it hot.

But if it's not that, then what? I can only think of one other explanation.

Before I can ask, our waiter arrives to serve us each a glass of chilled white wine. I give him our order at the same time and wait until he's gone before I pose my question.

"Anya, did I scare you on our first date?"

She seems taken aback by my question. Her eyes widen, and her lips part. She licks them nervously. "Um." An uncomfortable giggle bursts from her.

No matter what she says next, I know my guess must have hit pretty close to home.

"To be honest, you absolutely terrified me."

I did not expect that. "There's no way. I spent so long trying to make sense of you. You just seemed like an impenetrable wall. I didn't think you were afraid of anything."

Anya blushes. "I'll take that as a compliment."

"You should. Your feisty side is sexy as hell." Reaching across the table, I take her hand. "I don't want you to be scared of me." That might be the first and only time I've said those words.

I mean them with a sincerity I hadn't known I'd felt.

Anya's soft hand squeezes mine with surprising strength. "You don't anymore," she reassures me.

"Did I... hurt you in any way that night? I mean, aside from the obvious," I amend, realizing the question might not come across as I intended. I used a riding crop on her after all.

Again, a torrent of emotion ripples across Anya's face. Her lips part as though to confess, then they close. She does this two more times, seeming ready to tell me something, then thinking better of it.

I'm dying to know what it is. Obviously, I did something to hurt her, but it must be bad if she's struggling this hard. I fight the urge to command her to tell me. I might have in the past. But I'm trying. I want to be someone she can be honest with. Someone she feels safe telling anything. So I force myself to be patient.

Finally, she releases a deep breath and looks down at her hands, her cheeks turning a deep shade of crimson. "I guess you just hurt my feelings is all. I mean, I'd never done anything like that... with the bondage and the... whip. I didn't understand that it could be something... *other* than what it *seemed* to be. Then I saw how Whitney and her partner are together... And when you started mocking me about my virginity..."

Deep splotches of color rise across her chest. Her cheeks turn almost purple, she's so clearly uncomfortable. "Oh God, I'm doing a terrible job of explaining this. Please, just forget I said anything." She can barely look at me as she peers up through her thick lashes to gauge my reaction.

I can't help it. I burst out laughing. "I'm sorry. I shouldn't laugh," I say as my mirth rocks my frame. I fight to get it back under control as I give her hand a squeeze. "Thank you for being honest with me."

Inexplicably, her blush intensifies even more.

"Look, I'll drop it, okay? I just wanted to understand you a little better." *And get to the bottom of why you seemed uncomfortable when we came in.*

But now that I have, I can see why she wouldn't want to revisit our first night together. She's been scared enough lately. In all honesty, the last thing I want to do tonight is hurt her feelings.

I steer our conversation in a different direction as dinner comes.

Anya starts to loosen up, her humor returning as we talk and joke. Before I know it, it's time for us to head to the Civic Opera House.

Anya's eyes grow wide as we pull into the valet parking, and she peers greedily out the window at the impressive building. "We're going to a performance?" Excitement bursts from her lips.

"Something like that," I hedge.

I help her out of the car and hand my keys to the young valet before escorting Anya inside the grand building.

We make our way through the grandiose lobby to the theater itself. And I take her to the best seats in the house. Distracted by her program, Anya follows me without looking where she's going. When I stop her, gesturing for her to lead the way to our seats, she looks up for the first time and gasps.

"No!" she breathes. Her eyes grow round as she sees *Dracula* splattered across the curtain in what is meant to look like blood.

"You said you loved going to see ballets with your parents when you were a child. I thought maybe it had been a while. Do you like it?"

"Oh, Nico," Anya murmurs, tears shimmering in her eyes.

She flings her arms around my neck and kisses me passionately.

I'll take that as a yes.

The prolonged embrace makes my blood rise, and when we take our seats, I find my pants almost uncomfortably tight. But we settle in, and Anya's arm snakes around mine as we share an armrest. It feels like such a normal thing for a couple to do. Yet the gesture feels enticingly intimate.

As the lights dim and the curtain rises, I find myself more focused on the beautiful ballerina next to me than any of the dancers on stage.

I love how absolutely spellbound Anya seems by the performance. Her eyes never leave the stage. I wonder if she might have forgotten to blink on occasion as she stares adamantly, unwilling to miss a single moment.

I manage to appreciate the talented dancers as they move across the floor. But the tantalizing slit in Anya's dress keeps drawing my eye. And when she recrosses her legs about halfway through the performance, emphasizing just how revealing her skirt can be, I find I'm unable to control myself.

Letting my hand fall to her side of the armrest, I lay my palm on her bare leg.

The silky softness of her skin entices me to run my fingers lightly across her flesh. I'm rewarded by Anya's visible shiver.

Her eyes flick in my direction, leaving the ballet for the first time to acknowledge me.

The fire in their depths say I'm going to love taking her home with me tonight.

Forcing myself to behave, I keep my hand in the same place on her thigh. My fingers only stray ever so slightly to enjoy the feel of her soft skin. Tension crackles between us as the show unfolds. Even I can see it's an impressive display of art and athleticism.

Finally, after hours of mounting tension that puts my shoulders in knots, the final curtain drops. The audience bursts into applause. Anya rises to her feet, giving the dancers a standing ovation, and I join her. Smiling, I watch her from the corner of my eye.

"That was amazing!" Anya gushes as we make our way out of the theater. "I don't think I've ever seen such talent. I mean, did you see the way Mina and Dracula danced together? It was absolutely *haunting*."

Wrapping my arm around her shoulders, I pull her close to press a kiss to her temple. "I'm glad you enjoyed it."

"Did you?" she asks earnestly, glancing up at me.

"Definitely." My suggestive look tells her I very much enjoyed the foreplay.

Seeing her sexy legs on display and not being able to fuck her right then and there nearly killed me.

Anya blushes as a smile breaks across her face.

The valet brings my car right up to the front door of the opera house. We slide inside the vehicle and turn out onto the city streets of Chicago.

That electric tension crackles between us once more as I drive. I don't waste time slowing for yellow lights or easing around my turns as I make my way back to my penthouse.

Anticipation of what I plan to do with Anya has my pulse racing, my cock growing hard in my slacks. I know she must feel it, too, as she sits exceptionally quiet in the passenger seat. Out of the corner of my eye, I catch her glancing at me every so often.

As soon as I put my car in park, my self-control vanishes. I lean across the console to cup the back of Anya's head and bring our lips crashing together.

Anya responds hungrily. Shifting in her seat, she grips the collar of my suit jacket and pulls me closer. White-hot desire burns through my veins, and I feel like I might explode. I want her so badly. It takes all of my strength to pull back so I can look Anya in the eye.

She reads my thoughts. Releasing my jacket, she spins toward the car door, exiting hastily.

I follow suit, clamoring out of the car. I barely remember to lock it as I join her in front of the elevator doors.

As soon as I hit the call button, I'm on her again, kissing, nipping, fondling, groping. I feel like a horny teen with no experience or plan of action.

I want to feel every inch of her, and I can't wait to get up to my apartment before we start.

The doors ding open, and I guide her inside. Holding her hips, I walk her backward until she's pressed against the mirrored wall. I twine my fingers with hers and bring Anya's hands above her head. Grinding against her, I pin her in place, showing her just how much she turns me on.

Anya's breasts heave against me as she breathes heavily. She kisses me, intense and fiery. Keeping her hands pinned above her head with one hand, I find the slit in her dress with the other.

Then I work my way beneath the shimmering fabric. My fingers find the peak of her thighs.

I stroke her silken slit and groan.

"You're not wearing any panties?" I rasp.

The fucking spitfire smiles coyly against my lips.

Suddenly, I regret behaving myself in the theater. I should have fingered her right there in the middle of the performance. A reward for being the sexiest girl in the world.

I suck her lower lip between my teeth and bite down gently. I hardly register the ding of the elevator doors as they open to my penthouse apartment.

Only when Anya starts to giggle do I realize that I've missed my cue. I release her with a frustrated growl. Stepping back, I curl my arm around her waist to guide her into my apartment.

Gripping my tie, Anya leads me through the entry toward my living room couch. My cock throbs with anticipation as I admire her from behind. Her bare, athletic back, the narrow curve of her waist, the way her full hips sway as she walks confidently in her heels.

Fucking hell, the only thing sexier is that she's actually leading me by my goddamn tie.

Anya pushes me down onto the couch and straddles me, her thighs spreading to accommodate me. Her heels hit the floor with a muffled thunk.

Then she's kissing me, rolling her hips as she grinds against my swollen erection. Her hands slowly loosen my tie until she can remove it entirely. Then she starts on the buttons of my dress shirt.

I get to work on the strings holding the back of her dress together. It takes no time until she's naked on top of me, seeing as she wasn't wearing any undies–and the dress didn't allow for a bra. The sole piece of clothing slides easily up over her body.

It falls to the floor in a rose gold heap.

Anya works her way through my layers of clothing with tenacity, stripping me down until I'm sitting naked on the couch. My cock stands erect, waiting for her.

Easing down onto my length, Anya starts slowly. Her wet pussy wraps around my cockhead. And she sinks lower until I'm buried deep inside her.

I grip her hips as she starts to rock on top of me. Her breasts graze against my chest with each forward arch. Picking up the pace, she finds her rhythm. The roll of her hips allows for deep penetration before I slide out once more.

Following her motion with one hand, I support her. My other hand travels up to cup her firm breast. I massage it.

Anya moans, her head tipping back as she arches into my touch.

I lean forward to suck her other nipple between my lips.

Her motion grows more adamant as she rides me like a sexy cowgirl. One hand braces on my shoulder. The other combs back into her thick golden hair.

I don't know what unleashed this beast in her, but I want it all night long. I plan on fucking her until we're both so tired we can't keep our eyes open.

Anya's breaths come in sharp gasps as her walls start to tighten around my hard length. She's close to coming, and it drives me mad with lust.

As she pounds down onto my cock, I release her nipple from my mouth. Running my hand up her neck, I grip the back of her head and bring her lips to mine once more.

Electric pleasure jolts through me as we kiss.

I rock my hips up into her, intensifying the penetration as we both topple over the precipice.

Anya cries out against my lips, slamming down onto my cock. I give one final thrust and come hard. Burst after burst of cum pours deep inside her pussy. And she milks me for all I'm worth.

Slowly, her hips come to a stop as we cling to each other. We shudder with the intensity of our combined release. My kiss turns gentle as I continue to hold her to me. My cock twitches in response to the after-shocks of her orgasm.

Anya draws back with a deeply contented smile, her eyes hooded with the lingering haze of her release.

"Fucking hell, woman. I think I might have just died and gone to heaven."

Anya releases a lazy chuckle, and her walls tighten around me, making my cock pulse.

"Let's do that again," she murmurs, leaning forward to kiss my neck.

I skim her soft back with my fingers, raising goosebumps on her flesh. "I might need a minute to recover, but I have an idea of what we can do in the meantime."

"Oh?" She leans back to look at me curiously.

Wrapping one arm around her waist, the other beneath her hips, I hold her to me as I rise from the couch. Anya hooks her legs around me accommodatingly. She clings to me as I carry her to the bedroom.

I fall onto the bed with her, and Anya releases a girlish squeal.

Trapping her beneath me, I start to kiss her once again, my lips grazing hers, my tongue exploring rather than demanding.

Anya hums contentedly against my mouth. As we make out, my cock begins to stiffen inside her once again.

36

ANYA

I gasp awake to the tantalizing feel of Nicolo's tongue stroking between my folds. When I glance down, all I see are sheets, covering his sexy head of curls. His broad shoulders force my knees apart.

Taking the edge of the cover, I fling it down toward the foot of the bed. I want to watch the sexy Italian eating me out first thing in the morning.

My pussy's sore and stretched in the best way from a passionate night of sex. Every muscle in my body is weak and aching. I comb my fingers into Nicolo's thick black locks as I let my head fall back. My eyes flutter closed as I soak up the tingling pleasure that ripples up through my core.

Warm excitement blossoms inside me, and I rock my hips to the steady stroke of his tongue. I shudder every time he circles my over-sensitized clit, teasing me to life. Then his lips close around the bundle of nerves. He suctions it into his mouth, and I moan, my thighs quivering.

My body is so spent, I don't see how I can come again. Yet, as Nicolo teases me, licking and sucking and flicking me erotically, I find myself dangerously close to release.

"Nico," I whimper.

He hums against my clit.

His fingers circle my tender ass and pussy, bringing to mind all the different ways he fucked me last night. My core tightens at the memory.

"Fuck!" I gasp, my eyes flying open as my orgasm hits me out of the blue.

A fresh wave of arousal gushes from me, slicking my folds. My clit throbs and my walls pulse, searching for Nicolo's cock. I shudder, gasping with each wave of tingling pleasure.

"Good morning," Nicolo says, releasing my clit to smile up at me mischievously.

I hum contentedly in response as he crawls up to press a tangy kiss on my lips.

Then he collapses back onto the bed beside me and pulls me into his arms. He's as naked as I am, our clothes still lying on the living room floor. I can feel his arousal as his cockhead slides across my slick folds, pressing adamantly between my ass cheeks.

Reaching between my legs, I guide him toward my pussy entrance. Nicolo groans as I tilt my hips, initiating the first inch of penetration. Slowly sinking into me, he continues to spoon me as he fucks me from behind.

It isn't showy or fast or hard. It's sensual and almost sweet as he holds me close and slides in and out of me.

His hand runs down my arm to grasp my hand, and he guides my fingers to the peak of my thighs. Pressing my fingers against my clit, Nicolo silently instructs me to play with myself while he moves inside me.

I obey, circling my clit with my fingers as his cock finds my G-spot again and again.

"Come for me, Anya," Nicolo murmurs against my ear.

He bites down on the lobe, sending a zing of pleasure down my spine, straight to my core.

Whimpering, I circle my clit more adamantly and find my release a moment later. I explode around his cock as he starts to push more forcefully inside me.

With three erratic thrusts, Nicolo finds his own release. He pours his seed inside me as my pussy grips his cock like a vise. He throbs in my depths, drawing out my own orgasm. And his cum fills me so full it starts to leak out around him.

I don't know when or how my desire became so insatiable. But no matter how many times Nicolo fucks me, I'm always ready for more.

"Fucking Christ, if I could, I don't know that I would ever stop fucking you," he breathes as he holds me to his chest.

I love that his words mirror my own thoughts, and I breathe deeply as I take in this moment of bliss. Last night was one of the best nights of my life, and to follow it up with this morning seems too good to be true. I want to soak up every minute of it and solidify it in my memory.

Because I don't know if I'll ever have the opportunity to be with him like this again. Guilt tugs at me as I think about the massive, life-sized secret I've been keeping from him.

What once seemed like a justified decision, made out of fear to protect my daughter, now feels like an impossible hurdle to overcome.

What possible way can I tell him that we have a daughter together that doesn't end up with him hating me? I just can't see one.

I almost told him last night, when he started asking about our first night at Incognito. It would have been the right segue.

He even asked me if he had done something to hurt me. I had told him the truth. He hurt my feelings when he mocked me for not being a virgin. But what hurt most was that he never realized he was the one who took my virginity.

I was so close to telling him–to just putting it out there. If I'd confessed about our history together, I would have followed it up with the fact that he'd gotten me pregnant.

It was on the tip of my tongue, and then I chickened out. And now I feel like even more of a liar, a fraud. He just gave me the most wonderful evening, and still I haven't told him he has a daughter.

Nicolo doesn't ask about breakfast today. Instead, he showers quickly and prepares to drive me home once again. It's a silent understanding that Sunday morning is when I spend time with my family–though who that family is, he doesn't know.

Just like last week, he walks me right to my apartment door.

He gives me a kiss that melts my heart.

I walk inside and am greeted by my aunt and the excited chatter of my four-year-old daughter.

I know I can't keep putting it off. Nicolo deserves to meet her. He deserves to share this time with her, to watch Clara grow. Now I just have to decide how I'm going to tell him. And then I have to stick to it.

It's nearly impossible to eat my breakfast as I think about how Nicolo will react. The best I can do is break it to him gently. Sit him down and put it all out there.

Hopefully, he won't feel like killing me afterward.

While I don't actually think Nicolo would harm me, I do worry that telling him will ruin any chance of us being happy together. And right now, I hate the thought of letting go of what we have.

"Mama, can we go to the park today?" Clara asks as I carry our empty plates to the sink.

"Sure, baby," I agree, smiling at the way her face lights up. "Go wash your hands and get your coat."

"Auntie Patritsiya too?" Clara presses.

"I would love to go," Aunt Patritsiya says.

It's a short walk to Montrose Park, and the sun is shining, dissipating the chill brought on by the bitter gusts of wind. Clara skips between us, holding each of our hands as she chatters about what she and Auntie Patritsiya did last night while I was gone.

It's impossible not to smile at her rendition of *Toy Story* and why the "stringy dog" is her favorite.

Caught up in my daughter's exuberant tale, I lose track of my surroundings. I'm only vaguely aware of the harbor off to my right, the park all around us. I don't think about the people we pass or the dogs that chase their owners jogging by. This is the quality time I cherish.

"Anya?"

It's too late as I register the familiar voice. My eyes snap up to the tall, muscular man before me. My heart stops at the sight of Nicolo's devastatingly handsome smile.

"What are you doing here?" I blurt, all manners swept aside as panic sets in.

"I was just having a... meeting with a colleague," Nicolo says delicately.

His eyes drop to Clara, noting the way she's holding my hand and Aunt Patritsiya's. Then he looks up at my aunt, unleashing a charming grin.

"Hi, I'm Nicolo." He extends his hand. "Anya and I are..." His eyes flick to mine as if checking to see what word I would like to use in front of my family.

"He goes to Rosehill College. We have a class together," I provide quickly. "This is my aunt, Patritsiya," I introduce.

Aunt Patritsiya shake's Nicolo's hand. "It's a pleasure to meet you. I haven't met many of Anya's college friends, so this is a real treat."

He nods politely, and his eyes shift to Clara once again. "And that must make you... Anya's cousin?" Nicolo guesses as he stoops to address Clara.

His eyes move from her face to my aunt's and back, no doubt searching for the resemblance.

My heart hammers in my chest, and my palms start to sweat.

Clara releases a bright giggle. "No!" she squeals playfully, as if she thinks he must be teasing her. "This is my mommy." She looks up at me with round hazel eyes that hold all the innocence in the world.

My stomach drops as my heart comes to a screeching halt in my chest. This is the worst possible way Nicolo could find out about his daughter. I hardly dare to look at him. And when I do, I'm gutted by the anger and betrayal in his eyes.

"Funny, I don't remember you mentioning you had a daughter," Nicolo says with forced nonchalance.

Blood pools in my cheeks as my horror sends me reeling. "Oh, yes. Her name is Clara. Clara, say hi to Nicolo."

"Hi, Nicolo," Clara recites happily.

"Good girl. Now go take your auntie over to the playground and see if she'll push you on the swing. I'll be right there."

My aunt's eyes meet mine, her eyebrows raising in an unspoken question.

"I'll be right behind you. I just need to speak to Nicolo for a moment."

Clara leads my aunt by the finger, taking away my last barrier of protection against Nicolo's wrath.

"I can explain," I say as soon as they're out of earshot.

"That you have a daughter you never told me about?" Nicolo scoffs, his tone deeply wounded.

"No." Tears sting my eyes as I fight to hold back my emotions. "*We* have a daughter."

"What? What the fuck are you talking about?"

The vitriol in his voice lashes me like a whip, and I flinch.

"We went to high school together, Nicolo, for two years. You were so popular, and I thought I was invisible, but then I thought you really wanted to be with me. You invited me to one of your house parties, and when you took me up to your room to talk... well, one thing led to another... and I gave you my virginity. Afterwards, you made it perfectly clear that I was just a conquest, that you liked the challenge of getting virgins to sleep with you."

Emotion contorts Nicolo's face as understanding flickers in his eyes. Then, like a sunrise, his eyes light with recognition as he remembers me for the first time.

Why that's so painful even now, I don't know. But it cuts deep, knowing that he could go all this time without a clue.

"I got pregnant, and I decided to keep the baby. At the end of the school year, I transferred to a different school. I started late at my new school–after I gave birth." I shake my head, dropping my eyes to the ground. "I never thought I would see you again," I murmur.

"But you did. The first day of the semester–when you spilled your lunch on me–you recognized me right away. You've known for *months*," he hisses. "I was right there in front of you, and you didn't think to tell me I have a child?"

I flinch, then slowly force myself to meet his eyes. My anger bubbles to life when I do. "It's not like you gave me a good reason to tell you. You were an asshole, Nico. You were horrible to me in high school and even worse from the start of my time at Rosehill."

"And now?" Nicolo demands, his voice rising. "I'd say we're well past that excuse, Anya. God, you're un-fucking-believable!"

Tears trickle down my cheeks as my worst fears come to life. He's not going to forgive me for this. I can hear it in his tone.

"I was going to tell you," I insist, but my voice is too choked from the lump in my throat to hold any conviction.

Nicolo scoffs. "I'm sure. I can't believe I thought I was falling for you. You're just as full of shit as the rest of them, aren't you? Well, you can fuck right off. And you can't keep my daughter from me. You had no right to keep her from me as long as you have." Icy fury tinges his tone, and he leans closer, getting in my face. "Maybe I should just take Clara away from you as punishment for keeping her a secret."

My heart stops, and a strangled cry bursts from me. "Please, Nico," I beg. "Please don't take my daughter away."

"She's *my* daughter too," he rasps. His fingers comb into his hair as a snarl bursts from his chest. "Fuck, Anya! I can't even stand to look at you right now." With that, Nicolo spins on his heel and marches away.

I watch him go, struck dumb as my emotions consume me. I've lost him. There's no doubt about it. *But have I just lost my daughter too?* I don't think I could survive that.

37

NICOLO

"Silvia!" I call, storming into my father's house. I hope she's home.

She appears at the top of the banister a moment later, a broad smile on her face. "Nico, you're home!" she calls in delight. Then she takes me in, and her face falls. "What's wrong?"

I trudge up the stairs, my heart heavy. Shaking my head, I pull her into a bear hug and lift her off her feet. Silvia wraps her arms around me, giving me a tight squeeze.

"You want to talk about it?" she asks gently.

"I *need* to talk about it," I insist. I feel like I might explode from all the rage pounding inside me, demanding to be released.

"Come on. We can talk in my room," Silvia says as I set her down. Taking my hand, she leads me down the hall.

When we get there, she plops onto the edge of her mattress. Grabbing one of her colorful fluffy pillows, she hugs it to her chest.

The themes of her Paris-chic room jump out at me, the sketch of the Eiffel Tower that lines one wall, high-fashion women in fancy dresses posing like models. Even her bed cover has little images of the famous city drawn across its cream background.

"So... what happened?" she asks tentatively.

Now that I have her undivided attention, I suddenly find myself unable to say. Instead, I pace as I think about how I can possibly phrase everything in my head.

"Nico, what is *wrong*?" Silvia demands as I cross in front of her for the hundredth time.

I didn't know who else to turn to. I'm consumed by rage, distraught that Anya could keep such a monumental secret from me all this time. It's like she ripped my heart from my chest and stomped on it with a stiletto.

I have a daughter, an adorable little four-year-old girl. She has my hair, my eyes. I could see it as easily as I could see the guilt on Anya's face.

My kid sister is the only person I could even think about telling. She's the one woman in my life that I respect. Someone I trust inherently. She's always been honest with me, even when the truth is hard to swallow.

But now that I'm here, stalking across her bedroom like a caged tiger, I can't bring myself to tell her. I've never felt for anyone the way I feel for Anya. And to have her betray me so utterly–I can't even think straight, I'm so mad.

"Nico, *stop*," Silvia insists. She grabs my wrist and drags me down onto the edge of the bed. "I can't help you if you won't tell me what happened. Is it... the ballerina?" she asks tentatively.

I nod, dropping my head in my hands. I grind the heels of my palms into my throbbing eyes as I start from the beginning. "There was this girl I knew back in sophomore year of high school, Anya. A dancer. She was beautiful and kind of this enigma because she never came to parties. She didn't play sports or do extracurricular activities. I saw it as a challenge to... get to know her."

I hate myself as I say the words, ashamed to be telling my kid sister what I did to Anya when she was just my sister's age. "I slept with her, but I wasn't really interested in pursuing it after that. She, uh, comes from a poor immigrant family, and I knew Father wouldn't allow it to... go further."

"In other words, you were being a tool. And actually listened to our father. I might not have the leverage to stand up to Father, but you do. You're his heir, and if it matters to you, I'm sure he'll let you have your way. You're the golden child. Now, go on with your story."

Silvia's gentle chide drives a nail into my chest. I raise my head from my hands to try and get a read on her. She's grave, waiting for me to continue with my story.

"I never saw her after that year, and in all honesty, I completely forgot about her. I'd only been with her the one night, and four years is a long time... Anyway, she transferred to Rosehill this year, and I ran into her for the first time since sophomore year. I could tell she disliked me from the get-go, but I didn't recognize her, so I didn't know why. We ended up forming this sort of... rivalry."

"And then you saw her dance." Silvia says it with conviction, like a well-known fact.

I frown as I meet her eyes. "How did you...?"

"I was there, dummy. I've never seen you look at anyone the way you looked at her, like you just had to have her. I thought you might climb right over the theater chairs to get to her," Silvia teases.

I give her a weak smile, appreciating her attempt at levity.

"Well, we started dating, and... I dunno, Sil. I really started falling for her. I thought we might have something special. And then she just went and dropped an atomic bomb on me. She told me I got her pregnant back in high school, and she kept the kid. I have a fucking four-year-old daughter I hadn't met or even known about until today! But the worst part is, I get the feeling she never would have told me if I hadn't happened to run into them at the park." My rage boils up inside me once again.

It obscures my vision, and I curl my hands into fists to stop myself from breaking something.

"What did you do?" Silvia asks gently.

"I told her she could fuck right off. She lied to my face, Silvia. For months! She's kept my child from me for years. I told her she had no right, that maybe I should take Clara from her as punishment. I mean, four fucking years! My daughter walks and talks and has a fucking sense of humor, for Christ's sake. And Anya never once thought it would be smart to mention that I'm a fucking dad!"

"You threatened to take her daughter away from her?" Silvia asks, horror in her voice.

Guilt twists my stomach at the look of utter disbelief in my sister's eyes. Sighing, I bring my anger down a notch. "Maybe that wasn't the best thing to say," I admit.

"Nico, you abandoned her in high school. And then again today when she finally had the courage to tell you about your daughter," Silvia scolds me gently.

"It's not like she had a choice. I mean, the kid was right there in the park. We didn't plan on running into each other, and when Clara said Anya was her mom... I mean, I guess I didn't connect the dots right away, but Anya couldn't have kept it from me at that point."

"Still, it was probably terrifying to tell you about what happened. Think about it from her perspective. She's probably scared you'll abandon her again, forget about her like you did after high school. I'm sure she doesn't want her daughter to feel the same heartbreak she must have felt." Silvia's tiny hand comes to rest on my shoulder, a consolation after she just pared me down to size.

She's right. I hadn't thought about it like that before–that Anya might still be carrying what I did to her in high school. Suddenly, all her anger and resistance when I asked her to date me makes sense. She already knew I would probably fuck her and dump her like I have so many women over the years. When I look at it like that, I've been a downright prick.

"You're clearly in love with Anya," Silvia says softly. "And if that's the case, isn't it a good thing that you have a daughter together? Now is your chance to show Anya you can be a good man. You can show her that you'll stick with her even when things get tough. I know you have it in you, Nico. You might have the world fooled, but I know for a fact that you have a heart of gold."

I don't know what to say. At the mention of love, I want to draw back, to object, but if I think about it–truly focus on how I feel–my kid sister is right. I'm crazy about Anya.

What started as an obsession has transitioned into something much more intimate and real. Rather than losing interest in her, I find myself wanting to learn more about Anya every day.

Horror grips me as I realize what I've done. The words I just said to Anya.

Wasn't it just last night that I told Anya I don't want her to be afraid of me?

Then today, I went and threatened to take her child away.

I don't want Anya to look at me as a bad guy. I want to be a man worthy of her affection. When it comes down to it, I would rather try and work things out with Anya than be with anyone else.

And I don't really want to take Clara away from her mother. That would only traumatize my little girl. I don't want to be that kind of father. *I'm a father.* The realization hits me for the first time. For Clara's sake more than anyone's I need to see this from every possible angle, try to accept it, and keep moving forward.

It might hurt that Anya kept this secret from me for so long, but what matters is that she told me. Anya's trying, and I need to as well.

Pulling Silvia into a tight hug, I kiss the top of her head. "I don't know how you got so wise, but thank you. I really needed that kick in the pants."

"So, you're going to make things right with Anya?" she asks hopefully.

"Yes." I rise from her bed. "If she'll let me."

"Good." Silvia smiles warmly.

"Thanks, Sil. You really are the best person to talk to."

My sister flips her dark hair with false bravado, then she lets her humor slip. "You're my best person to talk to, too, you know," she says.

I snort as I chuck her gently under the chin. "That's just wildly unfair, then. How do I get someone who's so good at the whole talking thing, while you're stuck with me?"

"You're a wonderful person to talk to, Nico. Especially when you don't let your temper get in the way. I just wish I got to see you more often."

I pull my sister in for another hug. "I'll come back soon. Promise."

Then I head for the door. I can't let this conversation wait. I need to speak with Anya now and set things right. I want a future with her. I want to let go of all my anger to be with her. I want to meet the little girl she gave me. And knowing that brings an urgency to my step.

I race across town, hoping I haven't mucked it up so badly that Anya refuses to speak to me again.

38

ANYA

I hold Clara close, terrified to let go of her for fear that she might be ripped from me at any moment. We sit in my room at our apartment as I consider what my next move will be.

I took the time to fill my aunt in on the situation. I pulled her aside, out of Clara's hearing range, to give her the full story for the first time. I didn't want to scare my little girl.

Aunt Patritsyia thinks I should take Clara and run. Maybe she's right.

But the thought of leaving my whole life behind is as terrifying as the thought of staying to face the consequences.

Clearly, I've destroyed any hope of a relationship with Nicolo. Withholding the fact that he has a daughter is unforgivable, and waiting so long to finally tell him has destroyed the trust we built.

I understand why he's angry. I know I should have told him. I just couldn't find the courage. Not that I dreamed in a million years that he would threaten to take Clara from me. If anything, I had feared the opposite, that he would reject her.

And now he wants to take my daughter. I can't let that happen. Running would mean giving up my dream of dancing.

But my little girl is all that matters.

I don't know how serious Nicolo's threat might have been. He didn't take Clara from me right there at the park, thank God. But I feel the minutes ticking by until he comes for her.

Whatever I'm going to do, I need to do it fast. Urgency drives me to set Clara on the bed and stoop to pull my suitcase from beneath it.

"What's going on, Mama?" Clara twirls her hair nervously around her fingers as she watches me.

"We're going to go on a little trip," I say, working to keep the fear out of my voice.

I pull open my drawers and extract only the essentials.

I toss items carelessly into the suitcase. I don't bother to be neat about my packing as I prioritize speed over organization. Once I've packed enough clothes to get by, I close the suitcase lid and snap it shut to carry it to Clara's room.

"Come on, baby. Time to get your things."

I hold out my hand to Clara, and she slides off the bed to take my hand obediently.

Entering the common living space, I meet my aunt's gaze. Her lips turn down in resignation as she spots the suitcase. She gives a nod of encouragement, and I stride quickly across the room toward Clara's bedroom.

Pounding on the door to our apartment makes me yelp.

I nearly jump out of my skin as I turn toward the sound, my eyes growing round with fear. I'm too late. I thought I had a bit more time. I should have fled while I had the chance.

Now, the only way I'm going to keep my daughter is with a very convincing argument.

Silence falls, and I turn to meet my aunt's gaze. She shakes her head wordlessly. She doesn't have a solution for me either.

"Take Clara into her room for me?" I plead.

"I could call the police," she offers quietly.

As tempting as help might be, I don't know that they would help me. I'm not afraid that Nicolo will hurt me. And I wouldn't be surprised if they're in his back pocket anyway.

I shake my head. I need to face this head on. Aunt Patritsiya nods, holding her hand out for Clara to take. She reaches down with her free hand to lift the suitcase from my grasp.

Another round of sharp pounding rattles the door. I wait until my little girl is safely in her room with the door closed before I answer it.

Heart leaping into my throat until I can barely breathe, I draw upon my deep reserves of strength. I force air into my lungs and slowly let it out.

Then I unbolt the door and open it.

A stab of loss lances through me as I look up at Nicolo. Not twenty-four hours ago, he kissed me right here in front of this door. He left me feeling like I meant the world to him. That's all gone, my hopes of something real between us obliterated by my dishonesty.

His face is inscrutable, too many emotions shifting and morphing across it for me to know what he might be thinking. But I know it can't be good.

"Nicolo, please," I whisper, tears brimming in my eyes as I plead with him. "I'm so sorry. I know I should have told you sooner, but please, please, don't take Clara from me. She's all I have in this world. And she needs her mother–"

Nicolo presses a finger to my lips, silencing me as his green eyes warn me of his impending anger. I start to tremble, my anxiety consuming me.

But I don't step aside. I won't just willingly let him take her.

I bite down hard on my lip to silence the sobs that tear from my chest. And I'm consumed by how helpless I am to protect my daughter.

"God, what have I done?" he breathes.

For a moment, I'm not quite sure what he could possibly mean.

"Anya, I didn't mean it. I didn't mean anything I said earlier. I would never take Clara away from you. I've been so blind. I..." Nicolo falters, seeming lost for what else to say.

In the silence that follows, my mind manages to translate the meaning of his words. The tears come more quickly now, flowing down my cheeks as relief washes through me. An agonizing sense of loss follows.

"I'm so fucking sorry, Anya. Please forgive me," he begs. Reaching up to cup my cheek, he wipes away my tears with the pad of his thumb. "I've hurt you in so many ways over such a long time. If I could, I would take each of them back." Nicolo's eyes implore me, silently pleading for me to forgive him.

But I'm crying so hard, I can't manage to get the words out. Sobs burst from me so forcefully, I can't breathe. Sucking in air with each shuddering breath, I try to calm myself.

But I can't.

"I've been monstrous to you. And I understand if you can never forgive me. But I'm begging you, Anya. Give me another chance." Nicolo pulls me into his arms, tucking my head beneath his chin as he envelops me in his strong embrace.

"I've changed. *You've* changed me, and I want to be someone who deserves your love. I was wrong to treat you the way I have, and you were right to be scared of telling me about our daughter. This is all my fault."

Nicolo's fingers comb through my hair as he soothes me, murmuring a never-ending stream of apologies and assurances that only seem to make me cry harder.

Because I've already forgiven him. I knew I would before he even said he was sorry. The hours of thinking I'd lost Nicolo, that I'd ruined our chances of being together, had shown me just how lost and empty I would be without him.

Only fear of losing my daughter could diminish the pain of losing Nicolo. And once he assured me that he wasn't here to take her away, all those devastating feelings of loss had come crashing down upon me at once.

Finally, after agonizing minutes of being unable to speak, I manage to calm myself down enough to stem my torrent of tears. I force deep, shuddering breaths into my lungs to steady myself. Then I pull away from Nicolo.

I see the hope leave his eyes as he lets me go willingly. His hands slide from my shoulders, his fingers tightening almost reflexively around my arms before he forces himself to let me go.

"Please, Anya." His words are barely above a whisper as the fight seems to leave him all at once. His shoulders hunch in defeat. "I would do anything to be a part of your and Clara's life."

My heart squeezes at the promise behind those words.

I step forward to fling my arms around Nicolo's neck and kiss him.

He freezes, seeming momentarily stunned by my response. Then his hands press against my back, pulling me to him as he holds me close. His lips mold eagerly to mine.

When we break our kiss at last, we're both breathless.

A slow smile spreads across Nicolo's face as he combs a stray lock of hair behind my ear.

"Does this mean I'm forgiven?" he asks hopefully.

I laugh breathlessly. "Yes, I forgive you. Can you forgive me?"

"There's nothing to forgive," he assures me fiercely. His eyes roam over my face, as if to soak up every detail of me. "You did what you thought was best for our daughter. I couldn't ask for more than that. God, I love you, Anya."

My heart swells with joy at those words. "I love you too," I whisper as fresh tears sting my eyes.

Nicolo brushes a soft kiss across my lips before pressing his forehead to mine.

"Can I meet my little girl? Properly this time?" he asks gently.

A wide smile splits my face. "Yes, of course."

I pull Nicolo the rest of the way into my aunt's apartment and close the door behind him.

"Clara, Aunt Patritsyia, will you come out please?" I call.

After a moment's hesitation, Clara's door opens and my aunt peeks out to see if everything is alright. I smile, giving her a reassuring nod. Leading Clara out by the hand, my aunt meets us halfway as I usher Nicolo closer.

Clara hides shyly behind her auntie's skirt as she looks up at Nicolo, confusion in her eyes. Nicolo kneels down to her level and gives her a soft, comforting smile.

"Hello again, Clara. Do you remember me?"

"You're the man from the park."

"That's right," he says encouragingly.

That bolsters Clara's confidence enough for her to step out from behind her auntie.

"Clara," I say, kneeling as well and taking my daughter's hands.

She steps close to me, seeking comfort from her mom. Wrapping an arm around her waist, I hug her to me.

"Clara, this man is your father," I say gently. "He and I made you together, and he wanted to meet you."

"Why?" Clara asks, her innocence shining through.

"Because, Clara, I think you're very special, and I would love to become your friend. Would you like that?" Nicolo's tone is so tender.

Filled with a sense of wonder, it's the closest I've ever heard him to being emotional.

"Do you like dance parties?" Clara asks gravely, as though her decision hinges entirely on his answer.

Nicolo releases a deep chuckle. "I love dance parties," he assures her.

"Wanna have one right now?" she offers as her usual outgoing self comes out in full force.

"Definitely," Nicolo agrees.

"I'll put on the music," I offer, heading to the stereo and inserting Clara's favorite CD.

Clara springs into action as the music starts, and my heart melts as Nicolo joins her. She giggles every time he mimics her dance moves. That only encourages him to try more of them. Soon, the two of them are twirling and jumping, not so much dancing as rolling around the room.

Aunt Patritsiya steps up beside me to watch their dance party. "You're alright?" she asks quietly.

"Yes, I'm sorry, Auntie. I'm sure I scared the living daylights out of you. I just panicked. But we talked it out, and I think everything will be fine."

I smile as Clara releases another bout of contagious giggles.

"More than fine."

"Mama, come join us!" Clara demands. She jumps in place, looking impressively like a bunny.

"I'm coming!" I call, striding forward to meet them.

Clara grips my fingers with one hand. She wraps her other hand around Nicolo's pinky and ring finger—the most she can grip in her tiny fist. She starts to turn us in circles, skipping along as she does.

When my eyes meet Nico's, I'm astounded by the intense love and joy in his hazel gaze.

All at once, it's like my life has fallen into place, each stray puzzle piece coming together to form a beautiful picture. I have everything I've ever wanted, and suddenly I'm filled with hope at what our future together will bring.

EPILOGUE
ANYA

Six weeks later

I take a deep breath, settling into my pose in the utter silence of the auditorium. The classical sound of a violin starts, announcing the beginning of my choreographed number for the winter showcase.

Robbie comes to life behind me. Then the contemporary beat strikes, and I spring into action, transforming from a statue into a living, breathing piece of art.

The hush of the audience registers in the back of my mind, but I stay focused, rising up onto my toes as I dance across the stage. I twirl around Robbie as he leaps into the air at just the right time. After months of grueling practice and long hours in the studio, we're ready for this moment.

I'm so proud of how far my young dance partner has come, in strength, balance, movement. Where once, he was somewhat of an awkward teen, not quite sure of his body and how it might work with mine, we now fit as effortlessly as I once did with Fin.

I sprint toward Robby for our first lift and leap into the air. His arm catches me, using my inertia to push me high over his head.

For a moment, I hang there, suspended like a statue on its marble stand. Then Robbie releases me, letting me fall a split second before transitioning into our second lift. My feet touch down as if onto a cloud, and I spin away from him, my arms arching up around my head.

The music crescendos, and I shift into my chaînés, finding Robbie as my spot.

Every time I reach this point in the song, I think of Nicolo. That electrifying moment in the studio where I danced for him alone. The memory fills my motion with poignancy.

When I come to a halt in front of Robbie, my leg extended back in a deep split, my heart flutters.

As the beat comes to life once again, so do I. I weave my way through the choreographed piece with flawless ease. I could do this in my sleep.

In fact, over the past week, I think I have practiced the routine several times in my dreams. Nicolo tells me I've even started doing ballet moves beneath the covers in the middle of the night.

I'm still not sure I'm inclined to believe that.

It's bittersweet as the music slowly draws to a close. I arch backward over Robbie's arm as I'm suspended lifelessly once again, a doll unable to dance without my music. The auditorium bursts to life with applause.

After holding our pose for one last second, Robbie brings me back to a stand.

When we take our bows, my eyes skim the crowd that lies in shadow before me. It's so dim compared to the brilliant stage lights that I can barely make out Nicolo's beaming face. Next to him sit Clara and my aunt. Each cheers louder than the next, warming my heart with their approval.

Robbie and I take one last bow and exit stage right, making room for the next performance.

"We did it!" Robbie bursts as soon as we duck behind the curtain.

I can't help smiling from ear to ear. "We did."

"Oh, man. That was amazing!" Bouncing with enthusiasm, Robbie leads the way backstage.

"Beautiful, you two," Whitney compliments with a warm smile.

"You stayed to watch!" I pull my friend into a hug.

"Of course." She gives me a squeeze before releasing me. "You were breathtaking."

"So were you," I say.

I turn to head toward the dressing rooms and am greeted by the sight of Clara leading Nicolo by the pinky as she makes her way toward me.

"Hi, baby girl."

I bend, opening my arms to her. Clara releases Nicolo's hand to close the distance between us. Tutu or not, she doesn't care. Her legs and arms wrap around me like a monkey as I scoop her up.

"You were incredible," Nicolo says, his eyes dancing with a fire that makes my stomach quiver.

Leaning in, he wraps his arms around me and Clara both as he presses a chaste kiss to my lips. Anticipation builds inside me at the silent promise of what's to come later tonight.

If I had hopes for what my relationship with Nicolo might become, we have soared above them by leaps and bounds. I'm blown away by the level of commitment he has shown me and Clara since the day he found out about her.

Trips to the zoo, ice skating and hot chocolate at Millennium Park, he's been a part of all our fun family activities. And more than that.

My heart swells with love as I think about our simple movie night last night. We curled up by his gas fireplace as we watched *Frozen* for the third time in as many weeks. It's Clara's new favorite, and Nicolo has endured watching it on repeat like a true champ.

He's even spent considerable time winning over my aunt. She's given him the hardest time, presiding over our relationship with skepticism until Nicolo could prove he meant every word he said. Without a shadow of a doubt, I know he did.

At times, it can still be hard to wrap my mind around the fact that he is the eldest son born to a mafia family. I know he makes money through less-than-honest means. And while I still struggle with his life in the mafia, I can't see leaving him for anything.

I love too much about him to even consider it. And now I can both follow my dreams and be happy with the man I love. He's the father of my child, and every day, he becomes a better man.

With the winter showcase over, we now have three weeks of uninterrupted vacation time together as a family, and I look forward to it.

"What do you say I go get changed, and then we head home?" I suggest, giving Clara an eskimo kiss.

"Yeah!" she shouts enthusiastically.

I set her gently on the floor, and her tiny hand wraps around Nicolo's pinky once more. Every time, it makes my heart ache with happiness to see how close they've become in such a short time. Clara loves her papa, though she always assures me in a stage whisper that I'm still her favorite.

It never fails to make Nicolo laugh. "As is only right," he agrees. "Your mom is what makes the sun shine and the birds sing."

"Really?" Clara asked in awe the first time he said it.

"No, baby girl. He only means that I'm important to you both."

Still, those words melt me into a puddle every time. I never would have thought Nicolo could be so romantic. Charming, I never doubted. But I'm astounded by how tender and loving he's proven to be.

From a callous, ruthless bully, Nicolo has transformed into a man with incredible depth. I've loved every minute of getting to know more about him.

Who would have guessed that my gut instinct back in high school had been right all along? We are something special together.

More importantly, I think we might just stand the test of time.

Want the next installment in this sexy saga? Get Pretty Little Toy here. Want more Nicolo and Ana? Get a sizzling hot bonus scene here.

Made in the USA
Monee, IL
03 May 2023

32934385R00194